STALIN'S WITNESSES

by
Julius Wachtel

KNOX ROBINSON
PUBLISHING
LONDON • New York

KNOX ROBINSON
PUBLISHING

3rd Floor, 36 Langham Street
Westminster, London W1W 7AP
&
244 5th Avenue, Suite 1861
New York, New York 10001

Knox Robinson Publishing is a specialist, international publisher of historical fiction, historical romance and medieval fantasy.

First published in Great Britain in 2013 by Knox Robinson Publishing

First published in the United States in 2012 by Knox Robinson Publishing

Copyright © Julius Wachtel 2012

The right of Julius Wachtel to be identified as author of this work has been asserted by him in accordance with
the Copyright, Designs and Patents Act 1988.

A CIP catalogue record for this book is available from the British Library.

ISBN HC 978-1-908483-38-6

ISBN PB 978-1-908483-39-3

Typeset in Adobe Caslon Pro by Susan Veach
info@susanveach.com

Printed in the United States of America and the United Kingdom.

Download the KRP App in iTunes and Google Play to receive free historical fiction, historical romance and fantasy eBooks delivered directly to your mobile or tablet.

Watch our historical documentaries and book trailers on our channel on YouTube and subscribe to our podcasts in iTunes.

www.knoxrobinsonpublishing.com

Foreword

During the murderous frenzy of the 1930s known as the Great Terror, hundreds of thousands of ordinary Soviet citizens were summarily convicted of "counterrevolutionary" crimes and either executed or dispatched to labor camps. But perfunctory hearings wouldn't do for getting rid of those whom Stalin didn't trust. To justify their liquidation the General Secretary and his right-hand man, Procurator-General Andrei Vyshinsky staged the Great Moscow Show Trials of 1936, 1937 and 1938. Diplomats and journalists from around the world watched as top Party members and heroes of the Russian Revolution and Civil War took the stand and falsely confessed to participating in a series of completely fictitious plots to wreck Soviet industry and abandon the country to Germany and Japan. All fifty-four accused were found guilty; forty-seven were shot, each within twenty-four hours of the verdicts and with no opportunity to appeal. Only Trotsky was missing. Exiled to Europe in 1929, Stalin's arch-nemesis, who supposedly directed the intrigues from afar, would dodge the USSR's assassins for another few years.

That these victims – for that's what they were – cooperated so fully in their own destruction, to all appearances testifying willingly and with great sincerity, helps explain why the implausible tales were widely accepted. However, these capitulations also served to bring attention to what was missing. At the very first trial, which took place in August 1936, the evidence consisted nearly entirely of confessions. Its predetermined end – the conviction and execution of all sixteen accused – was greeted skeptically by some in the West.

To assure better reviews for the next trial Vyshinsky impressed five "witnesses" to corroborate the confessions of the key accused. Among the witnesses were two veteran Soviet intelligence officers who were performing dual roles as journalist/spies: Vladimir Romm, the Soviet Union's inaugural correspondent to Washington, and Dmitry Bukhartsev, his counterpart in Berlin. Rounding out the roster were Leonid Tamm, a high-ranking engineer whose brother Igor later won the Nobel

Prize in physics, Vladimir Loginov, a mid-level Soviet *apparatchik*, and Alex Stein, an expatriate German engineer, one of the thousands of specialists whom the USSR had recruited to build up its industrial capacity. Each was arrested, imprisoned in the Lubyanka, the dreaded home of the secret police, and "prepared" by interrogators.

This time world reaction was more positive. One key observer who applauded the verdicts was millionaire American Ambassador to Moscow Joseph Davies. With his assistance and President Roosevelt's encouragement Warner Brothers produced "Mission to Moscow." A glowing account of Davies' brief tenure as an envoy, the motion picture glorified the Soviet Union, disparaged Stalin's detractors and praised the trial and its outcome.

Once all seventeen accused stood convicted, the five witnesses literally dropped from sight. "Stalin's Witnesses" uses them as a looking-glass on the Soviet system. How did smart and to all appearances fundamentally decent men reconcile themselves to Stalin's ruthless machine? Why after enjoying stellar careers did they become its victims? In a greater sense, how did a transformative, ostensibly liberating ideology come to deliver a great land and its peoples into the arms of a pitiless, totalitarian regime?

I decided to address these questions with a novel, blending fact and fiction to create an informative and entertaining account that avoids doing mischief to key historical events. We follow along as Vladimir Romm, and to a lesser extent the other witnesses, navigate the minefields of Stalin's Russia, giving each a voice to express their dreams, fears and justifications. Interspersed with the main narrative is Romm's fictional prison diary, which suggests how the ruthless prosecutor Andrei Vyshinsky and his interrogator George Molchanov managed to create illusions so convincing that much of the world was fooled.

This is at heart a hybrid work. While in part fiction, great care was taken to assure that invented characters and conversations illuminate rather than muddle significant events. More is said about this in the "author's notes" section, which also includes a detailed guide that clarifies departures from fact and provides references to source materials.

At the risk of leaving someone out the author would like to name the friends, scholars and archivists in Europe and the U.S. who helped in the effort, with the proviso of course that any discrepancies in reporting and interpretation are the author's alone.

Without the assistance of Sergey Homich, a Belarusian scholar who resides in Minsk, there would have been little to write about. Sergey scoured Soviet-era archives in Russia and Lithuania, reviewed and translated Communist Party files on Vladimir Romm, Dmitry Bukhartsev and Vladimir Loginov, and with the help of the Blitz information center in Saint Petersburg gathered invaluable information about Romm and Tamm by locating and interviewing descendants.

Great thanks are also due to the archivists who dug up visa records, intelligence memoranda and other materials relating to Romm, Bukhartsev and Stein. Among them are Roseline Salmon and Christine Petillat of the French National Archives, Nathalie Fanac of the State Archives of Geneva, Blandine Blukacz-Louisfert of the United Nations Archives in Geneva, Dr. D. Bourgeois and H. von Rütte of the Swiss Federal Archives, Dr. Gerhard Keiper of the Bundesarchiv in Berlin, and Rosemary Switzer, Charles Greene and Christine Lutz of the Mudd Manuscript Library at Princeton University.

Naturally the proof of the project is in the writing, and to the extent that it meets expectations I must thank my reviewers. Among them are my wife Linda and daughter Jennifer, inveterate readers who provided valuable feedback through innumerable rewrites; my good friends John Morrill and Myron Levin; my mentors Dr. Hans Toch and Dr. Gary Marx; historians extraordinaire Dr. Dennis Dunn, Dr. Peter Solomon and Dr. Marian Rubchak; and of course my publisher Dana Celeste Robinson, whose generous commitment furnished the opportunity to bring this work to the attention of a wide audience.

Julius Wachtel
Garden Grove, California
July 2012

Lubyanka Prison Diary

Narrative

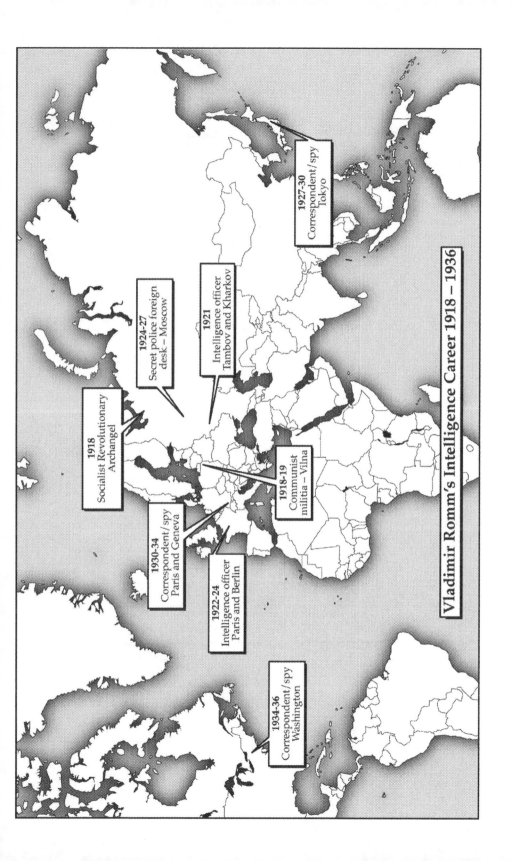

Vladimir Romm's Intelligence Career 1918 – 1936

1927-30
Correspondent/spy
Tokyo

1924-27
Secret police foreign
desk – Moscow

1921
Intelligence officer
Tambov and Kharkov

1918
Socialist Revolutionary
Archangel

1918-19
Communist
militia – Vilna

1930-34
Correspondent/spy
Paris and Geneva

1922-24
Intelligence officer
Paris and Berlin

1934-36
Correspondent/spy
Washington

Lubyanka prison, 27 November 1936

My cell is a narrow, rectangular affair, three meters wide by four meters in length, with a stained concrete floor, rude masonry walls and a sturdy steel door bearing the disquieting imprint of the labor camp where it was manufactured. There is one small window. High and out of reach, it is so encrusted with dirt that little light enters. My sole source of illumination is a single bulb that burns dimly around the clock, something that was at first bothersome but to which I'm growing accustomed. I sleep, or try to, on a rude metal cot with a thin, badly stained mattress. Into the little space that remains they've wedged a battered old desk and a flimsy chair, probably castoffs from some petty bureaucrat's office. What function they might serve eludes me as I've been denied the right to correspond. I leave for last my lodgings' most unpleasant feature, a metal pail euphemistically referred to as the "honey pot," which generates a stench so unpleasant that during my first days in this hellhole it was difficult to breathe.

Over the years I have heard tales of how prisoners adapt. Now that I've joined their ranks I'm not sure whether getting used to such indignities is something to celebrate. But I refuse to despair. I've done nothing wrong, and before long this horrible injustice will be sorted out.

I was notified of my reassignment three months ago, in August, while posted as *Izvestia* correspondent to Washington. There was little to suggest that anything was amiss. All who serve the Soviet Union are well aware of the pretexts that Moscow Center employs to recall officers who have fallen out of favor, like the sudden illness of a spouse or an accident involving one's child, but such events aren't normally celebrated with elaborate champagne receptions, good-bye gifts and congratulatory speeches by colleagues and well-wishers.

Moments after the embassy's communications officer decoded the message that brought to a close my two years of service, my superior, Ambassador Troyanovsky, announced that after a brief sojourn in the Soviet capital I would be sent to Great Britain. It would be disingenuous to say that I wasn't apprehensive, as sham transfers aren't exactly unknown, but his words seemed sincere, and after fifteen years in the Soviet secret service, much of it spent under the guise of being a foreign correspondent, it was easy enough to attribute my unease to a bad case of Bolshevik paranoia.

A few weeks earlier we had gathered in the embassy's projection room to watch clips from the trial this past August where sixteen comrades, among them several leading Party officials, took the stand and one after the other tearfully confessed that they had conspired to assassinate Stalin, wreck Soviet industry and abandon the country to its mortal enemies, Germany and Japan. That high-ranking Bolsheviks would participate in such a scheme seemed astounding – to me, it still does – but they spoke earnestly and their detailed accounts left little to the imagination. A few staffers actually fell ill.

As Soviet law prescribes, each of the accused was shot within twenty-four hours of the verdict, with no right to appeal. To execute comrades of high rank is an unprecedented step, and the auditorium remained quiet well after the projector ceased whirring. Troyanovsky tried to lift the mood with a small speech praising Procurator-General Vyshinsky's tireless efforts and brilliant investigation for thoroughly discrediting the plot's kingpin, the exile Trotsky, then in his seventh year of running around Europe, spouting off against the General Secretary and trying to spur a counterrevolution.

It's no secret that many loyal communists, myself included, favored Trotsky at a time when such sentiments were widespread and perfectly legal. It's also true that as the ambassador pointed out – I might add, with a glance in my direction – all had ample opportunity to recant their errors, so the few who failed to live up to their end of the bargain have only themselves to blame. Still, his comments were disturbing. Were any of us at risk? No one dared ask. Truly, all notions of "democracy in the party" vanished long ago.

Throughout the talk I spotted more than a few sallow faces, but as we filed out things livened up. Surely, went the whispers, treachery that severe left the authorities no option, especially now that fascists are breathing down our necks. Looking back on that day I suppose we just wanted to put it all behind us.

In the USSR the verdicts were celebrated with speeches and rallies. But world reaction was mixed. Troyanovsky told me to do what I could to counter the onslaught of virulent anti-Soviet propaganda, but nothing could stop the capitalist press from harping about our reliance on confessions, a curious posture as that is the main way of securing convictions in the West. As for calling the results "preordained," a smooth trial hardly seems something to criticize. Is it preferable that the accused deny their guilt?

Then the other shoe dropped. There I was, trying to sell my American counterparts on the wonders of Soviet justice when rumors began to float around the embassy about a second trial. Its scope seemed remarkably similar to the first, with Trotsky reprising his role as the enabler of an Axis-inspired plot to destabilize the motherland. What shook me up was that authorities kicked off their campaign by running *Izvestia* through the wringer, publicly disparaging my colleagues for their lack of patriotism, then added fuel to the fire by arresting the famous journalist Karl Radek and accusing him of being Trotsky's main go-between.

Radek and I – at the time of his arrest he was nominally my editor – go back a long way. Although not all my memories of him are pleasant, to argue that he was a fascist stooge seemed awfully far-fetched. Still, it was true that Radek was for a time Trotsky's most fervent disciple, at least until Stalin had them both exiled. In those days a bullet to the back of the head wasn't yet the preferred solution, and Trotsky was deported to Europe. Amazingly, Radek was allowed to remain and eventually clawed himself back into the General Secretary's good graces. I hadn't seen him since my going-away party in Moscow, and before that had steered clear of the man for years, so I managed to convince myself that his turn to counterrevolutionary activity was somehow plausible.

On a breezy afternoon only a month ago, as Washington enjoyed its last breath of fall, Galina, our son Georgie and I got together with Paul Ward and his wife at their fine home just outside the capital. While our wives took Georgie for a stroll, Paul and I sat in a "small" kitchen. Nearly the size of our Moscow apartment, it was equipped in typical American fashion with all the conveniences of a fine restaurant.

Affluence has not blinded Paul to his country's failings. The respected political columnist of *The Nation* was one of the first to point out Germany's threat to world peace and criticize as incredibly wrong-headed the isolationist tendencies of the American Congress. Regrettably, while many writers and intellectuals openly support the Soviet cause, neither Paul nor I had much success persuading legislators to join in, and he and I both fear that by the time the U.S. grasps that its future and ours are entwined it may be too late. Prick the skin of most Americans and out oozes European blood. What will it take for the most powerful nation on Earth to come to its senses?

Galina and I first set foot in America in early 1934. We were instantly overwhelmed by its apparent prosperity, the spacious apartments and fine homes, many occupied by persons of modest means, the abundance of inexpensive, high-quality consumer goods, and most of all the numerous automobiles clogging the roads, their fumes choking passers-by and casting an eerie pall. Yet in time the rough edges began to show. Coming from the USSR, where it is a serious crime to discriminate based on ethnicity, we were disturbed by racism so pervasive that even in the capital the colored ride in the back of public transport, hold menial jobs and live in the least desirable areas. I have written of the deplorable inequality in the distribution of wealth, with affluent areas bordering neighborhoods beset by the deepest imaginable poverty. Crime and violence are rampant, far worse than what one should expect in a civilized society. Yes, America did have its material comforts. Russians are perennially faced with a scarcity of conveniences – say, good soaps, nice toothbrushes – that could make everyday life a little more pleasant. Yet our sojourn in America convinced us that however well it might provide in the way of consumer goods, capitalism, particularly the unforgiving, every-man-for-himself kind practiced there, can have terrible consequences for those left on the outside.

Paul opened a fresh bottle of vodka and poured two shots. Not quite the Slav, he took only a small sip.

"To my good friend Vladimir Georgievich Romm, may you enjoy the pinnacle of success in whatever it is that you really do, now and in the future. *LeChaim!*"

"*Za vashe zdorov'ye!*" I downed my drink in a single gulp. Its unusual flavor prompted me to inspect the bottle. As I suspected, it was Smirnoff, from the Smirnov family, those infamous distillers who fled Russia during the Revolution.

I slid the tumbler forward. "Well, now that you've entrapped me I might as well have another."

I was expected to do much more than just take America's pulse. How could we assure its support in the battle against fascism? If war breaks out with Germany and Japan, as our generals are convinced it will, the Soviet Union will need the West's material support and, more likely than not, its armed might. I was to seek out persons of influence – journalists, capitalists, politicians – and bring them to our view of things. It was critical to overcome the isolationist sentiment, particularly noticeable in their Congress, which made it impossible for Roosevelt to fully embrace the USSR.

My relationship with Paul was much more than business, and because of it far more productive. I also had some nice chats with the *New York Times'* manicured, resplendently tailored Walter Duranty. Of course, both were already sympathetic to the Soviet cause. It's not that other reporters were hostile: it's that they didn't care. Most assumed that I spent all my time just like them, engaged in trivial concerns, and when I tried to steer discussions to issues such as the threats posed by fascism they usually groaned. Their editors were interested in drawing in readers, not putting them off. Pressures in the U.S. to return a profit imbue everything with a commercial flavor, affecting even newspapers, which as honest reporters will admit pretend to provide a public service while mostly chasing advertising dollars. American writers expend tons of newsprint and innumerable column inches reporting "juicy" events that lack any enlightening value or social significance, such as lurid crimes and the comings-and-goings of movie stars, topics that would be ridiculed in Moscow. Urging America to become involved in foreign conflicts is strictly taboo.

If newsmen were difficult, bureaucrats proved nearly impossible. Most were fearful that I might discover some horrible secret and were extremely tight-lipped, at least until a few shots of bourbon (a horrid drink to which Americans seem addicted) lubricated their tongues. Even then what I mostly got was nonsense. However, I did make inroads with one well-connected person. I first met Allen Dulles in 1932 at the disarmament conference in Geneva during that hopeful time when it seemed that world peace and prosperity was finally within reach. Dulles and I (he was legal counsel to the American legation) established a back-channel to smooth the way for establishing diplomatic relations between our countries. We became reacquainted when I was posted to Washington and he was spending time in the capital in connection with his famous brother's New York law firm. Dulles is rumored to be in line for a top intelligence post, and developing him as a source remains a very worthwhile objective.

But my fondest recollections are of Paul. He and I have a common outlook, a belief that under the right conditions America could transition into a just and peaceful society without artificial social and political boundaries; indeed, without a government of any kind. That's not to say that we are exactly of the same mind, as Paul had come to feel that the path chosen by the USSR was excessively centralized and authoritarian.

"When are you leaving?" he asked.

"Wednesday. We take the train to New York then sail for England the following day."

"Are you sure that you want to do that?"

My friend's somber tone took me aback. "What do you mean? Why wouldn't I be sure?"

Paul fiddled with his drink. "Everyone's heard about Radek. Could you be next?"

That was a startling thing for Paul to say, and it took me a moment to regain my composure. Was I being recalled under pretext? My conscience was clear. Indeed, I felt indebted to the USSR. Through its graces three citizens – Galina, Georgie and I – were participating in a great adventure, enjoying perquisites that would have been completely out of reach for Jewish persons under the Czar, and it seemed unthinkable to pay back that debt by turning our backs on communism.

"Why should I worry?" I asked, trying to convince the both of us. "I've kept my distance from Radek, and whatever the fool's done, or not, I wasn't in on it."

"I'm sure you had nothing to do with a plot, if there was one," Paul hastily replied. "But from what I heard there's a trial on the way. You know the man. If he's squeezed he's liable to..."

At that moment Paul's wife Dorothy rushed in. Georgie's brace was giving him trouble and I left to help. Paul and I never did finish that discussion.

Galina was overjoyed at the news of our return. Despite putting on a good show she dearly missed the homeland and was in fact quite miserable. My wife's absence from Moscow had forced her to give up a leadership role in a communist women's organization, and other than for an occasional lecture at the Soviet legation there was little in Washington to satisfy her thirst for political enlightenment. Her opinion of American culture wasn't favorable. She was badly put off by the preoccupation with wealth, the banal entertainments and careless form of speech and dress, and neither our spacious apartment, which in Moscow would be out of reach to all but the *nomenklatura*, nor the skilled therapists who attended to Georgie seemed to her worthy of squandering one more day in the hub of world capitalism.

Those, as best I can remember, were her exact sentiments.

Our travel plans coincided with the *Queen Mary's* schedule, and we secured a fine berth, a small luxury that, considering our little fellow's special needs, the ambassador was happy to indulge. Everything had been proceeding well until the evening before our departure, when after making my final round of farewells I returned to the apartment to find Galina hysterical.

"Why didn't you tell me that Radek was arrested?"

I took a deep breath. "I suppose I didn't want to worry you," I replied. Galina had called Dorothy to say her good-byes, and one thing led to another.

"Worry me? They shoot a score of traitors, and then two weeks later that repulsive little man who nearly manipulated you into collaborating gets picked up by the secret police!"

Galina was rarely frightened, and the depth of her concern got me thinking. What if, indeed? "Since those times all we've worked on together are a few newspaper articles," I insisted. "If there's anything even vaguely counterrevolutionary about them, give me a pistol, I'll save the bastards the trouble and do it myself!"

We had forgotten all about Georgie, and when our son heard these horrible words he began to sob. I took him into my arms and the three of us hugged for a very long time.

Cookies and a coloring book settled the little man down. But Galina was badly upset. My wife had always been the stauncher communist: deep down, did she think that I had somehow stepped over the line?

"Will you call the ambassador?" she asked.

Her plaintive tone threw me off balance. "What could I say without making him suspicious?" I protested. "Should I ask, 'Comrade Ambassador, exactly what kind of recall is this – the "good" kind or the bad?' Look, everyone knows that we're friends – he's the one who lobbied to bring me here – so if I was really in trouble he'd be the last person whom Moscow Center would tell. Only yesterday you and Elena were making plans to meet in London. Do you really think that Alexander Antonovich would knowingly lead us into a trap?"

My wife's tears returned, and when I tried to comfort her she ignored me and curled up on the sofa. I fell into bed, physically and emotionally drained. Galina had always been the more resilient. When doctors diagnosed Georgie's condition and warned there was already considerable damage she quickly took charge of things, learning everything there was to know about his illness and even arranging to have him treated in a French sanatorium, a placement that vastly improved his prognosis and probably saved our marriage as well. Now it was my turn to hold things together and I wondered if I was up to the task.

A few days later, after a nice send-off by the Troyanovskys and a good night's sleep in a fine New York hotel we stood in awe of the most magnificent steamship ever built, a vessel of such enormous dimensions that when Georgie asked how an object like this could float all I could say was, "It's a miracle!" The lengthy boarding process passed in the blink of an eye, and as I helped my son navigate the gangplank Galina squeezed my hand. Neither of us had brought up that unpleasant business again, and we let the excitement of the journey and the anticipation of reunions with family and friends carry us along.

The voyage was uneventful. Galina and Georgie passed the time reading and playing games while I wrote letters to colleagues whom I did not personally bid farewell. I particularly wanted to stay in touch with Allen Dulles, who remains influential even though his cronies are presently out of power. Sooner or later Allen will return to government, most likely in the intelligence service, which has long been his obsession. I had hoped we could work together when that day came, but that possibility now seems remote.

Our welcome-home celebration was hosted by my brother Alexander and his wife, Elena. Both are well-known Moscow art critics, and Alexander's biography of the French impressionist Matisse is due out as I write. Just before we left for Washington he and Elena were awarded a spacious flat in a Tverskaya Street brownstone, with high ceilings, a separate dining room and a splendid view of the Kremlin. Galina is terribly jealous, as our family, which includes her mother Ludvika, is stuffed into a tiny apartment that suffers from a bad case of Russian plumbing, meaning that we must often resort to buckets.

To my delight my other brother Evsey and his wife Esfir joined us. They live in Leningrad. Evsey is an engineer in the paper industry. He hasn't been in the best of health, and when I scolded him for making the long trip he responded by loudly bussing my cheeks, making the ladies laugh and reminding me of those times in Vilna when my brothers (I'm the baby of the family) would give me a big smooch as they snuck off to attend meetings of their revolutionary cell. Neither Alexander nor Evsey have children so they brought Georgie many gifts, spoiling him rotten, as uncles tend to do.

Every Russian family has a poet. Ours is Evsey. His passion, unfortunately, is for the Western-style romantic kind, which places him at odds with the proletarian ideals that the Soviet Union expects its artists to promote. It's an interest that he picked up from one of mother's artsy friends and which is bound to land him in hot water, even if he always does use a pseudonym.

Alexander, who has little tolerance for non-conformism, skimmed Evsey's most recent book of verse. "Can you show me which of these so-called 'poems' speaks to the struggles of the workers?" he asked, trying without much success to conceal his irritation. His attempts over the years to reform his liberally-minded sibling have had little apparent effect.

"What struggles do you have in mind, dear brother? Hell, even if you halve the figures the Commissariats are flaunting – no, if you quarter them! – every Soviet worker must be a Stakhanovite!"

Evsey's digs at the exaggerations of the Five-Year Plans and the glorification of Soviet workers riled Alexander. "Is it still your position, Evsey Georgievich, that art has no obligation other than to itself?"

"Please, call me "Sallo'. Everyone else does."

Alexander grinned weakly. "Very well, Sallo. You may call me 'Sasha'."

Evsey clapped in excitement. "Wonderful! Now that we're addressing each other as intimates let me explain why evaluating art through the prism of socialism does both a disservice. Better yet, why don't you ask your friend Shostakovich?"

That really was going too far. Everyone knows that Shostakovich is still on the mend politically after the inaugural performance of his "Lady Macbeth" led Stalin to publicly storm out of the Bolshoi. A biting editorial in the next day's *Pravda* pointed out that glorifying the murder of one's spouse to make way for a lover hardly qualifies as socialist art, and within days the Union of Soviet Composers announced a corrective campaign to assure that future productions support rather than disparage communistic values. A tempest in a teapot if you ask me, but don't get Galina going on it!

"Dmitri Dmitrievich's errors were the products of youth and inexperience," Alexander explained. "We recently had him over for dinner. He personally reassured us that he is working day and night to create more socially conscious works. Elena and I are doing all we can to help."

Evsey refilled his glass with a healthy dose of pepper vodka. "That's exactly my point, Sasha. Here the Government – I mean the critic – advises the composer, who writes a piece, which is criticized, then rewritten, then criticized some more, squeezing out whatever creative juices remain, so when the infernal cycle is done all you have left is a prune. No! Not a prune – the pit! But why worry? We've already let the Party decide for us in every other respect!"

The front door slammed. Galina and her mother were gone, taking Georgie with them. I couldn't blame them. After the ups and downs of collectivization, the wildly exaggerated goals of the plans, the struggles with Trotsky, the trials, and the looming war against fascism, there's precious little room left for differences of opinion, and with the risk of being denounced lurking around every corner it's best not to get into the habit of speaking too much from the heart. Tolerance for competing views is not a quality that Socialists have in abundance, and to that extent we could probably learn something from the West.

When I arrived at the apartment all were asleep. Early the next morning I woke to my wife's sweet breath, a steaming cup of tea and an excited eleven-year-old who couldn't wait to rekindle old friendships. All the unpleasantness seemed behind us. Galina was buzzing around the apartment, thrilled to be back and anxious to resume teaching at the primary school. Catching a glimpse of her fine figure and stunning profile, I considered myself a very lucky man.

On her way out she gave me a nice kiss. "You were right. I was silly to worry."

Ludvika was in the kitchen. As usual, she caught everything. "Worry? What's there to worry about?"

An hour later I was sitting in the reception area of *Izvestia* waiting for Nikolai Bukharin, the editor-in-chief. He never showed up, so the receptionist eventually turned me over to a preoccupied editor who knew nothing of my pending reassignment or really much of anything else ('we just placed someone in London, why would they send you too?'). He led me to a dusty, vacant office and told me to make myself at home. While cleaning out the desk of its prior occupant I found one of Radek's calling cards, an unnerving coincidence that left me a bit shaken. To clear my head I wandered around the news room. No one seemed interested in having a chat, which wasn't surprising considering what I later learned, in the men's room, when a reporter took pity and whispered the chilling news that Comrade Bukharin was confined to his home awaiting the findings of a Party inquiry into his alleged links with Trotsky.

Radek, then Bukharin. The dominoes were falling, all right.

The editor returned and we agreed that I would write a piece about American isolationism, a topic that was very much on everyone's mind. The hours passed quickly and it was soon time to leave. For a change of pace I tried the spectacular new Metro, opened only last year. As I walked down elegantly arched corridors lined with paintings and sculptures depicting robust workers, bountiful harvests and the USSR's military might it was impossible not to be impressed. Comrade Stalin may not be everyone's cup of tea, but his impact on productivity and morale has been nothing short of amazing. Moments later, seated comfortably in a shiny new railcar, I glanced out just in time to catch a fleeting glimpse of the General Secretary's likeness beaming down from the tunnel entrance. Public transportation in Washington was poor and there was no underground, so when I traveled it was mostly by car, one of those "freedoms" that Americans enjoy along with frequent jam-ups, breakdowns and accidents. One cannot truly appreciate the orderliness of Moscow without visiting the West.

I exited the train eager to get home and share news of my writing assignment and subway ride. My euphoria lasted all of a few seconds. Not more than twenty meters away, standing in a corner but making no attempt to hide, were the same two dour-looking characters who had been hanging around the paper when I left. I walked home quickly, their presence at the station instilling a sense of foreboding that not even Galina's warm greeting could shake.

I feigned a headache and took refuge in the bedroom. My mind was buzzing. What should I do? Under such circumstances what *does* one do? Pack a bag? Make a run for it? Destroy incriminating documents that don't exist? Time passed and I gradually relaxed. Maybe these were different men. Maybe my mind was playing tricks.

Alas, it wasn't. I'd been napping for an hour when a squad of secret police – yes, including my two shadows – barged in and spirited me away, their disinterest in looking around for proof of my guilt proving nearly as unsettling as my arrest.

Vilna (1905)

Rain began to fall. Soon the poorly maintained cobblestone path would turn into a pestilent river of debris and manure, trapping carts and horses and making passage impossible. There was good reason why Vilna once devoured eight-thousand of Napoleon's crack troops, all felled by typhus.

A spindly boy scampered by. Slowed by the muck, his shoes sinking to the laces with each stride, Vladimir tried to keep his mind on the praise that would come when he successfully completed his mission. He paused to take shelter under the eaves of a sturdy building. Established by his great-great grandfather David, the House of the Widow and Brothers Romm was once Eastern Europe's pre-eminent publisher of Jewish religious works. But when government officials began imposing onerous restrictions on the nettlesome faith – Nicholas II's payback, one assumed, for the assassination of his grandfather – the children of the Diaspora turned to a new secular creed that promised freedom from the yoke of the monarchy. In time religious interest faded and the printing house was sold. Neither Vladimir nor his older brothers were interested in the sacred, but their father insisted they continue taking Seder with their grandmother, who always made sure to set out the delicacies that the boys loved.

Vladimir adjusted his satchel. As he readied to leave a raggedy peddler pushed a cart piled high with junk in his way. Stretching a bony arm to within a hairs-breadth of the boy's face, the beggar intoned the familiar refrain.

"Please, your honor, for my family's supper."

Vladimir hesitated. Losing candy money was a disappointment, yet giving alms to the poor was the sort of thing that he had been taught to do, and after the briefest sigh he reached deep into his pockets and dropped a coin into the filthy palm. Vladimir Georgievich Romm would never inherit a royal title, for his father's Imperial rank, Collegiate Councilor, was too low on the pecking order to pass on.

Vladimir redoubled his pace. He was running late, and as darkness fell he worried how he would explain himself to Papa. Lying made him feel unclean, but under the circumstances telling the truth was impossible.

Like most structures in Vilna the crumbling tenement hadn't seen a coat of whitewash in years. Anxious to be done, Vladimir rushed straight to the apartment, a lapse in tradecraft that he would remember in later years, when being found out could mean a bullet.

A bearded young Socialist examined the leaflets. "Good job, Volya!" he beamed. "These will do fine. Be sure to thank Evsey and Alexander." And that would have been that, except that suddenly the front door burst open and a team of the Czar's men rushed in. More surprised than frightened, Vladimir realized that his negligence had led the secret police to the radical's lair. Overwhelmed with guilt, the budding young revolutionary reacted in the only way a nine year old could. He cried.

Hours later an open hack sped through the streets, its well-dressed passenger urging the white-bearded *izvoschik* to keep on the whip. George Romm was fifty. Stout but not fat, of medium height, with dark, deeply set eyes and a pleasant round face marred only by a long day's stubble, he was a physician at the Jewish Hospital in Vilna, the largest city in the Pale of Settlement, that western-most slice of the Empire where members of the untrustworthy ethnic group were being forced to return.

Romm was frantic with worry. His boys weren't home when the policeman brought the handwritten message. Thankfully it was from the Chief Inspector, one of the few ranking officers with whom he could reason. If, as the letter suggested, Evsey and Alexander had really involved their younger brother in running errands for radicals, well, that was unforgivable. If he could only forgive himself! Long shifts in the wards gave him little time to watch over the boys, and his joining an opposition party, even if it was only the mild-mannered Constitutional-Democrats, hardly set the proper example for three impressionable youths. Yet what *should* be done when spoiled royals wallow in luxury, ignoring the disease and malnourishment that were devastating the Pale? For the overwhelmed doctor it presented a moral dilemma worthy of the highest authority, perhaps the Gaon himself. But learned analysis would have to wait: the first order of business was to rescue his boy from the jaws of the *Okhrana*.

Romm read a crumpled flyer that announced a rally in honor of a condemned radical. "He took these to a Socialist Revolutionary hideout. They were printed, we're certain, at your people's high school." The inspector's eyes narrowed. "The same one, if I'm not mistaken, that Evsey and Alexander attend."

Opposing the monarchy in any way was a certain ticket to prison. What's more, the new Minister of the Interior had ordered that anyone who belonged to a faction that used violence, such as the Socialist Revolutionaries, be tried under martial law, meaning a summary proceeding and a prompt hanging.

Romm winced. "Please believe that…"

The officer held up his hand. "No need to explain, Doctor – I'm also a father. But this puts me in a tough spot. It's only been a week since Grand Duke Sergei's murder. So you can imagine the pressure!"

By then all of Russia knew the details. As customary, the Grand Duke was killed by dynamite, set off with an initiator sparked off by a flaming fuse. Because of the bomb's heft and crudity, Ivan Kaliayev had to hurl the lethal package at his target from up close. Actually he would have done so a month earlier when at the last possible moment he noticed that the man's wife and children were also in the royal coach. But on February 4, 1905 there were no innocents in the way. Minutes after the tremendous explosion shook Moscow, leaving citizens to think that an earthquake struck, the Grand Duchess was on her hands and knees gathering bits and pieces of her late husband from the pavement. Sergei Alexandrovich, uncle of Czar Nicholas II, was no more. Kaliayev somehow survived. Deafened, his skin peppered with shards from the carriage, the esteemed member of the Socialist Revolutionary Combat Brigade was promptly arrested and just as quickly hung.

The rotund officer leaned forward, affecting the mock-conspiratorial tone that Romm knew too well. "Look, Doctor Romm. The leaflets are in the garbage, so no real harm was done. A gesture to demonstrate your family's support for the police wouldn't be out of line, don't you think?"

George Romm found Vladimir sitting at the jailer's desk, getting the better of the man in a game of chess. On the way out the boy exchanged a friendly greeting with the desk sergeant. Had his father not been forced to enrich the "policemen's benevolent fund" with a month's wages he would have laughed.

They set off on foot. "They told me that you've been running messages for the Socialist Revolutionaries," George Romm said. "Is that true?"

"Yes, Papa."

"Well, you must stop."

Vladimir sniffled. "Please don't punish Alexander and Evsey. I begged them to let me help."

His father knew that was as much an answer as he was likely to get. Evsey and

Alexander might have thought of themselves as revolutionaries, but they were only play-acting. But his youngest unmistakably carried the soul of a fighter. It was a quality far too ingrained to reach with a whipping, even if one wished.

George Romm tried a different tack. "Volya," he asked, addressing his son by the diminutive, "what do your revolutionary colleagues want?"

"Why, that's simple, father," Vladimir replied, without a trace of self-consciousness. "We want justice for the peasants!"

"And the authorities? What are *they* seeking?"

Vladimir thought it over. "To stay in power?"

"So who would be in charge if the authorities lost?"

"I know! The Socialist..." Vladimir playfully poked at his father. "Ah, you're trying to trick me!"

"No, I'm just trying to keep you from being tricked. Men are always trying to lord it over each other, so you must be wary of everyone, Socialist or not. Do you understand?"

Vladimir smiled. "Father, does that mean I must also be careful of you?"

"Sure, I can be wrong," Romm conceded. "But you'll never have to question my motives."

He suddenly brought Vladimir close. Just ahead, two mangy dogs sniffed at a body lying in the dirt. Leaving the boy behind, the doctor shooed away the mutts and checked for signs of life. There were none. Noting the corpse's threadbare garments and frightfully thin physique, the weary physician passed it off as just another case of malnutrition.

Thanks to the Czar's *ukase* ordering their return, waves of dispossessed Jews poured into Vilna, besieging the city's social services and overwhelming its antiquated infrastructure. Overcrowding spread disease. Those who had scratched their way into the middle class suffered a particularly telling blow. Nice clothes, fine furniture, expensive musical instruments, the tangible symbols of a comfortable life vanished into pawnshops and secondhand stores, taking with them something even more important – a people's aspirations. Those with the means bribed officials for exit visas. Expatriates formed colonies in France, Switzerland, Palestine and America. However poorly they had been treated, many still considered themselves Russians, and the motherland tugged at their souls. Some would come back to participate in the new communist experiment or, appalled by its excesses, join oppositional movements overseas.

Romm led his son into a tavern, a well-worn spot favored by workers. Entranced by the atmosphere, Vladimir shyly glanced at the amused regulars and imagined how a man would feel in this place.

The bartender set down two glasses, vodka for the father and juice for the son. Romm downed his shot with a well-practiced flick of the wrist. Vladimir's enthusiastic attempt to imitate his father failed miserably, choking him and staining his shirt. His eyes reddened. Stifling a smile, Romm lifted the boy to his shoulders and began tapping his boots to a familiar beat. As he picked up the pace the patrons joined in with rhythmic clapping and the two Cossacks danced away their troubles around the bar.

Alexander and Evsey got home late, after a pleasant rendezvous with two comely sisters. Their good humor evaporated as soon as they saw their father's cryptic note. What had they gotten their kid brother into? Had their carelessness consigned the family to Siberia? They were about to go turn themselves in when Vladimir yelled from the sidewalk.

"Come help with Papa!"

Romm rarely got drunk, and never in front of his sons. "My gallant lads..." were his last words before passing out.

They undressed their father and put him to bed. His snoring came through to the kitchen. "Look, it's no big deal," Alexander said. "Father is for reform. He'll understand."

Evsey grimaced. "It's not about our politics, Sasha. It's all the lies, the sneaking around, getting Volya mixed up in it. How could he ever trust us again? Anyway, father's friends only demand a Constitution. They're not calling for the Czar's head. And for sure they're not running around tossing bombs."

"Neither are we!" Alexander protested. "That's the Combat Brigade! No one can control them, not even the central committee!"

Vladimir stepped in. "Father said that those who lie with dogs get fleas."

Evsey grinned at the wise counsel. "Maybe that's why we've been scratching so much. So what else do you know?"

"I heard a policeman say that they knew where the pamphlets came from."

Alexander was startled. "How's that possible?" he demanded. "Did you tell them?"

Evsey jumped to his little brother's defense. "Shame on you, Sasha! I've warned you about the school press: its plates have so many imperfections that we might as well be signing our work."

Alexander slumped. "So now what? Do we just wait until they come get us?"

"No one's coming for anybody," Vladimir said. "Papa fixed everything. But I think that he's seen your book."

Evsey scrambled to the boys' bedroom. He returned looking glum.

"It's gone, brothers. Now we're really in for it."

That next evening the family gathered for a meeting. Romm placed his sons' lovingly documented chronology of terror on the table.

"What's this?"

Evsey blanched. "It's a scrapbook, father. Of trials and such."

Romm had gone through the boys' appalling keepsake. It depicted the frightening handiwork of nearly every contemporary Russian terrorist, from Yevstolia Ragozinikova, the mentally unbalanced woman who strapped on a dynamite-laden corset to take revenge on a despised prison warden, to Yegor Sazonov, whose celebrated bomb-toss tore the much-despised Interior Minister Viacheslav Plehve to shreds.

He turned to Evsey, his eldest. His tone was frighteningly even. "What's your favorite account?"

Evsey knew there was no right answer. "Sazonov, I suppose. He threw the bomb from only a few paces away. He was severely wounded; it's a miracle he wasn't killed."

George Romm shook his head. "Miracles, if you believe in such things, are the work of a Creator. I know of no God who would endorse Sazonov's act. Do you?"

He wasn't surprised. Instead of the poets, writers and composers who had enthralled his generation, the new heroes were mentally unbalanced assassins. Some had even taken to wearing bombs so they could be certain of accompanying their victims to Hell. But what most disturbed him were the justifications. How could anyone with even a smidgen of conscience endorse let alone participate in murder? And lacking conscience, where would it all end?

Romm addressed his sons. "Tonight, you will tear this pornography in pieces so small that it can never be reassembled," he ordered. "You will then burn it and toss out the ashes. As your father I forbid you to ever consider violence. It's a poison that will corrode your souls."

There was a brief silence. Evsey spoke up. "You were cheated out of a promotion, Father. Do you really think that things will change peacefully?"

The physician sighed. His older boys were at heart gentle spirits and wouldn't survive ten minutes of a real revolution. Vladimir presented an altogether different challenge.

"Our family has always championed reason. It may not get you the same quick results or, God forbid, the same gratification as using force, but its effects are far more lasting. In the end violence will corrode socialism, just as it ravaged the monarchy, just as it has torn apart every society since the dawn of time."

The boys were asleep. Romm donned his fur hat and let himself out. It was bitterly cold. A thick blanket of snow draped the streets, the smoke from countless hearths generating a sulfuric stench that would linger until spring. Pausing frequently to make sure that he wasn't followed, the weary physician made his way to an address that he had been told was a closely guarded secret.

If his sons knew just how far their father had come in his political views they would have been shocked. Romm's warning about violence was sincere, yet he had become estranged from his mild-mannered constitutionalist colleagues, mostly well-to-do merchants who were more concerned with making a steady profit and maintaining the status quo than with pressing for meaningful reforms.

Still, he felt a pang of guilt. Before Alexander II's assassination the printing house had prospered. Ethnicity hadn't kept him from medical school, or from a coveted assignment to the capital, Saint Petersburg, where he met and married the daughter of a wealthy shopkeeper. Was he upset because of the repressions, or because their days of privilege had passed?

Romm paused before going in. What he had heard about Marxism sounded intriguing, if perhaps a bit utopian. Imagine: a proletariat, in charge of its own destiny, with no kings or potentates of any kind! Still, there were complications. Tired of the miserable conditions in Vilna and, perhaps, his fondness for a certain nurse, his wife Sofia had returned to the capital to resume her career as a concert pianist. The hospital was overrun with patients and he had three boys to raise.

Who was he doing this for, and why?

Lubyanka prison,
6 December 1936

My situation has evolved into something that Dante would appreciate. Yesterday a guard hauled me into a small, unkempt office where a haggard man in a rumpled uniform sat at a desk piled high with papers. When given my name the bored official, whom I took to be a magistrate, listlessly rummaged through the stack. In time he found what he was looking for, and without any further ceremony recited a remarkably brief, uninformative indictment that charges me with belonging to a counterrevolutionary terrorist organization, an offense that everyone in the USSR who is out of diapers knows is punishable by shooting. Naturally I was shocked to the core, but he refused to furnish a copy of the document, answer any questions or even assign a defense lawyer, which he said was not permitted until the "period of investigation" had run, whenever that will be.

Radek was my editor while I was in America, so I figure that my being here must somehow be connected with his arrest. Perhaps they're hoping that I'll testify against the weasel. Not that I wouldn't – he put me through a lot of grief in the past – but since that long-ago mess we've had no contact other than through *Izvestia*. As for any new intrigues, I would be the last person whom he would approach. It's well known that I repudiated both him *and* that scandalous document he once enticed me to sign supporting Trotsky, and if he's done any new mischief I know nothing about it. Still, considering the man's treacherous propensities, Galina's fear that he might have falsely denounced me, a threat that I once dismissed, now seems far more plausible.

It's a lousy state of affairs, all right. But over the years I've faced far worse, and if I've learned nothing else it's the importance of keeping one's wits. In the end there are many respected officials whose words count far more than Radek's who will gladly speak on my behalf. I'm undoubtedly here because he or one of his confederates peppered the authorities with a tall tale that put me in the bull's eye. What their motives might be I can't begin to fathom, but they've created a house of cards that a puff of truth will surely blow down.

Oh, yes. A few days ago the occupant next door took to tapping on the wall in an obvious effort to communicate. I've ignored him and he has apparently given up. Other than for guards' footsteps and the clanging of doors (who would ever think that such sounds would be welcome!) it's been quiet. Despite repeated requests I haven't been allowed to go outside to exercise or been given anything to read, leaving me to do nothing but sit, think and watch for the return of my occasional companion, a scruffy, glassy-eyed rat of whom I've grown unreasonably fond.

The Romms (1906-07)

An open carriage rolled down Nevsky Prospect. As the sun's rays yielded to the chill of a late summer's eve, the boys passed by more museums, theatres and monuments than one could visit in a lifetime.

"There! There it is!" Alexander eagerly pointed as the immense fortress came into view. Its splendidly arched façade polished to a lustrous hue, the famous Winter Palace, citadel of the monarchy, gleamed in the fading light.

Evsey turned to the driver. "Is the Imperial family in residence?"

"You didn't know?" the man replied. "The Tsar and Tsaritsa spend most of their time in the country, at Tsarskoe Selo."

"Why is that?"

The driver groaned. "It's more modest, at least by their measure. Maybe they're trying to convey the impression that they're just like you and me, only more so." His tone turned wistful. "You know, I used to make a fine living hauling guests to their balls. Ah, the decadence!" Years earlier the man wouldn't have dared to speak that way, but a near-revolution, frequent strikes and the Empire's disastrous rout in the war with Japan had spread a sense of gloom over the once-lively capital.

It seemed a fair match for Vladimir's mood. With his father in prison, Evsey at a university and Alexander soon to follow, the decision was made to send him off to live with his mother. Vladimir suspected that he wouldn't soon return to Vilna.

The coach pulled up to an elegant stone building. A well turned-out, grey haired butler rushed to greet the brothers.

"Your Honors...!"

Evsey and Alexander leaped from the carriage, enveloping the man in a hug. "You have no idea how much we've missed you," Evsey exclaimed.

"He means your cooking, of course," Alexander interjected.

Yasha was equally delighted. His return to the capital without the beloved boys had been a severe blow. He and his wife, both devotedly Orthodox, shared a bed for nearly forty years, and not once had he considered straying. Sadly, that's not how things played out with the upper crust. After tiptoeing around Romm's dalliances in Vilna, he now had to contend with his mistress's lack of discretion! Order and propriety were the touchstones of civilized life. What was it about the privileged that made such simple rules so hard to follow?

Sofia stepped outside. Middle age had lent her a special beauty. Her thick black hair, coiffed in the latest style, framed a slender neck unadorned by jewelry. Noticeably slimmer since arriving in the capital, she wore a dress made of the finest silk, its bodice cut modestly but not overly so. Her one concession to practicality, a prickly wool scarf that the boys remembered from Vilna, was their only reminder that this stunning woman, whose appearance made grown men blush, was, after all, still their mother.

Vladimir lingered behind with the driver. Evsey had to fetch him.

"What were you talking about?" Sofia asked, smoothing her little man's hair.

"Oh, nothing. Just boring political stuff."

The hack approached with luggage. He tipped his cap. "You've got a fine lad there, madame. Wish that everyone was as socially conscious."

Evsey took Vladimir by the hand. "Come on, Volya, let's get you inside before you spark a revolt."

Bailov prison was located in the walled city of Baku. Fortified in the twelfth century then captured by the Mongols in the thirteenth, the bastion held everyone from thieves and murderers to those, like George Romm, who thought they had come up with a better way to run things. As he awaited release, the physician was placing the final touches on a manuscript reflecting his experiences tending to prisoners and staff. Given its unavoidably critical tone he didn't expect it would be published, but writing it helped keep his mind off other things.

Nonviolent political prisoners found conditions remarkably relaxed. While taking up arms against the Empire was dealt with severely, those who confined themselves to rabblerousing were punished with relatively brief terms of confinement or exile. Most accepted their fates calmly, spending their enforced vacations reading, writing and quarreling over the finer points of socialist dogma. George Romm passed the time doing what he knew best.

His long day done, the physician made one last pass among the cots, taking temperatures, updating charts and making sure that no one had expired since the last round. He briefed the night orderly and headed back to his cell. Threading his way through the damp, forbidding corridors for what would hopefully be one of the last times, he concluded that the challenges of ministering in this prison with walls were not so different than what he experienced in the Pale.

Before the weary physician could rest he faced a final task: to attend to the ill prisoners who would line up by his bunk. A slight young man with dark, wavy hair and a neat mustache was last. He extended his hand. "Iosif Vissarionovich, at your service. Sick, but only of injustice."

Stalin – his adopted pseudonym meant "man of steel" – didn't cut a particularly inspiring figure. His face scarred by smallpox, his left arm shriveled by a childhood illness, the shoemaker's son hailed from Georgia, a lawless chunk of the Empire overflowing with ruthless characters who would do anything for a ruble. In the Bolsheviks, a Socialist faction that teemed with pretentious intellectuals, Stalin was one of Lenin's favorites, the go-to man, the one who got things done and let others worry about the justifications. That his work would occasionally land him in prison was an irritant, but it hardly made him useless.

"We heard that you'll be leaving us, Doctor Romm."

"You're well informed."

Stalin laughed. "Information is my specialty. Comrade Lenin says that our party could use your help."

"You've spoken with him?"

"How could that be possible? He's in Europe. But even in prison, there are ways to communicate."

A guard entered the cellblock. Romm gripped Stalin's wrist as though taking a pulse. "I can't help you," he whispered. "Governor Von Wahl has it in for me. Anyway, Vilna is Socialist Revolutionary country. Your chances there are slim."

Stalin replied calmly, as though he was without a care in the world. "Populist fantasies will get the SR's nowhere, Doctor Romm. Who ever heard of peasants making a revolution? Anyway, you can't substitute running around, tossing bombs for the real work of organizing. We're concentrating on the workers and soldiers."

Romm reeled at the audacious notion. "Soldiers?"

"And why not? Generals drink cognac, leaving the ranks to starve. Who's to say what one could persuade troops to do when the time comes?"

It was smart. Instead of fighting the Czar's army, Bolsheviks were planning to co-opt it.

"Do you really think they'll switch sides?"

"Even better, let them stay in their barracks!" The voice belonged to a young prisoner with thick glasses and prematurely gray hair. He offered George Romm a soft, manicured hand. "Andrei Yanuarevich, Doctor. Is my rude friend keeping you from resting?"

Stalin scowled. "Don't let Comrade Vyshinsky fool you. He's not even a Bolshevik! But he will be one soon enough. Andrei is like the girls in Saint Petersburg: they play hard to get but underneath..."

A guard passed by. He and Vyshinsky exchanged a polite nod.

"Isn't it amazing? If I was them, I'd shoot the lot of us!"

Stalin chuckled. "You, shoot someone? That would be the day! You'd dig up some obscure law, spend hours twisting it for justification, and in the end order a subordinate to have someone else go do it."

"Of course, but only if a Comrade Judge signed the paperwork!"

The Man of Steel and his pal laughed and drifted away. George Romm lay down. He wasn't sure what put him off more, Stalin's boastfulness or Vyshinsky's flip cruelty. But he suspected that if a revolution was to succeed, characters such as these would have to be at the helm.

It was visiting day. Alexander and Evsey stood in a long line of family members impatiently waiting to enter the yard. Everyone carried lunch baskets brimming with what inmates longed for the most, short of freedom – food, and plenty of it.

Evsey turned to Alexander. "How will we tell him?"

Alexander shrugged. "What's there to say? Mother's entitled to her friends."

"You know what I mean! He'll be upset."

"So keep quiet! Artsy people stay over all the time. How's this any different?"

Both knew why it was different. The young man – they met him when dropping off Vladimir – seemed to know his way around the house a bit too well. A talented artist, he was a good decade younger than his hostess, and judging from the gentle way in which they brushed past each other the purpose of his being there seemed perfectly clear.

Evsey persisted. "All I'm saying, Sasha, is that this fellow might be taking advantage..."

"Of *Mother?*" Alexander chuckled. "Oh, please."

A few minutes later George Romm was finishing his second cabbage roll and trying not to stare while his sons ate their first. "Have mine," Alexander offered. "I've been getting too fat anyway."

Romm eagerly snatched the delicacy. "Two more weeks and I'll no longer be stealing food from my babes."

Bored guards lazily strolled about. "Doesn't anyone ever try to escape?" Alexander asked.

"Ah, it's not so bad here. Most of the sentences are short. They chain the dangerous sorts in the dungeons. Believe me, it's nothing you'd want to see."

Thanks to an informer, the apartment where George Romm had gone to meet with the Marxist Bund was no longer so "secret." In normal times his presence during a police raid would have been settled in the usual way – with lots of rubles. But with his scalp still tingling from a crease placed there by a radical's bullet some years earlier, Vilna's Governor-General was determined to cool revolutionary ardor. Instead of letting Romm buy his way out, he imprisoned him in Bailov, sending a warning while obtaining the services of a talented physician, if only for a while.

Romm belched contentedly. He turned to Evsey. "You seem out of sorts, Sallo. Is there something you want to tell me?"

Evsey wriggled nervously. "Well, Papa, that artist...he's still there."

"So?" Romm's reply came out more sharply than he intended. He wasn't ready to tell his sons that he and their mother were divorcing, nor that he was thinking of remarrying and emigrating to Europe. He turned to Alexander.

"Didn't you tell me a couple months ago that a painter took an interest in Volya?"

"It's the same man, Father. He takes Vladimir to the museums."

"Well, that's wonderful! A boy needs the company of an educated man. Maybe he can help your brother forget all about politics."

Stalin was soon released. When he arrived in Georgia an urgent message awaited from Lenin, who was in self-imposed exile in Switzerland. A prolific writer and masterful ideologue, the Bolshevik leader was running short on money to print and distribute propaganda, so he was turning to his top fundraiser. His patron's request led the Man of Steel to turn to *his*. Semen Ter-Petrosian was the man's name. Most everyone knew him as the vicious robber Kamo.

June 26, 1907 was a gorgeous day in Tiflis. Pensioners, young couples and mothers pushing carriages took in the sunshine, admired the flowers and paid their respects to Pushkin, the revered Russian poet whose bust graced the ancient capital's central plaza. Named after its conqueror, Russian General Paskevich Erevanski, the square was ringed with ornate churches and opulent government buildings. One was the Georgia state bank.

About eleven o'clock in the morning two armored coaches approached the majestic repository. As the lead team of Cossacks clopped by, dozens of heavily armed men sprang from hiding places. Dynamite bombs sailed to their targets, their deafening explosions drenching the sidewalks with blood, human limbs and horseflesh. After finishing off the wounded with quick bursts of gunfire, the robbers made off with the lead Phaeton, which contained the tidy sum of 260,000 rubles.

Rescuers rushed to the grisly scene. One was not who he pretended to be. Dressed in the uniform of a police officer, the man who organized the horrific crime checked his handiwork. Whatever Kamo might have felt at the sight of dozens of innocent men, women and children blown apart no one will ever know. Satisfied that none who might testify had survived, he walked away. News of the massacre spread quickly. Stolen currency, recovered in Europe, promptly led to the arrest of several bandits. Fingers pointed at Kamo and, by extension, his well-known sponsor. Stalin fled to Europe.

George Romm spent a year at Bailov. When he was released he found his hometown of Vilna in an uproar. Chronic food shortages, the Empire's bloody defeat in the Russo-Japanese War, Nicholas II's stubborn refusal to allow even a smidgen of democracy, and, most importantly, his campaign against the Jews had turned the tired old city into a focus of unrest. Expelled from Moscow and Saint Petersburg, packed into the ghettoes of the Pale, the Jews longed for change. Revolution, actually a decade off, seemed only a question of when, not if. Romm was dismayed. If the military remained loyal to the Crown it would be a bloody affair for which he had no stomach. If they didn't, he had a good inkling of who might wind up in charge. He had no stomach for that either.

His career prospects were also bleak. Years earlier he had applied for the position of chief physician at the Vilna Jewish hospital, but the job went to an influential member of the Christian community instead. Now, with the stigma of a prison record, he felt like a marked man. Sooner or later they would find a reason to send him back.

Happily, the boys were prospering. Vladimir enjoyed the capital and was doing well in school. Evsey would soon earn an engineering diploma. Alexander's career choice was a surprise. Instead of pursuing a practical field like his father and older brother, Romm's middle son quietly applied to the renowned Moscow Art Institute, which awarded him a scholarship to study painting and art criticism. Everyone was shocked except for his mother and her artist friends.

George Romm was fifty-two. Now that his divorce was final he married the nurse with whom he had been keeping company, bribed all the right officials and bought passage for Switzerland. It would be the last birthday he would celebrate with his family for many years.

Lubyanka prison,
9 December 1936

Yesterday a corpulent, red-faced Ukrainian burst into my cell. I instantly realized that things were even worse than I imagined, for this was none other than Comrade George Molchanov, the legendary, dreaded interrogator who "persuaded" the accused in the 1936 trial to confess and thus forfeit their lives.

Molchanov shoved a document into my hands. He brusquely offered a pen. It wasn't intended for making corrections.

DECLARATION BY VLADIMIR GEORGIEVICH ROMM

I was born in 1896 into a privileged Jewish family in Vilna. My brothers and I were Socialist Revolutionaries. My father was a Bundist. I did not join the Communist Party of Bolsheviks until after the Revolution. Since then I have been employed as a journalist. Most recently, between April 1934 and November 1936, I was *Izvestia* correspondent to Washington. Between August 1930 and April 1934 I was *Tass* correspondent to Geneva, where I was accredited to the Disarmament Conference. I also spent time at the news agency's Paris bureau. Before then I was *Tass* correspondent to Tokyo.

I first met Karl Radek in 1922 in connection with the USSR's work in Germany. Radek was in close contact with Trotsky, then a top Party member. In 1926 Radek convinced me to join the Trotsky underground, oppose Stalin and illegally resist the Party. To these ends I signed the counterrevolutionary document, the "Declaration of the Eighty-Three". I later apologized for my behavior to a Party committee. My words were insincere. In my heart I remained a Trotskyite but I needed a job and intended to continue sabotaging the Party from within.

43

In 1930 Radek was still working for Trotsky, organizing an underground resistance inside the Soviet Union. I agreed to take advantage of my position as a foreign correspondent and secretly pass messages between him and Trotsky. Between summer 1931 and early 1934 I repeatedly met with Trotsky's son, Sedov, in Berlin and Paris and carried messages back and forth between him and Radek.

Sedov introduced me to his father in 1933, in Paris. Trotsky said that he was working for Germany and Japan, with the intention of weakening the Soviet Union and making it vulnerable to invasion. These objectives were to be accomplished in two ways: by assassinating the USSR's top leaders, including Comrade Stalin, and by sabotaging Soviet industry. I passed this on to Radek.

My last contact with the terrorist organization was in early 1934 when I met with Sedov in Berlin. He asked for a progress report from Radek. I brought it to him on my next trip.

I affirm that this declaration is true and correct.

The more I read of this horrendously contrived confession the more my jaw dropped. Everything has been twisted to make me seem as untrustworthy as possible. It's not surprising that they would have me denounce Radek, whom I actually hold in very low regard. What's astonishing is that they would have me condemn myself, and not just in a trivial way, but as a willing participant in a plot to murder the General Secretary. After what happened to the wretched defendants in the first trial one certainly knows what such an admission would bring!

How foolish do they think I am?

"This is ridiculous," I blurted out. "Who would believe such a preposterous tale?"

Molchanov held his temper. "Preposterous is a strong word, comrade. Communism has entered a critical phase. We've known since the assassination of the Leningrad Party chief that the Soviet Union is beset by spies and traitors. Fascists are eagerly waiting at the door. We must rally the people and keep them alert to treachery. Don't you agree?"

I could hardly believe my ears. Molchanov was referring to the late Sergei Kirov, a notorious womanizer. Rumors were that the man who shot him was a jealous lover, not, as the authorities insisted, a counterrevolutionary. (Of course, it's the latter that the killer said he was at the trial, thus dooming a passel of his alleged helpmates.) Surely Molchanov knows this, yet here he was, justifying the shameless fraud by engaging in the nauseating double-talk that has plagued communist discourse since the time of Lenin.

American Socialists would often ask why the Soviet government had neither "melted away" nor passed into the hands of the workers as communism promises. When I argued the official position, which I mostly believed, that a strong hand was needed to defend against internal and external threats, and that the transition to true communism would come later, their eyes rolled. Well, it's since become obvious that as far as our leaders are concerned "later" means "never." Maybe I'm demonstrating my naiveté, but until Vyshinsky's odious stooge appeared in my cell I never appreciated just how far our leaders were willing to go to stay on top.

Or maybe I didn't want to know.

I tried mightily to keep calm. "Look, Comrade Molchanov. There's no doubt that Germany and Japan are serious threats, and if I had evidence of a plot I would pass it on. But I don't. Other than knowing Radek and signing on to Trotsky's appeal many years ago, a stupid act that I promptly repudiated, this statement is pure fantasy. I didn't join a conspiracy. I know of none. I've never met Trotsky and have no idea who his son is, so I certainly couldn't have passed on any correspondence. Except for what I've been told and read in the papers, I am totally ignorant of any plans to topple the government and murder the General Secretary."

"A fantasy? If at this very moment you were confronted by witnesses who could corroborate each and every word of this declaration, what would you say?"

I replied without hesitation. "I would say that these 'witnesses' are liars."

Molchanov reddened. For a moment I was sure that he would turn to another means of persuasion. But he didn't. Like a teacher with a recalcitrant pupil he patiently pointed at the first paragraph. "Are these words true?"

"Yes," I replied, "but our family's 'privileged' status didn't keep my father out of prison. And calling me a 'journalist' is ridiculous – you know perfectly well that I served in the secret services."

"That's exactly why it can't be mentioned!" Molchanov pointed again. "How about these, regarding your errors with Radek?"

"Yes," I admitted. "It's what I told the committee in Tokyo..."

"And your assignments to Berlin and Paris? Are they factually correct?"

I wearied of the game. "My postings are a matter of record."

Molchanov threw the document on the desk. "I'll expect to find it signed when I return." He abruptly headed for the door.

His sudden leaving caught me off guard. "What about my family?" I blubbered.

Molchanov turned to face me. "Vladimir Georgievich," he sighed, "please believe me when I say that in time everyone cooperates. Stretching it out yields absolutely no advantage either to you, or me, or the Comrade Procurator-General, who is anxious to wrap things up." His voice turned ominously flat. "As for your family," he added, "their future is in your hands."

Well, I finally understand why the desk. As for the accursed document, it's still where Molchanov left it, glowing like an ember.

Journeys (1915)

In 1915 Vladimir was nineteen, enrolled at a technical university in Petrograd, the new name for the Russian capital. For the first time in his life, he was all alone. His mother had succumbed after a brief illness. Evsey and Alexander were married and pursuing careers, Evsey as an engineer in Leningrad and Alexander as an art critic in Moscow. George Romm was retired and living with his second wife in Switzerland.

Working odd jobs to pay for a small room and groceries left Vladimir little time to do anything but eat, sleep and spend what few kopecks he could scrape together amusing himself with the fairer sex. Ladies thought his olive skin and vaguely Asiatic features exotic and asked more than once if there had been Mongols in his past. Thinking the image of a brave warrior on horseback appealing he never denied it.

Still, he was in fact galloping nowhere. His day-to-day life, perhaps good enough for most, seemed insufferably dull, and he longed to reprise those exciting days dodging the authorities on the streets of Vilna. Now that the city was in German hands going back was impossible, but there were rumors that resistance to the Czar was building in Belorussia. Desperate for adventure, Vladimir impulsively abandoned his studies, packed his bags and headed to Minsk, where he took a clerical position at a *zemstvo*, one of a network of government-funded social service agencies whose employees' liberal propensities made them hubs of oppositional activity. That, he reasoned, would be his ticket to the political underground.

It was a chilly fall evening. Wrapped head to toe in blankets, Vladimir gazed out the window of his tiny room. He watched listlessly as pedestrians hurried along, their breaths leaving behind small puffs of condensation illuminated by the glow of streetlamps. After weeks of striking up conversations he hadn't met a single coworker, indeed a single citizen of any age who seemed interested in doing anything other than drinking and carousing, or in borrowing money to drink and carouse. Germany's menacing advance into Russian territory had sapped revolutionary fervor. It was all an able-bodied man could do to avoid the teams of military and police who scoured the streets for conscripts. Without his *zemstvo* identification card Vladimir would have already been drafted several times over.

Across the street a young woman waited for a wagon to pass. She carried a large bag but didn't seem to be shopping, and when she stepped from the curb and her features came into view Vladimir recognized his youngish superior. Anna, a robust, blonde Polish girl, was two years his senior. He found her attractive, although in an earthier, far less self-conscious way than the lissome coquettes he had courted in the capital.

A few minutes later Vladimir was counting his final week's wages while Anna returned the personal things he kept at the office. She glanced at a cheaply framed portrait.

"Your family?"

"It was taken soon after we arrived in Vilna. That's my father George Davidovich, my mother Sofia Evseevna, and my brothers Alexander and Evsey."

Anna looked closer. "Your mother was very beautiful. But her expression seems, I don't know...sad."

"Mother was a pianist. I was only a kid when she returned to the capital. She fell ill and passed away last year."

Vladimir's voice drifted. Anna impulsively took his hand. Her cheeks quickly flushed and she drew away.

"I'm sorry you're leaving. You know, I barely managed to keep the director from calling the police."

"Police? Why would he...?"

"Really, Vladimir Georgievich..."

"Please, call me Volya."

Vladimir's plaintive expression reminded Anna of why men were so dangerous. She steadied herself. "Volya, you forget there's a war on. Trying to strike up political conversations with everyone you meet draws attention. People have been whispering. Some think that you're a provocateur Petrograd sent to test their loyalty. Really, it's very disruptive."

Anna's warmth had knocked politics clean out of Vladimir's mind. Her resolve was also fading, and both found it difficult to keep suitably grim.

He brought out his last bottle. "Would you like something to drink?"

"Do you have any food?"

Vladimir rummaged through the cupboard. There was a half-loaf of bread and some moldy cheese.

Anna groaned. "You pour. I'll go get us a sausage."

It was early morning when Vladimir dragged himself from bed. Anna's scent still lingered. Considering the deft way in which she handled his firing, her tepid reaction to his political views, which for some idiotic reason he had felt compelled to convey, and the tender but decisive way in which she shattered the thin veneer of his pretense, he was more than slightly annoyed. His eyes were drawn to the photograph. What had really passed between his parents?

Was he destined to reprise all of his father's mistakes?

Anna took lunch alone. She smiled at the memory of the evening. When Vladimir learned of her peasant roots he grew excited, and after dinner he started babbling about how much more socially conscious Socialist Revolutionaries were than Bolsheviks. He was about to give her a headache when she playfully tried to distract him. Giving her would-be savior some practical experience with a real farmer's daughter did shut him up, but it also stirred something in herself that, considering their differences, might best be left alone. No matter how much he tried to pretend otherwise, her new boyfriend was *intelligentsia*. He wouldn't be the type to savor laboring in the fields, of that she was certain.

Vladimir spent the day looking for another clerical position. There were numerous vacancies but none carried a deferment.

"You could go back to school," Anna suggested. They were having dinner in her apartment, which was thankfully well-heated. She had nearly frozen to death the other evening.

"Not for a while. I left at the beginning of the term."

"Ah, impetuous youth! Well, you've finished two years of university. You could be an officer."

"They're not commissioning Jews. But dying for the Czar as an enlisted man – now *that's* perfectly acceptable."

"Then don't die," she grinned. "Look, if you'd like to get out of town, I'm going to the farm to help ready things for winter. There are fences to mend, a new barn to finish, lots of chores for a strong lad. All you can eat, great company, time to think things through. Want to tag along?"

"Sure. But I'm not...well...Christian."

Anna kissed him softly. "Work hard and I'm sure they'll overlook it."

Days later, after a long ride in a railcar reeking of cabbage and unwashed bodies a wagon deposited the couple at the entrance to an expansive farm. They were greeted by Anna's mother, a thickset woman with rosy cheeks and an engaging smile. She was followed at a discreet distance by her husband, a small, wiry man with a permanent squint from the outdoors, then by children of varying ages. Two of the girls, Vladimir later learned, were taken in after being abandoned on the farm's threshold.

Vladimir's presence was accepted without fuss. Two boys took their bags to the farmhouse, an impressively spacious brick structure with a steeply pitched tile roof. They were given the guest room on the second floor, an arrangement that made Vladimir blush but which their practical hosts thought perfectly reasonable.

The grizzled farmer and the idealistic city boy found plenty to admire in one another. Vladimir had never seen anyone labor as hard or skillfully, while the farmer was impressed with the young man's grit and determination. Vladimir was clumsy with tools but quick to learn, and when his unprotected, soft hands turned raw with blisters he donned a pair of gloves and got right back to it. Aware of their differences, Anna had warned both to steer clear of politics and religion, so in an abundance of caution they regrettably wound up sharing little of their true feelings.

Anna's father had asked Vladimir to give the blessing for the evening meal. Hurriedly thinking back to those visits with his grandmother, he recited the only Holy words he could remember.

"*Barukh atah Adonai Eloheinu melekh ha'olam.*"

A moment passed. Anna's mother smiled curiously. "You're done?"

"Actually, it's only a preamble, Mother," Anna said. "There would be more if we were eating Kosher."

"Really? What do the words mean?"

"It means 'blessed are you Lord, our God, sovereign of the universe'," Vladimir explained.

The farmer cleared his throat. "Well, that sounds like a very fine blessing to me. There's surely no reason to be long-winded!" Anna's father considered himself fair and open-minded and was reluctant to fault someone for things, such as their ethnicity, which were beyond their control. Their priest, who openly condemned religious and ethnic persecution, often reminded his flock that one could choose God but not their parents. Yet there were rumors that Jews, in particular, had been leaving the Lord, seduced by Godless Marxism. That was of course unforgivable.

Anna's father spread a thin, translucent layer of lard on a slice of bread and offered it to Vladimir. And with that they dug in.

"You know, Volya," the farmer said, "our property was once twice its size. Soon after the partition of Poland a Czarist official brought my great-grandfather startling news, that his boundary markers were off and that our land intruded on the adjacent farm. Now this seemed impossible, as the property had passed through generations without challenge, so my ancestor asked to see the records. He was told that the map for our plot was missing. It was the other map that supposedly revealed the discrepancy."

"Isn't it strange that only one was lost?"

"That's why the judge of the peasant court ruled in our ancestor's favor. But the plaintiff appealed to the Court of Cassation, and in his declaration made sure to mention that his family had converted to Orthodoxy while pointing out that the 'land grabbers' remained Catholics. As you might imagine, that pretty well sealed the outcome. Of course, you must know what it means to suffer for one's beliefs."

Until now Vladimir had heeded Anna's injunction, but the opportunity to talk about really important things was too enticing. "These injustices affect everyone," he said. "Whatever our ethnicity or religion we're all slaves to the Monarchy."

Anna and her mother exchanged a worried glance. It took only an instant for their fears to materialize.

"What did you say?" the farmer asked. "Slaves?"

Vladimir foolishly plodded on. "Well, not literally, but, yes..."

"Michal," the farmer said, addressing his oldest boy, "do you see any such persons here?"

Michal glanced nervously about. "No, Father. No slaves here."

Anna discreetly squeezed Vladimir's hand. But he felt compelled to explain. "Socialist Revolutionaries have the highest regard for those who work the land..."

"*Regard?*" the farmer bellowed. He slammed his fist on the table, sending plates clattering to the floor. "Under socialism we would have – nothing! Our land, our crops, our animals, everything we've toiled for, all that's been passed through generations would go to some Godless collective. We've managed just fine for hundreds of years. It's finally sinking into the Czar's thick skull that what we most need is to be left alone. We don't need radicals wearing shiny boots coming here, telling us how to live. You know," he added, "your people would be far more welcome if you tried to fit in." And with that he stomped off.

Anna's face turned into stone. She ran after her father.

Word of Vladimir's firing had reached the authorities, and a few days after his return to Minsk two stern-faced policemen showed up at his door with a draft notice. He had a week to put his affairs in order and report to a reserve infantry regiment near Petrograd.

On his last night as a civilian he was readying his things when Anna came to the door. Vladimir had left soon after the incident at the farm and hadn't heard from her since.

"Would you like to come in?"

"No, thank you." She handed him a small, neatly wrapped parcel and quickly pecked him on the cheek. "Please be careful."

Anna was gone. Vladimir opened the box. Inside were his well-used work gloves along with a warm note from the farmer and his wife wishing him Godspeed. Vladimir carefully packed the items in his suitcase. Even the secular could use some help now and again.

Lubyanka prison,
12 December 1936

What an evening it's turned out to be! Moments after finishing my meager supper the cell door cracked open and a prisoner stumbled in. Short, bald and frighteningly skeletal, there was no mistaking the thick glasses and formidable overbite.

Wonder of wonders – Karl Radek was in my cell!

I was in shock. Radek moved as if to embrace me, then apparently thought better of it and sat down. It promised to be a complicated reunion.

A rat of the four-legged variety helped break the ice. Wary of the stranger, it scurried as close as it dared and sniffed furiously. I tossed it some crumbs.

"Your pet?" Radek asked, exchanging a wary look with the creature.

"I named him Leon, after Trotsky," I said. "He's the perfect opposite. Ideologically primitive and completely trustworthy."

"Trotsky." Radek spat out the name. "What I would give to have never heard of the swine."

I felt the same, and not just about Trotsky. If anyone truly deserves to be in the Lubyanka it's Radek. This master of invective, with the sharpest of rhetorical knifes, has an uncanny knack for aligning himself with losing causes and dragging others down with him. When the Bolsheviks took power in 1917 Radek's polemical skills earned him a coveted slot in the Party Central Committee and a position as a propagandist. Only a year later he was helping organize workers in Germany, which some high-ranking Party idiots selected as a logical place for the next revolution. In the end German authorities quashed the half-hearted coup, shot two esteemed Socialists and booted Radek out. Why the Kaiser let the bigheaded scoundrel off is a matter of speculation, but it imparted a reputation for slipperiness that was confirmed years later when Stalin allowed him to return after he and Trotsky were exiled. Mark my words: whatever happens, Radek is by far the one most likely to land on his feet. His single-minded determination to stay in the game is what makes him so dangerous.

Radek handed me an envelope. Inside was a note in my wife's hand.

> My darling husband!
> Things are as you might expect. Every day there's a new story in the paper about a big conspiracy to murder Comrade Stalin. Naturally, your name has been prominently mentioned. I was fired from my teaching position and the landlady told us to leave. She wouldn't give me a reference so it was impossible to find another apartment. The government also stopped paying your salary (they said the law gives them no choice) so we are living off our savings. I didn't realize there was so little!
>
> We stayed with Alexander and Elena for a few days. It was very awkward since they frequently host important guests and can't afford to be distracted. So I took Georgie to Leningrad and moved in with Evsey and Esfir. We're sleeping in the front room and must pack and unpack twice a day. It's inconvenient and a terrible intrusion.
>
> So far I haven't been able to find regular work, since employers also want references. I'm doing some tutoring but parents are nervous about being associated with me, so I must keep lowering the price until the effort seems hardly worth it. Your brothers aren't rich and I worry about the future.
>
> I'm sure that you're innocent and that the arrest was a big mistake, but I also know that you're a proud man. Please, for everyone's sake, do what the Party asks so that we can be back together.
>
> Your brothers send their best Communist wishes.
>
> All our love, Galina.

Radek's unexpected appearance, then this, proved too much and my tears flowed as they had not since mother's passing. For a tiny moment I sensed the texture of ordinary life, of Galina's warm embrace, of little Georgie's sloppy kisses, and basked in the warmth of their imagined presence.

All too soon the daydream faded. I re-read the letter, which must have been censored if not dictated. "Do what the Party asks?" Of course, that's why they sent Radek, who was born without a conscience. He's a natural salesman.

"Karl Berngardovich, you know that I had no part in this. Why don't you tell them the truth? When I'm released I'll do what I can to help."

For a moment it seemed as he might laugh. "Volya, Volya," he said, carelessly invoking my pet name, "I appreciate your offer, but let the Procurator-General worry about the truth. You worry about yourself and your loved ones." He drew closer. "Everyone else is cooperating."

His words tightened on me like a noose. I grabbed the confession off the desk. "Cooperate? Is that how you're planning to save your neck? By having me offer mine?"

Radek scowled. "You think of yourself too highly, comrade. They're not after you. Have you heard of the 'conveyor'? Teams of goons harangue you day and night, as though they're riding on a belt, like in the mines. They douse you with water to keep you awake. It's not long before you're hallucinating. And if that doesn't break your spirit, they have lots more tricks up their sleeves. Believe me, I know."

For years my colleagues and I tried to ignore the disturbing signs of decay. Now that the evil could no longer be denied, the weight of the evasions, the far-fetched assertions, the implausible justifications came crashing down and I felt as though all hope had been sucked from my soul. What about the score of executions I diligently justified to Paul and the others a few months ago? My thoughts drifted to the newsreels, to the vacant expressions of the accused as, one by one, they took the stand and confessed.

Radek fidgeted. "Look, we're running out of time. Do you want to hear me out or not?"

I nodded weakly. What else could I do?

"Piatakov and I are the main targets. You're just a witness. Vyshinsky's trying to keep foreigners from raising a stink like they did the last time. He figured that bringing in some mid-level Party workers to corroborate the confessions would calm the Western press."

"Piatakov's cooperating?"

"Everyone's on board but you."

I was flabbergasted. All the accused at the 1936 trial were shot. What Radek was suggesting seemed tantamount to suicide.

"You want me to denounce you, and while I'm at it, myself? Are you crazy? Don't you remember what happened the last time?"

"Look, Kirov's murder had to be avenged. This is different." Radek lowered his voice. "Stalin assured me that he would spare our lives."

Stalin? That took a moment to digest. "He personally told you this?"

"Yes, *personally*. Look, both you and I have had our problems with the Party, and we've both been welcomed back. Just play along and it will all work out."

Radek's tone was so matter-of-fact that I was tempted to believe him. He and the General Secretary were once close. Were they in this together?

"But why involve *me*? I'm just a peon!"

"Everyone knows that Soviet agents have been hot on Trotsky's trail for years. The man lives in a fishbowl, literally a prisoner of European police, who guard his residence and shadow his every movement. How could a well-known Soviet official like me communicate with him? How was it kept secret from informers, our own NKVD and foreign security services not for a day or two, but for years? I would have needed an emissary who was free to travel to Europe without stirring suspicion. Ergo: a correspondent!" His pride of authorship was evident. "It's really quite simple."

So that was it. I'm to be the middleman, the link between Radek and Trotsky. It really *is* simple. All I'd have to do is stand in front of the whole world and falsely admit to being a traitor.

It was all too much to take in. I rushed to the door and banged furiously. "We're done," I yelled.

Radek was stunned. "Volya, please...think of your family!"

Think of my loved ones? What else did the scoundrel imagine I've been doing? Guards burst in just as I went for his throat.

The Commissar (1917)

A thin, pallid soldier approached an encampment in the hills just south of Petrograd. Dressed in a rumpled, ill-fitting uniform, he carried his rifle tucked under his armpit, muzzle down, as though he was a peasant chasing game in the woods. A freshly-skinned rabbit hung from his rucksack.

"Halt!" Vladimir ordered. "Password!" Although the nearest Germans were many kilometers away, he was on guard duty and rules were rules.

"Vladimir Georgievich?" the soldier called out, not bothering to break his stride. He knew that sentries were prohibited from inserting ammunition clips until the last possible moment, and he hadn't heard the characteristic thwack.

Vladimir lowered his weapon. "My name instead of the password? You're lucky I didn't fire!"

The dusty visitor leaned his rifle against a tree. "Shooting would have been a kindness. Maxim Feodorovich, at your service. I'm the personnel clerk at regimental headquarters."

They shook hands. "Excuse my appearance, comrade. You're still new, but you'll find that in this army every soldier is a hunter and gatherer. What they feed us isn't sufficient to sustain a dead man."

Vladimir stared. Something about the man seemed familiar, as though they had once met.

Maxim chuckled. "Don't you recognize me? I knew you the instant your file crossed my desk. You're little Volya, brother of the scoundrels who took advantage of my sisters and broke their hearts. Alexander and Evsey, if I'm not mistaken."

Vladimir was delighted. "Of course! You were in our revolutionary cell!"

"A cell is what it's turned into, all right," Maxim sneered. "Thanks to the Combat Brigade's suicidal antics, the authorities came after us with a vengeance. Nearly every Socialist Revolutionary I know is either in jail or the army, which is little different except they feed you less. Come by our camp when your shift ends and meet my little group." He held up the rabbit. "I'll save you some stew."

Late that evening Vladimir met with Maxim and two companions. "Is it just you three?" he asked, hungrily devouring a helping of the pungent dish.

"What were you expecting?" Maxim replied. "Political agitation is a hanging offense even for reservists. The mustaches despise socialism, so it's not like we can hold rallies. Just getting together is risky."

Vladimir turned to the others. "Can you read and write?" They sheepishly shook their heads.

"Fine. We'll start there."

Literacy, Vladimir knew, was a critical precondition for political enlightenment. With permission from their superiors, who thought the exercise a harmless way to pass the time, Vladimir and Maxim started holding classes. Their pupils soon numbered in the dozens.

Why Nicholas II chose that particular week to go for a ride in his personal train is a good question. Russia's sovereign had never labored in a freezing factory nor slogged through knee-deep mud dodging enemy bullets, so it probably didn't occur to him that the strikes and anti-war rallies that besieged Petrograd would turn out any differently than in the past. So when his timid advisors finally let on that unruly throngs had virtually shut down the capital, overwhelming its lightly-armed police and pillaging their stations, he ordered the customary remedy. But with the enemy on the march, the only available troops were newly-minted conscripts anxiously awaiting their turn to become cannon fodder for the mighty German army.

That they obeyed at all was a miracle. And like most miracles, it was exceptionally short-lived. After shooting more than two-score workers during a panicky confrontation at the statute of Alexander III, a site that came to be known as "Rebellion Square," the Czar's frightened peasant-soldiers had a change of heart, and the next officer who demanded that they fire on ordinary citizens was himself shot dead. Then, just as the Bolsheviks envisioned, the troops joined the strikers.

In the end the suffering and hardships brought on by the war accomplished what the assassinations and other shenanigans could not, breaking the people's bond with the Czar and stripping him of that most precious asset: his aura of infallibility. As the situation in Petrograd deteriorated Nicholas II finally heeded the advice of military commanders and abdicated in favor of his brother, Grand Duke Michael.

But a good look at the grim-faced throngs milling on the streets of Petrograd convinced him that the time for nobility had passed. Rebuffing his commission, the intended heir laid off the whole mess on the Duma, a powerless legislative body that the Czar created to placate critics. In February 1917, three centuries after sixteen-year-old Mikhail Feodorovich was installed as Russia's first sovereign, the House of the Romanovs was replaced by a liberally-inclined Provisional Government. Furious at being outmaneuvered, Socialists vowed that the so-called February Revolution would not be the last uprising of the year.

Word of the Monarchy's fall spread quickly. Orderlies ran around Vladimir's camp tacking up notices. "Look!" a newly literate soldier pointed out, "off-duty, we have the same rights as civilians!" Others crowded around. "That's right!" someone yelled. "All political prisoners will be freed! My brother will be released!"

Within weeks there was an even more startling announcement:

ORDER NUMBER 1
March 1, 1917

To the Garrison of the Petrograd Military District

The Soviet of Workers and Soldiers has decreed:

1. Every military unit is to elect a political committee
2. Every military unit of company size and above is to elect a single representative, who is to present his credentials to the State Duma
3. All military units are politically subordinate to the Soviet of Workers' and Soldiers' Deputies
4. Soldiers are to obey all orders except those that contradict the orders of the Soviet of Workers' and Soldiers' Deputies
5. All types of arms, including machine-guns and armored vehicles shall be under the control of soldiers' committees, and not of officers
6. On duty, soldiers are to observe strict military discipline, but off duty they shall enjoy the rights of any Soviet citizen
7. When off duty, soldiers cannot be required to salute officers. Officers shall always treat soldiers with respect and are prohibited from addressing them in the familiar "tu"

Although they were a minority, Socialists wielded substantial influence in the new government. Regulations were soon passed that authorized soldiers to form

Socialist political groups known as "Soviets" in schools, government offices and military units. Officers helplessly stood by as enlisted men anointed fellow soldiers as commissars to represent their interests. Whatever the reason for throwing the olive branch – many thought that the regime lacked the fortitude to confront revolutionaries – the move effectively turned Russia's armed forces into union shops, leaving ordinary soldiers to exercise veto power over everything from discipline to deployment. One of the newly anointed stewards was the commissar of the 177th Infantry Reserve Regiment, Vladimir Georgievich Romm.

"Tell us again, Comrade Romm, why we should worry about your numbing theories. Who cares if someone is a Socialist Revolutionary like you or one of Lenin's Bolsheviks like comrade Repin?"

Political education sessions were not going well. Soldiers were happy to gain protection from arbitrary treatment but most seemed numb to ideological appeals. They paid little attention during mandatory lectures, preferring to pass the time sleeping, chatting with friends or, as in this instance, trying to draw the speaker into a silly quarrel.

Vladimir could hardly contain his frustration. "As I've said, Bolsheviks want to make decisions for the people, while Socialist Revolutionaries feel that the people should choose."

"Do you mean," the soldier persisted, "that you would leave it to us, mere peasants, to decide?"

"That, comrade, is the populist way."

"Wonderful!" The soldier rose to address his colleagues. "I propose that we leave the fighting to the generals and return to our farms. All in favor?"

Cheers and hoots effectively ended the meeting. A captain approached Vladimir.

"Looks like leading the unwashed to their socialist destiny isn't as simple as you figured, eh?" Pleased with himself, the officer twirled the tips of the ample mustache that identified him as a career military man.

Vladimir stiffened. "One loudmouth doesn't reflect the whole group. I'm sure that..."

The officer laughed. "Please, Commissar, I'm not nearly as stupid as my epaulets suggest. You and I both know that the main thing these country-boys want is for the war to end so they can go home, and whoever promises that will get their support. Unless I've got my Socialists mixed up, that puts your faction in a pickle, doesn't it?"

Vladimir knew that the captain was right. Bolsheviks were mostly concerned with protecting Russia's urban centers, where their constituents – the workers – lived. Eager to extract Russia from a war that he attributed to Western stupidity, Lenin was determined to make peace with Germany even if it meant ceding large swathes of the countryside. That stuck in the craws of the Socialist Revolutionaries, for whom rural areas were the main base of support. Lenin wanted to play nice with the Kaiser; Socialist Revolutionaries were determined to kill him. Meanwhile ordinary soldiers were far less concerned with ideological distinctions than with surviving a war that introduced poison gas into the lexicon. Someone would still have to produce food, and if it had to be done under another flag, so be it.

Vladimir thought about his troops, nearly all conscripts fresh from the farm. Few were ready to take on the mighty German army, and fewer still seemed willing. None, including himself, would likely return from the front.

What should he tell them? Just as importantly, how did he feel?

Lubyanka prison,
13 December 1936

My head was still smarting from the guard's truncheon when Molchanov returned. His eyes drifted to my confession. It was on the desk, still unsigned.

He abruptly reached into a pocket, a move that I'm embarrassed to say caused me to flinch, and handed me an envelope of the kind used to convey confidential correspondence.

It was addressed to me. I ripped it open.

UNION OF SOVIET SOCIALIST REPUBLICS
PEOPLE'S COMMISSARIAT FOR INTERNAL AFFAIRS
Moscow, 3 December 1936

TO: Vladimir Georgievich Romm

You are instructed to extend your full cooperation, comply with all requests and directions, and maintain complete secrecy as to all matters brought to your attention by Comrade Georgi Aleksandrovich Molchanov of the Secret Political Department.

Nikolai Ivanovich Yezhov
People's Commissar for Internal Affairs

Molchanov picked up the confession. He thrust it in my face. "By authority of Comrade Yezhov, I direct you to sign."

"The Comrade Commissar is in charge of the police. He knows that there is a penalty for making false declarations," I objected.

Molchanov's veins nearly popped from his temples. "You *must* sign!"

"Why?"

For such an ungainly man he was surprisingly quick, and the next thing I knew I was on the floor. Something rattled in my mouth. I spat out blood and a tooth.

A New Order (1917)

Vladimir startled awake. Maxim was shaking his shoulder.

"It's the Bolshies," Maxim whispered, anxious not to rouse the other soldiers. "They're making their move!"

Vladimir quietly slipped from his bunk. He quickly dressed and joined his friend outside.

"I just got the message," Maxim said. "Our people say to keep out of it. They think the Bolsheviks will stumble."

"Stay out of it?" Vladimir was dismayed. "We're forbidden from supporting fellow Socialists?"

"If the Bolsheviks were so 'fellow' they would have asked their Socialist colleagues to join in, don't you think? Look, the Congress of Soviets opens tomorrow night. Knowing of Lenin's devious ways that's no coincidence. Just sit tight. If they don't pull it off we'll be in the driver's seat."

On October 24, 1917, as darkness fell over Petrograd, armed squads of Bolsheviks and renegade soldiers occupied government offices, police stations and the telephone exchange. Bolsheviks had worked for months to co-opt the capital's military garrison, and when the time came resistance was slight. Most civil servants peacefully yielded their posts, and other than for a few stubborn ministers who had to be forcefully dislodged from the Winter Palace opposition was slight. In the end that timid, unwieldy concoction known as the Provisional Government lived up to its label, lasting a mere nine months.

The next evening a slight, balding man climbed the steps of an old palace. Passing under majestic columns he entered the lavish hall where the Society for Education of Noble Maidens once taught etiquette to female members of the court. Energized by their leader's daring seizure of power, hundreds of Bolshevik delegates to the Second All-Russia Congress of Soviets jumped to their feet.

A badly outnumbered contingent of Socialist Revolutionaries sourly watched as

Lenin took the podium. Austere and erudite, the brand-new leader of the world's first communist state was a masterful orator, blending ideological profundities and calls to action into an intoxicating elixir that drove audiences to frenzy. Vladimir, who had never heard him speak, was electrified, and as Lenin's concluding words, "we shall now proceed to construct the socialist order" brought Bolsheviks to their feet he eagerly joined in the ovation.

Maxim was horrified.

Several weeks later Socialist Revolutionaries caucused in Petrograd. Vladimir and Maxim came to participate. They found conditions dreadful. Mounds of uncollected trash festered on the streets, drunks and beggars clogged the sidewalks, and wherever one looked citizens stood in endless queues seeking out the most basic necessities. If someone was in charge it wasn't readily apparent. For all their skill at organizing, Bolsheviks were few and their enemies many. How on earth they intended to stay on top was a mystery.

Delegates chatted quietly, waiting for the main speaker to arrive. A young man turned to Vladimir.

His tone was disarmingly genial. "Why did you applaud the tyrant?"

It grew deathly quiet. The question was obviously on more than one mind.

Vladimir replied carefully. "Tyrant is a strong word."

An older delegate joined the fray. "Not nearly strong enough!" he shrieked. "On nothing more than Lenin's authority Bolsheviks and their army stooges rounded up scores of so-called collaborators, including dozens of Socialist Revolutionaries. Who knows, maybe a few are guilty. But to let one man make up the rules is crazy! Considering what happened to his brother, he of all people should know that."

"That's right!" someone else chimed in. "Lenin's a lawyer, but who does he admire? A fine man like Comrade Steinberg? No! His idols are those murderous Jacobins of the French Revolution! If we let him decide who's acceptable and who's 'bourgeois' what comes next? Summary liquidation?"

Murmurs of approval filled the room. Maxim stepped in. "Look, it's not my colleague's fault that the Bolshies came out on top. If there's anything to blame, it's that infernal arguing amongst ourselves. What happened may not be to our liking, but it's a victory for socialism."

"Maybe not." A tall, impeccably groomed man carrying a lawyer's satchel entered the room and walked directly to the head of the table. Two delegates jumped to help him doff his luxuriant wool coat. Another quickly poured him a drink.

He raised his glass. "To the Revolution!"

One of the former Empire's most preeminent private lawyers, Isaac Steinberg was much beloved by the Socialist Revolutionary rank and file. For years he had made himself a pariah in the Czar's courts, assailing the Crown's legitimacy while trenchantly justifying the atrocities committed by his erstwhile clients, the assassins of the Combat Brigade.

"As you know," Steinberg began, "in a fit of making nice Lenin has appointed me Commissar of Justice. Although I was hoping to craft a model system of justice, all I've accomplished – and not altogether successfully – is to forestall a new Reign of Terror. Lenin hardly took a breath before he formed his own secret police, the Cheka, and placed his vicious acolyte Dzerzhinsky in charge. So instead of the *Okhrana* there's now a bunch of Socialist thugs rounding up dissenters and sticking them in the dungeons. Lenin's ruling by decree, and believe me, he has a fertile imagination."

Steinberg took a document from his satchel. "If you have the stomach, read this!"

PETROGRAD REVOLUTIONARY MILITARY COMMITTEE
28 November 1917
Proclamation
Leaders of the Party of Constitutional-Democrats are hereby declared to be enemies of the people and are to be immediately arrested and brought to appear before revolutionary tribunals.

V.I. Lenin

The document made its way around the room. A delegate rose.

"We appreciate you bringing this to our attention, Comrade. But this only applies to a few spoiled liberals. How is that a problem?"

"Because it bears all the signs of a dictatorship!" Steinberg roared. "Summarily adjudging someone guilty of a capital crime is a travesty! Not even the Czars went that far! And do you really think," he added, waving his spectacles for emphasis, "that there won't be other, more *inclusive* decrees in the future?"

"What do you mean?"

Steinberg shook his head in disbelief. "I mean, of course, us."

That got everyone's attention. The room stilled. A worried delegate rose. "What can be done, Citizen Commissar?"

"We can begin by slowing them down. They've set up a system of sham courts that convict without question. I badgered Lenin until he agreed to let me install some of our own people as lay judges." He passed a paper to Vladimir. It bore the Party seal.

"Congratulations, Comrade Romm. You are appointed to sit on a revolutionary tribunal. It's in Moscow, which will soon be the capital. Muster out of your regiment and report immediately."

Vladimir was stunned. "With all due respect, Comrade Steinberg, I am not qualified. I would prefer to remain at my post."

Steinberg scowled. "Not qualified?" He pointed at the other delegates. "Then tell me who is! Look, comrade, I would have preferred to remain an ordinary lawyer, but that didn't happen either. If your intention was to make a career out of being a commissar, forget it. Lenin's made his peace with Germany and conscripts will soon be heading back to their farms. You seem to get along with the Bolsheviks. Maybe you can encourage them to do the right thing. For now it's our best hope."

Vladimir's brother Alexander was newly married and living in Moscow with his bride Elena, a sculptress in her final year of studies. Vladimir gratefully accepted their offer to stay with them. Compared with the privations of barracks life, sleeping on a couch was like being in heaven. Nearly every night the apartment resounded with the excited chatter of young artists and musicians laughing, drinking and speculating about their roles in a socialist state. Those with families in the countryside often brought fresh game and produce. Alexander, a fine cook, would dump everything into a pot and at one sitting they would eat for a week.

Vladimir was enjoying his second helping of a spicy goulash when his brother tapped him on the shoulder.

"May I present Galina Alexandrova, of the Bolshoi."

Vladimir looked up from his bowl and fell into the sky. He would never forget that first glimpse of his wife's pale blue eyes, the tantalizing gleam of her perfectly formed lips or the provocative way in which her thick auburn hair fell across her shoulders. Nor the embarrassment when his brother swiftly kicked him in the shins.

"Volya, would you please stop drooling and inform the young lady of your name?"

A matronly woman with peasant features watched with interest as Vladimir's lips brushed over Galina's hand. She was accustomed to the effect that the young woman had on what should rightly be called the weaker sex. What she hadn't expected was that her daughter would blush. Ludvika set down her fork and went to her daughter's side.

Alexander made the introduction. "Madame Loukovicz, please meet my awkward brother Vladimir Georgievich."

Vladimir bowed. But as he reached for her hand the woman shied away. "Oh, my dear boy, you don't want to get that close to this gnarled claw of mine."

"But I insist," Vladimir said, in a tone so gracious that it stunned everyone.

Ludvika was impressed. "I'm surprised that young people still honor convention."

Vladimir gently kissed the matron's hand. "Socialists believe that *everyone* deserves to be treated like royalty."

Galina's smile lit up the room. Alexander whispered in his wife's ear.

"He's a dead man."

On the next day a different kind of drama played out in the dusty hall that served as headquarters of the Moscow Revolutionary Tribunal. Perched on an improvised podium, the tribunal's president, its only trained lawyer, reviewed a perfunctory, semi-literate arrest report. Done, he addressed a short, fat man with a badge pinned to his jacket. He was handcuffed to his prisoner, a shabbily dressed old man with rheumy eyes and a bobbing Adam's apple.

"For the record, please state why you hauled in this bundle of misery." The defendant had been unable to give the clerk a precise age or place of birth, other than it was a long time ago in a railcar not much different from the one that he lightened of a sack of sugar.

It was stifling hot. The secret policeman loosened his tie. "Well, your honor," he snickered, "our commander insists that we haul in at least two before lunch..."

Vladimir recoiled at the dreadful pun. As one of two lay assessors (the other was the judge's brother) he would vote on the verdict but wasn't expected to ask questions.

The president glared at the Chekist. "We're too busy to deal with trivial offenses. Please inform this tribunal why the accused should be charged with the counterrevolutionary crime of speculation rather than be turned over to a people's court and dealt with as a common criminal."

"Well," the secret policeman replied, "it's obvious. I mean, that's what thieves do with stuff, isn't it? Go off and sell it?"

"Was that your intention, Boris Kazimirovich?" the president asked. "To dispose of the sugar in the black market?"

The prisoner shrugged. "What else would I do with it, your Honor? Bake a cake?"

Vladimir couldn't keep still. "May I ask the officer a question?"

More prisoners were coming in, fouling the air with the odor of grime and sweat. "Make it quick," the president urged.

Vladimir turned to the officer. "How many did you see running off with sugar?"

"Um, ten or so. A few of the stronger were carrying two sacks, one over each shoulder."

"I understand. But why did you arrest this particular offender?"

The officer brightened. "Why, he was the slowest!"

The sharp sound of a gavel brought the hearing to an end. The court retired to deliberate.

The president opened with his conclusion. "There's no question of the man's guilt." He glanced at Vladimir, who after only a week had already gained a reputation as a spoiler.

"Of larceny, no," Vladimir agreed. "But to turn a simple thief into a counterrevolutionary..."

The president's eyes rolled. Weren't there enough Bolsheviks? Why did they burden him with a Socialist Revolutionary? "Look, what this 'simple thief' did is economic terrorism – the worst kind." He turned to his brother, who was communing with a flask of vodka. "Don't you agree?"

"Absolutely," the man nodded. He took a healthy swig. "A terrorist!"

"Fine, we have a majority, the accused stands convicted. For punishment I propose ten years at hard labor."

"But he's an old man!" Vladimir protested. "A decade in a camp is a death sentence!"

The president rose. "Comrade Romm, the Cheka has complained to the Commissariat of Justice about our tribunal's unseemly kindness towards anarchists and counterrevolutionaries. A firm hand is called for and this looks like a good place to start. But I'll defer to your wisdom. Five years in a work brigade, and not an instant less!"

Lubyanka prison,
15 December 1936

This morning the door clanged open and in stumbled yet another ghost from the past. This time my hollowed-out visitor was Dmitry Pavlovich Bukhartsev, most recently *Izvestia* correspondent to Berlin.

It turns out that he occupies the adjoining cell. So that's who was knocking!

Dmitry looked terrible. His eyes, already deeply set, appeared to have sunk back nearly to his vertebra. Thin as a rail, his sagging skin lent the once robust, garrulous ladies' man the appearance of a deflated balloon. On second thought, we probably look a lot alike. It's a good thing they don't allow us mirrors.

We had only crossed paths a few times. Dmitry's not a schemer like Radek, but he too was obviously on an errand. Before he could come to the point I asked him about his arrest. It turns out that we were picked up on the same evening. Unlike mine, his recall to Moscow came suddenly, supposedly to receive a medal for successfully completing a highly sensitive intelligence assignment. Dmitry declined to fill me in on the details – rumors are that they involved the family of the American ambassador. However, only an hour before the big event, just as his wife Raisa was pressing his best suit, secret police came knocking at the apartment they shared with her parents. They brought him here, and the next morning the same rumpled "magistrate" who I faced read some wild accusations. He then got back-to-back visits, first from Molchanov, who brought a ready-made confession, and then from Radek's co-defendant, Piatakov, who brought Dmitry a letter from his wife.

The similarities are stunning. Of course, they're working from the same script.

To his credit, Dmitry didn't try to pretend that the charges were genuine. "Look, they need a couple of dupes to fill in the gaps and we meet the specifications. I'm to be the messenger-boy between Piatakov and Trotsky." His eyes flitted over my missing tooth and lump on the head. "You were supposed to be Radek's go-between, but the man is scared to return."

I half-smiled. "My wife warned me about pride. As usual, I didn't listen."

Dmitry took hold of my shoulder. "Maybe you should have paid attention. It's not about *our* dignity, comrade. Our lives are done, and whatever happens, happens. But if we don't do what they want our loved ones will wind up in labor camps. You can bet on it."

No one with official authority dares convey such direct threats or acknowledge that these cases are a farce. No, that distasteful chore is left to one's fellow victims. Neat!

"How much time before the trial?" I asked.

"At most, a few weeks, so they're getting anxious. Look, these bastards have already auditioned and discarded plenty of witnesses. What they most fear is having someone backpedal on the stand in front of the whole world. Losing it with Radek was a bad move. Keep taunting Molchanov, and Vyshinsky might decide that you're too much of a risk. If they need a replacement he'd be brought in sooner rather than later."

Dmitry's matter-of-fact recitation was having its intended effect. I was scared to death, and not just for my family. "And what do you intend to do?" I blubbered, already knowing the answer.

"Hopefully, the same as you."

Socialist Reality (1918)

It was the evening of August 30, 1918. Fannie Kaplan was pacing outside a Moscow factory, nervously fingering the pistol hidden under her skirt. A veteran of Czarist prisons, where she spent a decade for transporting bombs, the wild-haired Socialist Revolutionary was determined to take revenge on the man who gave up vast tracts of her beloved homeland. Her only problem was to get sufficiently close, because at any distance Fannie was blind as a bat.

Applause signaled the end of Lenin's speech. Workers enveloped the leader of the Communist Party (that being the new name for the Bolsheviks) as he walked to his car. Fannie frantically made her way through the throng. She had just enough time to yell out his name.

"Vladimir Ilyich!"

Lenin turned. Fannie drew her pistol. Straining to make out his outline, she squeezed three times.

One shot hit a woman, who screamed and fell. But two others hit their mark, one piercing the upper torso, the other lodging in the neck. Lenin crumpled to the ground, grievously but not mortally wounded. Fannie was quickly arrested, tried and executed. Hanging being a relic of the Czar's era, her punishment was carried out in the new, neat fashion, with a bullet to the back of the head.

Vladimir's tenure at the tribunal was mercifully brief. Civil war loomed. To avoid battling on two fronts, Lenin had made peace with the Kaiser, ceding Ukraine and the Baltics to Germany. His move so enraged the Socialist Revolutionaries that they abandoned the cabinet. Stripped of his sponsor, Romm was quickly let go. As a non-Communist, the only job he could find was as a clerk in an obscure commissariat. Now, only days after Kaplan's execution, he was about to lose that job as well.

Vladimir was in his superior's office reading an alarming circular.

PEOPLE'S COMMISSARIAT FOR INTERNAL AFFAIRS
4 September 1918
Due to the murders of Volodarsky and Uritsky, the attempt on the life of V. I. Lenin, and the discovery of numerous plots by Right Socialist

73

Revolutionaries and other scoundrels against Russia's legitimate government, all organs are directed to stop dealing gently with terrorists. Each and every Right Socialist Revolutionary must be immediately arrested. Hostages are to be seized from the bourgeoisie and officer corps, the more the better. Suspected terrorists must be shot at the least resistance and without hesitation. Anyone suspected of taking up arms against our motherland must be shot without fail.

Quarreling split Vladimir's party into two: a Right faction that opposed Lenin and was actively cooperating with his opponents, and a Left, which included Vladimir, Steinberg and others, which was betting that Lenin and his Communists would realize that they couldn't go it alone and negotiate a compromise.

Vladimir returned the document. "How does this apply to me? I'm a Leftist."

"Yes, and so was Fannie," his boss countered. "Comrade, we could argue all day, but in the end it will all come to the same. Counterrevolutionaries are gathering in the countryside preparing for war. You've done a fine job, but the Party has ordered that your position be occupied by a Communist. Come back when you're ready to renounce your hooligan friends."

Vladimir, his brothers and their wives had tickets for the opening of Glazunov's new ballet, "*Stenka Razin*," performed by Galina's company. Vladimir and Galina had been seeing a lot of each other, always in the presence of her relentlessly protective mother. In a rare stolen moment he asked her to wait at the stage exit so they could have a private chat. She readily agreed. That, of course, was before his firing.

Vladimir found his affinity for the Socialist Revolutionaries hard to explain, even to himself. Was it because of Anna? Before setting foot on her farm he had known little about the countryside, all his well-honed homilies about the peasantry coming straight from a political tract. City folks gave farmers little thought, and when he told his former colleagues at the commissariat that peasants were Russia's soul they laughed and shook their heads. As far as Lenin was concerned farmers served two purposes: as cannon fodder, and as an easily exploitable means of feeding workers, the truly worthy denizens of the new socialist state.

His service on a revolutionary tribunal gave Vladimir a chilling insight into the ways of communism. It wasn't just the exaggerations, the making of petty criminals, mostly just miserable alcoholics, into dangerous "saboteurs." Chekists often brought in prisoners covered in bruises, and when he pressed officers to explain their usual response was that the accused "fell" or "resisted arrest." Naturally, few captives dared to disagree. And to a man they confessed.

It was intermission. In the washroom, Vladimir gazed at his reflection in the mirror and wondered what he would say. "It was an ordinary day. I wrote some reports and got fired." He mostly feared the reaction of Galina's mother, Ludvika, who held the keys to the castle. She was eager to find a prosperous son-in-law, and with several well-heeled suitors buzzing around it seemed unlikely that the widow would let her only child cast their lot with an unemployed radical, for there was the well-being of both mother and daughter to consider.

"Vladimir Georgievich! Is that you?" It was Maxim, his former colleague.

The friends exchanged a hug. "What are you doing here?" Vladimir asked.

"Looking for you."

Alexander and Elena hosted a reception after the show. "What's between Volya and his lady friend?" Elena asked while preparing tea cakes. "They haven't spoken a word to each other all evening."

"Maybe they're rehearsing for marriage," Alexander parried.

Elena threw her husband a withering look. "That fellow who Vladimir ran into said that you and Evsey were acquainted with his sisters."

Alexander carried off the samovar. "Really? Can't say that I remember."

Maxim hadn't taken part in such a stimulating conversation in a long time. Alexander and Elena waxed eloquent about the new realism in art, music and cinema while Evsey, who seemed quite the free spirit, delighted in challenging their positions. It wasn't long before he managed to offend.

"Take tonight as an example," Evsey said. "In real life *Stenka Razin* was a bloodthirsty, pillaging bandit. In the ballet, though, he's a revolutionary hero who battles the monarchists, all the while making love to the beautiful princess that his underlings kidnapped. Is that incongruous or...?"

"It was a great amusement, Sallo," Vladimir countered. "And the performances were wonderful!"

Evsey tried to backtrack. "Well, of course, I didn't mean..."

Galina stepped in. Her voice brimmed with the zeal of a convert. "Contradictions are at the root of socialist knowledge. It's in their resolution that we discover the underlying truths. *Stenka Razin* is far more than a love story. It's about how the privileged few exploit the masses. Finally, after years of mindless classical fantasies we can express feelings, give vent to emotion, act! Thanks to Comrade Lenin the ballet is making a place for real performers, not just impossibly thin children whose greatest talent is to execute ridiculous leaps."

Maxim was flabbergasted. Here was proof, if anyone needed it, that dogma was intruding into every aspect of Russian life. Even artists, who should by all rights be society's most independent thinkers were welcoming the new order. He almost felt nostalgic for the Provisional Government.

"I understand your point," Maxim said. "But aren't you taking a big chance by injecting politics into art? How will you preserve the quality of expression?"

Alexander breezily brushed the question away. "Marxism is a science. When one correctly applies its principles judging artistic merit should be no more difficult than counting sheep."

Evsey giggled. "Of course not, since that's what artists will have become!"

Maxim soon left. Vladimir walked with him outside.

Alexander sensed that something unpleasant was afoot when his brother returned. "That friend of yours, Volya, is looking for trouble."

Vladimir paused. It was now or never. "Maxim is on his way to Archangel, and I'm joining him."

It took everyone a moment to digest the stunning news. "Archangel?" Alexander shrieked. "You mean that frozen, God-forbidding place where the British and Americans landed?"

"You forgot the French, Alexander. Your brave communists ran as soon as they spotted the flotilla. Socialist Revolutionaries have been invited to form a government in exile. We're going to demonstrate that democracy isn't just for capitalists."

Ludvika was dismayed. "Vladimir Georgievich! Are you seriously considering abandoning your position to go off on some ridiculous adventure?" Vladimir's intelligence and roguish charm reminded her of her late husband. She had fervently hoped that her picky daughter finally found someone they could both accept. And now this!

Galina spoke softly. "There's nothing to abandon, Mother. Except..." She fled the room in tears.

Evsey jumped to his feet. He tipsily raised his drink. "Bravo, brother! Don't let them push you around! Loyalty to your comrades, above all!"

Vladimir left the next morning.

Lubyanka prison, 17 December 1936

Here's an unexpected little something that got served up with my breakfast:

Moscow, 8 December 1936
Dear brother!

Hopefully this finds you in good health. Please forgive me for not writing sooner but Comrade Yezhov didn't grant permission until today.

Galina and Georgie are well. As you know they're staying at Evsey's. The night of your arrest Galina came to our apartment in a complete panic but we were hosting foreign visitors and couldn't speak with her at length. The next day I made inquiries at the Lubyanka, but all they would do is confirm that you are there. It wasn't until I contacted the person in charge, Comrade Yezhov, that I discovered that you're charged with treason and will be confined until trial.

Naturally I was shocked. At Comrade Yezhov's urging I retained an excellent defense lawyer, Comrade Kutuzov, who has a lot of experience in such things. He will visit you as soon as the preliminary investigation is completed, which they say usually takes two months.

I will express myself frankly. Assuming (as I do) that you would never purposely endanger the Soviet Union, you must have said or done something, maybe to help a friend, that was seriously misconstrued. But what's past is past. According to Comrade Kutuzov the most important thing is to dismiss your case before it goes to trial, so he will do everything possible to that end. In the interim he urges that you assist the authorities so that your cooperation can be taken into account should they decide to proceed. Please think hard: is there any way that you can help? This also happens to be the advice given by the Commissar, who thinks quite highly of you but cannot, of course, interfere with the investigation.

Comrade Kutuzov and I are doing everything possible to resolve this mess. We are preparing a special pleading that cites your many contributions to the Soviet Union, which will be filed with the court should things get that far. We don't think so, but it's best to be prepared.

There is little other news. It's trivial considering your situation, but my book about Matisse is at the printer's. I will try to send you a copy in a few weeks in the event that you're still there.

I apologize for being repetitive, but the authorities have assured me that this ordeal will come to an end much more quickly if you cooperate. So please tell them everything you know.

Elena and I send our Communist regards.

Alexander

I should have been happy to hear from my brother, but in truth my feelings are mixed. Alexander can't be expected to understand my predicament – even I can hardly put my arms around it – but to suggest that I somehow brought it on...how could he be so naïve? Perhaps I'm being unkind. Having a close relative branded as a traitor threatens much more than one's career. Maybe he had no choice. Maybe he was afraid to express himself frankly because of censors. Maybe he's saying something between the lines and I'm just tone deaf. Maybe I should quit speculating.

Evsey is of a different sort. Nowadays children are glorified for denouncing their parents and teachers, but Sallo is still frozen in those times when loyalty to one's family and friends was paramount. If he wasn't so sickly he'd probably be organizing a jailbreak! In any case, it was good to read that all is well with my family. Whatever I do will be for them, and them alone.

Return to Vilna (1918)

Maxim and Vladimir reached Archangel in September 1918. It was an arduous journey. Trains and other forms of public transport took them as far north as Petrozavodsk. As they trekked on the climate turned increasingly bitter. Fortunately there were plenty of kindly peasants who for a few kopecks provided food, lodging and, most importantly, help in circumventing the communist Red Army's military checkpoints. Soon the adventurers were blending in perfectly, their groomed, city-boy looks, clean garments and soft hands a thing of the past.

A major port with direct access to the White Sea and the Arctic route, Archangel was locked in by ice most of the year. Now that the Russian Civil War was on, England, France and America had dispatched naval contingents to establish a beachhead from which they would help Whites fight the dreaded new scourge of communism.

Archangel's occupation presented Lenin with a major challenge. His Reds were in no shape to fight the renegade White armies and the British, French and Americans too. Unable to keep a rump Socialist Revolutionary regime from being established in the remote region, he ordered his field commander, Trotsky, to establish a land blockade. Beset by a painfully short growing season, their supply routes cut by Soviet troops, the inhabitants of the northernmost district of European Russia quickly started feeling the pinch.

Neither Vladimir nor Maxim expected a well-oiled machine, and what they found fell far short. In their fervor to establish a peasant's republic Socialist Revolutionaries wound up behaving no better than their predecessors, trampling over local customs and imposing their views by force. Eager to retake all of Russia – with Western help, of course – they instituted a draft, conscripting thousands of peasants into makeshift brigades. Results were at best farcical. Military commanders were mostly British officers who knew nothing about Russia. Ignorant of local customs, daunted by the indecipherable language, they were ill prepared to deal with the skeptical, stubborn *muziks*. Suspicious of foreigners, angry that a bunch of Socialist ideologues had turned their unique world upside-down, entire units of citizen soldiers rebelled, and the fledgling government quickly found itself struggling to get the counterrevolution back on track.

"If the Reds are stupid enough to come bother us we're ready. Why should we send our sons and brothers off to fight other Russians, even if they *are* communists?"

The peasant's words stirred his audience to hearty applause. Maxim struggled to be heard above the din.

"Our purpose isn't just to liberate one province but all of Russia..."

"That's exactly the problem," another peasant yelled. "Why should *we* care about *your* goals? We have trouble enough getting enough to eat when there's peace!" The man removed his cap. He rubbed his shiny, bald pate. "If you haven't noticed, nothing grows here in winter!"

The barn exploded in laughter; even a few horses neighed in. "Even if we didn't lack for supplies," he continued, "which we do, our entire population would fit into a corner of Moscow. How do you propose to make an army of it?"

Maxim stiffened. "There's the British, the French..."

Another citizen angrily shook his fist. "Yes, foreigners! I don't mind trading with them; now that you've turned Lenin against us, Lord knows we need their grain. But to be occupied by their armies is a disgrace! Better to starve or fall to a Red bullet than live under the British!"

More cheering erupted. Maxim turned to Vladimir, who hadn't said a word. "Why so quiet, comrade?"

Why, indeed. Vladimir knew that without foreign troops Archangel would have fallen long ago, yet he could hardly stomach the sight of the Western men-o'-war jamming the harbor, their arrogant soldiers and sailors strutting with impunity on sacred Russian soil.

"The citizens are right," Vladimir conceded. "We've only brought them grief. Communist or Socialist Revolutionary, we're all Russians. Any way you slice it, inviting the West to come in is treason."

Vladimir was caught in a dilemma. Estranged from the Socialist Revolutionaries, he knew better than to return to Communist-controlled areas while his loyalty was still in question. One day a friendly officer from the Inter-Allied Expeditionary Force mentioned that German troops had abandoned Vilna to the Poles and Lithuanians.

"Trotsky is supposedly gearing up to march on the town," the officer said. "I'm told it has a Communist cell, but what help they'll be able to offer the Red Army is questionable. Its members reportedly don't know their right from their left. Oh, I think I just made a little joke!"

After a punishing trip by train, foot and oxcart, Vladimir walked into his old neighborhood tavern, the same place where he once danced with his father. Things seemed remarkably the same. Their faces conveying the despair of hitting rock bottom, shabbily dressed laborers sat around crude wooden tables gulping down shots of cheap vodka. Vladimir's entrance was a welcome distraction, and for an instant he was caught up in the probing curiosity of ordinary people.

The regulars soon went back to their business. But an old-timer with a familiar face kept staring. Intrigued, Vladimir went to introduce himself. As he extended his hand the man suddenly yanked him close, bumping the table and upsetting the drinks.

"Ach, Misha, quit this foolishness," a companion said, grimacing at the spilled vodka. "We're no longer with the police. If this young man doesn't thrash you, I will!"

Vladimir gently freed himself. Something about the stranger struck a chord. "Were you the policeman who arrested me?"

"You're close," the man replied, grinning wickedly. "Think harder," he urged, twirling a coin in the light.

An absurd notion formed in Vladimir's mind. No, not the beggar! His startled look made the table of former *Okhrana* agents burst out in laughter.

"We made some very fine work in those days," the retired detective said. "We were smart, too – not like today, when they give pistols to thugs. Your comrades were flooding the city with posters. We examined them carefully for imperfections. It took time to find the right press. Then all we had to do was watch and wait." He poured Vladimir a drink. "You know, I came away from our brief encounter highly impressed. Revolutionaries with a heart – ah, those are the most dangerous kind."

Vladimir strolled through the city. Conditions were worse than he remembered. A pungent aroma of uncollected refuse burned the nostrils and made the eyes weep. Once-tidy neighborhoods were literally crumbling in front of one's eyes. In the business district every available vertical surface was papered over with political posters. Vladimir tested his rudimentary Polish on a notice emblazoned with the white eagle of the Second Polish Republic.

"It's nothing important, mister." A dirty-faced boy carrying a tub of glue elbowed him aside. In a blur of brush strokes he papered over the offending circular with a stark manifesto from the "Workers' Council" calling on the citizens of Vilna to topple their capitalistic (meaning Polish and Lithuanian) oppressors.

Vladimir watched the youth walk away. It was as though he was looking in a mirror.

As Vladimir suspected, and as the man who admitted him to the group's cramped offices readily confirmed, the Workers' Council was a front for the local cell of the Communist Party of Lithuania and Belorussia, a tiny group with so little influence that, while technically illegal, it was ignored by the authorities.

"Naturally, it's a double-edged sword," said the slight, thickly bespectacled comrade. "If we make waves the Poles and Lithuanians may come after us, but if we don't we might as well stay home."

Vladimir was introduced to Lev, a young man who was one of the cell's senior members. Impressed by Vladimir's account of his adventures in Archangel, Lev offered him a sleeping space at the country cottage that he shared with his wife. Vladimir gratefully accepted.

That evening, after enjoying several helpings of tasty borscht and the company of a loving couple, Vladimir made the decision that would shape his destiny. He was determined to be part of the Revolution, but the behavior of the Socialist Revolutionaries in Archangel made them lose their allure. His days with the party of his youth would end in the same place they began.

He was inducted into the Communist Party the very next day, at a ceremony that was comprised mostly of toasts.

"Your application reflects that you've had military experience," Comrade Kovalevsky said, opening a fresh bottle. Not yet thirty, the group's boldly mustachioed leader was, like most of his peers, a veteran alcoholic.

"Very little," Vladimir conceded. "After the February Revolution I served as a commissar in a reserve infantry regiment."

"With us, comrade, that would qualify you to be a general!" Kovalevsky walked around the table, filling glasses. "We drink to celebrate, and then we drink to erase the effects of drinking. Another of our beloved contradictions!" He raised his tumbler. "To the new leader of Vilna's Red Guards!"

Vladimir was stunned. "I'm...honored."

The comrades filed out. Kovalevsky pulled his chair close. "Some of the comrades are with us to eat and drink, others to fight for socialism. Ivan Feodorovich, whom you're replacing, was one of the latter. He was a good-hearted man, maybe too much so. The comrade had a large family, and when his farm failed he tried to make ends meet by working for others. Then his health turned. We tried to help, but he was very proud. Yet he couldn't bear to watch his wife and children go hungry. So he..."

Kovalevsky grasped an imaginary noose. He then shrugged and returned to his bottle.

In the following weeks Vladimir worked to transform an undisciplined, rag-tag people's militia into an effective fighting force. Although he had limited training and no fighting experience, his sincerity, good nature and natural skills won over the men and progress was steady. Vladimir broke down the two-dozen regulars into squads. They concentrated on small unit maneuvers and marksmanship, using the comrades' hunting rifles since the cell had no armaments of its own. Vladimir also organized a system of runners so that the group could be assembled on short notice. By themselves his men would be no match for the well-armed regulars of the Polish army, but they knew the lay of the land, and should Trotsky's army come to reclaim the province their knowledge could prove crucial.

And it did.

Lubyanka prison,
19 December 1936

Molchanov barged in this morning. He grabbed my confession from the desk, and when his eyes passed over my signature his cheeks literally glowed with pleasure. I had little choice. Bukhartsev was right: if I don't cooperate they will exile my wife and son, perhaps even my brothers and their families. And of course, shoot me.

If I do cooperate...who knows?

Molchanov sat on the bed. He positioned himself so close that I could smell the sturgeon on his breath.

He spoke as though we were comrades on an unpleasant but critical mission. "You were curious about *why*. Well, how the Devil should I know? You think that the Procurator-General asks my opinion? 'Oh, Comrade Molchanov, what do you think? Is this the proper approach? Do you agree?' Listen, to him I'm just another tool, like you. And perhaps easier to replace."

His soliloquy done, Molchanov grabbed my jaw. He inspected my mouth. "Good, it looks much better. Look, let's call a truce," he said, solicitously patting my knee. "I'll do my job, you do yours, and one day when we're both liberated, we'll have a drink, eh?"

He was on his way out when he spotted Leon in a corner, grooming himself. He went for the rat. I instinctively blocked him.

"No!"

Molchanov grinned as the frightened creature scampered away. I realized that he did it on purpose, as if I needed to be reminded who's boss. It's the madman's unpredictability that induces terror. I suppose that in some occupations being a lunatic does confer an advantage.

Guards later ushered me into a fenced yard and for the first time since my imprisonment I exercised in the open air. This unexpected pleasure – a reward, I suppose, for submitting to the inevitable – lifted my spirits, clearing my mind just enough to let new doubts sink in. Like every other ideology, socialism can't thrive without regular doses of deceit (and self-deceit) and I can't say I've never indulged. But to affix one's name to a horrendous fabrication, well, that's beyond the pale. Or so I used to think.

Father was by no means religious. Still, he strove to behave ethically, and was particularly fond of calling attention to Hillel the Elder's admonition, "what is hateful to you, do not do unto your fellow man."

Whose interests would *he* have sacrificed?

Communists (1918-19)

Vladimir was nearly done explaining the mission when a sullen youth blurted out the solution that was on everyone's mind.

"Why not just kill them? That's what Trotsky's men will do anyway. We can save them the trouble."

One day earlier a Red Army intelligence officer had snuck in to Vilna to meet with Kovalevsky. He was following up on a secret message delivered to the cell leader months earlier, instructing him to prepare dossiers on Vilna's civilian and military leaders so they could be quickly neutralized during the initial assault. Needless to say, the critical chore had not been done, and with the attack looming Kovalevsky, for once sober as a teetotaler, begged his Red Guard commander to help.

"These are the most important ones to track down," he said, handing Vladimir a hastily scribbled list. "Once they're neutralized resistance should crumble."

Vladimir was dismayed at the late notice but kept quiet. He now had to cool down a headstrong boy, but not so much as to demoralize him.

"We're not shooting anybody, at least not yet. Our orders are simply to collect information. How do they pass their days? Map where they live, follow them to work, identify whom they meet. Above all, be discreet. If anything changes I'll let you know."

Once the men left Vladimir turned to Lev. "If the Poles and Lithuanians get wind of what we're up to we're in trouble."

"We're in trouble anyway." Lev unrolled a brand-new poster.

TO THE CITIZENS OF VILNA

The Workers' Council declares itself the legitimate central authority of the Province of Vilna and has established a Provisional Government until such time as it is superseded by a higher authority. To this end, Vilna's Municipal Council and all lesser bodies are immediately dissolved, their officers and employees are discharged, and all properties, funds and accounts under their supervision are frozen.

With best Communist wishes,

Kovalevsky, Chairman

Vladimir was stunned. "Is this some kind of joke?"

"They're going up as we speak. Kovalevsky didn't want you to know ahead of time. He guessed how you'd react."

"And you?" Vladimir asked. "Where do *you* stand on this lunacy?"

Lev hesitated. He and his wife had grown fond of their thoughtful guest. Vladimir insisted on paying his way by preparing meals and watching over their young son. And yes, there was reason to be upset with the drunkard Kovalevsky, whose incessant bumbling had placed the cell in a tight spot. But he was still the boss.

"Look, Volya, Trotsky's on the way. Soon there will be lots more to worry about than some silly..." Lev's words were drowned out by a squad of Polish Legionnaires clopping by on fine stallions.

"They've got the latest repeating rifles," Vladimir pointed out. "How can we defeat that?"

"We can't. That's the Red Army's job," Lev replied. Both knew full well that once hostilities got underway the ill-equipped Red Guards would be at great risk. "By the way," he winked, "Tanya's coming for supper."

Olga, Lev's wife, had introduced Vladimir to an unattached cousin. Tanya was a winsome young woman whose earthy streak brought back fond memories of Anna. Their meeting came at an awkward time. A brief but affectionate letter from Galina had somehow made its way to Vilna, forcing the lonely youth into a different kind of conflict, a skirmish with his conscience that he was certain to lose.

A week later Lev suddenly appeared at Tanya's apartment in the middle of the night. He explained while Vladimir dressed.

"The Poles used Kovalevsky's decree as an excuse to shove the Lithuanians aside and declare martial law. I was alerted by your runners. My wife and son went to stay with her family."

"Should I come?" Tanya asked.

Lev shook his head. "You'd best stay out of it. If they knew about you two they'd already be here."

Vladimir kissed Tanya and rushed out. He noticed that Lev was trembling. "Well, out with it!"

Lev drew his comrade in close. "I didn't want to say this in front of her. They executed Kovalevsky. His brothers, too, even though they had nothing to do with it."

"Kovalevsky's dead?"

"That's how it's done around here. You trained your men well, so they should be all right. It's all we can do. Vilna's sealed up tight. There's no going back."

Vladimir realized he'd left something in the apartment. "Wait!" he yelled, running back inside.

They hiked cross-country to a small farm owned by Lev's in-laws. Olga and the boy were already there. A bed had been prepared for Vladimir, but he stayed only long enough to eat and pack a rucksack.

"You're crazy," Lev pleaded. "Trotsky's army is already on the march from Smolensk. Hang tight. They'll be here in a few days!"

"We don't have days," Vladimir said.

Armies are at their most unpredictable in retreat. This was doubly true for the Poles, who when not otherwise preoccupied enjoyed taking vengeance on the "enemies of Christ," a slur made popular by Empress Elizabeth Petrovna, the toxic offspring of Peter the Great. Olga's family was Jewish, and Vladimir hoped that in the confusion their ethnicity would go unnoticed.

Vladimir set out for the front. A day's hike found him at the edge of a ragged no-man's land tens of kilometers in width. Small arms fire clattered in the distance. Exhausted, he lay down to rest.

He was buried in the consuming intimacy of Galina's embrace, so near her heart that he could feel it mark off each beat. Suddenly the hand that so delightfully pressed on his back became the sharpest of blades. Vladimir awoke, crying out in pain.

"Should I finish him off, Comrade Captain?"

"Wait." A Soviet officer rummaged through the rucksack. He came across a list, neatly written in Russian, setting out directions to the homes and workplaces of Vilna's top police and military officials.

"Stop! He's one of us!"

Vladimir came to at a field hospital. He was lying on his stomach, his hands and feet bound to the corners of a bed. A large dressing covered the wound on his back.

He had no idea where he was, or why, the memory of his near-impalement by a Red Army scout having faded with the ether.

"Don't worry, comrade, you're not a prisoner. It's only to keep you from rolling over."

Vladimir turned his head. It was the same officer who visited the late Kovalevsky. "Those dossiers in your pack were very helpful," the intelligence man said. "Lev Alexandrovich also appreciated your prescient note about the farm. We got there just in time to keep it from getting torched by the Poles."

"What about the Red Guards?"

"They're fine. One of them – he's only a kid – shot a bunch of Legionnaires. They were stacked like cordwood at his place."

"I need to send a letter to Moscow."

The officer grinned. "If she's young and beautiful I'll deliver it personally."

"Actually it's to her mother."

Trotsky's army met with little opposition. Badly outnumbered, the Poles and Lithuanians decided to save themselves for another day. That it would come was not in doubt.

Euphoric at their triumph, communists rushed to transform the provincial capital into a model socialist community, nationalizing industry, installing party-controlled unions and political committees and even forming an official orchestra. War was expensive, so there was no sparing the principality its obligations to Mother Russia. Tax collectors visited farms to set their required "contributions" come harvest time, while committees impressed the idle and unemployed into labor brigades and the military. Neither did matters of faith escape official notice. Determined to keep competing ideologies from slowing the march to socialism, officials stripped priests and rabbis of their stipends, censored religious publications and closed houses of worship, even appropriating some for official use.

Communism was a jealous bride, indeed.

A week later Lev came to visit. "Hello, Volya. How are you feeling?"

"Better. I'll be on my way to Moscow soon. How are things at City Hall?"

"It's a tough slog. Comrades lack practical knowledge in running things, so we've had to let many officials remain in place, under close watch, of course. But that's the least of our problems." Lev handed Vladimir a document.

It was a list of new Party members admitted that month. There were only two. "Looks like you won't be needing office space," Vladimir teased.

Lev wasn't amused. "Before we liberated Vilna its workers had to kiss the factory owners' asses. Now they've been given their own union but refuse to attend meetings unless they're held during their shifts. And even when they show up, all they do is poke fun at the lecturers!"

Vladimir nodded. "It was the same in Archangel. We were accused of substituting one yoke for another. People were conditioned to hate us. They can't be expected to change overnight."

"But they must!" Lev insisted. "We can't tie troops down so far from home in the middle of a civil war! The Poles are regrouping; they'll be back any day. The citizens of Vilna must prepare to stand up and fight!"

Vladimir had come to realize that, in their own way, communists were as unrealistic as his former comrades. They didn't realize – or wouldn't accept – that abstract political notions carried little weight with ordinary people, and all the more so when they ran counter to established tradition. His friend's parting words, "maybe what's called for is less carrot and more stick!" offered little hope for conciliation. Like many of his colleagues, Lev was a true believer. An upper-class youth who turned to Marx while still at the university, he had never known manual labor. Of course, other than for his brief experience at Anna's farm, neither had Vladimir. Both carried the "soft hands" of the *intelligentsia*. Yet they unabashedly thought of themselves as saviors of the workers, whom they felt uniquely qualified to lead to victory.

But not everyone was fond of Communism. It was difficult enough to implement in central Moscow without resorting to force. Just how far was the Party willing to go?

Lubyanka prison, 20 December 1936

Early this morning guards marched me to the guards' bathhouse, where after weeks of collecting grime I was finally able to properly wash. I even got a new set of blue-and-white pajamas! Molchanov then came for me. We crossed the yard, entered the main building and took the stairs to the top floor. Sharply attired militiamen stood in the corridor at regular intervals, their reflections gleaming off the freshly-waxed tile floors. No, the display wasn't for my benefit, but I was still impressed.

We sat in a conference room. A large, brightly polished wood table was positioned at its center. Two portraits hung on the wall, one at each end. One was a likeness of Lenin, the other, of Stalin. I noticed that both were the same size. I hadn't been in a room like this since my days in America's capital, and for a moment I forgot all about my grumpy escort and imagined that I was still a senior operative of the Foreign Department of the Main Directorate of State Security (and supposedly, a correspondent for *Izvestia*) awaiting the start of the regular Monday morning meeting at the embassy.

My reverie was brief. A frumpy secretary with thick calves dropped off a file. She glanced in my direction and hurried away.

Radek walked in trailed by a beefy guard. He greeted us with a hearty "Good morning, comrades!" then turned to his escort and dismissed him with a curt "that will be all, Boris." From the guard's expression I was sure he would clobber the louse but he held his temper and took a post outside the room. I was shocked at what happened but it drew only a chuckle from Molchanov. What must pass between those two one can't begin to imagine.

Molchanov removed a lengthy typewritten document from the file. He gave it to Radek and left. It turned out to be an expanded version of my confession but formatted like a transcript (silly me – I thought those were prepared *after* one testifies). Radek and I spent a few hours methodically going over the questions I would be asked and the answers they expected, where necessary making adjustments and bringing dates and places into agreement with my actual travels. He seemed extremely familiar with the contents, leading me to believe that he was the author.

I had never met a man so eager to be condemned that he would coach someone to that end. It seems that odd rituals have become a Communist tradition.

Once we were done making corrections Radek walked me through the material, asking questions as though he was Comrade Vyshinsky.

"How long have you known the accused Radek?"

Radek's self-reference momentarily threw me. "Ah...I first met you – I mean, him – at the Trial of the Socialist..."

"No, no," he interrupted, reverting to his true identity. "Confine yourself to what's asked. Let the prosecutor tell you if he wants more."

"Fine," I replied, now thoroughly disoriented. "Since 1922."

"What was your connection with this man in the past?"

I was taken aback. "Connection?"

Radek testily set down the script. "You know, our *relationship*. We worked together in Germany, I was your editor at *Izvestia*, we conspired with Trotsky to bring down the Soviet Union. Simple as that."

I'm neither a political figure nor a big-shot journalist and theoretician. My career has been spent in the trenches. However Radek's cronies might view his confession, I know exactly what my friends and colleagues will think of mine.

We were done. I opened a window and let the refreshing breeze wash over my face. Citizens hurried along the streets below. Preoccupied with their personal affairs, few paid heed to the massive capitalist artifact in their midst. Erected in Imperial times to house a capitalist insurance company, the Greco-Roman fantasy became the Lubyanka, home to the secret police and its very own prison. As if to underline the point they plopped a likeness of Lenin's cruel buddy Dzerzhinsky out front.

For the briefest of moments a foolish notion crossed my mind. My thoughts must have telegraphed for I was rudely shoved aside. Molchanov was back. He slammed the window shut.

"Don't even think about it, comrade."

Guards brought lunch. We ate in silence.

Molchanov was the last done. He belched and wiped his lips. "Comrade Romm, do you understand your role in this case?"

"Yes. I'm supposed to be the middleman who passed messages between the conspirators and Trotsky."

Molchanov reddened. "What do you mean 'supposed'?"

Radek had already admonished me to follow protocol. "It doesn't matter what you think, just pretend it's all God's truth," he warned. Yet something in me stubbornly resisted going along.

"Comrade Molchanov, certainly you know that I'm not..."

Molchanov exploded. "*Know?* All I know is that you're a traitor, deserving of no more consideration than a flea, yet in its mercy the Soviet government is giving you an opportunity to..."

Our esteemed servant of State security belatedly realized that the secretary had returned. He quieted, but not without a glance that spoke volumes.

We were escorted to another, more intimate room. Procurator-General of the USSR Andrei Yanuarievich Vyshinsky walked in and briskly took a seat. His nose wrinkled, as if testing the air. If nothing else, I realized why the bath.

Our session was taken up with Radek's recitation of my edited testimony. Vyshinsky leaned back and listened. When the reading was done his gaze fell on me.

"Comrade Romm, is what you heard accurate?"

I glanced at Molchanov and Radek. They were holding their breaths.

"Comrade Romm?"

Deception in the service of my country used to be so simple. All I could manage was a squeaky "yes."

Apparently that was good enough. Vyshinsky checked his watch, scribbled a quick note and left.

Molchanov proudly slapped me on the back. "Splendid," he intoned, rubbing his paws. "Let's get to work!"

Tambov (1920)

A neatly dressed, meticulously-groomed man ascended the staircase of an elegant apartment building not far from the Kremlin. He rapped on a door with his left hand. For no reason other than habit his right was tucked in an overcoat pocket gripping his beloved Mauser, finger on the trigger guard, thumb on the safety. Precious few officers could as much as draw their weapon before he already had three rounds on the target, one on the forehead and two on the chest, just like during those endless drills at the academy.

Alexander answered the door. He admitted the visitor and went to the study.

"Someone to see you, Volya."

"Who?"

Vladimir's brother grimaced. "A tough-looking sort. All he would say is that he was 'a comrade from Vilna'."

Vladimir hurried to the front room. His face broke into a wide smile.

"You look like a new man!" the intelligence officer roared. "It seems that Moscow agrees with you."

"Not so much that I wouldn't return in an instant."

Both knew that was unlikely. Trotsky's Red Army troops were needed elsewhere, and only four months after the communists captured Vilna a regiment of reinforced Polish cavalry attacked, catching its remaining defenders off guard and routing them in a bloody defeat. Comrades were trampled by horses and spat on by resentful citizens. Lev wrote to Vladimir about the disaster. His words included the first hints that he, too, was wondering whether communism had as much appeal as they thought.

Alexander served tea. While the comrades reminisced Galina arrived with loaves of freshly-baked flatbread and large, succulent onions fresh from the farm. She took careful measure of her fiancée's formidable guest. It seemed that Vladimir's adventuresome days were far from over.

Her hunch proved correct. Vladimir was being recruited for the most prestigious of the Soviet security services. Founded by Lenin, military intelligence was the Communist state's premier spying organization, employing educated, rigorously trained agents, each personally sponsored by an existing member. In the years to follow many would be posted overseas to take on dual roles as journalists, embassy attachés, representatives of cultural and trade delegations and officials of the Comintern, the Communist International, the party arm that promoted the worldwide expansion of the uncompromising ideology.

When Vladimir's candidacy was discussed at Moscow Center, the intelligence service's highly-secret headquarters, some thought that he needed more seasoning. But the urgency of this particular mission could not be denied, and neither could Vladimir's unique qualifications. A peasant rebellion was in full swing in Tambov, a southern region a day's train ride from Moscow. No one thought that rural dwellers could have organized that well on their own, and suspicion immediately fell on their trenchant advocates, the Socialist Revolutionaries.

Vladimir had never formally broken with his old party. His role in Vilna was little known, so he seemed an ideal candidate for an undercover assignment. Yet the thought of betraying his former comrades left him uneasy.

"I understand why you're bothered," the officer said. "I'd feel the same. But look at it this way. We're not out to eradicate peasants; we're just trying to keep them from falling under the wrong influence. Agitators are encouraging them to deny our soldiers grain while secretly provisioning the Whites. If Socialist Revolutionaries aren't behind the revolt, you'd be doing them a favor. If they are, you'd be doing the Soviet people a favor. Someone must discover the truth – would you rather we send a die-hard sort or a comrade like yourself, with more balanced views?"

Vladimir and Galina recorded their marriage at the civil bureau the next morning. Alexander and Elena hosted a reception at their apartment a day later.

Evsey proposed the first of many toasts. "Volya, you must really be a Communist. Getting married to a beautiful woman on one day and enlisting on the next are absolutely contradictory."

Galina laughed with the others, though perhaps not as heartily. She remembered her surprise when Vladimir's absurdly formal letter arrived, addressed not to her but her mother, announcing that he was now a Communist and conveying his deepest regards to her daughter. In brief succession came his return, his awkward proposal and her somewhat hesitant acceptance. Vladimir suggested they wait to make it official until he was fully recovered and held a steady position. She readily agreed and they settled into a pleasant routine. Then his comrade unexpectedly arrived and her life was upturned once more. She was still reeling from her visit to Moscow Center, where Vladimir was sworn in during a brief ceremony. A serious woman in a drab uniform briefed her on security and had her sign a document that entitled her to collect her husband's pension should something "happen."

Vladimir detected the slight frown on his wife's face. He was as mesmerized by her beauty as ever. When he proposed he was uncertain that she would accept, and when she did, he worried that it seemed dutiful, as though he was asking for her mother's hand and not hers. He confided his fears in Alexander's wife.

Elena looked at him as though he was mad.

"Volya, you really must stop arguing with 'yes'."

On a bright spring day in June 1921 Vladimir was on his way to Tambov. He had no trouble fitting in. Its Socialist Revolutionaries readily accepted his long-expired party card, and only hours after settling into a filthy, vermin-infested boarding house he was attending his first meeting. Vladimir's familiarity with party etiquette helped him fit right in, and after toasting his anointment the comrades resumed debating an issue that had badly split the cell.

Moscow Center's analysts had wrongly assumed that the group spearheading the resistance, the "Union of Working Peasants", was a Socialist Revolutionary front. In fact, it was a completely separate organization comprised mostly of non-politicals, with a few wild-eyed radicals who happened to be Socialist Revolutionaries thrown in. In the end the Tambov cell neither encouraged nor discouraged its members from aiding the peasants' revolt, its indecision effectively entrusting the Party's reputation to those most likely to drag it through the mud.

The situation in the countryside seemed hopeless. While a handful of farmers (the so-called "*kulaks*") were doing relatively well, even holding back grain to stall for better prices, most plots had been subdivided to near-extinction, forcing peasants to hire themselves out and reducing many to unspeakable poverty. As if that wasn't enough, detachments from the Red and White armies thought nothing of commandeering a rural family's meager stores and butchering their only cow.

Vladimir knew that soldiers were also suffering, but condemning Russia's food producers to starvation seemed hardly a solution.

It was a brisk morning. Vladimir and the leader of the Tambov cell walked along a deeply rutted trail. Years earlier the man was snatched from the fields to fight in the Great War, then summarily discharged when a German bullet shredded his right arm, leaving a useless stump.

They crossed a dusty field and approached a dilapidated shack. A thin plume of smoke rose from the chimney. Vladimir's knocking startled a peasant family huddled around a pot.

A rail-thin farmer stepped outside. He quickly waved off the cell leader's canned speech. "Save your strength, comrade," he said, grinning through rotted teeth. "I know why you're here. And the answer is no: no to you, no to the communists, no to the damned Union, no to everyone."

Vladimir gazed at the fallow grounds. "You're not working the fields?"

"Why, so soldiers can strip it? Our animals and most of the seed grain are long gone. I hardly have the strength to turn the dirt. There's been no rain for months."

"We know – we're here to help," the cell leader said.

"Help?" the farmer sneered. He gestured at his visitor's limp arm. "How?"

A breeze suddenly kicked up, scattering the preciously little topsoil that remained. The farmer scooped up a handful of pale-looking earth. "We'd eat dirt, but it doesn't have enough nutrients to sustain a worm. A famine is coming, of that I'm sure."

"What will you do?" Vladimir asked.

The peasant gave Vladimir a solemn look. "You've got a touch of kindness, young man. Go home," he urged, returning to the shack. "Do it before the wind changes."

Several weeks later Vladimir was in a large, thickly draped office, its walls bare other than for a single portrait of Lenin. A sallow-faced, clean-shaven man in an unadorned uniform sat behind an intricately carved desk. His singular conceit, a thick mop of auburn hair that cascaded to his shoulders, suggested the soul of an artist or performer. But General Antonov-Ovseenko's reputation wasn't made on canvas or a stage. Trotsky's long-time confidant commanded the assault that dislodged the Provisional Government, and then helped lead the Red Army to victory in the Civil War.

Antonov-Ovseenko set down a thick report. "Your conclusions are puzzling,

Comrade Romm. You denounce the government for setting unreasonably low prices for grain and the Red Army for confiscating it, leaving rural families, as you report, to eat tree bark. Everyone gets blamed but the peasants and your former Socialist Revolutionary comrades. As for the Union, you insist that it's mostly a collection... let me see...of 'violent, opportunistic misfits' and suggest we deal with them not as an opposing military force but as common criminals. Is there something I'm leaving out?"

Vladimir grimaced. "No, Comrade General. Perhaps my report seems one-sided, but it reflected what I saw. Perhaps if I had more time..."

A grin creased the veteran leader's features. "Don't worry, Vladimir Georgievich, it's not your turn to be shot. At least not yet." He took off his spectacles. "Let me tell you a little story. Not long ago one of my regiments was cut off by the Whites. They couldn't be supplied and provisions ran dangerously low. Two requisitioning parties were dispatched to a nearby village; the first never returned and was presumably slaughtered, and the second came back with the soldiers beaten up and without their weapons. In a last ditch effort the commander assembled a third squad made up strictly of peasants and sent them off to the same village, unarmed and under a white flag. Imagine! The mighty Red Army, begging for food!"

"What happened?"

"The villagers felt badly. They gave the soldiers potatoes from their cellars, shared a few bottles of vodka and sent them on their way. It was enough to keep the men going until we broke through the encirclement."

Antonov-Ovseenko threw Vladimir's report in a drawer and slammed it shut. "I can't think of anything more useless than an officer who only says what his superiors want to hear. So, Vladimir Georgievich, how do we fix things?"

Vladimir thought back to the old farmer and his miserable family. "There is so much hunger and desperation. Maybe if we could help the peasants ..."

"With what? We don't have enough food for our own men! And who would supply us, the West? I'm sure you've heard of Archangel." The General got up. He drew the curtains, flooding the room with the light of an early summer's day. "Comrade, your work is done. I appreciate your intentions, but there are no easy solutions. And may I offer some advice?"

Vladimir snapped to attention. "Of course, Comrade General."

"Maybe the Socialist Revolutionaries are to blame, maybe not. Either way, nothing promotes unity like having a common enemy." He looked at Vladimir evenly. "Lugging around all that honesty is a heavy burden. Be careful that it doesn't break your back."

An iron fist wasn't the general's first choice, but Lenin decided that it was time to bring the unrest to an end. Secret policemen and soldiers fanned out through the countryside. Scores of peasants and resisters were arrested, brought before perfunctory tribunals and summarily executed. Rebels responded by shooting suspected collaborators, executing captured officers and murdering their families. In the end the general with the unruly hair unleashed a merciless military campaign that pacified rural Russia, but at a human cost that would haunt the Soviet Union for eternity.

A divided nation was at risk of consuming itself.

Lubyanka prison, 21 December 1936

Leon has been visiting me regularly. He grooms himself endlessly – most Russians I know would be well advised to spend half as much effort on their personal hygiene. He's also taken interest in a maze and other rat playthings that I've made to while the time away.

Confinement is a boring business. During the brief periods in which I'm let out to exercise there's been no one but a guard, with whom conversing is strictly forbidden. Happily, this morning a trustee pushed a cart full of books into my cell. Amazingly, the Lubyanka has a library! Unfortunately, most of the titles are either nauseating political tracts, mind-deadening biographies of Marx and Lenin, or trashy novels that glorify Stakhanovites, the heroes of Soviet labor. It's said that the man behind that label, Aleksei Stakhanov, mined more than a hundred tons of coal in less than six hours, all by himself.

A good man with a pick could come in handy about now!

I selected a couple of novels and placed an order for something more literary, say, along the lines of Tolstoy. The trustee, a historian in his previous life, warned me that such titles are few. Serious works apparently have many ambiguities, making censors doubly careful. I wound up on a long waiting list. Hopefully I'll be gone before my turn comes up.

Meals are much improved. Although the borscht is still watery, my last two dinners have included potatoes, some leek-like greens and small portions of meat. They're obviously rewarding me for cooperating. On the downside I now have something else to lose.

The Comrade (1921)

By 1921 the Civil War was won and Lenin indisputably controlled Russia. Both sides had committed innumerable atrocities, many during the latter stages of the struggle. Perhaps the worst of the massacres occurred in Crimea, where in a frenzy of bloodletting Chekists and Red Army troops made good on Lenin's promise to punish the alleged "reservoir of spies and secret agents," hanging and shooting more than fifty-thousand, innocent and guilty alike.

Not all secret policemen were equally vicious. Known only by his family name, Comrade Severny was by all reports a sensitive man, not given to the violent, profane outbursts common among his peers. So fond of drink that he rarely arrived at work before noon, the rotund policeman was known for his leniency, and whenever he thought that someone was innocent he pressed for their release. Severny's impact on the brutal system, although slight, occasionally put him at odds with his more brutal superiors, requiring that his close friend, Grigori Zinoviev, the chairman of the Communist International, ride to the rescue.

Severny's most flagrant faux-pas took place while he was secret police chief in Tsarskoye Selo, a sleepy village located near the palace used by the Czars and their families as a summer home. There was good reason for stationing secret policemen. During its brief tenure the Provisional Government had coddled the Imperial family, giving it access to diplomatic pouches which they promptly used to sneak off jewelry and other valuables to relatives in Europe. Furious that a good chunk of Russia's patrimony had been spirited off, Lenin ordered his security services to keep a close tab on the spoiled aristocrats until time came for their liquidation.

One of the displaced royals was Princess Olga, whose husband, Grand Duke Paul, had been rotting in prison since the Revolution. Olga and her daughters were living in a cottage on the palace grounds at Tsarskoye Selo when orders came for their eviction. Since no one in the town dared rent them a room, the princess asked Comrade Severny for permission to relocate to Petrograd where she and her

105

children could stay with friends. Severny promptly issued the family a safe conduct pass. Indeed, he was apparently so smitten with the princess that he dispensed with inspecting her luggage and, according to the coachman, even bussed her hand while bidding her a safe journey.

Thanks to his buddy Zinoviev, Severny's "punishment" for his unseemly behavior was to leave the Cheka and be reassigned as chief of military intelligence in Kharkov, Ukraine. He and his men were supposed to help pacify the region in preparation for its formal absorption by the Soviet Union. However, an officer sent to gauge Severny's progress reported that neither his work habits nor unseemly indulgence of "counterrevolutionaries" had changed an iota.

Yan Karlovich Berzin was chief of Soviet military intelligence. A decorated veteran of the Revolution and Civil War, General Berzin could look how he pleased and wear what he pleased, and what pleased him most was to be clean shaven and dress in tailored Western suits. The contrast between his appearance and that of his bearded, ostentatiously bemedaled peers couldn't be more pronounced, and that's exactly how he wanted it.

Berzin nodded for Vladimir to sit. "I've been told that you have a taste for telling things as they are, or at least as you think them to be," he began. "Is that true?"

Vladimir could only guess where that came from. "Yes, Comrade General. It's a habit that I find hard to break."

Berzin smirked. "Then this assignment should please you. Despite your junior status I am appointing you Assistant Chief of Ukrainian military intelligence. We've been hearing disturbing tales from Kharkov. It seems that Severny's men spend their time throwing wild parties while their spineless boss drinks himself silly. We had an inspector make inquiries. Three days later Severny sent me a long, apologetic message begging for a strong-willed deputy with ideas for improvement. Let's see if he really means it."

Vladimir had been doing a lot of pencil-pushing since his return from Tambov. Sick of being an office-boy, he longed for a field assignment. But the notion of tangling with Severny wasn't appealing. Everyone knew that the man was politically connected.

"What if the comrade resists my advice?" Vladimir asked. "He has friends in high places. They could cause me a lot of grief."

Berzin nodded thoughtfully. "So they could," he agreed. "Of course, so could I." He stood and extended his hand. "Good luck, comrade. We're counting on you."

Vladimir's arrival was uneventful. Comrade Severny greeted him warmly and seemed interested in his ideas. There was no question that he faced immense challenges. After passing through the hands of the Germans and Poles, Ukraine was about to become a constituent republic of the USSR. Police and Red Army troops were doing what they could, but it was impossible to liquidate every troublemaker. Severny and his crew of young, inexperienced military intelligence officers were a crucial part of the process. If Vladimir could help them become more effective so much the better.

Vladimir didn't have to wait long for signs that not all was well. His arrival was celebrated in the unit's new clubhouse, an elaborate, bricks-and-mortar affair that seemed wildly out of place for a "secret" organization. His second inkling of trouble was when he spotted the prominent, engraved plaque that named the facility in Severny's honor. His third was Severny's portrait, which hung beside those of Marx and Lenin. Not only that, but all were the same size!

As the night wore on the enormity of the challenge became obvious. Egged on by his men, Severny downed one shot after another, becoming for all purposes indistinguishable from his subordinates and losing whatever vestiges of dignity remained. Vladimir was appalled. He was convinced that a healthy dose of fear in one's superiors was vital for maintaining discipline. Yet Severny was utterly convinced that his unorthodox approach worked. How could he be made to understand that his own troops didn't take him seriously?

Vladimir's introduction to the unit had been marred by an unfortunate episode. After bunking in a supply shed for a week Severny finally gave him keys to an apartment, but when Vladimir walked in he discovered it was occupied by a young woman who said she had been living there with her baby for months, with permission. Severny conceded that he had felt sorry for the lady, who was in some way related to someone he knew. He urged Vladimir to go back and ask to be taken in as a lodger, and authorized him to kick her out if she refused. But the second time around the woman wouldn't as much as come to the door. In a moment of frustration Vladimir forced his way in, yelling and making rude threats that he had no intention to carry out. All this commotion brought out a militiaman, who tipped his cap and withdrew when Vladimir flashed his identification.

Angry with himself for acting the bully, Vladimir returned the next day to apologize and tell the tenant she could stay. He found the premises vacant and a scrubwoman at work. Vladimir had a premonition that the episode would come back to haunt him.

Vladimir spent hours reviewing the unit's records. Severny had clearly been no more successful in Ukraine than in Tsarskoye Selo. Secret police were catching spies and saboteurs right and left. Meanwhile military intelligence was generating bountiful reports that seemed more a product of its leader's vivid imagination than anything else. What Severny's flowery prose couldn't obscure was that his unit hadn't arrested a single terrorist in recent memory.

Vladimir made an appointment with Severny to share his concerns. When he arrived he heard gunfire from the woods. For the first time during his visit, the men were practicing with their weapons.

Severny nodded thoughtfully and made copious notes. He didn't seem in the least offended. "Your points are very well taken, Comrade Romm. It just so happens that only this morning the men secured a warrant to search the home of the leader of a counterrevolutionary cell. Why don't you take the rest of the day off and come back at eight?"

Vladimir suspected that this mission, like the impromptu weapons drill, had been cooked up for his benefit. Yet he had no choice but to salute and leave. His doubts increased when he returned at the appointed time and learned that Severny wouldn't be coming along because of "other important obligations."

Their quarry lived in a dank, moldy apartment building with his wife and three daughters. Vladimir watched as the men made a big show of employing tactically correct procedures, bursting through the door and pouncing on the frightened family like a pack of hyenas.

As it happened the so-called terrorist was inebriated to a stupor, a condition that his spouse confirmed was his normal state. Despite a thorough scouring the men found nothing even remotely counterrevolutionary: no weapons, no pamphlets espousing rebellion, no lists or suspicious writings of any kind.

Before the search got underway the frightened wife voluntarily surrendered an extra ration card, which the team leader snatched as though it was the pistol that shot Lenin. Once it was clear that the raid should have never been mounted, he ordered that the couple be dragged off on the basis of that card alone. His men, who were by this point playing with the children, stared uncomprehendingly. Vladimir did the only reasonable thing: he grabbed the card from the team leader's hands and tore it into bits. The woman fell at his feet and kissed his boots.

Severny called him in the next day.

"You kept our officers from making not one arrest but two! Why?"

"These citizens posed no threat to socialism. There wasn't a kopeck in the place and little food or clothing. I know full well how revolutionary tribunals work. What would happen to the children?"

Severny jumped up, clearly overjoyed. "Thank you, comrade, for making my case! It's been less than a year since the Cheka rampaged through Ukraine, cutting down thousands of innocents. *Of course* the poor woman licked your boots! Normally we would have left those people alone, but Moscow Center seems convinced that a plot lurks around every corner, so we thought that making an arrest would get you off our backs. Can you blame us?"

Vladimir had seen enough of Severny to be skeptical. Just because the man had a good heart didn't mean he wasn't lazy. And under pressure he was willing to sacrifice others to save his own hide. "Are you saying that there's not one real terrorist left in Kharkov?"

"Say there is. How far are you willing to go to find him?"

Vladimir was recalled to the capital the next day.

Berzin waited until Vladimir finished reading the accusations. "Well, comrade, what's your answer?"

"Bringing too much luggage? Being rude to subordinates? Why would they concern themselves with such trifles?"

"The Ukrainian Communist Party is questioning everything: your past affiliation with the Socialist Revolutionaries, your family roots, your privileged upbringing, your wife's occupation..."

"Her...what?"

"Communism is about workers," Berzin sighed. "It's not about ballerinas from well-off families."

Vladimir almost laughed. "Comrade General, my wife is even more socialistically inclined than me."

"What about that woman's statement? Did you really force her and the child from the apartment?"

"It's grossly exaggerated. I never raised my hand to strike her – that's a complete fabrication. I even went back to apologize!"

Berzin was at wit's end. Comrade Romm was bright, honest and sincere. He was also possibly the most naïve Communist he had ever met. "Look, Vladimir

Georgievich, this wasn't supposed to be about you. It was about getting Severny off his butt! My superior likes to brag to the Central Committee about all the terrorists we catch, and I try to give him what he wants. You finally got our men in Kharkov to do something, then you pulled the rug out. It confused everyone."

"I apologize, Comrade General. But it just didn't seem...I don't know...*fair*."

Berzin looked stunned. Who knows what might have happened had a mop of hair attached to a man's body not bounced in. General Antonov-Ovseenko wrapped Vladimir with a bear hug.

"See where truth-telling gets you?"

Berzin sighed and poured drinks. He turned to his visitor. "What did Zinoviev say when you showed him Severny's file?"

"What could he say? Kissing the hand of a princess would turn any communist into a frog. Comrade Romm is no longer welcome in Ukraine, and Comrade Severny is no longer chief of Ukrainian intelligence. More than a fair trade, I would say."

Vladimir was greatly relieved. "I keep my party card?"

"Barely," Berzin admonished. "Use your leave to think about what I said."

Vladimir left. Berzin opened a fresh bottle. "A fine comrade, but he still sees too many shades of gray."

Antonov-Ovseenko downed a shot. "The rot hasn't set in yet. Give him time."

Vladimir, Galina and Ludvika settled into a utilitarian two-room apartment not far from where Alexander and Elena lived. Ludvika slipped into her role, impatiently waiting for the day in which her daughter, who was recovering from yet another dance injury, would tire of the ballet and start a family. Galina and Elena became fast friends, and several times a week the couples, accompanied by a feisty *babushka*, found themselves sipping tea and playing cards well into the night. Vladimir greatly enjoyed the idyllic interlude. He suspected it wouldn't last.

Lubyanka prison,
23 December 1936

This morning a guard took me to the room where Radek and I met the other day. It was now arranged like a courtroom, with places for a prosecutor, judge, witnesses and spectators. My heart sank in anticipation.

I sat in the spectator section, next to Bukhartsev. A prisoner was slumped in the witness chair, his hands folded on his lap. It took me a moment to realize that the forlorn-looking figure with the shrunken physique and sharply pointed beard was none other than that famous leader of Soviet industry, Georgi Piatakov! He had disappeared from the Communist stage not long after Radek, fueling a lot of speculation as the two were reportedly close. Unlike his fickle, mercurial friend, Piatakov never let his position go to his head and enjoyed excellent relations with nearly everyone, from ordinary workers to his colleagues on the Central Committee. (I say "nearly" because it was no secret that Stalin was jealous of Piatakov's popularity.) Piatakov had by all accounts performed admirably as deputy head of the Commissariat of Heavy Industry, and other than for an unfortunate past dalliance with Trotsky, an affliction that many of us once shared, the notion that he would become a traitor is simply unbelievable.

Piatakov glanced in my direction. He didn't appear to recognize me, which wasn't surprising as we hadn't run across each other in years, and then only briefly. I suppose that my looks have also changed, and not for the better.

Outside a light snow fell, dusting the landscape and covering up the bird droppings on Dzerzhinsky's statue. Moscow's pigeons defer to no one! The scene reminded me of a favorite anecdote. One day Stalin noticed that his pipe was missing and asked his secret police chief to investigate. Days later Dzerzhinsky returned to give his report. He found his boss contentedly puffing away. "Iosif Vissarionovich, did you get a new pipe?" he asked. "No, I found my old one only minutes after we spoke,"

Stalin replied. Dzerzhinsky was stunned. "But comrade, we've already arrested a dozen who admit to stealing it! Should we release them?" Stalin was enraged. "Let them go?" he barked. "Absolutely not! It would only *embolden* the scoundrels!"

Footsteps signaled Radek's arrival. He was momentarily followed by Molchanov and Vyshinsky. The dreaded interrogator stepped to the lectern. He would play prosecutor while the real one watched.

Molchanov resumed where they left off.

"In your statement you mention that several groups were preparing terrorist acts."

"Yes." Piatakov's voice was barely audible. He was pasty-faced and looked about to collapse.

"Speak up! What was the purpose of the Moscow organization?"

Piatakov's forehead scrunched, as though he was trying to remember his lines. "To assassinate Stalin and Kaganovich, the railways commissar. Other groups had other missions. One was led by Radek." His voice quavered, as it should. Imagine testifying to this rot in open court!

Molchanov swiveled dramatically. He honed in on Radek. "And what was *your* goal?"

"To investigate the possibility of destroying the entire Soviet leadership." Radek's voice was loud and clear. Here is a man who enjoys his work!

"*All* the leaders?" Molchanov's voice dripped with sarcasm.

"Yes. Every last one."

Molchanov affected shock. He paused dramatically before continuing. "Did you know that other terrorist groups were also active?"

"I knew of several; for example, Loginov's Ukrainian group."

Loginov? The name means nothing to me. Is he a witness? An accused? I've got the feeling that I'll soon find out.

"Were you and Piatakov preparing to commit terroristic acts?"

"Piatakov and I discussed whether our objectives could be achieved, whether they were reasonable."

"Did you settle this matter?"

"We could not settle it because we had not spoken with the field commander of the terrorist organization for six months."

"Everything depended on this leader?"

"No, it depended on facts that we did not have and that only he could provide."

"Stop avoiding the question! Preceding Piatakov's return from Berlin in 1936, were you or were you not preparing for terroristic acts?"

"Yes," Radek spat out.

"Yes to which?" Molchanov demanded.

"Yes, to terrorism!"

Leningrad Party chief Sergey Kirov was shot dead two years ago by a crazed young Communist, a rival, some whispered, for the affections of the same young lady. But Stalin and his cronies had a different idea. They pointed to the murder as proof of a wide-ranging conspiracy to assassinate Soviet leaders and used it to justify the campaign of arrests and repressions that culminated with the 1936 trial. Since then no other Party official has succumbed to anything more than a bad liver, so Radek's theatrical warning that a terrorist strike was imminent is probably intended to make up for an embarrassing lack of corpses.

The rehearsal was done. All in all, a fine performance; had I not known better I would have thought that the duel between the faux prosecutor and all-too-real witness was real. Vyshinsky actually applauded. "Much, much better!"

Molchanov looked like he was in heaven.

Radek approached. "You see? When everyone cooperates things go smoothly. You two will get your chance soon."

"When do we get the scripts?" Bukhartsev asked.

"They're being fine-tuned. Don't worry," Radek grinned, "you'll have plenty of time to memorize. Just be sure to insert some 'ums' and 'ahs.' It helps things look authentic."

A Struggle Within (1922)

Some say that Grigori Semenov was a genuine Socialist Revolutionary. Others insist that he was a spy for Lenin's secret police, the Cheka, from the very start. What's for certain is that in October 1917, when the Revolution brought Lenin into power, the Bolsheviks placed Semenov in the same prison cell where they had confined a dozen leaders of the peasant-loving Party of Socialist Revolutionaries. Semenov then dropped from sight. He didn't reappear until after the Civil War, and then not in prison but as an ostensibly free man in Europe.

How that came to pass was never explained. More improbably, after having accomplished this near-miracle, Semenov called a press conference where he tearfully and with apparent sincerity admitted that he and his former cellmates, who were still locked up without charges, had plotted from prison to undermine the Russian Revolution. In a remarkable act of sacrifice (or treachery, depending on who's to be believed) Semenov and his paramour Lydia Konopleva, who some also considered a Bolshevik spy, voluntarily returned to the Soviet Union and went through the motions of surrendering to the Cheka, Lenin's secret police.

Lenin was once a lawyer. Eager to demonstrate that socialist justice had moved beyond the summary arrests and punishments of the Revolution, he presided over the adoption of a thick set of legal codes. They were quickly put to use. Charges of counterrevolutionary activity were filed against the Socialist Revolutionary leaders. Semenov and Konopleva were also arrested and became government witnesses. It wouldn't be an ordinary trial. Lenin ordered an open proceeding, inviting Socialists, journalists and diplomats from around the world. As chief judge he selected Georgi Piatakov, a noted engineer and Communist theoretician. Fifteen years later Piatakov would appear at another show trial. That time it would be on the wrong side of the bench.

After his aborted mission in Tambov, Vladimir was assigned to a desk job at Moscow Center, summarizing reports from agents stationed overseas. As a former

Socialist Revolutionary he closely followed reports of the forthcoming trial. Press coverage was extensive, with ever-more frightening accounts of the defendants' perfidy coming out every day. The case had been assembled by a massive new organ of internal security, the GPU, which had absorbed the functions of the Cheka. Dzerzhinsky remained in charge. By Lenin's design the GPU's functions overlapped those of military intelligence, creating competition and turf battles. Vladimir and his colleagues in military intelligence thought of the secret police as a bunch of uneducated thugs, which they were, while the secret police looked on military intelligence as a bunch of overeducated poseurs, which was also mostly correct.

Vladimir wasn't personally acquainted with any of the accused, nor with Semenov or Konopleva, yet he worried that his dalliance with the Socialist Revolutionaries would come back to haunt him. His fears were confirmed when, one day, General Berzin's aide dropped a copy of Semenov's "confession" on his desk.

"Dzerzhinsky wants your comments. He thinks you might be able to add something."

"What could I know? I wasn't in jail with them!"

Like most of his colleagues the aide hated Dzerzhinsky and his goons. He lowered his voice. "Look, the trial's in trouble. European Socialists aren't toeing the line. They're screaming about how shoddily Lenin has treated the accused, keeping them locked up for years. Now that he's got the whole world coming, the scramble is on to find witnesses who can corroborate Semenov and Konopleva. I mean, everyone knows they're collaborators."

"That's for sure," Vladimir agreed. "How did Semenov waltz out of prison and wind up in Europe? And why would he and that disgusting woman willingly plop their heads on Dzerzhinsky's platter?"

"It gets better," the aide said. "The prisoners suspected that Semenov was a Bolshevik spy and gave him the cold shoulder. Now to a man they're calling him a liar. Of course, it's way too late for Lenin to back down."

Vladimir read Semenov's "confession" at length. The stooge was never a key player in the Party of Socialist Revolutionaries, yet he was claiming to have been present at so many important junctures and high-level discussions as to defy the imagination. Vladimir laughed at Semenov's claim that the Socialist Revolutionary central committee ordered him to give Fannie a pistol to shoot Lenin. No one in their right minds would have let the feral, half-blind woman as much as hold a gun, let alone entrust her to assassinate the best-guarded man in Russia. But it wasn't until later in the story, when Semenov gave a first-person account of how he and other Socialist Revolutionaries instigated the Tambov uprising, a "fact" that Vladimir personally knew was false, that the statement's insidious nature became indisputably clear. Semenov could have never dreamed up the details on his own. From its implausible beginning to its ridiculous end, the "confession" had to be the handiwork of prosecutors and the GPU. Vladimir knew just how elastic the truth was in revolutionary tribunals. But that the pre-eminent organ of state security would sponsor such an out-and-out fraud was deeply disturbing.

He set it all down in a memorandum to Berzin. Within weeks the ranks of the accused swelled to more than forty. Several had participated in the rump Socialist Revolutionary government in Archangel. One was Maxim.

Vladimir was summoned to meet with the prosecutor. Nikolai Vasilyevich Krylenko was on his way to becoming Russia's top legal authority. Brusque and so dogmatic that he stood out even in a nation of ideologues, his speeches and writings mocked the "reactionary pretense" that the legal system had any purpose other than as an instrument of class struggle. Had he been more polished he might have held off the far smoother Vyshinsky, perhaps even survived.

Krylenko got right to the point. "Comrade Berzin says that you doubt Semenov's account."

"If he's all you have there is no case. Semenov is a liar."

Krylenko was momentarily stunned. "You...you never occupied a high position in the Party! How can you challenge Semenov's account of his dealings with the Central Committee?"

"If they ever took place," Vladimir sniffed.

"*If?*" Krylenko bristled. "I'm a prosecutor. I deal in facts. What kind of 'fact' is 'if'?"

"Tambov is a fact. I was there. Semenov utterly distorted the role that Socialist Revolutionaries played in the uprising. They didn't encourage violence: they tried to prevent it."

Krylenko forced a laugh. "Socialist Revolutionaries avoiding violence? That's ridiculous. Have you never heard of Savinkov? The Combat Brigade? Anyway, from what I hear you botched your assignment so badly that you were recalled."

"All the facts about Tambov are in my report. Of course, a Chekist might have written it differently."

More than anything Krylenko was a practical man. Romm was far too risky to call as a witness. He gathered his papers.

"You define your role too narrowly, comrade. In bourgeois society trials are supposedly based only on what is heard or observed, but crucial information is often missing or distorted, allowing innocents to be convicted and evil-doers to go free. In socialism we have a far more powerful tool for finding the truth – our political consciousness. We make decisions according to the principles set out by Marx and Lenin, not just on fleeting 'facts'."

Krylenko's repulsive vision was still very much on Vladimir's mind when he and his wife visited Alexander and Elena at their new apartment.

Galina admired the spacious sitting room. "It's beautiful!"

Elena beamed. "Thank you. We often host foreign visitors, so the Party gave us more space."

The doorbell rang. Alexander opened the door to a frumpy, middle aged woman. She was wearing a stained cotton dress.

"I'm Nastasia Feodorova. Is this the residence of Alexander Georgievich?"

Moments later Maxim's hungry sister was in the kitchen devouring a plate of pork-filled dumplings.

She belched demurely. "Thank you. I haven't had a thing to eat since arriving."

Alexander was worried. Everything in Soviet life was imbued with political meaning. His brother's dalliance with the Socialist Revolutionaries was no secret, but that trip with Maxim to Archangel – no, that was something best left buried.

Vladimir knew he had to explain. "I gave Maxim your address in case of emergency."

Alexander exploded. "You did – *what?* My wife and I are official art critics! We host foreign delegations! Do you know the position you've put us in?"

Nastasia felt dizzy. Her brother was about to go on trial. What kind of people were these who cared more about their positions than with saving a comrade's life? "Please," she implored Alexander. "Your name is in the papers. You have influence. They will shoot him!"

"My wife and I are art critics!" Alexander protested. "There's nothing I..."

"Who else can I turn to?" the woman sobbed, grabbing his shirt. "My brother did nothing! He is innocent!"

Vladimir pulled the distraught woman away. He sat her in a chair. "Please, there is no need. Your brother will be released."

Her eyes fixed on Vladimir. "But, how...?"

"He'll be fine. You have my word."

Nastasia settled down. Elena tucked a loaf of bread under her arm and gently led her to the door. They watched from the window as the forlorn figure boarded a streetcar.

Alexander turned to Vladimir. "Volya, how could you promise such a thing? Didn't Comrade Lenin just demand the ultimate penalty for everyone, including Semenov?"

"No one's executing anybody," Vladimir insisted.

"How can you be so sure?"

"Lenin isn't stupid. Shooting socialists would isolate the Soviet Union and make the work of the Communist International impossible. It would dry up the foreign investments that are finally starting to trickle in. Sometimes the best way to demonstrate one's power is to be merciful. This is no time to look like a butcher."

As expected, nearly all the accused were found guilty, and twelve were ordered to be shot. But within days Lenin commuted all the sentences to brief terms of imprisonment or internal exile. Semenov promptly returned to his career as a spy, his self-professed role in the affair conveniently forgotten. Years later he would become useful in another trial. By then the Soviet Union had a new leader and the idea of killing one's own was no longer unthinkable.

Lubyanka prison,
24 December 1936

Bukhartsev joined me at exercise. While strolling we talked about that appalling bit of theater involving Radek and Piatakov. It's become obvious that resisting is useless. When the accused are so determined to confess and point the finger at each other (Radek admittedly more so than Piatakov) who are we to stand in their way?

Next to being separated from our families the most difficult aspect of this ordeal has been our political estrangement. Nothing prepared us for the anguish of being alienated from our comrades, and after spending so many years in the Party's good graces we feel utterly lost. Radek, Piatakov and others who used to have real influence are probably the worst affected, but even for bit players like Bukhartsev and I the desire to get back in the game is overwhelming.

Looking back on my time in America I am amazed at how easily their citizens can switch political allegiance, say from the Republican Party to the Democratic. It's like picking out a new coat! That no doubt helped keep party leaders mindful of their constituencies, for if there was too much dissatisfaction their underlings could – and did – vote with their feet. In our system, though, there is no other option, so the big shots are much less likely to be concerned with the views of the rank and file.

One safety valve we do have is a long-standing tradition of self-criticism. Party cards are literally accompanied with instructions for groveling. No matter how offensive a comrade's behavior may be, if they sincerely and openly recant the door is nearly always open for their return. Even Radek, Trotsky's number-one man, was readmitted. Bukhartsev doesn't think so, but when this trial is done, why not us?

Moscow Center (1922)

Berzin motioned for Vladimir to sit. He got right to the point.

"Comrade Romm, the only similarity between your reports and those of your predecessor is in the color of their covers. Are you trying to shock me?"

Vladimir, the newly minted chief of Moscow Center's European section, was responsible for assembling a monthly intelligence summary. Vilna remained a big issue. Two years had passed since the Red Army's thrashing and memory of the humiliation was bitter. Soviet generals insisted that the West, and particularly the Poles, were determined to finish off communism before its dangerous ideas infected the world. They expressed themselves so adamantly and with such conviction that the analysts at Moscow Center felt compelled to go along, issuing increasingly dire predictions that made an attack seem all but imminent.

Vladimir was skeptical. Agents on the ground were reporting no signs of a build-up. Lenin's move to boost the civilian economy and reduce spending on the military suggested that the generals' concerns were prompted by more than a smidgen of self-interest. While most of Vladimir's colleagues privately agreed, they nonetheless warned him not to stray from the accepted line. "It's what the General wants," they cautioned. "Who are we to disagree?"

Keeping quiet ran counter to Vladimir's nature. He was determined to stop the runaway train before any more of the fledgling nation's resources were squandered preparing for war, let alone the wrong one.

"Comrade General," Vladimir began, "none of our foreign officers report unusual mobilizations or exercises, a *sine qua non* in preparing for large-scale operations. Now that the war has ended, Europe's economy, forgive the expression, is in the toilet. France and Belgium are at Germany's throat over war reparations, while Poland and the Baltics have gone their own ways and can't agree on anything other than to avoid entering into agreements. Westerners may not be pleased that our heart still beats, but they have more pressing issues..."

Berzin groaned. It wasn't the first time he had to remind a junior officer that the first word in military intelligence was "military."

"Comrade Romm, can't you see that you've put me in a pickle? Bukharin and his pimply-faced accountants can't wait to feast on our bones. What do you expect me to tell our colleagues when their budgets are slashed?"

Vladimir knew better than to tangle with Berzin. "Very well, Comrade General. I'll redo the report."

Berzin sighed. As of late the Party was pressing him to ignore more and more "facts." At some point they might as well do away with spies and just make it all up. "Let's talk about that other conclusion of yours," he said, his tone softening. "That the *real* threat to Russia comes from its only friend."

Germany and the Soviet Union had recently exchanged diplomats, a shocking development inasmuch as they had been on opposite sides during the war. In truth, this union of outcasts was a matter of necessity. Germany was reviled for its aggressive militarism, while Russia was both feared and reviled: feared, for sponsoring world socialism, and reviled, for refusing to make good on the huge foreign debts run up by the Czars, a not inconsequential matter during a time of worldwide economic hardship.

Vladimir resumed his briefing. "As you know, we've inserted numerous agents into Germany's government and military; we even have a spy in President Ebert's household staff. Each day my in-basket overflows with coded radiograms that reveal the innermost thoughts of..."

Berzin yawned. "Comrade, your loquaciousness makes me sleepy. Please get to the point."

"Germany says they want to help us modernize the railways and develop Siberia. They're desperate for a source of coal, to replace what the Armistice requires they send to France."

"Yes, I know. Well, that's what happens when you blow up someone's coal mines – while retreating! But you think that there's more to it?"

"Comrade General, we're no more Germany's partner than they're ours. Another war is inevitable. If we go along with their plans, they'll be able to run their trains right into our heartland. And not just to fetch coal."

Berzin chuckled. "You tell me nothing I don't already know. The Czars may have been evil, but they weren't stupid: there's a damned good reason why our track gauge is wider than the European standard and will remain so. Germany and its *lebensraum!* They'll be our mortal enemy until my grandchildren's grandchildren are Soviet generals, and beyond."

And that was that. After another warning to keep whom he worked for in mind, Vladimir was dismissed. He left with the distinct impression that Berzin had tested him, and that he passed. But about what?

He discovered that evening when Karl Radek came calling.

Vladimir had never met the famous Communist journalist, and when he unexpectedly appeared at the door it took a moment to recognize the small, misshapen man with the Napoleonic swagger. In those days Trotsky's confidant wielded great influence, his facility with words, remarkable intellect and encyclopedic knowledge of Communist minutiae making him someone with whom few cared to tangle.

Galina and Ludvika were thrilled at the presence of the famous intellectual and ran off to get refreshments. Accustomed to star treatment, the visitor settled into a chair. His gaze fell on the photo that once caught Anna's eyes.

"Our family, shortly after it arrived in Vilna," Vladimir explained. "A friend once remarked that my mother looked sad."

Radek inspected the picture. "She seems like a woman mourning for her lover."

Vladimir was stunned. That oddball Radek, a romantic?

Galina came in with a tray of desserts. "I'm a great admirer of your writings, Karl Berngardovich. We often refer to them during study sessions."

"Very kind of you to say so." Radek greedily wolfed down a tea cake. "Excellent! You know, Madame Romm..."

"Please call me Galya," she blushed.

"You know, Galya, that I'm a great fan of the Bolshoi, which is by any measure far more entertaining than anything I could possibly write. So we're more than even."

Galina reluctantly withdrew. Radek took a pipe from his coat pocket.

"I'm Comrade Zinoviev's deputy at the Communist International, specializing in German affairs. My good friend General Berzin says that you have some interesting views on the Reich."

Vladimir quickly put two and two together. Military intelligence officers were often sent abroad under guise of working for the International. Was this his chance to escape the drudgery of Moscow Center?

"Russia and Germany haven't always seen things eye-to-eye, so it makes for an uneasy alliance. But we have much in common. We're both hemmed in by hostile states and share borders with a mutual enemy, Poland. We've exchanged military liaisons and are working on a security pact – secretly, of course, as Versailles forbids Germany from having an offensive capability. In my opinion the danger is in the long term. Germany's under the magnifying glass of the accords, which impose all sorts of onerous conditions. But England seems to have little appetite for enforcing its provisions. That worries France and Belgium, who know all too well what can happen when the Reich is on a long leash. Sooner or later – and I figure sooner – the Germans will be on the march. You can bet on it."

Radek bit into the pipe, which as usual remained unlit. "When do you think they'll make their move?"

"Their economy is in dire straits, and their government is weak. Beaten-down lands always tilt to the right. Give the fascists a couple of years to worm their way in, then a few more for the country to rearm. Then watch out."

Radek was impressed. Most military men were so preoccupied with pleasing their superiors and advancing in rank that they dared not think outside the box. Just like Berzin said, this officer was different.

"Comrade Romm, since you've generously shared your thoughts, I'll fill you in on a little secret. The Politburo's been funneling large sums through the International to help the German Communist Party, the KPD, try to counter the right. I'm in charge."

Vladimir was surprised. This wasn't Radek's first time at meddling in the Kaiser's affairs. That other occasion was a well-known debacle. "You really think that Socialism can take hold in the Reich?"

"It took hold here, didn't it? I'm only worried about acting prematurely. What happened in 1919 is a perfect example. You know that after the Revolution Lenin sent me to Berlin to find out if a worker revolt was possible. Really, the situation was hopeless. German leftists were too dispirited and confused to accomplish anything meaningful. No one here wanted to hear that, and they passed word to the German Socialists – not through me, mind you – that if they rose we would back them. Naturally, that was a complete fantasy."

Galina brought more pastries. Radek greedily wolfed down a cake. "And they say that Russians can't make sweets!" He waited until she left. "I'll always be blamed for what happened, but it wasn't my fault! Comrade Liebknecht incited the workers with a foolish speech. They ran home for their pistols, and soon the streets of Berlin echoed with gunfire. It was utter chaos. There had been no planning or coordination. German troops reacted with overwhelming force and butchered thousands. Liebknecht was killed right off. His good friend Rosa was hunted down like a dog. They dumped her body in a canal and then came after me. I was lucky to only be jailed. And even luckier to be expelled."

Radek had a reputation as an adventurist. His account of the disaster was suspiciously self-serving. Had he learned his lesson, or not?

"Forgive me, Comrade Radek, but I feel as though we're speaking in code. Are you suggesting that Lenin favors another, perhaps better organized attempt?"

Radek smiled sheepishly. "Oh, I'm no longer in that circle. Anyway, he's still convalescing from the shooting and Trotsky's the only one who sees him. My task is to prepare our German comrades for all eventualities." He carefully wrapped several sweets and got up. "I understand that you have experience training insurgents."

"A bit."

"Good. Brush up on your Deutsch, Herr Romm. We'll meet in Berlin."

Lubyanka prison,
27 December 1936

Dmitry and I have been exercising together. There's only so much we can say about our situation without going crazy, so we've been talking a lot about our families.

Dmitry is two years my junior. He is married to Raisa Gerchikova, a schoolteacher. They are childless. A few years ago Dmitry's father, an industrial chemist, was disabled by heart problems. His wife, who worked as his assistant, stayed on at the plant to supplement her husband's meager pension. Dmitry's paycheck was not large but he also contributed when he could.

He recently received a letter from Raisa. It turns out that shortly after his arrest both she and his mother were fired from their jobs, so in desperation they hired themselves out as cleaning women so they wouldn't starve. That, together with the withholding of Dmitry's entire salary forced him into what he bitterly describes as a bargain with the Devil.

Dmitry and I have similar backgrounds. My grandfather ran a Jewish printing house while his was a strict Hassid who devoted his life to studying the Torah. Yet we were both raised in non-religious homes. Our fathers were scientific men (mine was a physician) who concerned themselves with the empirical world. That doesn't mean they didn't care about ordinary people – far from it. Both were committed to ending poverty and inequality, so they naturally stood against the monarchy. Like many other liberal thinkers they fell under the spell of a radical political philosopher of the era. As they studied his ideas they discovered that he was very much like them, a secular man with a pious Jewish background who resented oppression in all its forms, whether by priests, rabbis or self-serving bureaucrats. His solutions were steeped in a dense, pseudo-scientific rhetoric that promised to upend the social order and crush the mutually reinforcing tyrannies of church and state. If it turned out that his theories or calculations weren't quite up to snuff, or that his disciples would be consumed by the same lust for power that they attributed to their enemies, that would be something to worry about later.

Well, Karl Marx is gone. But later happened.

Berlin (1922-23)

Vladimir arrived in the German capital in October 1922. The train chugged in to the Lichtenberg terminal precisely on schedule and his baggage was delivered intact and without fuss. While waiting for the embassy car he watched a stern, neatly attired policeman making his rounds, tipping his brilliantly polished, spiked helmet to citizens whose tidy appearance and impeccable manners made the officer's presence seem superfluous.

En route to the embassy Vladimir got a preview of that other Germany. Everywhere he looked dour-faced citizens stood in endless queues grasping bags stuffed with bundles of near-worthless *marks*. A loaf of bread cost several thousand; within months its price would be several million, and by the following summer several hundred million. Their savings wiped out by hyperinflation, Germany's once vigorous middle class struggled to survive. Money depreciated so quickly that as soon as workers were paid – ultimately, as often as three times a day – they rushed to buy food or, if none was available, as was often the case, anything that might hold its value and could be used as barter. A bag of clothespins was perfect: if peddled one by one they could feed a family for days.

Through it all Germans remained remarkably stoic, dressing each morning and reporting to work even when there was nothing to do or no way to pay them. Their resilience allowed most functions of a civil society to continue; trash was dutifully collected, streetcars ran on time, mail was delivered. When Vladimir wandered off the main thoroughfares, though, the malaise that gripped the proud metropolis was readily apparent. Peddlers and street urchins pestered anyone who looked remotely like a foreigner. Families frantically scoured trash bins, carting away their treasures to tenements crowded in a way that Vladimir had never experienced, even in chronically overcrowded Moscow.

And there was yet another Germany. As night fell platoons of service workers attired in the usual uniform of patent leather boots, the shortest of shorts and briefest of tops took to the streets. Not even layers of rouge and makeup could disguise that many of the girls were barely in their teens. Music halls and cabarets offered entertainment for all ages and sexual preferences. Vladimir had never thought of himself as prudish, but even he blushed at the sight of a perfectly formed chorus of *fräuleins* clad in nothing but pasties, each prepared at a moment's notice to provide a more personal service for a gentleman of means.

What Germans most wanted was foreign currency, especially dollars and pounds sterling, but even the lowly ruble was welcomed in the luxury stores and restaurants of the Kurfürstendamm. Vladimir wandered into one of the many Russian-themed coffee houses, its air so redolent with cigarette fumes that, as one of the few non-smokers, he was quickly nauseated. Soviet diplomats and members of trade missions sat along one wall. Along the opposite wall, assiduously avoiding eye contact, were a mix of exiles and less affluent members of the purged Russian nobility, meaning those who couldn't spirit away enough cash and valuables to finance comfortable lives in France and Switzerland. Vladimir felt embarrassed at the grotesque manifestation of the rift that plagued his homeland. He could only wonder: how had it come to this?

Early the following morning Vladimir sat in a dusty, cheaply furnished office looking through photographs. One depicted a company of raggedy-looking troops in dirty, ill-fitting uniforms.

"Are these the *Freikorps*?" Vladimir asked.

"Yes," a local Communist answered. "Thanks to the armistice it's what passes for a German military. They're mostly jobless vets who signed up for pocket change and a hot meal. A scruffy bunch, but like dogs dangerous in a pack. They're not our main concern, though."

The comrade pulled out another photo. It depicted a squad of sharply-attired troops goose-stepping in parade formation. They carried pistols and batons and were dressed completely in brown, their sleeves sporting red armbands with a black swastika emblazoned on a circular white field.

Vladimir grimaced at the intimidating sight. "*Sturmabteilung*. Storm troopers."

"Some fought in the war, others came from the *Freikorps*. Nazis give them a nice uniform, three squares a day, all the beer they can guzzle and a dry, warm place to sleep it off. What more could an unemployed hooligan want?"

"Why do the authorities allow it?"

"This weak joke of a social-democratic government is scared to death. The Nazis would have the *Freikorps* for breakfast. Fascists are completely out of control. Every week they murder another comrade. If we don't do something, and soon, they'll wipe us out."

Vladimir's official purpose in Germany was to provide ideological instruction to members of the KPD, the German Communist Party. That was perfectly legal. But his real mission had little to do with dialectics. He was there to assess the "Proletarian Hundreds," a Communist militia much like Vilna's Red Guards. Local cell leaders were certain that given enough training and materiel their comrade-soldiers could rid Germany of its fascists once and for all.

Vladimir's first step was to get a lay of the land. As he and an interpreter inspected Communist cells around Germany it was readily apparent that the KPD was far from being able to take on the enfeebled government, let alone the countless Nazis and assorted rightists who would surely spring from the woodwork. Contrary to the KPD's assertions, there were few truly functional detachments of Hundreds, and nearly all that existed were woefully ill-prepared. Only a handful of their members had served in the war, most of the remainder being young, unemployed ruffians who lacked discipline and basic military skills. What few weapons they had were small-caliber, bolt-action rifles useful only for game. Authorities generally ignored the scruffy bands; although they were technically illegal, the biggest threat they posed was to themselves.

Hamburg was the last stop. While by no means prosperous, the commercial and shipping hub offered more opportunities for employment, and Vladimir saw less of the forlorn, hungry-eyed look that was common elsewhere. His first impression of the local Communist cell was also favorable. A neatly attired, well-spoken official took them on a tour of the Party's own building, pausing at a wall of honor that portrayed the feats of comrades who perished during earlier uprisings.

Vladimir was about to deliver a lecture. A good-sized crowd of comrades were in attendance, imparting the meeting hall with a revolutionary fervor that he had not experienced in years. When time for questions came he recognized a young man wearing the insignia of the local Hundreds brigade.

The eager, bright-eyed Communist warrior jumped to his feet. "How far will the USSR go to support our revolution, Comrade Romm? With troops and matériel or only with your mellifluous voice?"

Laughter filled the hall. Vladimir realized why Radek made himself scarce. German communists feared a replay of the prior fiasco, that when the time came they would do all the heavy lifting while the Soviets waited to see which way the wind blew.

Vladimir's aide quickly interceded. "Comrade Romm isn't..."

"That's all right." Vladimir didn't want to lose face with a promising audience. "Considering recent history, it's a fair question. Our countries are allies. We have pledged not to interfere in each other's affairs. But as a Communist let me address your concerns from a different perspective. When the Provisional Government took charge some Socialists collaborated and became enemies of the workers. Bolsheviks chose a different path. They seized on the setback as an opportunity to coalesce around a common cause, and by assiduously adhering to the precepts of Marxism brought us to where we are today. In the end, it's all about *will*."

There was more clapping than snickering. A sallow-faced comrade stood.

"Those are stirring words, Comrade Romm, but they're subject to different interpretations. Consider our situation. We lack weapons. Our cadres are woefully unprepared. If you haven't noticed, the economy is so bad that workers are leaning right, not left, so we can't even count on their support. Without the Soviet Union's help..."

The aide jumped in. "Please, our guest isn't here to..."

"So what do we need him for? Send him home!" someone yelled.

Vladimir waited for the hall to quiet. "I'm aware of our differences," he assured. "That's why I would never encourage you to act until you're ready. When that time will come I don't know. But I can personally attest that your unswerving commitment to the cause will impart a strength far in excess of your numbers."

A few days later Vladimir and Radek sat at the famous Bolshevik's customary table in Berlin's celebrated Allaverdi restaurant, enjoying a Ukrainian meal to the soft tunes of a balalaika quartet.

Radek caught the waiter's eye. Two clean glasses and a chilled bottle of German vodka instantly arrived.

The server bowed stiffly. "Will there be anything else, comrades?"

Radek politely shook his head. The waiter clicked his heels and left.

"That's the former Count Andrei. Too far down the royal food chain to lay claim to anything but a title."

Radek poured shots. Vladimir took a small sip. The pale liquid was surprisingly smooth. "Prunes?"

"Figs, actually. They grow wild here." Radek daintily patted his lips. "It seems from your reports that we're of the same opinion."

"German communists are in no shape to take on the government, now or in the foreseeable future. Of all the cells only Hamburg seems the least bit prepared. With guns and training they might even avoid being slaughtered."

Their table began to shake. Trucks blaring martial music passed the restaurant. They were followed by hundreds of goose-stepping workers wearing swastika armbands. A protective ring of storm troopers marched along casually swinging batons.

Radek frowned. "That's what happens when you bring a nation to its knees. As things stand there's not a swallow's chance of a successful revolution from the left. Trotsky's convinced that we need an alliance."

"An alliance? With whom?"

Radek clenched his pipe. "With the Nazis, of course. Trotsky doesn't care that they think of him as half-human. He says that the first order of business is to topple the government; then there will be plenty of time to go our own way. He's got most of the Politburo behind him. Actually, nearly everyone except the General Secretary, but he's always against anything that Trotsky favors. Stalin's been making noises as though he should be in charge. Imagine that: a rude Georgian running things!"

Radek suddenly checked his watch. "Whoops!" He led Vladimir to a lounge. They arrived just as a young woman in a flowing gown took the stage. She tucked a brightly lacquered violin under her chin.

"Have you heard of her?" Radek whispered. "I understand that she's marvelous!"

Indeed she was. Their quarrels temporarily forgotten, Soviet bureaucrats and extravagantly mustachioed members of the displaced nobility sat peacefully side by side, lost in the melodious strains of Stravinsky's "Song of the Nightingale," performed by the brilliant Elisheva Kramer, a German Jew.

As 1922 came to an end Galina took leave from the ballet and joined Vladimir in Berlin. Vladimir was delighted by his wife's beauty and poise. As always, Galina took great care with her appearance, eating moderately, exercising vigorously and spending too much time applying a dizzying mix of concoctions before declaring herself ready to go out. Yet in their physical relations, her hesitant lovemaking, her newfound reluctance to keep hold of his arm on the street, he sensed an unnerving distance. Fearful that his wife had found someone else – for that was the only explanation that came to mind – a prideful, jealous husband retreated into his shell.

For days the unhappy couple sought relief in the capital's musical and artistic pleasures. They distracted themselves with Furtwängler and the Berlin Philharmonic, took in the enchanting new art form called jazz at a bawdy cabaret, and watched Doctor Caligari and his fellow villains of the German cinema perform their on-screen antics at fancy movie palaces along the Alexanderplatz. Their schedule left little opportunity for contemplation or idle talk, and when their days came to an end they literally fell into bed. But one afternoon husband and wife found themselves free and decided to pass the time in a park. As they strolled down a trail Vladimir impulsively took his wife's hand, and her slight squeeze was all the encouragement he needed to guide her to a bench.

They sat close. "Galya, are you seeing someone? Please, just tell me. I won't scold. I promise."

Galina was bewildered by what had spilled from her husband's lips. She took a letter from her purse. It was addressed to "Vladimir Georgievich Romm," care of the postmaster, Moscow.

Dearest Volya!

I hope this finds you well. I thought of writing every time a squad of soldiers trotted by. At last I decided to wait no longer. I didn't have your address but hope that this message will somehow reach you.

You remember the farm. We were praying that our little corner of Ukraine would be overlooked, but in 1919 a Socialist committee came, took away the animals and confiscated nearly all the grain. I left the *zemstvo* and hurried home to help. Conditions were frightful. Starving peasants overran the fields, ripping out anything that dared poke through the soil, and between them and the soldiers the land was denuded. Other farmers had decided to plant only enough for their own needs, but I refused to let my parents give up and used my savings to help them buy seed. Somehow we managed to hang on. Then father fell ill. He passed away in February

1921 and we buried him near his favorite spot, where he would sit for hours watching the horses graze.

One other bit of bad news. Do you remember my brother Michal, the one who brought you gloves when your hands got raw? He was only fifteen when the Red Army took him away to fight in the civil war. They buried him in a common grave near Kharkov.

Now for better news. I am an old married woman! My husband Idzi and I have twin boys, Jarek and Mikolaj, who will be happy to pester you and ask all about your adventures when you visit. Things are much better, too much so, if you look at my waist! Under Lenin's new program – who would think that he'd introduce capitalism? – we're using profits from selling grain to hire help and buy machinery. We even have a tractor! It's old and Idzi is always tinkering with it, but it does the work of several horses. We have a few of those too, which the boys like to ride, and some pigs and cows. Idzi is very handy and built a machine that helps in the milking, so there is plenty to sell. Michal's twin, Marusha, is still on the farm, working alongside Tanya and Lidia. (Remember the toddlers who followed you everywhere?) My other sister, Katja, married a fellow from Minsk who I began seeing after, well, you know. They live on a collective where he fixes machinery. They already have three children!

Here's a surprise for you. Do you remember the land that was stolen from father's ancestors? My husband is the owner's son! He's older and fought the Germans. By bringing our holdings together we assembled a spread that's large enough to prosper. Hopefully things will stay like this for a long time.

How I wish Papa could be here. He would be so proud!

Now I must go. Please write and tell me all about you and your family.

All my best, Anna Mikhailovna

Vladimir carefully folded the letter. "I'll write something that you can mail from Moscow. Maybe you can include our photo."

"Who is she?"

"Please, Galya, it was so very long ago!"

Galina softened. "Why didn't you tell me about this part of your life? Don't you think that I would have understood?"

Give me a GPU inquisitor any time, Vladimir thought. "I don't know. She was the first woman for whom I had real feelings, but we lost touch during the war. Maybe I thought it best to leave things be."

"Well, she still has feelings for you. That's plain to see."

Vladimir drew his wife close. "Look, I freely admit to being an idiot. You'll just have to be smart enough for the both of us."

"Funny. That's what mother said."

Galina left for Moscow in mid-January. Her train had just left the station when Vladimir's interpreter ran up to the platform frantically waving a newspaper.

"Comrade Romm, it happened! They invaded!"

Lubyanka prison, 28 December 1936

It's been snowing heavily and the weather's turned bitterly cold, making outdoor exercise impossible. One of the older guards took pity and let Dmitry and I linger in the hallway. We used the time to reminisce.

We became acquainted in the late 1920s while I was at *Trud*, the mouthpiece of the trade union movement, and Dmitry was at *Komsomolskaya Pravda*, the organ of the Communist Youth League. Dmitry was also working for the state planning board and had just completed his first book, a political hit-piece that criticized the Allies' stranglehold on Germany. Those were the days when the Reich was supposedly our friend, a relationship that we all knew wouldn't last.

I heard no more of Dmitry until 1936. One morning I was having breakfast at our Washington embassy when Ambassador Troyanovsky walked in with an *Izvestia* fresh from the diplomatic pouch. Alexander Antonovich had a big smile on his face, and when we asked why he read an article out loud. It was so hilarious that it brought everyone in the dining room to their knees. Our correspondent in Berlin was researching a piece on food shortages and caught up with an official from the Nazi health ministry. When he asked the flustered man why strict rationing had been imposed the explanation he got wasn't about production difficulties or the effects of the economic crisis. No, the measures were a necessary corrective as German citizens had been endangering their health by overindulging!

I looked at the article. Its author was Bukhartsev. During his two years in the Nazi capital (his tenure roughly coincided with mine in America) Dmitry's dispatches mocked everything German, from their obsession with the famous composer and notorious anti-Semite Richard Wagner to the Nazi's appalling stiff-armed salute and its lesser cousin, the wrist flip, invented by some genius so that the torch-bearers of Aryan purity could properly greet each other in close quarters. Dmitry reserved his most acerbic comments for the S.A. and the S.S., the jack-booted thugs who ran around the capital keeping a watchful eye lest someone of a lesser kind – like Bukhartsev – contaminate the Führer's seed stock. Naturally, the Nazis suspected that Dmitry, a Jew, had been purposely sent to tweak their noses. Why they didn't find an excuse to expel him is hard to say. Maybe they didn't want their own man kicked out of Moscow. Or maybe they figured that the Soviet Union would cut short his tenure soon enough.

Two prisoners were led by as Dmitry and I returned to our cells. One was a middle-aged Russian. The other's age was hard to guess because his face was badly bruised, probably the result of some recent "encouragement." Guards called him "Fritz," a common way to disparage Germans. Bukhartsev recognized the pair and whispered that they were being auditioned for roles as witnesses. That the idiom of theater should aptly describe what's taking place is an outrage, but we've accepted it without batting an eye.

Adapt or perish!

Essen (1923)

Germany was in serious trouble. Beset by food shortages and hyperinflation, yet legally bound to keep making war reparations, it was using every excuse imaginable to delay meeting its ruinous obligations. That was a dangerous game to play, and particularly with the French, whose land the Kaiser's troops mercilessly plundered during the Great War, destroying what they couldn't haul away. Finally, after repeated ultimatums to ship overdue trainloads of coal were ignored, French and Belgian forces occupied the Ruhr, a vast industrial region that was Germany's main source of raw materials. The squeeze was on.

What the invaders didn't expect was the determination of the German people. Miners and railroad men staged wildcat strikes and work stoppages; if the interlopers wanted coal they would have to dig it up and transport it themselves. Their patriotism galvanized the besieged country, prompting the ineffectual government to shake off the cobwebs and actively support the resistance. Berlin instituted a massive relief effort, shipping food to needy areas and reimbursing strikers for lost wages. Unable to borrow, the treasury financed the move by simply printing more *marks*, stripping the currency of whatever value remained.

The Reich was running on vapor.

One week into the occupation Vladimir was summoned by his embassy's military attaché, who served as his link to Moscow Center. He walked in to find the official consoling himself with a bottle of vodka.

Vladimir turned down a drink. His host helped himself to another.

"Here's the problem, comrade. Now that France and Belgium have carried out their threat they show no inclination to pack up and leave. Moscow Center is plenty worried. Problem is, we have no one in position to collect intelligence. That's where you come in."

Vladimir was dismayed. He sure wasn't looking for a reason to extend his stay. "What about the GPU? Doesn't the secret police have foreign operatives?"

"Of course they do," the attaché replied, forlornly gazing at the nearly empty bottle. "But they never share anything with us. Their boss Dzerzhinsky reports only to Stalin, and the General Secretary keeps everything to himself. Meanwhile I've got Generals screaming for answers. What do the Gauls have in mind? Just getting what's owed them or something more?"

The attaché spun the dials of a safe. He took out a diplomatic passport and a quantity of American currency, perhaps a month's wages in the U.S. but worth a small fortune in Germany.

"You'll be our eyes and ears in the Ruhr." He gave Vladimir a slip of paper bearing two addresses. "This one's our trade mission in Essen. Use their pouch to communicate with Moscow Center. The other is the *gasthaus* where you'll be staying. Your passport identifies you as a member of the Soviet trade mission, so pretend that you're a businessman looking for customers, raw materials, whatever. Lodging is scarce so you may have to share a room."

Vladimir frowned. "Everyone thinks that 'trade delegates' are spies. We have no relations with France. If they arrest me..."

The attaché finished the thought "...you're screwed. So don't get arrested."

Vladimir went to bid Radek farewell. He found him ensconced in a fine hotel, registered under a pseudonym. Radek was hardly recognizable. For once the hirsute schemer was clean shaven.

"I'm not really supposed to be in Germany," Radek explained. "Since my last visit they've kept 'losing' my visa application. They probably suspect we're up to something."

Vladimir felt a chill. "Are we?"

"Trotsky decided to help our German comrades prepare for a *putsch*. We're to do it without the Nazis."

Vladimir detected a trace of ambivalence. "No coordination?"

"No knowledge, no cooperation, nothing. They outnumber us and are still growing, and Trotsky fears that they might opt for a quickie divorce. He's sure that if we seize the initiative it will make up for a lack of numbers. Like in the Revolution."

"But it's *not* the Revolution. Not ours, anyway. Any way you slice it it's an act of war, and against our only ally. What does Lenin think? Stalin?"

"Vladimir Ilyich isn't long for this world, I'm afraid. Maybe taking out that bullet wasn't such a great idea. Trotsky, who seems to be the only one who's spoken with

Lenin, insists that the boss is on board. Comrade Stalin, as you can probably guess, is dead-set against the idea – he calls it 'unbridled adventurism'."

"And you? What do *you* think?"

"Me? Why, Vladimir Georgievich, I'm just the messenger."

Passenger trains were still running when Vladimir made the trip north. His first glimpse of the new order came when French military police boarded his car as it rolled into the occupied zone. Vladimir's passport immediately caught the officials' attention.

An officer sneered. "What business would a Soviet have in the Ruhr?"

"Trade. I come for coal."

The Frenchman laughed heartily. "Really? Us, too!"

More security checks followed. When the train finally pulled in to Essen it was hours late. Vladimir struggled with his luggage to the taxi stand. He noticed that a uniformed dispatcher was turning away one prospective passenger after another.

"Passport, *bitte*."

Vladimir displayed his credentials.

The dispatcher carefully reviewed each page. He pointed to a waiting cab. "*Danke*."

The taxi swung into the Hollestrasse. Although it was early afternoon a sulfurous pall made it seem like sunset. Vladimir tried to breathe as shallowly as possible. "I thought a strike was on," he said, speaking in broken German.

The cab driver sneered. "France is bringing in their own workers. You might have noticed that we refuse them service. Is this your first time in the Ruhr?"

"Yes."

"So your nostrils have already informed you that this is no resort. Mines and industrial plants are lined end to end for a hundred kilometers. Everything belongs to those filthy Krupps. As long as their exports keep hard currency coming in they're allowed to do as they please, the unions be damned. They'd be playing footsie with the French if we let them."

They entered a working-class area. Groups of strikers huddled on sidewalks, staring down passing squads of French cavalry. Suddenly the cab swerved. The driver cursed at a drunk staggering down the roadway.

"Our police refused to swear allegiance to the French so they were told to go home. Now we have no order, to go along with no food."

"I thought that Berlin was paying compensation."

The cabbie roared. "Sure, they've made us millionaires! I've got sacks of *marks* at home. Once there's enough for a truckload I'll go stand in line for two hours to exchange it for a sausage – if any are left. The French have first dibs on everything. We've evacuated children to other regions so they can have milk. My girls are with their grandparents in Heidelberg."

They pulled up to a run-down boarding house. Vladimir gave the cab driver an American twenty-five cent piece. He accepted it gratefully.

"Thank you. And be sure to tell your comrades that Germany will never give in to invaders. We will starve first!"

A wheezing desk clerk examined Vladimir's passport with interest. "We don't get many 'diplomats' here," he snickered.

"Actually, I'm a businessman..."

The clerk snickered again. "Sign here," he instructed. "Follow me."

Vladimir was led to a tiny room with two beds, a table and two chairs. Wall hooks served as a closet. Most of the floor space was cluttered with another occupant's belongings.

"You're sharing," the clerk said, pointing out the obvious. "He's also Russian, got here right after the invasion. Toilet's down the hall. Be careful, as it overflows."

"Is this all you have?"

"It's the last room with only one occupant. French officers grabbed every decent space weeks ago. They even seized homes. You're lucky not to wind up in a dormitory."

Vladimir was looking for a place to hide his money when the door swung open.

"Greetings, comrade!" A robust, clean-shaven man with wispy brown hair and sparkling blue eyes sauntered in.

"Lev!"

Vladimir had not heard from Lev since their adventures in Vilna, and to run into him in Germany, of all places, was a shock. Curiously, Lev didn't seem at all surprised. Vladimir quickly realized that their meeting was no accident.

Lev confirmed as much while pouring drinks. "When the trade mission informed me of your assignment I volunteered to share my humble lodgings. You are posing as a..." Lev pretended to search his memory. "Forgive me, I can't remember."

"I'm an accountant. And you?"

Lev laughed. He refilled Vladimir's glass. "You've probably guessed that I'm with the GPU. Can you believe that? Lev Alexandrovich, a secret policeman! You know, it's insane that our bosses don't coordinate their efforts. How far is it between our offices at the Lubyanka and yours at Moscow Center?"

Their conversation was interrupted by a knock on the door. A matronly woman in a stained apron pushed in a cart piled high with delicacies.

"Behold our bounty!" Lev exclaimed. "A loaf of pumpernickel, a slab of butter, a dozen soft-boiled eggs and a liter of beer." He playfully tweaked the woman's pink cheeks. "And, of course, a comely *fräulein!*"

Vladimir gave the woman ten cents American. She gushed and left.

"You over-tipped," Lev scolded. He popped a whole egg into his mouth. "In my next report I'll threaten to do like the Germans and go on strike; unless, that is, I'm given hard currency like my comrades in military intelligence. What do you think?"

Vladimir slathered butter on a thick hunk of bread. "I think that if I keep eating like this I might need a new wardrobe."

For several weeks two Russian "businessmen" frequented taverns favored by French officers and bought countless rounds of drinks. By the end of the experiment all that Vladimir knew for sure was that the French liked to drink and that they passionately hated the Germans, two facts that hardly required coming to Essen to discover. As for what the invaders intended to accomplish and how long they planned to remain, there were as many opinions as willing drinkers.

"Stay?" bellowed the very drunk *Capitaine*. "Not even Marshal Poincaré knows!"

Vladimir's temples throbbed from the previous evening's excesses. Nearly half his money was gone, and with precious little to show for his efforts. His reports to Moscow Center were appallingly thin and it seemed only a matter of time before Berzin would question his usefulness. He longed for the assignment to end, but hopefully not in disgrace.

"It's rumor on rumor, speculation on speculation, from those least likely to know," he complained.

Lev looked up from another improbably copious dispatch. "Ah, you're too picky. Surely there's more you can write. What about their threats to blow up the mines when they're done, just like what was done to them? Or the rumors about partitioning Germany, half for France, half for Belgium?"

Vladimir groaned. "There's no need to feed our superiors any more garbage. They make plenty enough bad decisions as it is."

Lev bit into a juicy apple. It was amazing what an American coin could buy. "Ah, you must be talking about Comrade Radek! There's a rumor that he and Trotsky want to use Germany as a platform for conquering Europe."

Vladimir knew that Lev was pumping him for information. Stalin bitterly opposed

Trotsky, and with Lenin on his deathbed an epic confrontation loomed. Anything that discredited Radek would likely finish off Trotsky as well. He went on the offensive.

"Is it true that your boss Dzerzhinsky is Stalin's boy?"

Lev snickered. "Touché." He sealed his message in a security envelope. "I'm off. Seriously, Volya, are you sure you don't want to send something? I promise not to read!"

"Just the letter home, thanks."

Early the following morning the roommates were awakened by a great commotion. Hordes of workers singing Germany's new national anthem, the *Deutschlandlied*, tromped by the rooming house, shaking it to its foundations. Many grasped lengths of pipe.

Vladimir quickly dressed. "Hurry!"

Lev seemed uncertain. "Are you sure? If we're arrested..."

"Then I'll finally have something to report!"

They joined the march. From what they could learn a battalion of French engineers had commandeered an idled steel mill in the middle of the night, overpowering the few strikers who the union posted as guards. Soldiers made off with the plant's machinery, but in the confusion an infantry squad was left behind. Workers learned what happened and rushed to the scene. After a tense confrontation the scared, lightly armed troops barricaded themselves in an empty building.

Vladimir and Lev climbed atop a storage shed and watched agitators exhort the crowd. Speeches drew cheers and shouts of "Death to the French!" Before long a mob advanced on the building where the troops had taken refuge. Fearing for their lives, the soldiers took aim from the windows and fired. Several strikers fell. Mistakenly thinking that the French were mounting an all-out assault, protesters stampeded for the exits, trampling each other in a desperate rush to get away. At the main gate they encountered heavily armed French cavalry who had come to rescue their colleagues. A melee broke out and by the time it was over dozens of workers lay dead.

When fighting broke out, Vladimir and Lev jumped down from the shed. Lev landed poorly, twisting an ankle, and in the delay a squad of French cavalry rode up and blocked their escape.

"*Nous sommes les diplomates Russes!*" Vladimir yelled, skipping over the part about being a businessman.

A soldier leveled his rifle. "*Non, monsieur,*" he replied. "*Vous êtes prisonniers de la France!*"

Lubyanka prison, 30 December 1936

This morning they took Dmitry and me back to the mock courtroom. When we arrived Piatakov was just coming off the stand. He stumbled to a chair, looking unwell. I understand that he has heart problems. This show better get on the road, and soon.

It was Bukhartsev's turn. I sat next to Radek in the spectator's gallery. Vyshinsky was off in a corner, deep in thought. Maybe he was thinking of those halcyon days in pre-revolutionary Russia when he and Stalin shared a prison cell. Or maybe he was just wondering what to have for lunch.

Molchanov cleared his throat. "You are Bukhartsev, Dmitry Pavlovich?"

Dmitry shifted nervously. "Yes." I winced at the absurdity. This was to be a trial under Soviet law, yet here we were, rehearsing our lines. Is this what socialist reality has come to?

"Please relax, comrade. Keep in mind that you're a witness, not an accused."

"Excuse me," Bukhartsev said. "But I *am* confessing."

For a moment one could have heard a fly land. Vyshinsky was furious. "No!" he barked. "Accused confess, witnesses give testimony!" I was happy to hear the Procurator-General make the distinction, as fatuous as it may be. One must find comfort where they can!

Molchanov gave Dmitry the sternest of looks. "You have been called as a witness in the case against Radek, Piatakov and others. You must testify truthfully. Please inform the court of your last official position."

Bukhartsev took a deep breath. "Between 1934 and 1936 I was *Izvestia* correspondent to Berlin."

"Do you know Karl Radek?"

"Yes. He was my editor at *Izvestia*."

"Are you acquainted with Georgi Piatakov?"

"We met in Berlin in 1935."

"Did you have occasion to enter into relations with Piatakov in connection with the performance of underground Trotskyite work?"

"Um...what?"

The pretend prosecutor tried again. "How did you bring Piatakov and Trotsky together?"

Bukhartsev brightened. "Ah, yes. Trotsky was in Oslo. Radek introduced me to a Viennese journalist who was Trotsky's contact in Berlin. He told me that Trotsky wanted to meet with Piatakov. I passed this on to Piatakov when we met."

"Did he agree to go to Oslo to see Trotsky?"

"Yes. But first we had to meet with the journalist to make arrangements."

"Tell me about Piatakov's meeting with Trotsky..."

Vyshinsky broke in. "Wait a moment! Shouldn't we be more precise about when all these meetings happened, and where?"

Radek unexpectedly piped up. "We'd best not get into too many specifics, Comrade Prosecutor. Some of the schedules don't coincide. Germany keeps precise entry and exit records and the press would be thrilled to rub our noses with any inconsistencies."

Vyshinsky's cheeks flushed. "Are you suggesting, prisoner Radek, that the witnesses and accused should testify incorrectly?"

Molchanov threw Radek a withering look. "Not at all, Comrade Procurator-General. We're merely trying to keep our enemies from distorting what took place."

"So get the right information to begin with!" Satisfied that he covered his tracks, Vyshinsky sat down. "You may continue."

Molchanov resumed the questioning. "Comrade Bukhartsev, please tell the court what Piatakov said about his meeting with Trotsky."

"When Piatakov returned from Oslo..."

Vyshinsky was clearly dissatisfied. He broke in again. "Piatakov made a secret flight from Germany to Norway. Is that correct?"

Beads of sweat formed on Molchanov's forehead. "Ah...yes?"

"Yes or no?"

"Yes."

"Fine. So how did Piatakov, a well-known Soviet diplomat, manage to travel to a foreign land and meet the notorious exile Trotsky without anyone noticing? Was Piatakov wearing lipstick and a wig? If he was using false documents, where did he get them?"

Molchanov turned to Piatakov. "You heard the Procurator-General's concerns. Did you carry a false passport?"

Piatakov struggled to infer the correct answer. "Yes?"

"Did you alter your appearance?"

"Um...I cut my hair. Yes, that's it! Shaved it clean off. Made me look years younger!"

"That's helpful," Vyshinsky said. He turned to Molchanov. "Now all that's left to know is where this mysterious flight originated. It certainly didn't come in from Moscow! And what about fuel stops, flight plans, clearances to take off and land? Do you intend to leave those details hanging so they can be thrown in our face by the capitalist press?"

Radek had been furiously scribbling on a pad. He suddenly looked up. "Comrade Prosecutor, I may have the answer. Everything was arranged by a Viennese middleman whom Austrian authorities refuse to concede even exists. Naturally they must be hiding him, if he isn't dead. And of course there are no documents, as the journey was completely illegal."

Vyshinsky frowned. Radek's invocation of yet another ghost was not a perfect solution, yet unless someone could travel through time to synchronize schedules, create flights and bring non-existing persons to life, it would have to do. And that's where things were left.

I later asked Dmitry when Piatakov's visit with Trotsky actually took place. He looked at me as though I had gone mad.

"Good grief, man, you bought it?"

"I mean when it *supposedly* happened. Was it in the summer? Fall?"

Bukhartsev thought for a moment. "It would have to be in January."

I was incredulous. "Flying into Oslo in the dead of winter? That's crazy!"

Dmitry chuckled. "Maybe they fitted skis on the plane and slid right up to Trotsky's door. Look, the script sags with inconsistencies. Explaining each triggers three more. It's what drives them to make up characters from thin air. You were in America during the first trial. Did you really think that dedicated comrades like Kamenev and Zinoviev sold us out?"

I pondered my embarrassing embrace of the implausible. "To not believe would have threatened my Communist identity. It's how we all felt. So I put your "inconsistencies" out of mind."

"Of course you did," Dmitry said. "So did I."

The Colonel (1923)

We were in a makeshift prison cell. It was freezing cold. Lev huddled in a corner, trying to ignore the stench wafting from a hole in the floor. "Have you ever been locked up before?"

Vladimir was walking in place to keep warm. "Once, as a kid. I passed the time playing chess with a policeman."

"Lucky you."

"Lucky *us*, Comrade. We could have been shot."

A French lieutenant had recognized the pair as the free-spending Russian "businessmen" who had been pouring liquor down officers' throats. He ordered Vladimir and Lev bound, blindfolded and hauled off to a military base a few kilometers from Essen.

The door creaked open. A guard burst in. "*Sortez!*"

Vladimir and Lev were hustled to a small office. Filing cabinets secured with thick metal bars and padlocks lined the walls. The room's exact center was occupied by a desk, its top bare but for a cheap metal lamp and a framed photograph of a familiar-looking middle-aged man and his well-fed family.

Moments later the official depicted in the photo came in. He was wearing an inexpensive suit that, considering his girth, lent him the look of a poorly-dressed bowling pin. He dismissed the guard and sat at the desk.

"Did I ever thank you fellows for the schnapps?" He spoke in passable but heavily-accented Russian.

Vladimir recognized another beneficiary of their hospitality. "You're welcome. As I recall you only had a couple shots before leaving."

"It's all the time I needed," the official replied. "You may call me Otto. Don't let it fool you – I'm named after my grandfather – but in my heart I am one-hundred percent French. I'm a senior inspector with the *Sûreté*, the national police. We're the

151

intelligence arm for French forces in the Ruhr. Running into Soviet intelligence – and I use that term with the utmost respect – is always a pleasure."

Vladimir protested. "Like we've repeatedly told your men, we're..."

Otto raised his hand. "Please! Let's not get off on the wrong foot. Be assured that we know the both of you quite well." Otto held up two thick folders so that his guests could recognize their photographs tacked to the inside covers.

"Did you fellows really think you could run around Essen unobserved?"

Lev bristled. "Why should we care who's watching? We're not breaking any laws!"

"Really? I daresay even the Reich prohibits spying. And everyone knows what happens to secret agents who get captured during wartime."

A heavyset German woman in a chef's hat walked in with a tray. It held a heaping plate of Wiener schnitzel, a loaf of bread and a stein of ale. She set them in front of the policeman.

"Please forgive me," Otto said, patting his ample midsection. "I've been trying to lose a few pounds, so I skipped breakfast!" He tucked a napkin into his collar and ravenously attacked the meal.

Vladimir and Lev hadn't eaten for a day. They hungrily watched the portly policeman wipe the plate clean with the last chunk of rye. He pushed the dishes aside. "Well, back to business! Comrades, would you please tell me why you were sent here?"

"We're Soviet citizens," Lev insisted. "We demand to be treated in accordance with international law."

Otto nodded agreeably. "That is your right," he conceded. "Or rather, that *would* be your right had you been wearing a uniform, which you weren't, or if our countries enjoyed diplomatic relations, which they don't. But if you insist, I will be happy to turn you over to the adjutant to be court-martialed." His voice turned grave. "Regretfully, we didn't pack guillotines, but I guarantee that you would be shot before sunset."

Lev paled. Otto gleefully thumped the desk. "Relax, my friend, relax. We French aren't animals! Our Revolution – the one that Comrade Lenin used as his template – has been over for more than a hundred years. Still, I wouldn't hesitate to make your lives as miserable as possible. A few months in our 'hotel' would make a mute man sing. So how about it? Why are you here?"

"You have our passports," Lev said. "Like they say, we're with the trade mission."

Otto sighed. He flipped through one of the files. "You, Lev Alexandrovich, were assigned to the GPU team stalking the exiled Grand Duke Kyril in Munich. Apparently he has visions of assembling an invasion force and returning as Czar. Isn't that right?" Without waiting for a reply he removed a photograph out of the other file and held it up for Vladimir to inspect. It depicted Radek in the restaurant watching the Nazi demonstrators march by.

"Amazingly, Comrade Romm, the man you were with shouldn't even be in this picture. I don't think he's held a German visa for years! Or that's what our men in their foreign ministry say."

Vladimir did his best to act nonplussed. "I'll be sure to bring that to Karl's attention, Inspector."

"Good, good." Otto took on a conciliatory tone. "Look, comrades, France and the Soviet Union have a lot in common. You despise the Germans, and, miracle of miracles, so do we! France and the Soviet Union will soon be exchanging diplomats, perhaps as early as next year. Of course, that can only happen if your Politburo gets Trotsky to forget about conquering the world. Regrettably, every time things seem on track you Bolshies spring another surprise. Like that insane proposal to form an alliance with the Nazis."

"Us cooperate with the Nazis? That's crazy!" Lev blurted out.

"Of course it is!" Otto agreed. "Anyone who thinks they can negotiate with the likes of Hitler suffers from a bad case of historical amnesia. Don't you agree, Comrade Romm?"

Vladimir was appalled. What secrets didn't the French have? "I watched your sailors roam the streets of Archangel while French frigates lay at anchor in Russian waters. If we're going to reminisce, let's not do it selectively."

A plate of pastries arrived. Otto greedily plopped a cherry strudel in his mouth. "Ach, delicious! Well, time for coffee!" He summoned the guard. "Drop them off wherever they wish."

"We're releasing them, Inspector?"

"*Pourquoi pas?* The greatest risk these two pose is to the Soviet treasury."

Hours later Vladimir and Lev were taking turns in a tub vigorously scrubbing off jailhouse grime.

"I think we could work with this guy," Vladimir said. "Give a little, get a little."

"I don't know, Volya. Near-death experiences give me chills."

Vladimir laughed. "Well, you're not dead yet. Say, I didn't know that you had spied on the Grand Duke. I heard that he's a real nitwit."

"He's the next nitwit in line to the throne. Kyril is so intent on restoring the monarchy and becoming Czar that he's volunteered to be the figurehead for an invasion. As long as he runs no personal risk, of course."

"An invasion? By whom?"

"You know, the same enemies of the state who justify Dzerzhinsky's position, Berzin's, yours, mine..."

Their laughter was interrupted by an insistent rapping. A large middle-aged man with dark, deeply-set eyes stood at the threshold clutching a large valise. His long woolen coat, collar turned up, lent him a vaguely sinister appearance.

Lev instantly recognized the visitor. "Comrade Colonel!"

Colonel Iosif Stanislavovich Unshlikht rose through the Cheka and GPU to become Dzerzhinsky's top deputy. Surprisingly, he recently transferred to military intelligence as second in command to Berzin. His reassignment, rumored to be Stalin's handiwork, was feeding a lot of speculation.

Lev promptly excused himself. "I've got plans tonight, comrades. Don't wait up!"

Unshlikht would spend the night. He unpacked a bottle of Ukrainian vodka and a smoked, heavily marbled Russian sausage.

"Quite a coincidence to run into Lev Alexandrovich. I hired him when I was with the GPU. A fine officer, don't you think?"

"Yes, Comrade Colonel."

Unshlikht sliced the meat wafer thin, serving Vladimir first. "So, Comrade Romm, what did the fat Frenchman have to say?"

Vladimir was dazed. How did this man find out, and so quickly?

Unshlikht chewed slowly, savoring the fatty delicacy. "Never assume you're the only layer of cake, comrade. Now tell me everything." The Colonel listened carefully as Vladimir related the account of their arrest. He came to the end. "Right at the point where you'd expect Otto to put on the squeeze he cut it short and had us dropped off."

Unshlikht poured drinks. "Perhaps he's reaching out. You know, I'm intrigued by his mentioning of diplomatic recognition. Our best guess is that the French will wait for the British, and they for the Americans. Do you think he was trying to open a back door?"

"It's possible," Vladimir said. "Would you like me to pursue it?"

"Unfortunately, no. You're going to Hamburg."

Lev straggled in the next morning looking much the worse for wear. "I think I used up eight lives, comrade." He looked around. Unshlikht was gone and Vladimir's suitcase was half-packed.

"I figured you'd be leaving. What the heck, maybe Otto and me can be pals."

"Sounds like a plan." Vladimir lobbed Lev the rest of the sausage. "Maybe this can help butter him up."

Lev collapsed on his cot. "It doesn't make sense. Stalin's close to the GPU. He and my boss Dzerzhinsky are thick as thieves. The General Secretary hates Trotsky, and by extension his chum, your boss Berzin. So how is it that the Colonel, who was Dzerzhinsky's protégé, winds up number two in military intelligence?"

"Ah, they're all a bunch of connivers," Vladimir said, skirting the subject. "I'll be working for Moishe Stern. He's a straight military man, utterly non-political. Germany is now a theater of operations and he's in charge of the Northwest sector. My job is to transform Hamburg's Proletarian Hundreds into something resembling a military organization."

Lev whistled. "Only the Politburo can designate a theater. Maybe the Man of Steel was outvoted. But I guarantee that he wasn't outmaneuvered. Stalin inserted Unshlikht to make sure that Berzin and Trotsky fail. And you, my friend, are caught square in the middle." Lev switched off the lamp. "Volya, Russia is bone-tired of war. There's room for you at the GPU. Think about it."

Vladimir had thought about it. His past affiliation with the Socialist Revolutionaries was bad enough. Thanks to Radek he was now caught up in another adventurist scheme. When would it ever end?

Lubyanka prison,
1 January 1937

Early this morning our keepers came by with thimblefuls of cheap vodka to mark the New Year. Guards and prisoners alike stood in the hallways, savoring the stinging liquid as though it was from the General Secretary's private reserve. For an instant we were all comrades, caught up in a predicament far and beyond the power of any ordinary mortal to comprehend. And when the last drop was gone we returned to our cells without fuss, clanging the doors shut behind us like the well-disciplined herd that we've become. What more could a dictator want?

Galina and I had looked forward to my new post in England. French and American doctors managed to stabilize Georgie through diet and medication, and we heard of promising new therapies in Great Britain. Forget the Party's boasts: despite an abundance of physicians, medicine in the USSR is, like nearly everything else, terribly backwards, a shame considering our poor diets and unhealthful living conditions. I'm sure that my brothers are doing what they can, but sitting here powerless to intervene while a dreadful disease threatens my son is driving me crazy.

At exercise, Dmitry told me that after the last rehearsal he, Molchanov, Radek and Piatakov spent hours discussing how to make the secret rendezvous in Norway seem more plausible. Radek, that despicable creature, suggested that the *Izvestia* correspondent to Vienna be "recruited" to play the role of a journalist. If not, prosecutors could invoke the excuse of State secrets and have an actor testify from behind a screen. In the end Molchanov decided against both options. He considered it too late in the game to bring in (meaning, arrest) another witness, especially since it might prove necessary to audition several, while using a stand-in was impossible as it would force the Procurator-General to concede, even if only to a few, that the trial is nothing but theater. In the end they merely fiddled with the script. Radek named the phantom Viennese newsman "Mr. Stirner." He will otherwise remain a cipher.

Dmitry and I figure there are at least three reasons for the trial. Stalin wants to prove to the two powers that count – England and America – that Germany and Japan pose an imminent threat. He's determined to remove long-standing political irritants, meaning anyone once aligned with Trotsky, and replace them with obsequiously loyal young communists whom he's been inserting into posts made vacant by the purges. And to deter competitors he's also sending a powerful message about who's in charge. To accomplish it all without making the regime look like a machine of terror is where the art comes in. It's where *we* come in.

But can Vyshinsky pull it off? His reliance on crude stratagems demonstrates just how little we understand the West. In the Soviet Union the issue of guilt or innocence is settled during the preliminary investigation, where defense lawyers are not permitted. Trials merely place an official imprimatur on what's already been decided. That's not true in America. During my time in Washington I occasionally sat in on criminal cases, observing defense lawyers cross-examine police and witnesses and argue the law, both unknown here. Judgment was rendered by ordinary citizens, and I was present on a couple of occasions when the accused were actually acquitted. And, believe it or not, findings of innocence cannot be appealed. Imagine that!

That's the good news. In reality, ordinary people are at a serious disadvantage. My American colleagues told me that most defendants can't afford to hire their own lawyers so they make do with overburdened public defenders. Most cases are settled with guilty pleas, often to reduced charges. One can't help but take away the impression that in some cases the accused, particularly the poor, are innocent but plead guilty to avoid being exposed to the possibility of much more severe punishment should they be convicted at trial.

As for the role of the press, it's also mixed. Serious crimes often provoke media frenzies, with commentators leading "string them up" campaigns that would make our General Secretary blush. Still, I've observed more than a few occasions in which the press championed the underdog, and others where reporters took authorities to task at the merest whisper of official wrongdoing. While their system has many faults, it does breed some pugnacious journalists, and if anyone thinks that simply planting a few witnesses will fool them they're sadly mistaken.

Incidentally, Bukhartsev is convinced that Radek's cold-blooded suggestion to arrest the Austrian correspondent for the sake of enhancing the script proves that it was his idea to reel us in. Wish that I could have finished him off back when!

Hamburg (1923)

The worker thrust his rifle forward. Vladimir moved to take the weapon but the man wouldn't let go. Military drill was obviously not the company's strong suit.

"Loosen your grip," Vladimir whispered. The would-be guerrilla fighter hastily released the gun. Vladimir barely caught it before it hit the ground.

Vladimir examined the weapon. It was filthy and in ill-repair.

"When did you last clean your rifle?"

"Never. Today was my first turn to carry it."

Vladimir's forty-odd men were assembled indoors. Unlike Vilna, where nearly every Red Guard had a rifle or shotgun to bring in game, few of Hamburg's Hundreds owned a firearm, and what few rifles there were had mostly rusted away. As he looked out on a sea of pretend weapons fashioned from scraps of wood, Vladimir realized why the police didn't look on the communists as a credible threat.

"Men with real rifles, one step forward!" Vladimir patiently waited for the handful to comply. "From this point forward treat these weapons as your own. Take them home and clean them thoroughly. Your life and the lives of your colleagues may depend on it!"

An armed worker timidly raised his hand.

"Yes, comrade, what is it?"

"My wife doesn't want guns in the house. May I give it to someone else?"

A few days later Vladimir went to Stern's office to submit his weekly report. On his way he glanced at a small display honoring the cell's martyrs, murdered over the years by rightist assassins. He could only imagine how many would fall if Moscow Center's foolish plans went forward. Sending ill-equipped, unprepared comrades to fight a regular army was little different than murder.

"Come in, come in." Moishe Stern left his desk to give Vladimir a warm embrace.

A large, charismatic man with thick eyelashes and a boyish grin, the hero of the Russian Civil War was a soldier's soldier, simple and direct. His office was unadorned except for a large, carefully framed portrait of Lenin.

Stern lapsed into Yiddish. "*Nu?* What do you think of Hamburg's finest? Are they ready for battle?"

Vladimir frowned. "Comrade Stern..."

"Please, drop the formalities! I'm Moishe. Moishe!"

"Very well, Moishe. Here's what I think. I think that a squad of Young Pioneers could defeat the whole lot before lunch."

Stern's eyes narrowed. For a moment the legendary military intelligence commander said nothing. He then erupted in laughter. "Yes, exactly! Well put, Vladimir Georgievich, well put!" Stern took out a fresh bottle of vodka and poured two healthy shots. He raised his glass.

"To a socialist Germany!"

Vladimir's task was to prepare Hamburg's Proletarian Hundreds to seize key police and government facilities. They and their counterparts around Germany would hold their gains until Germany's workers rose to the occasion, like in Essen. Assessments by the German Communist Party, the KPD, predicted that the masses would come over to the Communist side within a few hours. Vladimir was deeply skeptical. Just that week massive strikes and protests over food prices had toppled the central government, yet new officials quickly assumed control. Military units remained in their barracks and not even the bellicose Nazis dared make a move.

Stern sensed his subordinate's doubts. "I've begged Unshlikht for weapons and hopefully some will soon be trickling in. We've barely had time to get organized. Really, no one wants to catch blame for a disaster. Berzin told the Politburo that at this early stage sponsoring a revolt is out of the question, and they agreed. Of course, we must get ready as quickly as possible. He can't say 'no' forever."

"How much notice will we get?"

"One week, minimum. Moscow Center will send a coded message to the military attaché in Berlin. Detailed instructions will be carried to each cell by a motorized courier, who will phone the embassy to confirm that the message was conveyed. Same process if an order is modified or cancelled."

"Sounds clumsy."

"There are security concerns. Germans are tapping phones and monitoring radio transmissions, so face-to-face contact is essential."

Vladimir was unconvinced. "What if a courier is detained? What if they're in an accident or their vehicle breaks down?"

"Look, every operation has its 'what if's'. In all likelihood we'll drill for a couple months, the Politburo will get sane, and we all go home without medals." Stern paused. He knew that his reply was unlikely to satisfy a good officer like Romm. And he had even more troubling news to convey.

"By the way, if the plan is implemented, you and I won't actually participate."

Vladimir was aghast. "We won't fight?"

"Remember that Germany is our ally. There must be complete deniability in case the revolution collapses. We can't afford to get caught."

It seemed insane, but they would have to prepare their men to go it alone. Stern had been admonished to do nothing that could draw attention from the police. Naturally, that made it difficult to properly train the men. Equipping them was even trickier. Smuggling weapons from the Soviet Union to Hamburg was rejected as dangerous and impractical. Small arms would have to be acquired from local entrepreneurs, a risky, inefficient way of doing business that would lead to many close calls.

Vladimir spent the next month doing what he could, giving talks on military tactics and occasionally sneaking a few men into the woods for hurried target practice. One day he brushed past a courier who was hurriedly leaving Stern's office.

"Close the door," Stern ordered.

Vladimir felt his chest tighten. He guessed what would come next.

"We move in ten days."

All the frustrations of the past weeks poured out. "Moishe, we're not ready! We finally have a few rifles but the men haven't learned how to properly use them. They don't know how to work together. They'll be shooting each other! Please," he implored, "let me take them into the woods. If we're challenged we'll say we're hunting."

Stern took a deep breath. "All right, but do only what's absolutely necessary. Unshlikht has absolutely forbidden maneuvers, and if you're caught we'll probably be court-martialed."

Vladimir had been dismissed. But his feet didn't move. He simply had to know where his superior stood. "Comrade Stern, are you in favor of this? What are your feelings?"

Stern looked up. His officer deserved a response. "Comrade Romm, I'm a soldier and do as I'm told. To avoid confusing my men I'm always in favor. But my feelings? Have you ever pulled a trigger and watched a man stagger as your bullet pierced his chest? Or cowered under a fusillade so powerful that it felt as though your head was being ripped clear off your shoulders? And once the terror of battle subsides, have you broken into tears and experienced guilt so profound that you doubted your own humanity? So if you're asking my personal opinion, why that's always no: no to cruelty, no to war, no to all the madness! Why in Heaven would anyone say 'yes'?"

Vladimir led his men into the woods. He broke them into squads and demonstrated how to coordinate movements and advance on the enemy. An abandoned shack proved an ideal place to practice assault and defensive techniques. He set up targets and taught the men how to steady their weapons, take aim and squeeze the trigger so as to place accurate shots. It wasn't until they were done and on their way back when they ran into trouble. It was in the form of a pair of startled game wardens. Shocked to find a band of armed men traipsing around, the keepers of the forest were even less amused that only one had a hunting license, and out of season at that. Suspicious that no one had bagged any creatures, the officials gave everyone a stern talking-to and let them go. Vladimir suspected that this wouldn't be the end of it.

He was right. Police were informed of the encounter and quickly identified several of the involved as Socialist rabble-rousers. An official protest from the German Chancellery soon followed.

"The Politburo is furious," Stern said. "Berzin had to cancel the attack. Unshlikht went crazy. He only cooled off when I threatened to resign."

Vladimir didn't feel the least bit chastened. "What do they expect us to do? Our men are supposed to take over government buildings, seize police stations, kidnap officials, even kill if necessary. If they're not properly prepared…"

"I know, I know, it's the same as shooting them ourselves," Stern agreed. "Comrade Romm, I can't pretend to understand where the Politburo is going with this. It's as though they've said 'yes' but with their fingers crossed behind their backs. All I'm sure of is that without you, and perhaps me, the men would be far worse off. Let's try not to be dismissed before whatever happens, happens."

Several more go-orders were issued that summer. Each was promptly rescinded for one reason or another. In time Vladimir and Stern assumed that the scheme had been abandoned. Perhaps the Politburo was finally coming to its senses! The men grew lazy and some began skipping drills. Vladimir exercised, wrote to Galina and impatiently awaited his recall to Moscow Center, where there might be something useful to do.

During the second week of October 1923 another go-order arrived, with execution set, as usual, in ten days. Stern and Vladimir cajoled the men to get ready. Objectives were scouted and plans refreshed. Surveillance was established on the handful of local officials whose neutralization in case of war was deemed essential.

To insure that Stern and Vladimir were nowhere near the combat zone the go-order directed them to be at the Soviet embassy in Berlin no later than twelve hours before the uprising's scheduled start time. In so doing Unshlikht made certain that the only communists with any military experience wouldn't be present when the epic struggle got underway.

Stern and Vladimir assumed that the attack would be called off in plenty of time, just like all the others. This time, though, no courier showed up. With only a day to go, they hurriedly met with their squad leaders, helped them finalize their plans and wished them all the best.

That the rebellion would go forward seemed inconceivable, yet there they were, speeding along in Stern's supercharged sedan with three-hundred kilometers to cover and only a few hours left on the clock. They kept a sharp watch for the courier's vehicle. Surely the man would drive past at any moment with the message canceling this idiocy. What could be holding him up?

They pulled into the embassy garage shortly before daybreak. An orderly was scrubbing the floors. Things seemed quiet, with no signs of the activity one would expect if a coup was underway.

Stern barked at a sleepy soldier manning the reception desk. "Where is the ambassador?"

The man ignored him. "Good to have you back, Comrade Romm. Who's the rude character with you?"

Vladimir suppressed a laugh. "Is the boss in?"

"He and his staff left for Moscow last night. Why, is something wrong?"

Vladimir and Stern rushed for the stairs. They exited on the top floor and ran down the hallway, nearly colliding with a cleaning woman sweeping crumbs from a birthday celebration.

"Bureaucrats in a hurry? What will they think of next?" she muttered.

A lone military cadet manned the communications room. He jumped to his feet.

"We're from Hamburg," Stern announced. "Where is your superior?"

"Uh...at breakfast?"

It seemed like a peculiar way to manage a revolution, Vladimir thought. He glanced at a message still in the teletype. It was a routine summary of news articles from that day's newspapers.

"Was the order for 'Operation Freedom' recalled?"

"Of course, comrade, just like always." The cadet checked a clock. "About this time yesterday." He seemed as perplexed as his visitors.

Stern became enraged. "*Yesterday*? Was every command notified?"

"Of course," the cadet replied. "It's not the first time this has happened, you know."

Vladimir grabbed the burn bag and dumped its contents on the floor. He and Stern pored through all the inbound messages but couldn't find the one they sought.

"Did Hamburg confirm the order to stand down?" Vladimir asked.

The cadet paled. He was starting to put it together. "No, comrade. The officer I relieved said it was the only one outstanding. We assumed that..."

An alarm rang. The youth shut it off. "That's the signal for 'Freedom'. I guess they forgot to reset it."

Lubyanka prison,
3 January 1937

Radek came by to get me ready for my own run-through. After all that's happened being with the man should feel awkward, but at this point there's little reason not to work together. One man standing alone has no chance of influencing this travesty. Vyshinsky will get what he needs one way or another, if not from my lips then from another's, and the only thing being recalcitrant would accomplish is to place my loved ones at risk.

As I write Leon's rat eyes gaze unblinkingly into mine. It's comforting to have another warm-blooded creature around. Guards promised that as soon as they haul in a veterinarian they'll send him over to give my companion a checkup.

It's been getting noisier. There has apparently been a new round of arrests, and Dmitry and I have overheard the guards talking about another trial. Stalin's purges are depriving the Soviet Union of some of its finest comrades. Once he and his vicious prosecutor are through no one may be left to take on the fascists.

Today during exercise Dmitry and I talked about my former superior, Ambassador Troyanovsky, a man whom I still regard highly. Like us, Troyanovsky is Jewish. He is reportedly close to Stalin, who for a time lived with the Troyanovskys while in Switzerland. That's when the General Secretary, whom few would credit as an intellectual giant, wrote his famous thesis about the coexistence of Russian and non-Russian ethnic groups, an article whose authorship many credit to his far more erudite host. Indeed, while I was in America Troyanovsky traveled around the U.S. giving speeches that gushed about the USSR's designation of homelands for Jews, Kazakhs, Volga-Germans and other minorities. He was particularly effusive about Stalin's grand creation, the Jewish Autonomous Region, a tiny, forbidding space wedged next to China that some regard as a Pale of Settlement with a pretty bow. Troyanovsky explained that the Region was a way to atone for what the Jewish people endured under the Czar, and that it gave the pious a place where they could follow their traditions unmolested. It goes without saying that the ambassador never had the honor of living in the Region, and the last I knew his son was attending an exclusive school in Washington favored by the wealthy.

Dmitry and I were raised in the Pale of Settlement. We know from personal experience that living apart can reinforce the idea that one is fundamentally different, both to oneself and others. We didn't embrace socialism to get a special place in the sun but because its precepts explicitly reject ethnic and racial stereotyping. We became revolutionaries to fight injustice, not promote it! True, so far no one is being forced to live in the USSR's ethnic regions. Even so, with the very concept of tolerance under siege, the possibility that they might become ghettoes doesn't seem so far-fetched.

Why would supposedly enlightened, well-meaning persons like Troyanovsky champion separateness? Dmitry spoke of some Jews he met in Germany, who even after being stripped of citizenship seemed convinced that given time the Nazis would mend their ways and come around to reason. Self-deception is truly our Achilles' heel.

City of Light (1924)

Vladimir was welcomed back to Moscow Center as though nothing unusual had happened. What he wasn't offered, and knew better than to seek, was an explanation. Why had Unshlikht, until recently a secret policeman beholden to Stalin, been placed in charge of a military operation whose success would have advanced Trotsky's agenda? While few knowledgeable insiders believed that the plan had much of a chance, the manner in which it was executed virtually guaranteed failure. Perhaps the answer lay in examining who might have benefitted from the calamity.

Hamburg revolted alone. The official explanation was that the courier arrived late. Confident that they were participating in a general uprising, the Proletarian Hundreds and the few workers who ultimately rose in their support seized a few police stations, holding out for three days before they were overrun by German troops. Dozens of Socialists were killed, and within a few hours those unlucky enough to survive had told their captors everything there was to know. Yet to Moscow's surprise – and relief – Germany chose mostly to look the other way. Vladimir, Stern and a handful of other Soviets were expelled. And that was about it. Authorities officially attributed the stillborn revolt to the work of a few incorrigibles, citing its outcome as clear evidence that the German people supported their government and despised socialism. As an isolated island in a sea of hostility, Germany thought it best to avoid divorcing the only ally it had.

Trotsky was once thought to be Lenin's favorite. But his fecklessness and thirst for conflict raised concerns about his suitability among the upper reaches of the party bureaucracy. Hamburg made an indelible stain. As Lenin's health worsened a council of three caretakers was appointed to oversee things. One of its members was Stalin. When Lenin died on January 21, 1924 the General Secretary became the Soviet Union's dominant force.

Trotsky wasn't the type to fold his tent. Diminished in stature but by no means contrite, he turned his back on the party hierarchy to form a boisterous opposition. Stalin had his own problems, not the least being rumors of a letter that Lenin supposedly wrote on his deathbed severely chastising Stalin for being rude to Krupskaya, Lenin's wife.

Vladimir and his colleagues were firmly on Trotsky's side. To be sure, the radical's ambitious (some might say, megalomaniac) plans for world domination made him a natural target for ridicule. But many committed Socialists, especially among the youth, found his enthusiasm infectious. Despite a pretentious *nom de guerre*, Stalin spent the Revolution and Civil War in safe, noncombat roles, damaging his reputation with military men who admired Trotsky and considered the prospects of having a coward at Russia's helm unimaginable.

Vladimir was awarded two weeks' leave. With Galina in rehearsals he spent most of his time running around with his hyperactive mother-in-law. Ludvika had been something of a tomboy in her youth, and sure enough one morning the woman grabbed her late husband's ancient rifle and dragged Vladimir to the countryside, where by reason of her failing eyesight she anointed him the triggerman in a rabbit hunt. During their trek they managed to bag two of the poor creatures, which she dressed right on the spot, wielding a razor-sharp knife with impressive flair. Her simple, straightforward approach to life reminded him of Anna.

Alexander and Elena hosted a party to fete Vladimir's return. Evsey and his bride Esfir came in for the occasion from Leningrad. Under Ludvika's expert hand a Polish hunter's stew of rabbit, cabbage and sauerkraut took form, its pungent aroma lending the large and by Moscow standards luxurious apartment the ambiance of a peasant's hut.

They were finishing off the last traces of the savory dish when Alexander began reminiscing about the brothers' life in Saint Petersburg. "It was marvelous. The parks, museums, everything so safe and orderly. We were terribly disappointed to leave for Vilna. Sallo, do you remember that huge chandelier?"

"Sure," Evsey replied. "Father always felt guilty about how much Grandpapa's wedding gift must have cost. But what I remember best were the parties, mother playing the piano, the men standing around in their tails, smoking cigars, the ladies so beautiful in their jewels and petticoats."

"I don't remember any of that!" Vladimir teased.

Alexander chuckled. "You weren't born yet. Sallo, what's all this about petticoats?"

"Ah, I was just a kid!"

Esfir patronizingly patted his head. "He still is." She raised her glass. "To Saint Petersburg!"

Galina didn't join in. "It's been 'Leningrad' for more than a month," she frowned.

"In our hearts, Galya, it's still Saint Petersburg," Evsey said. "Not that ridiculous 'Petrograd,' nor the fawning 'Leningrad,' but a name worthy of the most beautiful city in Europe – no, in the world! The universe! Let your comrades shoot me for calling it that, I don't care!"

Alexander offered a peacekeeping toast. "To a Chekist with steady aim, lest my crazy brother Evsey Georgievich suffer!"

Galina was miffed. If only citizens didn't take the Revolution so lightly! Evsey and Esfir were hopeless. As for Alexander and Elena; well, they always said the right things, but their tastes for nice things and foreign-made conveniences made her wonder about their commitment to socialism.

They gathered in the drawing room. Elena, a fine pianist, limbered up with "Flight of the Bumblebee." After much begging Galina took off her shoes and in stocking feet danced a scene from "Sleeping Beauty," a bourgeois piece that wasn't one of her favorites, but which her husband and his brothers had loved as children.

Vladimir proudly watched his spirited wife glide around the room. For a moment he forgot her distracting and at times irritating preoccupation with the new communist etiquette. His wife and her comrades in the Bolshoi's political committee had enthusiastically taken up Stalin's call for reform in the arts, and were demanding, among other things, that the ballet supplant its classical repertoire with works that conveyed the reality of class struggle. Then what? Would picks and shovels become ballerinas' everyday props? He knew that Galina's attitude was shared by many educated women, who were delighted with the official policy of full gender equality. Naturally, they weren't the ones who would labor in factories all day, then go home to do the cooking and housework that Soviet men still scoffed at.

Alexander brought out a gleaming samovar. They sat for sweets and tea.

"Well, Volya, when can we expect a revolution?"

"Things aren't so simple." Alexander wasn't the only who one had bought into the propaganda mill's assurances that despite the recent setback, Germany was only a short step from communism. "Nazis are if anything more popular now that Hitler's in jail. There's little support for an insurgency, and none for one from the left."

"That's all the more reason to step in! If not now, when?"

Alexander had received a student deferment. Vladimir was at the end of his patience. "Sasha, do you have any idea what fighting looks like? Let me quote from an expert. His name is Moishe."

Vladimir had shared little with Galina about his experiences in Germany, and his heart-felt recitation had a profound effect on his wife. When they went to bed that night she curled up close. For the next hour the mentally and physically drained officer of military intelligence poured out his soul. He mentioned his narrow escape from the massacre in Essen, his arrest by the French, who seemed as perplexed by their mission as he was of his, and of Hamburg's Proletarian warriors, those brave young men who were set up to be butchered in a tragedy for which he was partly to blame.

The next morning Galina made Vladimir a hot breakfast, and when he left she warmly kissed him good-bye. Ludvika found the display of affection heartening. Her daughter had been spending far too much time at political meetings. Only the other day she had for no apparent reason prattled on about a provision in the USSR's marvelous new Civil Code that allowed women to sue for divorce without their spouse's consent. Not that a breakup seemed imminent, but still...

Vladimir's first day back at work began with a pleasant surprise.

"Welcome, comrade!" Instead of summoning his favorite officer, Berzin greeted him at his desk. They shook hands.

Berzin noticed the open envelope. It contained a message from the German Foreign Ministry, indefinitely barring Romm from the Reich. "You've read it?"

"Yes, Comrade Colonel."

"A note like that would normally earn its recipient an extended desk tour," Berzin bantered, "but I figure that's something you'd welcome. So I decided not to reward you."

Vladimir kept the tone light. "I apologize for being caught, Comrade General. Please tell me how I can make up for it."

"You'll regret those words. Come to my office."

Berzin spread a set of grainy surveillance photographs on his desk. "These were recently taken by our officers in France."

Vladimir examined the images. He pointed to a roguish-looking figure. "Savinkov the assassin. He once led the Socialist Revolutionary Combat Brigade. I understand that he's become a hopeless alcoholic."

"That hasn't disqualified anyone from sitting on the Politburo, has it? Do you know any of the others?"

"That one's Grand Duke Kyril. I thought he was in Munich."

"He and his wife recently moved to France. They bought a cottage in Brittany. The fool dreams of a glorious comeback. He's declared himself Emperor and is shopping around for someone to lead an invasion force."

"Good luck to him. Exiles despise the pretentious bastard. Word's out that he waited for his first cousin to divorce, then quickly married her."

"Really? Well, if they want to breed a passel of indolent hemophiliacs, why stand in the way?"

"Kyril's mother, the Grand Duchess, is German, Comrade General," Vladimir corrected. "Tsarevich Alexis' bleeding disorder was passed on through the English side of the family."

Berzin laughed. "I guess I should have paid better attention at general's school, eh?" He pointed to another exiled Royal. "There's that other rich brat, Grand Duke Nikolai Nikolaevich. He's been seen with some of the White officers I fought during the Civil War."

Berzin put the photos away. "So, Volya, what do you think?"

Vladimir knew that most officers would kill for an opportunity to work in France. But another prolonged absence would not sit well at home. Or maybe it would, and he'd rather not find out.

"Please do yourself a favor and never play cards," Berzin quipped. "This tour is accompanied, meaning you can bring the wife and your boy. You can also drag your mother-in-law along, but her upkeep comes out of your salary."

"That's very generous, Comrade General."

"Don't thank me too soon," Berzin cautioned. "There's a tricky aspect. You're aware, I'm sure, of the special relationship between the General Secretary and the secret police. Dzerzhinsky prevailed on Stalin to give the GPU exclusive jurisdiction over exiles, meaning that military intelligence is technically out of the picture. They're supposed to keep us informed if they spot a military threat. Hah! As if they would! Anyway, I refuse to be treated like a mushroom."

Bureaucratic squabbles truly were the bane of communism. Vladimir rose to attention. "I am at your service, Comrade General."

Berzin walked him to the door. "I understand that your father is in Paris."

"Yes. He and his second wife moved there from Switzerland. She passed away last year and we've encouraged him to come back. My brother Evsey and his wife have offered to let him stay with them in Leningrad. But Papa's been putting us off. He enjoys his freedom."

A few weeks later Vladimir and his father were strolling down the Boulevard du Montparnasse. They were accompanied by Galina, Ludvika and Karla. George Romm's latest female companion, the sprightly Russian émigré was nearly three decades his junior.

George Romm paused at a café. He addressed the ladies. "My son and I have some things to talk over. We'll see you at the hotel."

He led Vladimir to a specific table. A waiter promptly deposited two *café au laits* and a chessboard.

"You know," George Romm said, "we're sitting at the exact spot where Trotsky used to hold court." He gestured at a nearby table. "There's where Lenin sat. He was an excellent player. When there were no suitable challengers he'd take out a chess book and study moves for hours."

"Did you ever play him?"

"Only once. He was much too intense for my tastes. It really bothered him to lose."

Vladimir was entranced by the atmosphere. It was a typical Parisian coffee house scene, a mix of businessmen, shopkeepers and government officials sipping drinks and stretching *l'heure du déjeuner* well into the afternoon as though they had not a worry in the world. Indolence seemed perfectly reasonable. Electricity was on when the gods willed, transport schedules were useful mostly for wrapping baguettes, and public places and sanitary facilities were so poorly maintained as to make visiting Russians feel nearly at home. Happily, food was abundant, but getting it involved some odd rules. *Boucheries* sold nothing but beef and lamb, chicken was available only at dairy stores, and fruits and vegetables could only be obtained during certain hours and never on weekends. Soon, though, the inconveniences began making perfect sense. Floating down the Seine, past Notre Dame and the majestic buildings rising from the *Île de la Cité*, Vladimir and Galina succumbed to the city's seductive pace, and in the process rediscovered each other. Whether this way of life would stand the test of time – and of the ambitions of Germany's future Führer – was the question.

George Romm slid a knight forward. "I'm curious what you, of all people, would be doing in a trade delegation. You never struck me as someone who was interested in buying and selling things."

As Vladimir struggled to form a comfortable lie a slender, blue-eyed dowager swooped down on their table. "Doctor Romm, how de-light-ful to see you!"

Vladimir's father and the woman traded air kisses. "Duchess, my youngest son, Vladimir Georgievich. Son, may I present the Grand Duchess Victoria Feodorovna."

Vladimir brushed his lips across the finely manicured hand. Kyril's wife – "Ducky" to her friends – was a fine-looking woman indeed.

"*Enchanté*," she giggled. "Are you visiting from Russia?"

"Yes, with my wife and mother-in-law."

Ducky smiled wanly. George Romm changed the subject.

"Duchess, are you picking up things for the estate?"

"Actually, I'm looking for my Emperor *sans Empire*. Have you seen him?"

"Is Kyril Vladimirovich missing?"

Ducky sneered. "Missing? I wouldn't think so. How could one get lost in a hotel?"

The duchess excused herself to return to her friends. George Romm quietly explained.

"It's a poorly kept secret that Kyril keeps a mistress at the Continental. Ducky gives the scoundrel an allowance to play with, but not so much that it threatens what's left of their fortune."

Vladimir peeked at Imperial Russia's flesh-and-blood monument to self-indulgence. She returned a coy smile.

"Don't even think about it," his father admonished. "None of these people are worth a gob of spit."

"About that we're of the same mind," Vladimir agreed.

George Romm drew out his son's king. It was soon cornered. "Checkmate! Done just like your communists: by sacrificing the pawns."

Vladimir reset the pieces. "The war's over, father. Things will settle down as soon as Lenin's succession gets worked out."

"Whose side are you taking?"

"Me? I have no influence. But if you're asking for a prediction, my money's on Trotsky."

George Romm glanced at his boy. Well, Vladimir was no longer that. But what had he turned into, exactly? "Just remember to use your head, Volya. Stalin may have the intellect of a gnat, but his memory is like an elephant's."

Lubyanka prison, 6 January 1937

My turn finally came. Best I can remember, this is how the dress rehearsal went:

"What is your name?"

"Vladimir Georgievich Romm."

"What was your last official position?"

"*Izvestia* correspondent to Washington."

"You are a witness in the case against Radek, Piatakov and others. Providing false testimony will subject you to criminal prosecution."

We all should have burst out laughing, but Molchanov's nonsensical admonition didn't draw even the faintest smile. We've become so inured to lies that the only way to get a reaction would be for someone to accidentally lapse into truth.

"What was your connection with Radek?"

For once I pointed to the man with genuine relish. "He recruited me to be a Trotskyite!"

I was of course referring to the occasion in 1926 when Radek prevailed on me to sign a petition supporting Trotsky. It was an idiotic move that will probably haunt me to eternity.

"What did Comrade Radek ask you to do? And what *did* you do?" Vyshinsky, Molchanov, Radek, the whole rotten gang was on the edge of their seats. Would this Romm fellow go through with it, or not?

Well, he did.

"Not much happened until 1930," I said, the rubbish literally pouring from my lips. "Radek approached me when I was *Tass* correspondent in Geneva. He said that the struggle against Stalin had resumed and that we Trotskyites had to stick together. I agreed to serve as a courier between Radek and Trotsky. One year later, when passing through Berlin, I met with Trotsky's son, Sedov. I later received a letter from him in Paris; it contained a message for..."

Vyshinsky cleared his throat. He gestured at Molchanov and Radek to follow him into the hallway. They returned shortly.

Radek approached me. "Don't be so eager," he whispered. "It sounds rehearsed. Make the prosecutor do his job."

He was of course correct. I was rushing through the lies to make them less painful to utter. That wouldn't do. Each mouthful had to be savored like a fine meal.

Molchanov continued. "This letter to Radek that you spoke of..."

"Excuse me," I corrected, "but I never said to whom it was addressed." If they wanted obstinacy, I was happy to oblige.

"Excuse *me*, witness Romm, for anticipating the obvious. For the sake of the record, could you please confirm the identity of the intended recipient?"

"As you said, Radek. It was from Trotsky."

Molchanov glared. "Are you aware of the instructions it contained?"

"Only from what Radek told me. He said that Trotsky was urging him to use terroristic means against the Party Central Committee, particularly Comrade Stalin, and against the Commissar of Defense."

"Terroristic? What does that mean?"

"To kill them, I suppose. He was also directed to combine his efforts with those of Zinoviev's group. Become part of them, if you will."

I was referring to the fictitious terrorist cabal that was supposedly led by Lev Kamenev and Grigori Zinoviev, Stalin's partners in the *troika* that took charge when Lenin was disabled. Of course, linking anyone to them was like passing a death sentence, and that's exactly what I told Radek – that he was effectively committing suicide. But he seemed oddly nonplussed.

Molchanov pretended to address the court reporter. "Please let the record indicate that witness Romm is referring to the two traitors who were tried, convicted and executed in August 1936." He returned to me. "What happened next?"

"In 1932 I met Radek in Moscow. He told me that he and Piatakov wanted to form a separate group, to provide a fallback option in case the main group was discovered." I remember nearly choking on these words. Not simply because they were untrue – I mean, it was all a lie – but because of the depth of the fabrication.

"Did Trotsky agree with this new approach?"

"Radek composed a letter to Trotsky asking for approval. He hid it inside a book, which he gave to me. I mailed the book and note to Trotsky's son, Sedov when I returned to Europe."

"Then what happened?"

"At the end of July 1933 Sedov telephoned me in Paris and we arranged to meet at a café. He confirmed that he received everything. He then took me to meet his father."

Molchanov paused for emphasis. "You met with Trotsky?"

My voice faltered. Uttering bold-faced lies still doesn't come easily, which I suppose is a good thing.

"Yes," I said weakly. "Trotsky agreed to the backup group. He said that it must not merely stand by but that it should actively support the work of the main group through terrorism and sabotage."

Molchanov feigned shock. "Didn't he realize that this would undermine the Soviet Union's defensive capabilities at a time when our country faces great peril from the fascists?"

And so on and so forth. Vyshinsky was anxious to allay skeptics and establish the plot's wickedness from the start. It fell on me as one of the lead-off witnesses to provide context for the lies that followed. But there was one thing that I absolutely refused to do. Radek's original script had me testify that I actively supported the counterrevolution while posted in Washington by supplying secret materials from the embassy, thus sullying a period of service of which I am proud. I objected so vigorously that they relented: I would testify that I agreed to stay in touch with the traitors, but that I never followed through.

Radek then took the stand. He confirmed my account, making only a small correction regarding the contents of one of the letters that passed between him and Trotsky. It was just another of the many staged disagreements that were sprinkled throughout the script to further the illusion that those testifying were speaking the truth.

Well, enough. Stalin's determined to stage this monstrosity, and it's up to criminals like Vyshinsky, Molchanov and Radek and fools like Bukhartsev and me to make it convincing.

How could that noble experiment called communism have sunk to this?

Savinkov (1924)

Other than for his chance encounter with Grand Duke Kyril's flirtatious spouse Vladimir's first weeks passed uneventfully. Certain that the *Sûreté* was keeping track, he tried to behave like a real commercial attaché, spending mornings at the trade mission reading newspapers, doing minor chores and occasionally calling on legitimate clients on matters that required little commercial expertise. For lunch he took the Métro to meet Galina and Ludvika, who were volunteering at Communist Party offices. Afterwards he usually joined his father at one of the coffee houses favored by expatriates, where they'd while away the afternoons playing chess, chatting with acquaintances and watching former members of the Russian nobility come and go.

Intelligence work calls for a lot of patience. In a milieu flush with spies and informers fresh faces drew suspicion. As the run-in with Ducky demonstrated, knowing an insider was crucial for being accepted in émigré circles. Vladimir hadn't intended to exploit his father as an entrée, but his usefulness couldn't be denied. To salve his conscience he tried not to press for any more information than was absolutely necessary.

George Romm slid a knight into place. "Checkmate!"

Vladimir had yet to win a game. He signaled the waiter for more coffee.

His father checked his watch. "Don't bother. I've got to go to the hospital."

"Is your lady friend sick?"

"Sure, of me. Actually, I'm working at a children's clinic."

Vladimir froze. The Soviet Union's number-one fugitive was headed for their table. "Doctor, good to see you!"

Boris Savinkov and George Romm exchanged a hearty embrace. Vladimir noticed that the depraved assassin was even more rumpled and boozy-looking than in the photograph.

His father made the introduction. "Boris Victorovich, meet my youngest, Vladimir Georgievich. He's a Soviet trade delegate."

Savinkov's handlebar mustache quivered with pleasure. Having emptied the pockets and exhausted the patience of every Russian expatriate in Paris, the former leader of the Socialist Revolutionary Combat Brigade was thrilled to find a new someone to buy drinks and listen to his tales of murder and intrigue, many actually true. A bitter enemy of the Bolsheviks, Savinkov had conspired on numerous half-baked invasion schemes, none yet carried out for lack of funds and willing martyrs. Knowing that he was at grave risk of being snatched, he nonetheless remained supremely confident in his ability to distinguish between friend and foe.

George Romm stepped into a balmy Parisian afternoon. He glanced back to the coffee house where Vladimir and the adventurer were engrossed in conversation. The retired physician took a deep breath, hoping to clear his mind. Marxism once seemed like such a wonderful notion, but it turned out to be just another way for men to impose their will. He didn't worry about Alexander, who seemed to be an expert at navigating the rapids. As for the other boys, he wasn't so sure. Evsey was a hopeless anarchist, but he kept mostly to himself. Vladimir, though, liked to be in the thick of things. He was also a chronic truth-teller, and in the relentlessly dogmatic climate of the Soviet Union, truth could bring a lot of grief. All he could do was to warn Vladimir about not depending so much on his high-ranking friends, even those who were Jewish, or whatever it was they now considered themselves. Of this he was absolutely sure: that when push came to shove not one of them would come to his son's defense.

Nearby, a vigorous-looking young man with Slavic features greedily drew the smoke of a pungent *Galouise* deep into his lungs. France had its advantages, he thought, not the least being its cigarettes. He waited until George Romm left in a taxi before approaching the café. Through the windows he watched Savinkov wildly gesticulating to his companion. Maybe he was reminiscing about the bomb-laden lunatics he once dispatched to blow up the Czar. Or maybe he was bragging about his accomplishments during the Civil War, when he urged on Polish irregulars to their doom in a hopeless campaign against Trotsky's Reds. For a moment he considered walking right up to the pair. But there had to be a better way to deal with this unexpected gift. Savinkov was a major target of the secret police, and here he was consorting with the Romms! No, it had to be handled with care.

Days later, Vladimir was taking an after-lunch stroll when he sensed that he had a shadow. Not only that, but his watcher was making only the most perfunctory attempts to keep out of sight. He bought a newspaper and took a seat at a café.

Lev arrived at his table ahead of the waiter. "Greetings, comrade!"

The friends exchanged a hearty embrace. "I thought that you looked familiar!"

"You're very observant, Volya. Our little adventure in Essen aged me a decade."

They ordered coffee. Lev waited for the server to leave. "So, what did you think of Ducky?"

Vladimir flinched. He hadn't noticed a tail on that day. "Far too much makeup for my taste. She could also do with more of a chin."

Lev laughed heartily. "You haven't changed a bit. You find fault in one of the most handsome women in Paris!"

Vladimir sipped his *café au lait*. It wasn't particularly surprising that the secret police would be interested in his doings. Still, Lev's behavior seemed unusually bold.

"Why are you following me, Lev Alexandrovich? Did Otto flip you? Are you now with the *Sûreté*?"

Lev laughed. "Otto and I did become friends. I fed him the Colonel's sausage, and he filled me in on France's plans. Like we figured, they never intended to stay. It was all a gambit to get the Germans to pay up. When Otto came home my superiors had me tag along. Say, maybe we could have a reunion!"

"No, thanks. You know, no one wins turf wars except for the enemy. Whites have been cooking up invasion schemes for years. Last I heard that's well within our jurisdiction."

Lev nodded agreeably. "For sure, for sure! My boss would kill me for saying this, but I personally couldn't care less who gets the credit. Say, we could partner up! This time the tables are turned: I'm the one with unlimited resources."

"Great! What's the plan?"

"Grabbing Savinkov would be a real coup."

Vladimir groaned. He hadn't spotted anyone on that occasion either. "I can't deny that he's a worthwhile target. But his brain's pickled in vodka. Not that he wouldn't like to, but the man's in no shape to lead a passel of Pioneers, let alone a military expedition. He's already run through my budget. If you've got the *francs* to waste I'll be happy to introduce you."

"My friend, you have a deal."

On a warm evening several weeks later Vladimir escorted Galina and Ludvika to the opening performance of *Le Train Bleu*. Staged in the baroque, gilded splendor of the magnificent *Théâtre des Champs-Elysées*, the production featured one of his wife's favorite dancers, the great Bronislava Nijinska.

Le Train was a celebration of showmanship from beginning to end. At the overture an enormous backdrop depicting two naked, bosomy nymphs cavorting on a beach was lowered to the stage. Crafted in Picasso's studios, the astonishing canvas, far more graphic than what would be permitted in the USSR, led Vladimir's wife to turn away. But as the performance unfolded and its underlying message became clear – a biting satire of the Parisian upper crust, the ballet's theme is not far removed from the concerns of socialism – Galina relaxed, and when the first act ended she and her mother heartily joined in the applause.

At intermission Vladimir strolled through the lobby, admiring the beautifully rendered posters depicting the company's principals in their celebrated roles. Diaghilev's Ballets Russes would never stage a production in the Soviet Union, the land from which it drew its dancers and artistic inspiration. Renowned for its commitment to creativity and self-expression, the company refused to perform in a place where every activity had to have an acceptable political interpretation.

Lev awaited Vladimir at the bar.

"It went down like clockwork. Dzerzhinsky sends his regards," he whispered before slipping away.

Vladimir felt lightheaded. The next thing he knew Ludvika had hold of his arm.

"Son-in-law, are you all right?"

Vladimir realized that he had spilled his drink. "Yes, of course!"

She shook her head reprovingly. "Your wife isn't feeling well and here you are drinking!"

"Did she eat something...?"

"No, Volya. It's not something you get from eating..."

It took a moment for Vladimir's overloaded mind to process the information. He bolted for the lobby. Galina was sitting on a bench, looking pale as a ghost.

"Wait here!" He ran to summon a taxi, and then gently led his wife to the cab. "Drive slow!" he barked.

George Romm was pacing outside the apartment building lobby when they arrived. His sour look telegraphed why he was there.

Galina was in bed when the men walked outside. George Romm could hardly contain his anger.

"How could you betray me like this? I introduced you to the man in front of everyone! Where do you think that leaves me? You and your friends might not think much of the Russian exiles, but they're the only community I have!"

Vladimir took a deep breath. He felt like a worn-out pugilist about to go the final round. "Are you being accused of setting him up?"

"What else could they think? Savinkov was living with a young woman. I went to see her. She said that two men – her description of one perfectly fits you – had been coming by, filling Boris full of tall tales about a new Russian revolution. Then one day he's gone. Poof! My God, Volya: who other than the secret police would offer a stinking drunk command of some ridiculous 'Army of the Peoples of Russia'? Anyone in their right mind would know that's a one-way ticket to the Lubyanka!"

"But I didn't mean for you..."

"Stop it! You're my son, for God's sake! You were seen introducing Savinkov to a stranger. Next thing anyone knows he's in Moscow, charged with treason. Your hands stink of this mess. Mine, too!"

An urgent cable from Moscow Center awaited at the trade offices. Vladimir could guess at the message. His tour was over. And very possibly, his career.

Savinkov's capture brought great acclaim to the secret police, and especially Dzerzhinsky. That of course infuriated Berzin. But as much as Vladimir dreaded explaining what happened to his boss, as the moment approached he felt oddly at peace. Roping in Boris was just plain fun. He hadn't felt so alive since Vilna. He regretted involving his father so deeply, but George Romm was better off without those Russian expatriate leeches.

As he expected, Berzin was highly displeased. "I've been told to make you available for the pre-trial investigation. Do you know why?" His superior disliked being told what to do, and the thought that one of his officers would be assisting the GPU stuck in his craw.

Vladimir tried to play down his involvement. "They had Savinkov under watch and know that we met. They probably want an account of what he said."

"They've asked for your reports, and I told them to go straight to hell. Not that there's anything in them that Dzerzhinsky hasn't already told reporters."

Berzin obviously suspected his loyalty, and Vladimir wasn't sure that he cared. Unlike the secret police, whose exploits were glorified in cheap novels and the press, military intelligence lumbered along, its activities so hush-hush that officers joked regulations prohibited them from knowing what they were doing. That old saw, that the benefits of their work would be apparent in due time was looking more and more like an excuse for accomplishing nothing. Neither the unhappy episode with Comrade Severny, nor the abortive mission in Tambov, nor the fiasco in Germany had given Vladimir a smidgen of the satisfaction that he felt from trapping the bloodthirsty braggart.

Lev was basking in glory: why shouldn't he?

As it happened, there was no need to call any witnesses. Savinkov was nothing if not a survivor. In keeping with the socialist tradition of self-criticism he eagerly confessed, recanting his sins with such eloquence that prosecutors invited several favored correspondents to sit in on the secret trial's last day to hear his final plea.

Radek, still licking his wounds from Essen, came in his capacity as Communist journalist-of-record. By his side was the *New York Times'* Walter Duranty. A handsome man, not quite middle-aged but already nearly bald, his worldly bearing and personal charm impressed colleagues and enthralled the ladies. Duranty owned an apartment in Moscow where he kept a matronly American wife and, rumors had it, a young local woman who served as their cook and, reportedly, his lover. He got away with it because he was a great fan of Stalin, and made sure that the General Secretary knew it. One of the Soviet Union's earliest and most passionate boosters, Duranty's zest for socialism suffused his writings and earned him incomparable access to the Great Leader. He was eight years from earning a Pulitzer.

Bailiffs hustled Savinkov to the podium. Jailers had trimmed his mustache to a nub, and his eyes lacked the feral luster that Vladimir remembered. But being away from drink for a few months had done him a world of good. His voice was strong and his words flowed smoothly.

"When Lenin ruled out a Western-style democracy my hopes were shattered. When he made peace with Germany I was infuriated..."

Savinkov paused. It was as though he spent his entire life preparing for this moment. An accomplished orator, he had the courtroom enthralled, and knew it.

"...Blinded by drink and, yes, personal ambition, I refused to accept what should have been clear from the start, that the Bolsheviks – and only the Bolsheviks – understood the needs of the people of Russia. Thanks to the brave agents of your

GPU I gave up my dissolute life and saw, as though for the very first time, the joyful faces of the workers and peasants as they labored together in this glorious socialist state..."

Radek nudged Duranty. "I'd shoot the rascal now," he whispered, "before he fools the court. Did you know that the sycophant recently wrote to Dzerzhinsky, offering to work as his assistant?"

Duranty was intrigued. "Can you get me a transcript of the letter? My editor would go crazy over it!"

Boris droned on. "...I know that it's over for me, yet even in the breast of the most treacherous soul there is always a kernel of worth, and if you can find it in your hearts to forgive the sins of an old, worn out counterrevolutionary..."

So it went for an hour. Then the judges recessed. They came back with the foreordained decision within minutes: guilty on all counts, sentenced to be shot. A thin smile graced the condemned man's face. It was as though he, too, was pleased that justice had been done.

Lev and Vladimir watched as Savinkov emerged with his guards. Russia's most famous terrorist was led to a van, smiling at the well-wishers and curious who lined the way.

Lev blew him a kiss. Savinkov replied with a rude gesture.

"My brothers kept a scrapbook on revolutionaries," Vladimir said. "I can't remember ever seeing his picture."

"You only get your photo in the papers when you're caught. It wasn't like Savinkov to personally shoot anyone or throw a bomb. But he was more than happy to get others to do it. Hey, look at that!" Radek and Duranty were about to board a tram. They were in deep conversation. "Trotsky's boy and Stalin's stooge. An odd pair, don't you think?"

"No stranger than me and Berzin."

Lev treaded carefully. He felt guilty about landing his friend in a jam. "Since you've brought it up, how are things at Moscow Center?"

"Oh, I can get lots of stuff done now," Vladimir snickered. "No one bothers me."

Lev didn't smile. "Well, comrade, your future's not a joke. My people are ecstatic about Savinkov. I've been asked to tell you that the offer is still open."

Early the next morning Vladimir reported to the Lubyanka to be sworn in as a GPU man.

Lubyanka prison, 8 January 1937

Molchanov brought us in to critique the run-throughs. He praised our performances and said that Vyshinsky was also pleased. All this official happiness led me to ask about my own case. Our beloved interrogator instantly reverted to his stiff old self, saying that he couldn't comment as that was a completely separate matter.

There's still a catch. In any normal trial lawyers try to trip up each other's witnesses. Considering all the rubbish that we're testifying to, a competent defense lawyer could give us fits. To set us at ease Molchanov explained that due to the nature of the charges the trial will be conducted before a panel of military jurists, who aren't the type to tolerate mischief. Even better, fourteen of the seventeen defendants have declared themselves so confident in Soviet justice that they've declined legal representation. Neither does Vyshinsky anticipate any problems with the three token defense lawyers who will be there. In other words, the fix is in. One would think that to make the process even more efficient they would have already shot the accused, but, silly me, socialist legality doesn't permit it. This isn't like the West where citizens can plead guilty and be done with it. In the USSR a trial is required!

Father was sympathetic to the Marxists, but he didn't buy into the notion that materialism and class struggle explained everything. He was appalled by ideological blather of whatever stripe, predicting – correctly as it turned out – that Socialists would eventually turn to force as the only way to get skeptics on board. All through the Civil War we were reassured that "extraordinary methods" of social control were necessary because powerful class enemies would stop at nothing to enslave the workers, and that as soon as Chekists managed to squish the last counterrevolutionary the State would simply "melt away." Naturally, as soon as one "class enemy" was vanquished another would magically take its place. Troublesome concepts like morality were derided as bourgeois artifacts, enabling unprincipled *apparatchiks* like Vyshinsky and Molchanov to do things that no right-thinking person could possibly justify.

Will forcing people to falsely confess help bring back the dream? Are obstinate types like me blocking the way to Utopia? What will people think of this in fifty years? One-hundred?

I posed these questions to Dmitry. His jaw dropped. "Your problem, Vladimir Georgievich, is that you're still looking for meaning beyond the four corners of your cell." We were in the exercise yard under the loose watch of a bored guard. "Me, I'm resigned to pass time as painlessly as possible, burying my head in whatever trashy novels they send my way." Bukhartsev is a voracious reader, and I occasionally overhear him yelling at the trustee for showing up with the same tired batch of books.

"Maybe you're right," I admitted, "but you'll never convince me that you're all that unaffected."

"Perhaps I'm not," he conceded. "But if you'll allow me my fool's paradise I'll grant you yours."

"And what might that be?" I asked.

Dmitry scooped up a handful of dirt. He blew off a thin layer of snow.

"They'll never let us go, you know. They can't."

Trud (1924-25)

Major changes had swept through the secret police. Although it still had its share of what military intelligence derided as "Dzerzhinsky's goons," Stalin's patronage and generous funding enabled it to hire scores of educated officers with language skills. In short order the USSR had a network of spies that was second to none. Great Britain was so thoroughly penetrated, it was said, that not even the Queen's bosom could safeguard the despised Empire's secrets.

One of the GPU's top operatives, Styrne (his given name was also Vladimir) was only in his twenties. A clean-cut, wholesome-looking fellow with a ready smile, his disarming manner belied a fearsome reputation gained as an interrogator. Rumors had it that he had ordered his own parents executed for counterrevolutionary activities. Most everyone believed it.

Vladimir had spent several weeks decoding and passing on dispatches from spies in Europe. He was now in Styrne's office to receive a permanent assignment. Their meeting didn't turn out exactly as expected.

"Pack up your things. You're being discharged."

Vladimir was stunned. "Discharged? But...why?"

Styrne chuckled. "Well, 'discharge' may be overstating it. We're placing a few of our more intellectually gifted officers in the newspapers as writers and editors to keep an eye on things. Mind you, you'll have to do enough journalism to allay suspicion. Do your job, and I don't expect that anyone will challenge someone who comes highly recommended by the Party. Be careful not to get too caught up in things, in office politics and such. Always remember that your primary responsibility is to us."

Vladimir's first assignment was at *Trud*, the newspaper of the Central Council of trade unions. Like other dailies it carried some general news, but its principal

189

objective was to boost productivity by enlightening workers about their socialist roles and obligations. Since nearly every occupation from construction to dancing had a union, *Trud's* circulation was second only to *Pravda*, the Communist Party daily.

Against all odds, he found journalism a perfect fit. Unlike the uncertain world of the secret services, where accomplishments were few and far in-between, each day at *Trud* yielded tangible results. Publishing a great newspaper was a noisy, oftentimes chaotic process that required the cooperation of everyone from the editorial offices to the printing plant.

Vladimir trained under an experienced editor for several weeks. A middle-aged stump of a man, with thick glasses, an even thicker German accent and a disturbing tendency to tear reporters' copy to shreds at the slightest provocation, his coach initially took to the burden like a cat to water, which is to say quite poorly. Over time, though, his pupil's earnestness and good humor won him over, and the experienced newspaperman tried his best to break in the newcomer to the intricacies of the craft. Naturally, the old-timer was concerned about this intelligent yet somewhat edgy young man with a foggy past. Why would a journalistic rookie be made an assistant editor? But when he brought up his suspicions to his wife she warned him to keep his misgivings to himself. He knew it was sage advice. Wherever the new comrade really came from, he was a quick student, accepted criticism and bathed regularly. If they're all to be like Comrade Romm, he concluded, let the Party send whomever they wish!

Galina was on leave from the Bolshoi. Not yet halfway through her pregnancy and already beset by backaches and frequent bouts of nausea, she was distressed to watch as her fine physical form, gained through years of dieting and exercise, quickly deteriorated. Galina was so disturbed by her new image that she turned the bedroom mirror to the wall, forcing Vladimir to adjust his tie in the bathroom.

He quietly shut the door, slipped off his shoes and took to the couch. The women were snoring, Galina's softer pitch interspersed with her mother's spasmodic growls. Reassured by the sounds of life, the exhausted journalist/spy reached for his earplugs and fell fast asleep.

Vladimir startled awake. In the early morning light he detected the outline of Galina's hovering belly. It was like one of those new airships, he thought.

"What's so funny?" she asked.

He struggled to think of something she would find humorous. "I...I just remembered an anecdote that I heard from the late crew."

"Well?"

There really was an anecdote, but he wasn't sure that his wife would enjoy it. But he was too fuzzy-headed to think of another.

"It's the middle of winter. Three condemned prisoners, a Frenchman, a Soviet citizen and a Jew are in the Lubyanka. Each gets a last request. The Frenchman asks for wine – no problem. The Soviet asks for vodka – no problem. Then the Jew asks for strawberries."

"Strawberries?"

"Yes, strawberries. Of course, the warden tells him that they're out of season. So the Jew says..."

Galina smirked. "Yes, yes, I know: "that's all right, I can wait'. Don't be repeating that nonsense, Volya, it could be misconstrued! Get dressed and come to breakfast. We have eggs!"

Ludvika served the welcome treat. "My cousin brought them from the farm. There was a plump chicken, too. If you hadn't been so late you would have had a fine dinner!"

Vladimir dug in. Food shortages and hoarding were forcing ordinary Muscovites to do without or spend their last kopeck in the black market. Morning "coffee" was a bitter brew, ninety-nine percent chicory. So one had to look for their pleasures elsewhere. He glanced at his wife. Although she was wearing a frumpy bathrobe, her hair was tied in a towel and her cheeks glowed so red that they seemed to be on fire, Galina was looking very pretty.

"How are you feeling?" he asked.

"Fat."

On his way to work Vladimir checked the designated spot behind a bakery for any messages from Styrne. He found an envelope containing an article published in the Communist Party's youth newspaper. Its author was a worker-correspondent named Bukhartsev:

"Any reasonable person would have found the barracks unsuitable for human occupancy. Windows were jammed shut to trap the heat. The air reeks of coal dust, unwashed bodies and dirty clothes. Every square centimeter is packed with row after row of rickety metal cots, their torn straw mattresses stirring with bugs and vermin. Toilets are holes in the floor and lack partitions. And that's not the worst of it. Singles, couples and families share the same space; lacking dividers or other concessions to privacy no act of intimacy passes unobserved. One could go on, but it's hardly surprising that this factory, which manufactures work clothes, just posted its largest quarterly profit. The only question is – who benefits?"

GPU agents had swooped down on the plant and arrested its owner, who now faced trial for profiteering and exploitation. Vladimir's curiosity was piqued. Why not cover the affair?

He arrived early on the appointed day. A bailiff directed him to a large, utilitarian courtroom with rough benches for spectators, an elevated table for the judge and assessors and a metal desk for the prosecutor. There was no defense table as defendants routinely waived their right to a lawyer.

It seemed that the push to raise the profile of these cases was succeeding. Spectators packed the gallery. Among them were union representatives, reporters from *Pravda* and *Izvestia*, a fellow he knew from *Tass*, and correspondents from worker and peasant publications.

The hall quieted. An intense young man with small, dark eyes, an aquiline nose and hair that fell to his shoulders took the prosecutor's seat. Moments later a militiaman brought in a sallow-faced fellow in thin jailhouse garments and rudely sat him in a chair. A bailiff appeared and bid all to rise.

A judge wearing a robe and two civilian assessors in suits entered and took their seats. It was time for the show!

The opening argument ran a full thirty minutes. The prosecutor described each alleged episode of abuse in excruciating detail, from laborers pulling double shifts for only a day's pay to workers standing helplessly by as their rightfully-earned bonuses and health contributions went straight into their greedy employer's pockets. He frequently referred to the defendant's lengthy confession, reading selected paragraphs out loud, as necessary modulating his tone to emphasize particularly juicy aspects.

Next up, a series of citizen witnesses delivered riveting, plain-spoken accounts of the miseries they suffered at the hands of their heartless boss. And when it seemed as though the evidence couldn't get any more damning a thin young woman in her twenties took the stand, her face obscured by a veil. In a soft, halting voice she painted a portrait of lechery and forced servitude that took the spectators' breaths away. Her employer, she said, regularly ordered her to come to his apartment, where he forced her to drink and engage in acts that the president of the court excused her from describing. If that wasn't enough, she also had to come by on her days off to wash her torturer's clothes.

Dazed by the damning testimony, the prisoner buried his head in his hands. And when his turn came to take the stand he broke into tears. Led by the prosecutor through his litany of misconduct, he sobbed that yes, everything was true. Then after a brief recess came the moment for which all had been waiting: his plea for mercy. He faced the bench and read a prepared statement:

"Your honors, had I been present as a spectator rather than as the accused and heard these eloquent and most correct presentations by the prosecutor and the witnesses, I would demand nothing less than the Court impose the harshest sentence authorized by law. But I'm not a spectator: I'm the one whose avarice destroyed the lives of innocent workers. And for that I deserve to be severely punished. How I wish that I had never been exposed to the temptations of capitalism, to the lure of material possessions, to the twisted reasoning that made me think that I was entitled to a life of comfort and pleasure..."

"Yes, yes, thank you, prisoner." It had been a long day and the judge was eager to be done. He and the assessors were gone only ten minutes. On their return he delivered the verdict: guilty as to all charges, with a sentence of six months hard labor, the leniency due to the defendant's cooperation and evident remorse. It was ordered that all his worldly possessions be sold, that the proceeds, along with the contents of his bank accounts be distributed to his victims, and that the plant be forfeited to the union and reopened as a Socialist cooperative.

Vladimir left with mixed feelings. He wasn't surprised by the verdict, which seemed justified by the evidence, and thought the sentence appropriate. Yet forcing the scoundrel to participate in his own ritualized humiliation – and without a lawyer, at that – was troubling. The proceedings seemed more like a gussied-up version of the revolutionary tribunals than a forum for discovering the truth. Was that to be an example of the new Soviet justice?

And there was something else. After the verdict, the prosecutor assured reporters that the decision to dismantle a legally chartered for-profit business was a necessary corrective, not a repudiation of Lenin's agenda. Later, when Vladimir discussed the outcome at the newspaper, the consensus was the opposite, that Stalin, who wielded great influence over the security services, was deploying them to undermine capitalism. Editors felt free to say so because the USSR was still ruled by a committee and the straightjacket of dogma had not yet pervaded every aspect of Soviet life.

Vladimir was amazed at his colleagues' naiveté. Here they were, pretending that freedom of the press was as inviolate a principle in the USSR as in the West. Meanwhile key agencies of social control, including the secret police and judiciary, had been co-opted by a man who insisted that his nose belonged in everything – even the arts! Unless something changed the descent into totalitarianism that his father predicted seemed inevitable.

Yes, there was another way. His name was Trotsky.

Lubyanka prison,
10 January 1937

Dmitry's comment shook me up. Do Vyshinsky and Molchanov really intend to throw us overboard once we've done their bidding? Bukhartsev says that he only keeps going for the sake of his family. He insists that we're radioactive, that we know far too much to ever be released.

I've given it a lot of thought. Maybe I'm just fooling myself, but if the authorities are really that worried about someone spilling the beans they'd have to shoot half their own men. The world has a short attention span, and as soon as the accused are liquidated this whole sordid business will be quickly forgotten. Dmitry emphatically disagrees, but he does have a tendency to look on the dark side of things.

Well, moving on. Our jailhouse librarian brought me Victor Hugo's fabulous novel, "Ninety-Three." It's supposedly one of Stalin's favorites. Set during the French Revolution, it tells of the struggles of Lantenac, an exiled Royalist who sneaks troops into France to stage a counterrevolution. His adversaries are his grandnephew Gauvain, an army general, and Cimourdain, a prominent politician who was Gauvain's childhood tutor. Gauvain and Cimourdain couldn't be more different. Gauvain is an honorable soldier, while Cimourdain is a bloodthirsty ideologue who would have the military slaughter every man, woman and child who gets in his way. He tries to bring Gauvain around to his way of thinking, counseling that, "In times like these, let's leave to justice its most fearsome form." Cimourdain is of course referring to the guillotine.

The time comes for Gauvain to pursue Lantenac and his brigands. Suspecting that the kind-hearted general might stop short of total victory, France's new rulers ask the ruthless Cimourdain to keep an eye out and make sure that Gauvain does *all* of his job. Their concerns are well placed, for as the battle rages Gauvain helps

Lantenac escape certain death. Cimourdain, who has sworn to obey his own rules, orders his beloved pupil's execution. Then, heartbroken, he commits suicide.

What's the moral of the story? When pursuing a cause, it's folly to form personal attachments. Stalin's clearly learned that lesson well. For him the book isn't a novel: it's a text.

The Manifesto (1926-27)

Vladimir's prediction that his father would grow weary of rich idlers was correct. Not long after the Savinkov affair George Romm gave up on Paris' self-absorbed expatriate community and moved in with Evsey and Esfir.

At his first opportunity Vladimir went to Leningrad to visit. He and his father had lunch at a restaurant near a children's clinic where George Romm volunteered. It wasn't until aperitifs that Vladimir finally indulged his curiosity. Why had his father, who cherished female company, come home alone?

"I thought that you and Karla were a pair."

George Romm theatrically beat his chest. "Ach," he grimaced. "We were! Then one day I came home and she was gone. Took her clothes, everything. A few weeks later I ran into her and this fellow arm-in-arm in the Marais. They were newlyweds! Let me tell you, it was quite a shock."

Vladimir was speechless. His father forced a laugh. "That's all right, Volya, I'm mostly over it. She was young and wanted children, so I expected to be dumped sooner or later. But *mon Dieu*, her choice!" George Romm paused as though the facts were too revolting to convey. "When I was in prison," he grimaced, "there was a jailer, a nasty young fellow named Ivan. He tried the best he could to live up to his namesake, and mostly succeeded."

"Don't tell me that...!"

His father nodded vigorously. "Karla introduced her groom as 'Count Ivan Ivanovich.' Of course, we instantly recognized each other. The fool's eyes got big as melons! I, too, was dumbfounded. But she seemed so proud of her title that, after a bit of stumbling, I shook the impostor's sweaty palm and walked on."

Vladimir was impressed. He raised his glass. "You're a real *mensch*, Papa. I don't think I could have done it."

"Oh, it wasn't easy. She looked terrific, all dolled up like a real countess. Look, I wouldn't have hesitated to plunge a blade into that sadist's heart for a minute. But to act like a jealous lover and spoil her happiness – no. If that's to happen, let it be his doing."

A waiter set down two shots of vodka. He discreetly gestured at a severely attired, shapely woman sitting alone. "The comradess wishes to convey her gratitude to the esteemed surgeon for his work with the children."

George Romm and the woman exchanged a polite smile. "Katja is with the political committee at the hospital," he explained. "They had to confirm that I wouldn't ideologically poison my patients."

"Are you seeing her?"

"What, are you crazy? She's a Communist. And nearly *my* age!" His tone became sheepish. "Well, once or twice."

The woman noticed the men's smiles. Whatever the joke, she hoped it wasn't at her expense.

Vladimir went to a monthly meeting with his counterparts from the other Moscow dailies. During a break he was approached by Dmitry Bukhartsev, an editor at the newspaper of the Communist Youth League.

"A Babylonian Talmud was passed down through our family," Bukhartsev said. "It was published by the 'House of the Widow and Brothers Romm.' Are you by chance a relation?"

"Why, yes! My grandfather David was the widow's husband."

Vladimir and Dmitry were both raised in the Pale of Settlement. Dmitry's birthplace, Dvinsk, a town ninety-five miles to Vilna's northeast, was second in size to Vilna and an important center of Jewish art and culture in its own right. They laughed about the subject of their communities' rivalry, which would have seemed inconceivable to modern ears. It wasn't which town had the best university, orchestra or sports team. It was which boasted the wiser chief rabbi.

Another thing they had in common couldn't be as openly discussed. Dmitry was at *Komsomolskaya Pravda* for the same reason that Vladimir was at *Trud*, on assignment for the secret police.

Bukhartsev returned to his office. He had to think. The situation in the Politburo had reached a boiling point. Sick and tired of being treated like underlings, Kamenev and Zinoviev, Stalin's ostensible partners in the ruling *troika*, left to form a bloc with Trotsky. Their platform called for rapid industrialization, stern action against peasants who were withholding food and, in a salvo directed at their former ally, "democracy in the Party," meaning an end to autocratic decision-making. There was just one hitch. To accommodate the firebrand and his disciples, the duo had to endorse the wild man's signature cause, a worldwide workers' revolution. It was a notion that many young communists found simply marvelous.

Dmitry wasn't one of them. While he admired Trotsky's intellect, the notion of converting the planet to socialism was, if not inherently outlandish, at least ridiculously premature. That a movement to do just that was picking up adherents was driving Stalin crazy. Luckily, Menzhinsky, the new secret police chief (Dzerzhinsky had recently passed away from a heart attack) also happened to be on the General Secretary's team, and he was taking his marching orders – to complicate Trotsky's life at every possible turn – quite seriously. Instructions were passed to the Lubyanka's journalist/spies to start writing articles ridiculing Trotsky.

Bukhartsev stared at his typewriter. Who might turn out the winner in this high-stakes duel was still very much up in the air, and at this stage of the conflict placing one's byline on a hit piece seemed needlessly risky. Memories in the Party were long, and what if the Man of Steel *didn't* prevail?

Dmitry sighed. He would have to choose wisely.

The birth of a child had a profound effect on Galina. While she did not seek out the role of being a mother, she quickly succumbed to the pleasures of tending to a creature that had been as firmly embedded in her body as her own heart. Galina had looked on breast feeding as an annoyance, certainly nothing that an educated Communist woman must do herself, but when the nurse placed little Georgie in her arms for his first meal she didn't hesitate, and instinctively succored her newborn with great delight.

To prevent the spread of disease relatives were not allowed to set foot inside maternity wards, so it was commonplace for expectant fathers to gather outside hospitals in view of the wards and chalk greetings on sidewalks for the new mothers to read. Some of the messages were simple, others were embellished with hearts and flowers, yet all were equally precious.

Galina's labor was normal and the delivery went without complications. Tuberculosis was rampant, and the doctor, a serious young woman just out of medical school, urged that Georgie be kept away from anyone who was even the slightest bit ill. Galina thanked her for the well-meaning advice, which she knew was useless. Who wasn't sick with something or the other?

Vladimir was rocking Georgie the way he did every night before going to bed. He felt at once elated and a bit left out. Ludvika and Galina spent all their time caring for "the little man," and whenever he tried to do something as simple as change a diaper they watched closely. That was fine with him, as like most new fathers he was terrified of accidentally hurting the baby. Vladimir's thoughts drifted to the man whom Moishe Stern mentioned, the enemy soldier who staggered when a bullet pierced his chest. That man too had been rocked by his father.

Galina gently lifted her newborn from her dozing husband's lap. Surprised to see tears trickling down Vladimir's face, she felt her own eyes moisten, for no particular reason.

Vladimir had become a creature of the newspaper. Thanks to an unnamed but clearly influential patron he was soon appointed to *Trud's* editorial board, where he helped shape policy and steer the publication through political minefields. At the time it was considered unseemly for a paper to openly favor one faction over another, so other than occasionally asking that he intercede in a hiring or foreign assignment the Lubyanka mostly left him alone. But as the year 1927 approached things began to change. Emboldened by his growing influence, Stalin boldly purged the Politburo of his opponents. Trotsky was out. Enraged, he cranked up the volume, holding rallies and making caustic speeches that did everything but call the General Secretary a dictator.

As the defining struggle between the Soviet titans reached its peak, freedom of the press finally gave way. *Pravda*, the Party organ, launched the first salvo, running a biting piece that accused Trotsky and his supporters of splitting the country. Other newspapers quickly fell in line. Dispassionate analysis became a thing of the past. *Trud's* free-wheeling atmosphere was no more, its fearful staff members taking extreme care to couch their writings and public utterances in terms that left no doubt of their fidelity to Stalin and their contempt for Trotsky and his handmaidens.

Vladimir's stint at the paper turned sour. As Trotsky's position weakened the Lubyanka began demanding detailed reports on the fidelity of his colleagues. He watched what he wrote and tried not to pass on anything that could conceivably compromise a co-worker. Still, every issue of the paper brought new articles and opinion pieces, each open to be construed in many ways. Caught in an impossible predicament, the unhappy spy turned to the only form of relief he knew.

"Done early?" It was mid-afternoon. Galina was at the sink preparing Georgie's meal when she heard the front door open.

"The board met. I didn't feel like going back after." Vladimir stroked the infant's cheeks. His son was underweight. Doctors found nothing amiss and prescribed more frequent feedings.

Galina heard the clink of glassware. Vladimir had been coming home early. He had little to say about *Trud* and no longer even bothered to bring a copy home. And now he was hitting the bottle. Her father had also been a smart, sensitive man. And he too had drunk himself to death.

Vladimir stepped out right after supper, giving no clue as to where he was going. He boarded a bus, rode for a bit, then switched to a tram and hopped off well short of his destination. He walked briskly. Satisfied that no one was following, he ducked into a nondescript building and climbed a flight of stairs. Moments later he was in a darkened room sitting opposite Karl Radek.

"Your experiences at *Trud* aren't unique. Similar pressures are being felt by comrades throughout government. Many like you are choosing to resist. That's not to say that we can afford to be careless. Make no mistake: this is a critical moment. We don't draw a breath without taking precautions."

Vladimir hadn't known where else to turn. For weeks he had been sidestepping the Lubyanka's increasingly pointed demands to slant coverage to favor Stalin and to denounce the Trotskyite traitors and counterrevolutionaries who must surely work at the paper. He considered various stratagems, but in the end decided that the time was drawing near to choose one camp or the other. He took his concerns to the editor who broke him in to the paper, and now he was here, in one of several secret apartments kept for that purpose, facing a decision every bit as momentous as the one he took at Archangel.

Radek slipped an elaborately bound document from his briefcase. "It's called the Declaration of the Eighty-Three, after the eighty-three comrades who initially signed it. There are now hundreds of signatures, including many from old Bolsheviks who have risen to denounce Stalin. Trotsky intends to personally present it to the Party Central Committee. That should rattle some cages!"

Vladimir read the celebrated manifesto. His idol seemed as arrogant and determined as ever. Democracy in the party! Defeat the rich peasants! Reverse the slide to capitalism! And while you're at it, world revolution! Trotsky's incendiary language and pointed accusations literally bubbled with energy, and it was easy to see why his broadside touched off waves of euphoria among his supporters. Their hero might be outnumbered and outgunned, but he was taking the fight directly to the enemy. It was impossible not to be impressed. Nor to realize that Trotsky and his cronies were drawing a line that could never be erased.

Vladimir returned the document. "It reads like a declaration of war."

"Maybe, but only against those who turned their backs on the principles of bolshevism. When Trotsky called the General Secretary a 'mediocrity' he was being generous. It's not just the dictatorship he's imposed at home: his ignorance of foreign affairs could fill volumes! What's tragic is that he's managed to convince many in the Central Committee that the USSR can prosper as a socialist island. What did he do when that madman Chiang Kai-shek – whom we helped install, by the way – purged our allies from the Kuomintang? Nothing! What's he doing now that Chinese communists are being threatened with extinction? Nothing! Not to worry, he says, he could 'squeeze the Chinaman like a lemon.' What kind of answer is that? So I go to the newspapers to publish a warning but not one – not even yours – can spare the space to defend our common interests. When I speak at the Communist Academy hoodlums drown me out while Stalin calmly watches, a beatific grin on his fat face. If this isn't tyranny, please tell me what *is*."

"Won't it play into the hands of those who accuse Trotsky of trying to split the party?"

"It's been split for a long time. We're determined to replace a plodding, self-serving bureaucracy with a living, breathing communism that will fulfill the promises of the Revolution. The only decision, comrade, is whether you want to be with those who seek to shape the future, or with those who are bound to the failures of the past."

Radek bit on his pipe. He offered Vladimir a pen.

Lubyanka prison,
11 January 1937

Thanks to an influx of prisoners it looks like everyone will be double-bunking. Dmitry introduced me to his new cellmate at exercise. His name is Vladimir Loginov. Sallow-faced, with a prominent Adam's apple and skin stretched so tightly that his cheekbones show, Loginov hails from Kharkov, a mineral-rich region whose foul air he blames for a chronic dry cough. He will also be testifying as a witness. But that's where the similarities end. Even in private conversations Loginov steadfastly insists that he really did participate in a conspiracy to overthrow the USSR, pouring out the nonsense with so much fervor that it could fool anyone who didn't know better. Well, Bukhartsev and I *do* know better, but when we confront Loginov with specifics he clams up, saying that he must save the details for court.

Dmitry initially suspected that the man was a stoolie planted by the authorities to check up on us. But after observing him for a couple days he changed his mind. He's convinced that Loginov is so terrified of being permanently kicked off the socialist train that he'll do anything to stay in Vyshinsky and Molchanov's favor. That's what makes him such a good witness.

Loginov was a mid-level *apparatchik*, the head of coke production at a mining complex. One would think that considering his plunge from grace he would comport himself modestly. It's just the opposite. Stiff and self-important like the bureaucrat he once was, he boasts of being an original Bolshevik, meaning that he joined the "correct" party before the Revolution. Loginov likes to brag about an Order of Lenin that he received for motivating underlings to exceed production quotas. In the USSR it's well known how such "progress" happens, so Loginov might as well admit that he purposely risked worker lives for the sake of getting a shiny piece of metal. At least that confession would be truthful.

Bukhartsev said that Radek came by to help Loginov prepare his testimony.

Dmitry was stunned at the size of the script, which is several times thicker than ours put together. In one part Loginov and two other witnesses, a Soviet engineer and a German fellow testify that a string of fatal mining mishaps (thanks to the killer quotas of the five-year plans there are plenty to choose from) were caused by sabotage. Transforming horrible accidents into acts of terror is a brilliant move, the kind one would expect from Vyshinsky. Now that he's brought in some corpses – the last real "victim" he could point to was Leningrad Party leader Kirov, the centerpiece of the 1936 trial – Trotsky and the accused aren't just conspirators. They're murderers!

It's not a new approach. During the late twenties and early thirties secret police arrested dozens of Soviet citizens and European contract workers for blowing up mines and sabotaging machinery. They were accused of trying to slow down production and enrich foreign companies by forcing the USSR to buy replacement equipment. Most everyone admitted their guilt, but to my knowledge no one was shot and the foreigners were simply expelled. I then heard rumors that the confessions were coerced, which knowing some of the brutes in the secret services didn't seem completely out of the question. One of my former colleagues also alluded to the possibility of falsification. But the notion that everything had been staged seemed implausible. And that's after suffering through the trial of the Socialist Revolutionaries, a truly wicked frame-up under an earlier regime.

Perhaps I was only being naïve. Or maybe I purposely made myself stupid.

Lev (1928)

It took only a single cycle of the "conveyor," just two consecutive twelve-hour periods of interrogation for the skinny, sunken-eyed engineer to talk. Now the frightened, exhausted man was presenting yet another challenge: he seemed utterly without imagination. "Please," he begged, "just tell me what it was that I did. I would be so grateful..."

"Let's begin again," the interrogator ordered. He would have turned to a different approach, but an officer from Moscow hovered nearby. "Tell us where you got the money."

"Money? What money?"

"The money that you used to pay the wreckers, the saboteurs! Did it come from the capitalist mine owners?"

"Ah...yes?"

"Very good. So who did you give it to?"

"Ah..." The engineer was stumped. To whom could he have given money that he never had?

"Who were your pals?"

"Um...I worked with Odrof, Kolodoob..."

"Good! So, who did you give the money to?"

"Ah...Odrof?"

The interrogator relaxed. "Excellent! Now we're getting somewhere!" He winked at Lev. "Would you like to take over?"

It was February 1928. Stalin, the Politburo's "first among equals" had crushed the opposition and expelled its members from the Party. Trotsky and Radek were sent off to Siberia. Radek scratched around a remote village for more than a year, writing letter after letter begging to be let back in. After writing a fawning piece about Stalin, he was. Trotsky, a far more problematic case, was eventually exiled to Europe. It was a move that the General Secretary would later regret.

Trotsky never returned to the USSR. But much of his agenda was implemented. Stalin brutally collectivized agriculture, dispossessing the *kulaks*, the so-called "wealthy"peasants and impressing them into forced labor. A massive industrialization campaign sought to achieve parity in machinery and armaments with the West. Unrealistic quotas, antiquated equipment and poor training soon proved a lethal combination, leading to a rash of mishaps.

Mineral extraction proved especially lethal. Coal mine explosions in the Shakhty region killed many workers and badly impaired output. But there was no column in production reports for "accidents." Secret police promptly stepped in, arresting forty-nine Russians and three Germans for participating in an elaborate plot attributed to mysterious "foreign elements." It was an unprecedented move. Many accused held out, insisting that the only crime was in their managers' frantic efforts to meet productivity goals. Provincial secret police asked Moscow for help. They sent Lev.

He was there when Berezowsky gave it up. In truth no more guilty of the charges than his inquisitors, the miserable engineer started naming names. Pretty soon he wouldn't shut up. More innocent men fell. They in turn named others. Soviet newspapers began running lurid accounts of the conspiracy.

The proceedings were about to get underway. Lev threaded his way through a throng of reporters. For reasons that he couldn't fathom, Moscow had invited foreigners to observe the trial. Leading European and American dailies eagerly sent their leading correspondents to take a rare peek into the world of socialist justice.

"Lev Alexandrovich!" It was Walter Duranty of the *New York Times*. In contrast to most other correspondents, who were skeptical at best, his writings had come to reveal a deep sympathy for the Soviet cause. "Have all the accused admitted their guilt?"

"Come to the trial, Walter. You won't be disappointed."

Lev had always been proud to carry the emblem of the sword and shield. He knew that in practice not everyone confessed willingly nor, truth be told, accurately. Even so, those he investigated were usually guilty of something, and if it was occasionally necessary to smooth a few rough edges, so be it. Here, though, the evidence was wholly lacking; when laid end-to-end the confessions simply didn't add up. How could a few rubles induce dozens of miners to stage accidents that imperiled their lives and those of their colleagues? Never before had he been ordered to deliver the goods "or else," and not even a stiff drink and a long soak in the bath house could restore his sense of well-being. Yes, explosions did happen. Yes, scores of miners were killed. That was all true. As for the rest, he chose not to know.

Soon after returning to Moscow Lev received an unexpected visitor. Citizens normally steered clear of the Lubyanka, so he assumed that Galina's presence was an act of desperation.

"My husband wasn't surprised when the end came," Galina said. She tried to sound matter-of-fact but her concern was palpable. "One morning the guards in the lobby kept his ID card and gave him a box containing his personal things. He got three months' severance pay and a snippy letter from the journalists' union bidding him good riddance and suggesting that he pursue a different vocation."

"Do you know why he was fired?"

"No, but I can guess. A few months ago he began coming home early and heading right for the bottle."

"Well, if it's simply a matter of alcoholism..."

Galina's temper flared. "Excuse me, Lev Alexandrovich, but it must be much more than that. Volya was never a drinker. He is a wonderful man, but childishly trusting. My husband really has no idea of the duplicity of which some people are capable."

"Who do you mean?"

"Radek, for one."

Lev stood. He extended his hand. "I'll look into it."

"Thank you. And please don't tell Vladimir that I came. He is a very proud man."

Sometimes change comes suddenly, other times it sneaks up like a guilty dog. Before Georgie's arrival Galina could not have imagined that rocking her baby to sleep could give her a pleasure far more profound than the rhythmic applause at a curtain call. Sure, she was upset; these were tricky times and her husband had made a mess of it. But the situation wasn't hopeless. His collapse forced her to find new strength, and she was determined to do whatever it took to make things right. So when two somber men in cheap suits appeared at the door, she welcomed them inside.

"Please come in. My husband will be home shortly."

Vladimir wasn't expecting a visit from the GPU, but neither was he shocked to find them waiting. His surprise came later. Instead of being hustled into a dank interrogation room, his escorts deposited him in a spacious, nicely appointed office. Once they had gone, probably to haul in another chump, a fashionably-attired secretary asked if he wanted tea! It didn't make sense, but he was happy to sip a warm beverage and wait for what came next.

Lev walked in. "I see that you've made yourself at home."

Vladimir nearly spilled his drink. He hadn't seen his friend for months.

Lev sat at his desk. He flipped the intercom. "Please give us privacy."

The box squawked. "Very well, Comrade Colonel."

Lev removed a thick folder from his safe. "Look through this."

It was Vladimir's confidential Party file, something that one wasn't supposed to see much less freely peruse. He flipped through the pages. A neatly handwritten log tracked his career, from his induction in Vilna, through his adventures in France and Germany, and finally to his assignment at *Trud*. Curiously, there was no mention of his leaving the paper. His exit evaluation and the letter from the union were also missing.

Lev noticed his friend's confusion. "Some things are better left out."

Vladimir was stunned. Rising stars like Lev didn't take chances, and if he was found out the repercussions could be severe. "I appreciate what you're doing," Vladimir stuttered, "but..."

Lev came around the desk. "*But?* What kind of word is that? What do you think would happen to your beautiful wife if you became our permanent guest? Your child? Things are changing, Volya, and not for the better. Surely you heard about Shakhty!"

"*Pravda* reported a dozen Soviet workers were sentenced to death."

"The exact number was eleven. If their families and friends hadn't risen in anger, Stalin might have actually allowed it! They sent me there to expedite things. When I arrived the case was in turmoil. Most of the accused steadfastly insisted that they were innocent. All I could accomplish was to get the interrogators to use psychological methods instead of brute force. That of course took time. Chief Judge Vyshinsky was greatly irritated by the delay. The prosecutor, too. I think you met him once."

"We had a few words when he was railroading the Socialist Revolutionaries."
Lev sighed. "Plenty of officers aren't thrilled with what's happening. But what can
we do? The old Chekists are still in charge, and their allegiance is to the General
Secretary. As for me, I'm thinking of transferring to the militia. Let those with
stronger stomachs handle political cases."

"You want to be a policeman? Blow a whistle and chase hooligans?"

Lev shrugged. "At least I'll be able to look at myself in the mirror." He wrote a note
on official stationery. "Take this to the languages department. They'll assign you a
tutor. *Tass*, the news agency, needs a correspondent in Tokyo. It's not accompanied,
meaning your family stays here, but it will have to do."

"Tokyo?"

"It's exactly what you need – a fresh start, and far from here. We'll soon send a
new ambassador. He said he'd be happy to have you, warts and all. It seems that you
two share a certain heritage."

Lev's kindness reminded Vladimir of an earlier time, when Socialists held all the
ideas but none of the power. Now a different kind of Czar was in charge. Would
Socialist Revolutionaries have done it any better? He wasn't sure. Championing
the collective over the individual has unpredictable consequences, especially for the
individual.

Vladimir was grateful for Lev's help. But his experiences had soured him on the
security services. So he hesitated. "Will I still report to the Lubyanka?"

Lev laughed. "Volya, Volya. One way or another, we *all* report to the Lubyanka!"

Over the next weeks a kindly old Japanese woman immersed Vladimir in the
complexities of a language that required memorizing more than a thousand symbols
to make sense of the simplest text. With her encouragement he soon stopped
trying to read the characters and began visualizing them, as his tutor suggested,
as individual works of art, each with its own meaning. Under her guidance he
learned to recognize and correctly pronounce simple phrases. He also memorized
all the stops on the Tokyo subway line, a practical skill that would one day prove
very useful. By month's end he was even making a little small talk, addressing
others in the proper Japanese way, according to their age, gender and social status,
a surprising accomplishment that earned the proud teacher's hearty *Jouzu desu ne!*

Galina had taken a job in a primary school, leaving Ludvika to tend Georgie during the day. Although he was almost two, the child was still reluctant to take to his feet, so his grandmother dragged him from one doctor to another to find out what was wrong. Every physician said the same thing: children develop at different rates, and even if the little fellow didn't turn into a champion gymnast he was bright, an early speaker and intellectually precocious. Indeed, Georgie paid such close attention to adult conversations that it seemed as though he understood everything. In time his parents thought it best to switch to Yiddish when discussing things that they didn't want him to know. Little did they realize that the old Jewish-German dialect was the first language the little man learned, sitting innocently on Grandma's lap, listening raptly as she schmoozed with friends.

On a brisk September day Vladimir and his family said their good-byes at the Moscow train station. Soon the new man from *Tass* would be on the Trans-Siberian railroad on his way to line's end, at the edge of the Pacific Ocean at Vladivostok. He would then transfer to a ferry for the last leg of his journey to the Land of the Rising Sun.

Lubyanka prison, 12 January 1937

Looks like I'll soon have a guest. Just this morning guards had me rearrange things to make way for a second bunk. Hopefully its occupant will be someone who likes toothy creatures.

Loginov was missing from exercise. Dmitry said that his cellmate has been working on a new aspect of the case. According to the most recent version of the script, Piatakov asked Loginov to destroy a nitrogen plant. Loginov enlisted two workers to help carry out the scheme. I'll refer to them as "Mr. L" and "Mr. R." (Yes, a nitrogen plant did blow up, but it was undoubtedly an accident caused by unskilled workers, broken equipment or taking dangerous shortcuts to meet a wild-eyed quota. Or, as usual, all three.)

Now here's where it gets interesting. Unless they're from another planet, Messieurs L and R know full well what happened to the accused in last year's trial – heck, they probably toasted the verdicts with their coworkers. Naturally, they're terrified. So fearful, in fact, that Radek is having fits calming them down enough so they can be properly coached. That's where ever-helpful Loginov comes in. Molchanov has him visiting the poor fools to convince them that testifying is in their best interest! As one might expect, Dmitry's cellmate took to his assignment with zest and from all indications is well on his way to succeed, that is, to get them to literally commit suicide.

I remember when word of the first trial reached Washington. By then Stalin's buddy Duranty had already bought into the "wrecking" and sabotage business. Many other journalists weren't far behind. (Regrettably, their number included my good friend Paul Ward.) But a few newsmen remained skeptical and besieged me with questions. I'm sorry to say that I did my best to reassure them that everything was on the up-and-up. Did I believe it? In a few instances it did seem that events were given a more sinister interpretation than what the evidence warranted. But it never occurred to me that it was all made up. Perhaps it wasn't convenient for the horrible thought to cross my mind. Self-deception is truly the worst kind.

Stalin supposedly worries what America thinks. That's why they're shoring up the trial with witnesses. But will our testimony prop up the façade enough to avoid offending delicate Western sensibilities? In the end I don't think it matters how much phony corroboration Vyshinsky and his underlings generate. However nicely it may be wrapped, garbage still stinks.

Siberia, Ukraine, Tokyo (1928)

Trotsky's tumble from grace had serious consequences for his followers. One day Vladimir Loginov was assistant chief of the State Bank of Ukraine. The next he was in a stinking, overstuffed train on his way to the Buryat-Mongolian Republic in southeastern Siberia. He would spend the winter of 1927-28 in a village near Lake Baikal alongside nomadic herders whose way of life had not changed since the dawn of time.

Loginov had never experienced such bitter, unremitting cold, the winds whipping across the ice, instantly freezing any carelessly exposed flesh. He spent his days in a drafty schoolhouse teaching the Cyrillic alphabet to native children. Most evenings were whiled away in a ramshackle tavern, drinking bitter Siberian vodka in the company of other exiles, assorted ne'er-do-wells and the occasional adventurer. Early one morning, as Loginov set off for the crowded dormitory where he slept, he lost his bearings, and as he leaned on a fence to catch his breath the railing collapsed, sending him to the ground. Stunned by the impact, too drunk to feel the numbness setting in, he surrendered to an inexplicable urge to take what could have been his last nap.

Loginov was in a child's cart bouncing along snow-covered fields. Misha ran ahead, pulling him with a rope. Suddenly a wheel struck a rock, ejecting him from the cart and landing him in a drift. He thought that he heard laughing, yet when he got up his beloved older brother was nowhere to be seen. Then the voice faded, and his memory returned of that terrible day when his grief-stricken parents announced that Misha was dead, felled by a bullet fired by an idiotic soldier in an idiotic war.

Loginov came to. He gazed at the frozen landscape, the ice-encrusted soil gleaming eerily in the moonlight. Realizing that another moment's rest might well turn into an eternity, the proud Bolshevik struggled to his feet. Moments after shuffling into the boarding house he wrote yet another plea.

JULIUS WACHTEL

20 March 1928:

I was born in 1897 in Kiev. My first political involvement was in 1915 when my older brother and I joined a Socialist worker's group in a shoe factory. In 1917 my brother was drafted into the army and joined a Bolshevik military committee. He died fighting the Whites in 1921.

I joined the Bolshevik Party in February 1917. I fought in Ukraine and was captured by German mercenaries, who were supporting the Whites. After my release I held many responsible political positions. My last assignment, in 1923, was to lead the Department of Political Education for the Communist Party of Ukraine.

I have always worked hard to promote the party line. But the shock of Lenin's death depressed me. In confusion and despair I joined a fringe discussion group and began supporting Trotsky. I have since learned that he and his fellow-travelers are nothing more than counterrevolutionaries. It's true that I didn't completely sever my ties to Trotsky before the Fifteenth Congress, which he tried to co-opt for his own criminal purposes, but neither did I actively participate in the opposition. All I did was go to meetings, sign a meaningless declaration and shoot off my stupid mouth.

I am truly sorry for letting down my comrades and pledge my absolute loyalty to Comrade Stalin even if I am not readmitted. But I beg that the Party reconsider my application for reinstatement.

Vladimir Feodorovich Loginov

My old Party card no. 0923284

Loginov put down the pen. He was shivering, not from the cold but from fright. Was he still dreaming? He dared not close his eyes.

Stalin's exhortations to go after "rich" farmers were reaching every corner of the USSR. In their remote corner of Ukraine all Anna and Idzi could do was watch, wait and pray. By no means wealthy, yet more prosperous than most, they shuddered at each hushed reference to the General Secretary's despised new bogymen, the *kulaks*. What was so wrong about producing in abundance and earning a profit so that one could give work to others? Fortunately they and the children were healthy, and as spring approached the promise of a fine harvest lifted their spirits. They convinced each other that their beloved country was just suffering from an ordinary illness that would soon run its course.

Anna was in the kitchen stirring a fresh vat of buttermilk when she noticed three strangers approach. Two were no more than boys, eighteen if that, wearing ill-fitting uniforms of the reserve militia. One fidgeted with a rifle. They were accompanied by a middle-aged man in a cheap suit. Clearly a minor official of some kind, he affected that puffy, self-important look characteristic of Communist hacks.

The bureaucrat paused and scribbled in a notebook. Anna's heart skipped a beat. As the keeper of the farm's books she instantly recognized his purpose.

He was making an inventory.

Idzi and the twins were on their way back from the equipment barn when they came across the visitors. Anna's husband had just finished tuning up their new tractor, a splendid, powerful workhorse that he bought on credit, a wonderful opportunity made possible by the economic reforms. Idzi recognized that capitalism was no panacea, and there were plenty who would squander their profits on drink and carousing. But every ruble he and his wife earned was used to pay down debt or reinvested. Nothing would keep them from passing on a model farm to a new generation.

Idzi had the boys stay behind. He approached the men.

"Good morning, comrades. How can I help you?"

The official flashed his identification card. "I am from the People's Commissariat for Interior Affairs. Are you Idzi Nikolayevich?"

"Yes, I'm the owner, along with my wife, Anna Mikhailovna."

"Owner?" The bureaucrat grinned malevolently. "Haven't you heard? From now on the proletariat own everything." He looked around. "Where are the ones who do the *real* work?"

Idzi recoiled at the insult. "We all labor, comrade. Well-paid men and women are tending the fields as we speak. Is there a problem?"

"Not as long as you don't interfere. This farm and everything in it belongs to the State. We're making a list so that nothing 'disappears.' You'll get a copy to use when petitioning for compensation. But don't get your hopes up too high. In the USSR we don't reward exploiters. All you're entitled to is what you've done with your own hands."

Anna anxiously watched from the farmhouse. At a recent meeting of the peasant council, on which she and Idzi served, a delegate from the Agriculture commissariat warned that change was coming. This time, the nervous man said, it would go far beyond expropriating grain and forcing farmers to accept lower prices. Just how drastic the new way of doing things would be was soon apparent. Within weeks a collectivization campaign began in earnest. Idzi vowed not to let anyone take the farm without a fight, and Anna believed him. All she could hope for was that in the confusion they'd be somehow overlooked.

Her husband and children came in the house. From Idzi's expression she feared the worst. "Is it really happening?"

Idzi ignored the question. "Go pack your rucksacks," he told the boys. Jarek and Mikolaj were only eight, yet already serious farmers. "Mother's taking you on a trip. Hurry!"

Their sons scampered off. "Take them to the village and find Boris Ivanovich. He will drive you to the train station. Wait for me at your brother's in Dnepropetrovsk."

Anna had seen him like this once before, and in the end a would-be bandit lay dead. "Let them have the farm!" she implored. "We'll take what they give us and start over."

Idzi gently touched his wife's face, roughened like a man's after years of exposure. "Please go. It's just a precaution, for the children's sake. I'll join you soon."

Anna and the boys were loading a horse-driven cart when the official walked up.

"Nice animal," he said, patting its rump. He jotted a quick note. "You may keep it, and the cart, too. You'll discover we're not the ogres they make us out to be."

Idzi and his visitors watched the cart leave. "Take us to the machinery shed," the official barked.

These would be the man's last words on Earth. Idzi had decided to hold his temper for the sake of his boys when, on the way to the shed, he caught the boy with the rifle sneaking glances at him the way that scoundrels do. He wasn't surprised. All that chatter about "compensation" was an empty promise, a stall while the rascals worked up their courage.

Idzi opened the door and stepped aside, letting the youngster with the gun go in last. As he fell in behind the youth he swiftly drew his knife, the one with the sharp blade for neutering sheep, then in a single swipe neatly slit the boy's throat, instantly severing the vocal chords, a fearful trick that he learned as a scout during the Great War. It all happened so quickly that the official didn't realize anything was amiss until a thirty-caliber slug from the dead reservist's rifle slammed into the back of his head.

Stunned by the mayhem, the other boy cowered in a corner. Idzi's hands shook uncontrollably.

"What was to be the excuse for murdering me? That I resisted?"

"I refused!" the petrified youth screamed. "That's why he had the rifle!"

Idzi stared at his beloved tractor. He fell to his knees and began to weep.

The embassy car sped along the Showa-Dori, swerving and honking as though its occupants were late for an audience with the Emperor. Vladimir was in the back, hanging on for dear life. All bets were off when these gentle, good-natured people got behind the wheel. A city-full of citizens careening through the streets, accelerators mashed to the floor. One had to live it to believe it.

Ichiro skillfully double-clutched his way through an intersection. It seemed that half of Tokyo was on its way to the opening ceremonies of Japan's first subway. *Tass's* interest in the event was puzzling. All he could figure was that his boss was trying to make up for that story about the death of the Taishō Emperor, a mordant piece that rubbed the Interior Ministry raw and nearly got Vladimir-san expelled before he even got started. Gleefully published by the papers in Moscow, and bitterly denounced by the Japanese press, the biting salvo criticized the desultory way in which the divine leader's passing was mourned, the shopgirls and salary men going about their daily routines even as cemetery workers hoisted the coffin into the Imperial Mausoleum. What particularly galled the Foreign Ministry was Vladimir's critical analysis of the Emperor's troubled reign. In a society where embarrassment was to be avoided at all costs, nothing was more shameful than mental illness, an affliction that for decades kept the half-man, half-God from the public eye while the real power was exercised by then-Regent, now-Emperor Hirohito, the newly enthroned ruler of the Shōwa period of "enlightened peace."

Police waved the embassy car into a reserved area near the line's Asakusa terminus. Vladimir exited and bent down as if to tie his shoe. Sure enough, their shadow was parked not more than a hundred meters away. Notwithstanding the Foreign Ministry's infuriatingly polite reassurances to the contrary, the USSR compound at Minato-Ku and every official vehicle that left it were under constant watch. Grim plainclothesmen went so far as to delay departing taxicabs to see who was leaving, and often as not they'd mutter a pretext and ride along. Every Soviet official was under watch, some around the clock, while lesser employees such as

Vladimir got "escorts" during the day and whenever circumstances allowed.

Japan had reason for concern. A recent exchange of diplomats created new opportunities for the Comintern, which greatly ramped up its support of the Japanese Communist Party. Thanks to the island country's weak economy, its recruitment drive was meeting with considerable success. Protests by Japanese authorities fell on deaf ears, with the Soviets insisting that the Communist International was an autonomous entity outside government control. But of course they'd be happy to pass on any concerns!

Vladimir found ordinary Japanese citizens gracious and helpful. They always smiled and made way for the *Gaijin*, and whenever he got lost or disoriented someone would promptly offer to help. If it wasn't for the language! One month's study proved ridiculously insufficient. Excepting for the simplest needs, like finding a bathroom, the slightest lapse in phrasing or pronunciation could make his intentions incomprehensible or, as was often the case, hilarious. When Ichiro wasn't present he learned to resort to pantomime, which was usually accepted with giggling and good cheer.

His job was to develop contacts, the more influential and well-positioned the better. But Japanese officials were reluctant to meet with foreigners outside formal settings lest it draw suspicion. Not only was it impossible for a European to blend in, oversight of everyday life was more than a match for anything that the GPU might dream up. Legions of police, intelligence agents, informers and all-purpose busybodies were always on alert for signs of the slightest indiscretion. Of the security services none was more of a nuisance than the Tokkō, the brutal political police, whose agents tailed Soviet staffers and listened in on telephone calls. They could be shaken off quite easily, but the threat of being observed hung over every encounter.

Vladimir and Ichiro entered the gleaming new six-story office tower positioned over one end of the underground. After the disastrous Kwanto earthquake and fire of September 1923, which leveled much of Tokyo's core, the Japanese switched to building with concrete rather than the more traditional wood, so other than for some nostalgic touches like the terminal's pagoda-roofed staircase Tokyo began taking on the appearance of a Western metropolis.

They descended to the station. In contrast with Russians, who were accustomed to wait in line for everything including their daily bread, the Japanese seemed to have no concept of a queue. Despite a tradition of unquestioned obedience to authority, hundreds of eager riders mobbed the platform, pinning a skirmish line of Tokyo's finest against the gleaming new subway cars as they pushed and shoved to be the first aboard.

Ichiro plunged in. He elbowed his way through the crowd yelling *gaishu*, which depending on pronunciation and context meant either foreign minister or whore. He and Vladimir were soon exchanging bows with an impeccably dressed official.

"Vladimir-san, I wish to present the Chief Engineer."

Ichiro was pleased that Vladimir followed his instructions, bending fully from the waist and not, like an ignorant European, from the shoulders, and that he extended the courtesy of leaving his pen and notebook in his pocket until introductions were done. Vladimir then began the interview. As his driver translated, the man from *Tass* asked about the line's length, its cost, projected ridership, and so on, according the engineer the proper respect by writing continuously and treating every response as a gemstone. In short time they were done, but as Ichiro moved to thank the engineer Vladimir posed an additional question.

"Please ask the Chief Engineer how they intend to keep riders from being pushed onto the tracks."

Ichiro's voice cracked. "Pushed? You mean, like, accidentally?"

"How else?"

Ichiro reluctantly translated. The engineer grew instantly suspicious.

"A red line will be painted to keep passengers from getting too close to the edge. No Japanese would be so rude as to purposely cross it, and guards will be posted to guarantee that no one does so inadvertently."

Romm jotted down the reply. "Please ask how they will keep persons from jumping in front of a train on purpose."

Ichiro's mouth fell open. "Vladimir-san, I can't..."

Vladimir took over. Smiling politely, he thrust his arms out, mimicking a leap. The shocked bureaucrat flushed deeply, mumbled a few words, bowed and left.

Ichiro was dismayed. How do these insufferably rude people avoid murdering each other before breakfast? "The Chief Engineer begs your leave as the ceremony is about to begin. His assistant will escort us to one of the cars for the inaugural ride."

An hour later Vladimir and Ichiro were in a restaurant at the other end of the line. They were enjoying heaping bowls of *oya-ko*, a hearty workingman's lunch of chicken and egg mixed with rice.

Ichiro poured tea. "Vladimir-san, please forgive my impertinence, but I don't understand why you insist on pushing things so far. You must realize that the Chief Engineer felt insulted."

"Well, then please convey my apologies. Still, it's well known that suicide in Japan, especially among the young, is a serious problem. My editor would expect me to ask, so I did. Now if you don't mind, let me ask *you* something. Why would a fine young person with a degree from a prestigious university be chauffeuring a rude, smelly Soviet official?"

Ichiro laughed. What Vladimir's comrades disparagingly called the "Oriental mask" momentarily faded.

"You're not so smelly, Vladimir-san."

Ichiro's overseers at the Tokkō had warned their rookie agent not to let his guard down. Vladimir-san's case file left no doubt that he was first and foremost a spy. But Ichiro detected other aspects to the man. Vladimir-san always treated him with respect, often seeking out his advice and on occasion even taking it. His most endearing quality, though, was the courtesy he unfailingly extended to those of lower station, all the way down to the embassy's wrinkled old scrubwoman. It reminded Ichiro of his father. A military veteran and descendant of a Samurai family, he had always cautioned against the temptations of elitism, warning that excessive pride in caste and nationality led good people to muzzle their conscience and commit unspeakable acts. It was left unsaid, but Ichiro assumed that the warning was based on personal experience.

Ichiro decided that opening himself up a bit would do no harm. "You asked about my background, Vladimir-san. Because of the depression there were few good opportunities when I graduated, so my father, who's in the import-export business, sent me to keep the books at his branch in Vladivostok. I was there three years."

"So that's where you learned to speak Russian! Your pronunciation is excellent."

"Thank you, Vladimir-san. I became a great fan of your literature. There's no greater pleasure than to read Pushkin in his native tongue."

"Pushkin? You'd enjoy meeting my brother Evsey Georgievich. He's an engineer, and in his spare time, a poet."

"I would be delighted, Vladimir-san. You know, there's so much more to feed than a stomach."

Lubyanka prison,
13 January 1937

I now have a cellmate. Early this morning guards brought in Leonid Tamm, a tall, thin fellow a few years my junior. Fortunately he's nothing at all like the fool who poor Dmitry got stuck with. Leonid is quiet and polite, and when the best judge of character in the Lubyanka scampered up for a sniff I was delighted to see that he instinctively offered it some of the stale bread prisoners hide for snacking. I was embarrassed to admit that the rat's name is, well, "Leon." My new companion was delighted. He said that considering all the scoundrels with his given name (Trotsky springs instantly to mind) he was honored that at least one was an honest sort.

Leonid's arrest came unexpectedly, at the end of a regular workday at the Commissariat of Heavy Industry, where he was engineer in charge of fertilizer production. He at first assumed that it was all a mistake, an outgrowth of the arrest of his commissariat's number two man, Piatakov, who was unexpectedly dragged off one morning by two burly secret policemen wearing black coats. Naturally that scared the heck out of everyone, as Piatakov was a celebrated original Bolshevik. If they can do that to such a famous and influential comrade, no one is safe.Leonid has a fascinating background, which lacking other things to write about I'll describe in some detail. He is of German descent. His grandfather emigrated from Thuringia, married the daughter of a wealthy landowner and settled in Elizavetgrad, a provincial capital in Ukraine. Their son Evgeny (Leonid's father) became town engineer. He put the community on the map, installing modern lighting and one of the first tram systems in Russia. Evgeny and his wife had three children: Igor, Tanya and Leonid, the youngest. Tanya is a housewife. Igor, a well-known scientist, is one of the directors at the Lebedev Physical Institute, a pre-eminent research center in Moscow.

Elizavetgrad happens to have an interesting pedigree. Named after the Empress Elizaveta Petrovna, the headstrong daughter of Peter the Great, the city was renamed Zinovievsk to honor its native son, Grigori Zinoviev, member of the *troika* that ruled the Soviet Union while Lenin was incapacitated. He and a second member, his friend Lev Kamenev, were liquidated in the 1936 trial. That presented Stalin, the third and only surviving member, with a dilemma, as one cannot allow a town to carry a counterrevolutionary's name. The General Secretary handled it with his usual aplomb, re-christening it Kirovograd, in honor of Kirov, the popular party leader whose murder Zinoviev and Kamenev supposedly planned. Naturally, this convenient if circular solution now smells like day-old meat. Maybe when they get around to denouncing Kirov they'll rename the place Vyshinskygrad!

Leonid told me an interesting family story. Elizavetgrad changed hands several times during the Civil War. At one point while the Reds were in control officers ordered his father to start up an idle electrical plant, a wood-fired monstrosity that could devour a forest in a fortnight. Most improbably, he refused. You see, the town's poor depended on the trees for fuel, and they would have frozen to death if he complied. The mild-mannered graduate of the Petersburg Technological Institute was hoping that Red Army generals wouldn't be so stupid as to shoot the man who made the town tick. Thankfully, his hunch was proven correct, and both he and the forest were spared.

Leonid spoke wistfully of his wife, Nina. They have no children. He reminisced about their courtship and marriage, which caused quite a stir, as his family is upper-class – his mother is a General's daughter – while Nina comes from ordinary Russian stock; the peasantry, if you will.

Welcome to communism, Leonid Evgenevich! Here there are no artificial barriers of any kind. Everyone is equally miserable!

Despite his high civilian rank Leonid never joined the Party. He said that his father's experiences persuaded him to stick with what he knows best and leave politics to others. Well, that hasn't worked out so hot either, but Leonid is hopeful that his beloved Commissar, Sergio Ordzhonikidze, a favorite of the workers, will step in to fix things as soon as he recovers from whatever malady has been keeping him from coming to the office.

What I didn't tell Leonid – why upset him further? – is that not long before I left America Ambassador Troyanovsky told me that Ordzhonikidze was confined to his home because he protested the arrests and questioned the justifications for the first trial. So I'm not sure that there is a remedy for what ails him.

In this regime there's no faster way to get into trouble than by being loyal to one's underlings, nor any better way to get ahead than by denouncing one's superiors. Of course, it's wise to wait until your target is already *in extremis*. As I learned the hard way, things can change quickly!

Oh, I almost forgot. Radek came in to alert us that the trial is set to begin in ten days. It won't come too soon to please me!

Fumiko (1928)

Ichiro dropped Vladimir off at the entrance to the Ueno subway terminal. His boss had taken to slipping away on Friday evenings. He usually carried a small bag, so his driver assumed, correctly as it turned out, that Vladimir-san found someone with whom to spend the weekends.

Vladimir's search for female companionship had taken him to Asakusa, where prostitution was legal and sex workers got regular check-ups. Out of curiosity he also visited a few of the unlicensed areas that Ichiro politely warned him to keep clear of. Vladimir didn't understand why all the fuss. Even the bawdiest of Tokyo's red-light districts was no match for the backstreets of Berlin, where skimpily-attired *fräuleins* openly solicited clients on the sidewalk, fighting viciously over the chance to service prosperous-looking foreigners. There was otherwise little to distinguish between the flesh trades. Behind the makeup the despair seemed the same. Much as he enjoyed a woman's touch, Vladimir found commercialized sex profoundly disturbing.

His dilemma was resolved in an unexpected way. Not long after arriving in Tokyo Vladimir paused to hand the cleaning woman a few yen when she wrapped his fingers around a note. It bore nothing more than a telephone number. That's how he came to know a procuress who supplied courtesans to wealthy Japanese. Although her usual prices were far beyond his means, Vladimir-san came highly recommended, and there just happened to be an apprentice whose companionship could be offered to a refined Russian gentleman for a moderate fee.

Vladimir met with the madam at a tiny Asakusa café. Older and thickset, she wore heavy makeup, a style long passé in the metropolis but still favored in the provinces. The woman scribbled out the contract on a sheet of perfumed stationery, writing in their common language, French. Payment was due the first of the month, in advance. Vladimir was not to arrive at the apartment before six o'clock Friday and had to leave before six a.m. Monday. Under no circumstances was he to take the girl outside Asakusa without prior notice. "Special services," which the procuress explained in embarrassing detail, carried a surcharge. Without skipping a beat she also made it clear that rough treatment would bring on serious consequences, their precise nature being left to his imagination.

Vladimir hesitated. His visits to the districts had increased in frequency. Taking up with a consort, though, was something else altogether. It certainly couldn't be rationalized as a "slip." Sensing his indecision, the procuress brought out Fumiko's photograph. Her name, meaning "beautiful child," seemed a perfect fit. Vladimir gazed at her delightful features, the smooth skin and full lips, and most pleasingly, her flawless figure, its curves flattered by a provocative Western-style bathing suit just sufficiently immodest to stir the imagination. He felt obliged to ask the girl's age. Fumiko was "near" twenty: just how "near" the madam didn't say.

He was lonely. Street encounters weren't his cup of tea. So he signed.

Fumiko's apartment was on the second floor of a building occupied mostly by pensioners. Located in a residential area not far from Asakusa's thriving entertainment district, the hideaway was a safe and comfortable place to spend the weekends. Its kitchen and bath boasted Western-style conveniences, while in deference to custom the living areas were mostly furnished with mats, cushions and screens. A locked closet and a few men's toiletries suggested the apartment had other uses during the week, but like the issue of Fumiko's age Vladimir thought it better not to ask.

Fumiko cracked the door open to let him pass. After a long, frustrating week of playing cat-and-mouse with the Tokkō, Vladimir longed to bring her close. But a long ride in stuffy subway cars while repeatedly exiting and boarding to throw off a tail left him a sopping mess. Laughing at his disheveled appearance, she gave him a quick kiss and drew a bath. No sooner was he in the tub than she came in and modestly arranged herself on a mat. Draped in an exquisite, daringly sheer silk kimono, an outrageously expensive garment intended for a single purpose, she had taken to letting her hair fall loosely on the shoulders, the way that he preferred. She was slimmer than the photograph suggested, her legs bony, cheekbones higher and more pronounced, hair not nearly as dark. Undisguised by makeup – a light touch was Vladimir-san's preference – Fumiko at times seemed nearly child-like.

Vladimir was cautioned against asking too many questions or, worse, becoming romantically attached, but after enjoying weeks of pampering by this delightful young woman he was eager to know more.

"Where are you from, Fumiko-san?"

Fumiko always rebuked him for asking personal questions. For reasons that she would later wonder about, this time she chose differently.

"Do you know where Hiroshima is?" she asked. Her French was silky and without noticeable accent.

Her earnest response caught Vladimir off-guard. "No...not exactly."

She laughed. "Then I'll give my dear *Gaijin* a little geography lesson. Japan is divided into middle, near and far 'countries' according to their distance from Kyoto, the Imperial capital. Chūgoku is a 'middle' country on the southern tip of the big island – the one we're on. Hiroshima is its largest city. It was once very beautiful but it's now full of smelly factories and industrial plants. My father unloads freight at the port."

"And you?"

Fumiko's smile faded. For the first time she addressed him as something other than a playmate. "I study law at the university."

It took a moment to digest the surprising news. "I'm glad to hear that. I was hoping that this wasn't your...um...'career'."

"You mean like a Geisha? Oh, no. They're ridiculously expensive! Auntie's mother said that you were a kind man and deserved someone nice but were very poor."

So the procuress was the cleaning lady's daughter? Japan was a constant surprise! "Forgive me, but I don't understand. You're young, smart and beautiful. I'm, well..."

Fumiko placed her fingertips on her patron's lips. "You're a wonderful man who's helping pay for my studies. But since you're feeling guilty, may I ask a very important favor?"

"Of course."

Fumiko dashed off. She returned with a Russian primer.

Vladimir was stunned. "You want to learn Russian?"

"It's become a very important language. Please forgive me, Vladimir-san, but Russians speak terrible Japanese. Exchanging diplomats was the first step. Once trade relations are normalized, lawyers who can speak Russian will be very much in demand."

Vladimir leafed through the book. "I'm not much of a teacher, Fumiko-san, but I will be pleased to do what I can."

Fumiko bowed deeply. She rinsed off her honored guest. Then with a quick, adept shrug the budding lawyer slipped off her kimono.

It was midnight. Vladimir glanced in the mirror. He badly needed a shave and his hair could stand a vigorous brushing. Perfect! He scuffed a pair of shoes and sprinkled sake on a rumpled suit he brought for just this purpose. An expertly forged French passport in the name of a deceased citizen of *la République*, enough hard currency to send inquisitive policemen merrily on their way, and he was set to go. This night he would be just another drunk foreigner looking for amusement on the streets of Tokyo.

Vladimir strolled through Asakusa's cinema district. Japanese loved the movies. Each weekend eager throngs jammed screenings of the latest silent films from Europe and America. Vladimir was especially fond of American gangster films, especially those starring James Cagney. And when the action lagged he never failed to be amused by the enthusiastic interpreters on stage, whose antics conveying story lines and translating dialogue frequently surpassed in entertainment value anything that took place on screen.

He approached the subway entrance. Sure enough, there was the man in a grey fedora that he gave the slip to earlier. Vladimir took his time descending the stairway, then paused at the bottom to watch for his train. Timing it closely, he sprinted on board just as the doors closed, leaving the frustrated plainclothesman behind. Vladimir rode to Inaricho, then crossed over and boarded a train headed in the opposite direction. Satisfied that no one was on his trail, he exited at his intended destination, Tawaramachi. The platform was empty. Not even the Tokkō could afford to post men at every terminal around the clock. Thank goodness for the subway, and for a tutor who suggested he memorize its schedules.

Vladimir walked through the darkened streets. He was soaked in perspiration. As summer approached, the rain, while more frequent, lost its ability to cool. He was warned that typhoons would soon batter the island, uprooting trees and flinging them through the air like they were matchsticks. Then again, for a people accustomed to earthquakes, flying trees were probably not that big a deal.

Only a few minutes passed before tree-lined sidewalks and well-tended buildings gave way to a narrow dirt lane, rickety shacks and the stench of human waste. A small pack of hungry-eyed dogs warily tagged along, hoping that the stranger might give them something to eat.

It was his first visit to the junkyard. A middle-aged Japanese man answered the bell.

226

"I'm a friend of the workers," Vladimir announced, speaking in Russian. "And you?"

"A friend of the workers' friend," the man answered, also in Russian. "Come in."

Vladimir was led to a shack. Inside, a woman bundled in dirty blankets lay listlessly on a mat. Empty medicine bottles were scattered at her feet. A lone, flickering candle illuminated the lamentable scene. People may be different, Vladimir thought, but poverty always looks the same.

"Is this your first visit to one of our honorable slums?" the man asked.

"Yes," Vladimir said. "I had no idea..."

"Of course not! When capitalists rebuilt Tokyo their real purpose was to drive the poor to the fringes. As you see, they succeeded. My wife caught ill because of the filth."

The woman stirred. In her half-open eyes Vladimir recognized the signs of a fading life.

The man tenderly applied a wet cloth to her forehead. "I was an accountant. She helped me. With our extra earnings we bought a few noodle carts to rent out. Everything was going well until some crooked tax collectors started coming around, demanding payoffs. They took all our profits. It was like we were working for them! I complained to the police but only got beat up for my troubles."

Vladimir had heard many such stories. Corruption was the party's best friend. "Is that why you became a Communist?"

"We both did. Then a few weeks ago the roundups began. Comrades started disappearing without a trace. When I went to inquire the Tokkō bastards were very sly. 'You say that so-and-so is missing? How dreadful! No, we know nothing about it. Please, let me take a report.' One day later a body covered with cigarette burns turns up in the dump! We fled just in time. My wife's cousin owns the yard. He let us use this shack. And what's Moscow doing about this outrage? Nothing!"

Vladimir was angry. And embarrassed. That same inexplicable timidity that kept the USSR from confronting the treacherous Chiang Kai-shek, leading to the torture and execution of scores of Chinese cadres, was leading to an even greater disaster in Japan. He tried to explain.

"We filed objections, but they've banned the Party, so the Interior Ministry insists that the arrests are perfectly legal."

The woman lapsed into a spasm of coughing. Her husband rushed to her side. "We've run out of medicine and the doctor won't come back unless I pay. If we go to a clinic they'll arrest us."

Vladimir felt lost. He pressed all his cash into the man's hands. "I'll be back."

An hour later, as a Soviet spy settled back into his hideaway, a supervisor in the Tokkō approached his boss.

"Our friend was up to some late-night mischief, Inspector-san. They lost him between Ueno and Asakusa."

"Running around so late? He must be shacked up somewhere close. At my age," the inspector winked, "I leave no bed unless I must."

"Let me put a team on him. They'll find out where he's hiding."

The inspector looked at a wall map. Colored pins identified homes not yet searched and Party members not yet arrested. "We're already stretched thin. Everyone not in the field is tied up in interrogations. When's he due to go on leave?"

"In two weeks."

"Wait until he returns. In the meantime put a new face at Asakusa and tell him to keep out of sight. I want the Russian to think that things have cooled."

"I understand, Inspector-san. Give a man enough rope, he'll reveal himself."

His superior grimaced. "Something like that. And have his driver come in. We need to talk."

Lubyanka prison, 14 January 1937

A guard delivered another letter from my wife.

Dearest husband!

Georgie and I are still at Evsey and Esfir's apartment in Leningrad. I don't know how they put up with it, but they do. Yesterday your lawyer Comrade Kutuzov came to see me. He brought good news. The authorities informed him that you've been very helpful, and he's sure that this will speed settlement of your case. In his words, if you "keep on course" it's likely that your salary will be restored. I was greatly relieved to hear this since Evsey and Esfir can't keep feeding and lodging us indefinitely. Your lawyer said he will visit you after you testify. He will bring documents for you to sign, including a petition for release and so forth.

Georgie's health seems stable. You know that he's never had the energy he enjoyed after his treatments in France, and I'm looking forward to taking him back to the sanitarium in Berck-Plage when you return.

I telephoned Alexander to thank him for paying the lawyer. He said not to worry, that his new book has drawn good reviews and is bringing in royalties. A copy is on its way and will hopefully get past the censors.

Evsey and Alexander asked me to convey their personal greetings. Alexander also passes on his enthusiastic endorsement of how Comrade Kutuzov is handling your case. He's certain that if you continue cooperating everything will turn out well.

That's all I can think to write. Please remember that you are always in our thoughts.

All our love, Galina

So there you have it. This lawyer Kutuzov ('cooperation is essential!') will come see me, but *after* I testify. He's apparently convinced my family that I'm being held for legitimate reasons. Naturally, once I take the stand I'll never be able to persuade them otherwise. Galina will be perfectly within her rights to divorce me, and even if she doesn't I'll never be in her good graces again. Once these reprehensible lies become part of the record there will be no convincing anyone otherwise.

The one blessing is that dear Georgie seems to be holding his own. Going to France would be wonderful, but even if my marriage survives there's little hope of getting an exit visa. Would Moscow want someone who knows what I know running around Europe?

Well, enough – I'm beginning to sound like Dmitry!

It's amazing how quickly captives start sharing their most intimate thoughts. Leonid and I have chatted endlessly. He speaks of nearly all his relations with great fondness. One exception is his brother Igor. A highly respected scientific man, he is the one family member who might be in a position to intercede. So far, though, there's no indication that he's tried. My best guess, and what I told Leonid, is that Igor's probably been warned to keep out of it. Vyshinsky is unlikely to let anything stand in the way of doing the General Secretary's bidding, and coming out on Leonid's behalf could have serious repercussions. Moral satisfaction can't feed a family.

There's another possibility. It may be that the authorities downplayed the seriousness of Leonid's situation to his brother. Maybe they've convinced Igor that this will blow over and that protesting would be counterproductive. From what I detect in my brother Alexander's letters that might explain his posture as well.

Of course, Leonid and I are different. All he wanted was to practice his profession, tend to his loved ones and be left alone. He purposely steered clear of politics, kept mum during worker meetings and never questioned Stalin's policies. In these respects he was my precise opposite. And his life would have taken a wholly different trajectory, too, except that one day there was an accidental explosion at the mine where he worked, and an evil genius decided to use it as evidence of a ridiculous conspiracy.

How many loyal Soviet citizens must be cut down before the General Secretary is satisfied? How has such rot come to consume our great socialist experiment? Why are such questions even necessary?

Georgie (1928-29)

Vladimir suspected that something was seriously amiss when he noticed that Alexander was alone on the platform. As the date of his home visit approached Galina's letters had taken on an increasingly distant quality, and her absence from the station fueled his anxieties. Had she found out about his indiscretions? How could that even be possible? But when he exited the railcar and his sibling hugged him in a way usually reserved for greeting children, Vladimir realized that he had steeled himself for the wrong catastrophe. Alexander wasn't the type to shed tears over a woman, and most assuredly not someone else's.

In 1905 the Nobel Prize in Physiology or Medicine was awarded to the German physician Robert Koch for culturing and identifying the slender, rod-shaped bacillus Mycobacterium tuberculosis. Known since Greek times as phthisis, or "consumption," the disease was endemic to Eastern Europe, periodically ravaging its overcrowded cities. Other than for Dr. Koch's tuberculin remedy, a concoction made from dead bacilli that ultimately proved useless as a cure but a lifesaver as a diagnostic device, tuberculosis was mostly treated with rest and nutrition, and in cases where it settled in bones and joints, through immobilization.

When the brothers entered the ward Galina was sitting by the bedside, watching her three-year old sleep. Georgie's leg was in a plaster cast to the knee. Alexander had already informed Vladimir of the basics. His son's reluctance to get on his feet had nothing to do with his being slow to develop. After Ludvika's insistent demands for a more thorough examination doctors discovered a tubercular pustule deep in the child's right ankle.

Galina turned her head. She took quiet measure of her husband. He had been away fifteen months, and the passage of time had done him well. His face, no longer puffy from too much drink, had regained some of the angular, boyish qualities she once found so attractive, and his physique seemed leaner and more robust. For once he seemed healthy and vigorous. If that could only be said about their son!

231

"I didn't want to frighten you about nothing," she explained, gently pulling away from her husband's embrace. "When we found out for sure you were already on your way home."

Vladimir felt unbearably guilty, as if Georgie's condition was his punishment for carrying on an affair. It was all he could do not to throw himself at his wife's feet right then and there and beg her forgiveness. Then he looked at his boy, and his thoughts turned to someone other than himself.

They sat down with the physician, a middle-aged woman whose eyes reflected the strain of caring for patients for whom available treatments held little promise. "There is some good news. The infection doesn't appear to have spread. We haven't detected any pulmonary involvement."

"Are you certain it's tuberculosis?" Vladimir asked.

"I'm afraid so." The doctor held the X-Ray to the light and pointed to the ankle. "It's readily observable. There's severe bone damage, but the bacilli appear well encapsulated and we've detected no changes since the first radiogram. Unless a patient's defenses are compromised for some other reason these cases need not become generalized. With proper care – and God's will – it won't."

Vladimir and Galina exchanged an apprehensive glance. The physician realized that invoking the Lord's name only managed to frighten the couple.

"I'm sorry. All I meant was that the capsule seems intact. The disease doesn't have to spread."

Vladimir inspected the image closely. "Can you take it out?"

"Surgery is risky; the bacillus might spread. Look, most of us carry the bug, but no more than ten percent get sick. Why it struck your son and lodged where it did we'll never know, but be thankful it's not in his lungs. With plenty of rest, good air and proper nutrition he'll outlive us all."

The physician picked up a shiny brace, of the kind used by the seriously disabled. "We're fitting it tomorrow." She tried to ignore the horrified look on Vladimir's face. "Your wife is familiar with its use. Listen to her. She's been devouring the literature and is as well informed about treatment protocols as anyone on staff."

Ludvika came to the hospital. She settled into a cot next to her grandson and sent his parents away.

Vladimir and Galina took a taxi to their apartment. He was stunned by the city's shabby appearance. In reality nothing had changed, but after his time in bustling Tokyo, Moscow seemed extraordinarily dull. That led to another jolt of guilt, and the distraught husband nearly blurted out everything in the back seat. His self-absorption was so complete that it never occurred to him that his wife might be dealing with her own demons.

Galina took out the special bottle of vodka that her mother bought for the occasion and set out two glasses. Fifteen months had passed, and the thought that she and this near-stranger would be sharing a bed seemed oddly distasteful. She filled the tumblers and downed a shot. That went down so well that she had another.

She was about to gulp a third when a hand gently stopped her. "Why don't you go to bed, Galya? I'll make myself comfortable out here."

"Thank you. Maybe I should."

Galina couldn't sleep. She switched on the light and reached for one of the journals from the hospital library. She turned the page.

The performance came to an end. Rhythmic applause surged through the hall as the corps of ballet took to the stage. For a few blissful moments Galina and her colleagues set aside the pains, the sprains, the torturous exercises and endless, wearying rehearsals they endured for the sake of that most demanding of art forms. When the principals stepped forward with their exaggerated curtsies she remained in place, for she was also a soloist, and when the other soloists withdrew she held fast, for she was the prima ballerina, the one whom the composer had in mind when he put pen to score.

She woke to a soft, melodious baritone. A tipsy man sat on the edge of her bed. He was singing the ballad of *Stenka Razin*.

"...*A ana, patupiv ochi,*
Ni zhiva i ni mertva,
Molcha slushait jmelny,
Atmanavi slava..."

Vladimir paused. "Remember? We argued, and then I left for Archangel."

Galina's defenses crumbled. She gently stroked her husband's stubble. "So, does the drunk Ataman really intend to drown me?"

"According to the score, only if you're a princess."

"Well, no problem there, comrade." She patted the mattress. "Come to bed and we'll discuss it further."

Vladimir let his wife sleep in and returned to the hospital by himself the next morning. He found Ludvika on the cot, snoring.

"Shhh," Georgie cautioned. "Nana sleeping."

Vladimir was pleasantly surprised. He had never heard the child say anything but gibberish. He placed Georgie's hand to his lips. "Daddy."

Georgie flashed a large smile. "You're my daddy."

"That's right, I am."

"Daddy went far away."

"Yes, and I've come back."

Georgie's face contorted. He struggled for the right words. "Stay...?"

"For a while. When I come back again, it will be forever. I promise."

Georgie seemed puzzled. "Forever," his father explained, "means a very, very long time."

Georgie stretched out his arms. "This long?"

Vladimir stroked the boy's hair. "Yes, that's about right."

Ludvika readied to leave. She summoned Vladimir into the hallway. "What have you been spending your money on, son-in-law?"

Her harsh tone cut to the quick. "Um...nothing special. Wasn't I sending enough?"

"Don't take me for a fool, Volya! You know that you weren't! Do you intend for the marriage to last?"

"Of course."

"Then finish that business in Japan and get yourself home."

Vladimir smiled weakly. "You know, I had that conversation last night."

Ludvika's expression didn't change. "Someone came looking for you while you were in Japan."

"Really? Galina didn't tell me..."

"She doesn't know, Vladimir Georgievich. And won't, unless you spill it. A woman came to the door in the middle of the night. Frumpy, maybe a little crazy, too. She said her name was Anna Mikhailovna."

"Was she alone?"

"As far as I could tell. I asked, but the woman wouldn't tell me what it was about. She was very disappointed, almost panic-stricken when I said that you were away."

"But Galina knows all about Anna! Why didn't...?"

Ludvika seemed surprised. "She does? Well...your wife wasn't home. She was at a...political meeting."

Vladimir sensed that Galina was leaving something unspoken. His curiosity turned into dread. It took him a moment to catch his breath. "A late-night political meeting?"

"I might be mistaken about the hour, Volya. Anyway, be happy that she wasn't home. This person was acting very strangely. Who knows who might have sent her."

"Did she leave an address? A way to contact her?"

"No, nothing. She kept looking around. It was like she was hiding."

Georgie quickly adapted to the brace. Within days the boy was scurrying around, surprising everyone who had become used to his passivity. Galina devoted herself to working with the child. Through research she learned of sanatoriums which had achieved remarkable success in prolonging and improving their patients' lives and keeping bone tuberculosis at bay. She wrote to a well-regarded children's clinic in coastal France to inquire about a placement. If there was a way to help the boy she was determined to find it.

On a day when his family was busy running errands Vladimir paid a visit to the headquarters of the Moscow militia. A policeman directed him to an office in the detective bureau.

Lev greeted his comrade warmly. "I've been reading your dispatches in *Pravda*, Volya. They're fascinating! Who would think that socialism would find such an enthusiastic response among Japanese workers?"

"Thank you." Vladimir noticed that boxes of personal belongings were scattered on the floor. "Are you coming or going?"

"Going. I'm taking charge of the homicide squad in Leningrad."

"It seems that police work agrees with you. Last I heard you were an ordinary detective."

"Fighting crime isn't glamorous but at least our scalawags are really that. Militiamen are mostly good men but terribly uneducated. My superiors think that I can introduce a more modern approach. But that's not why you're here." Lev produced a thick file. "No notes," he cautioned, waiting until he got a nod. "You have thirty minutes. And please give my regards to Galya."

Lev left. Vladimir opened the folder. Inside were reports from the militia and GPU, the surviving reservist's statement, three autopsy findings, a memorandum describing a technical examination by a firearms expert, and a jailer's declaration. There had obviously been a serious effort to get at the truth. Only the suspect's true cause of death was unknown. Vladimir read the closing memorandum by a supervisory inspector from the Lubyanka.

JULIUS WACHTEL

SECRET
JOINT STATE POLITICAL DIRECTORATE
14 August 1927
Subject: Review of investigation by Ukraine militia and GPU
into the murders of reservist Repin and committeeman Bazhenov
by kulak Idzi Nikolayevich Rutkowski.

There is no controversy that on 6 June the kulak Rutkowski
disarmed reservist Repin and slit his throat, then used Repin's
pistol to kill committeeman Bazhenov. This conclusion is based on
the statement of Repin's partner, reservist Melnikov, observations
of militia and GPU officers who went to the scene, autopsy
findings, and the conclusions of the expert who compared the
bullet removed from Bazhenov's head to unexpended ammunition
in Repin's pistol. However, it cannot be confirmed to the same
degree of certainty that kulak Rutkowski's death was a suicide.

According to the original inquiry, kulak Rutkowski shot Repin
and Bazhenov dead. He then told reservist Melnikov to alert
the authorities. Melnikov left. He returned with militia and
GPU. Rutkowski surrendered without incident and immediately
confessed. Melnikov read the confession and affirmed that it was
an accurate account of what took place.

Kulak Rutkowski was held in a temporary cell in the militia
office. Jailer Nikolsky, who works during the daytime, insisted that
as a matter of routine he removes and tags belts and shoelaces to
prevent suicides. Jailer Nikolsky was present when Provincial GPU
officers Frenkel and Tikhonov arrived and took the kulak to an
interview room. Frenkel and Tikhonov said they interrogated the
kulak for approximately five hours, then personally returned him
to his cell because the jailer had left. When Jailer Nikolsky came
back the next morning he found the kulak Rutkowski dead, hanging
from a crossbar with a belt around his neck. Jailer Nikolsky couldn't
determine if this was the same belt that he took from the kulak.
It did not have a tag. His records confirm that he took a belt and
shoelaces but he could not find either item in the storage cabinet.

At the autopsy the physician found a large welt on the right side

236

of kulak Rutkowski's head. Examination revealed that the kulak would have died from cerebral hemorrhage had he not asphyxiated.

The undersigned re-interviewed reservist Melnikov, Jailer Nikolsky and GPU officers Frenkel and Tikhonov. None remembers this injury. All insist that their original accounts were correct. Other relatives and workers who were at the farm told police and provincial GPU that they were in the fields when the murders took place and have no idea what happened. None knew of any preexisting injuries to kulak Rutkowski's head. By the time I arrived all had been transported to camps in the Far East and could not be re-interviewed.

During the search for kulak Rutkowski's wife Anna Mikhailovna and their two minor children the undersigned interviewed her brother Iosif Mikhailovich. He confirmed that his sister and her children lived for a brief period at his apartment in Dnepropetrovsk but left without notice while he was at work. He said that he does not know where they went and has not heard from them.

There being no further leads it is recommended that Iosif Mikhailovich be transported for failing to report his sister's odd behavior to the authorities, that Jailer Nikolsky be disciplined for failing to remove the prisoner's belt, and that Ukraine GPU officers Frenkel and Tikhonov be admonished for not noticing that the prisoner was wearing a belt when they placed him in his cell.

Tarasov

Inspector for Internal Affairs

Vladimir left the file on Lev's desk. None of it brought him any closer to Anna, and trying to track her down was far too risky. Neither was he in any position to help her brother, who was probably in a Siberian labor camp for doing nothing more than giving his sister a place to stay.

A few days before Vladimir's return to Tokyo the family got together at Alexander and Elena's apartment. George Romm was not feeling up to the trip so Evsey and Esfir left him in care of a neighbor. Ludvika prepared a feast of boiled dumplings stuffed with a delicious mixture whose ingredients she coyly refused to divulge. "Everyone is entitled to take one secret to the grave," she insisted.

Alexander helped himself to a second serving. "What I don't understand is why you're going back, brother. Let them find someone else to write about young women leaping off cliffs."

Evsey was curious. "Leaping from cliffs? What's that about?"

"There's an epidemic of suicide among young Japanese," Vladimir said. "Girls forced into unpleasant marriages, failing students who fear facing their parents, that sort of thing. Youths are under tremendous pressure to fulfill their obligations to their families and the Emperor. Some can't handle it."

"That's what makes our system so much better," Alexander boasted. "Socialism doesn't suppress initiative – it channels it for the public good."

Evsey scowled. "Is that what you call driving peasants from their ancestral lands? 'Channeling'?"

"Every peasant has the opportunity to participate in a collective. If they choose not to..."

Evsey stood his ground. "I don't think it's that simple, Sasha. If you want to feed a hungry nation, disparaging successful farmers and exiling them because they refuse to hand over their hard-earned gains is hardly the solution."

It was a reasoned reply. But Alexander refused to be shown up. "Look, excesses happen in every movement. You can't hold up progress because of a few mistakes." He turned to Vladimir. "You're awfully quiet, brother. What do you think – unofficially, of course?"

Vladimir collected his thoughts. "There are arguments on both sides. Maybe collectivization is the way to go. But the revolution's no longer in diapers. One would think that we might have learned how to proceed less cruelly."

"Brother, you amaze me!" Evsey exclaimed. "Of course, I agree wholeheartedly. Yet all your work in Japan emphasizes our superiority. For example, that piece about their subways..."

"The 'kilometer to nowhere'," Alexander laughed. "It was very amusing."

"Only if you ignore the inconvenient fact that we have nothing to approach it," Evsey snapped. "Japan has department stores, with restaurants on top! Meanwhile we stand in line to buy cigarettes. If they awarded decorations for wasting time, I'd be Hero of the Queue!"

The thought of Evsey with a chest full of medals made everyone laugh. Ludvika seized on the opportunity to bring out a tray of blueberry-stuffed pastries. Vladimir playfully grabbed her.

"Come with me to Tokyo," he implored.

Husband and wife lay quietly in bed. Nothing between them seemed close to being settled.

"I'm glad you told me about Anna's visit," Galina said. "I feel terrible about not being here when she needed us."

"Her situation isn't your fault, Galya. Lev Alexandrovich showed me the investigation file about her husband."

"What did it say?"

"Do you really want to know?"

Galina moved closer. "If there's to be any hope for us, maybe I should."

Vladimir sat up. For the next few minutes he described in exacting detail what happened on that dismal day in a once prosperous corner of the Ukrainian countryside.

His voice trailed off. Galina touched his arm. "You must have really loved her."

"Maybe. What I was really infatuated with were big ideas. Robust, red-cheeked peasants gazing at fields redolent with grain, a look of steely determination in their eyes. We were so enthusiastic! A society without caste or rank, everyone laboring in harmony, not one child denied the necessities of life."

"It will happen. I'm sure of it. We must give communism a chance."

They heard knocking. Alexander and Evsey were at the door, their faces drawn with sorrow. Evsey spoke first.

"I'm so sorry, Volya. We just got the message. Father had a heart attack and passed away."

Lubyanka prison, 15 January 1937

Radek brought news about the trial. It will begin in eight days and last one week. Bukhartsev and I will be the first to testify. It's our job to build the "edifice" on which the house of cards will rise. Should everything go well – meaning, if we lie our butts off – we can expect to be released as soon as our own cases get "tidied up," whatever that means. Then, who knows? I can't imagine simply waltzing back into the newsroom. ('Hello, how are things?') At this point even Siberia sounds good.

Radek left with Leonid. I feel sorry for my cellmate; he's much too gentle a soul to be among those wolves.

During exercise Dmitry and I ran into a balding, middle-aged fellow with deep-set eyes, high cheekbones and a dimpled chin. It took us a moment to realize that he was the beat-up foreigner whom we watched being led down the corridor. The man introduced himself in excellent though heavily-accented Russian. He is Alex Mikhailovich Stein, a contract engineer from Germany. Interestingly, he grew up in Russian-occupied Latvia. And yes, he is also a witness in the trial. That makes five: myself and my cellmate Tamm, Dmitry and his cellmate Loginov, and Stein.

Stein was arrested while working at an electrical station that was supposed to furnish power to the mines in Leninsk. I say "supposed" because broken equipment and a scarcity of spare parts caused frequent interruptions in the generation of electricity, disabling, among other things, the pumps that sucked water from the pits. There was no money to fix things, so the situation festered. When heavy rains came there was no juice for the pumps, so the mines flooded and dozens of miners died unspeakable deaths. Truly, there can be nothing worse than drowning.

Naturally, the bosses couldn't admit the real reason for the disaster, so they called in the GPU. They promptly "proved" that Hitler orchestrated the sabotage of German machinery so the Soviet Union would have to buy more! But how could the Führer's tentacles reach all the way into the Soviet Union's heartland? That's easy: the German contract workers were really agents of the Nazis!

Our brilliant guardians of State security quickly put a bunch of German engineers and technicians through hell. Stein at first denied everything, but they beat him half to death, so he signed everything the bastards put in front of him. It was then off to Moscow.

Stein's bruises have healed, but he very much remains a beaten-down man. I'm not naïve – there have always been officers who use force during interrogations. Most I knew frowned on the practice, as you can get a lot more out of people by treating them decently. But whatever one thinks of beating criminals, abusing innocent persons to make them falsely confess is unforgivable. That's when one knows that the apparatus of justice has been completely perverted.

The Tokkō (1929-30)

Alexander Antonovich Troyanovsky wasn't the type to stand out. Short and slightly-built, clean shaven, hair neatly trimmed and parted on the left, he seemed just like another among the legions of functionaries who congested the Soviet bureaucracy. But on meeting the man opinions tended to change. Few officials seemed as poised and well-spoken, and fewer still as immaculately attired, the gleaming cufflinks poking out just so from the sleeves of a bespoke, finely tailored suit that would set back an ordinary civil servant half a year's wages.

For Troyanovsky was no ordinary bureaucrat. Years before the Revolution, when the young Stalin was on the run from the Czar's secret police, it was Troyanovsky, Lenin's man in Vienna, who gave the rude, unpolished Georgian a place to stay. The USSR's future Ambassador to the U.S. then spent months helping the Man of Steel produce his first (some would say, last) significant tract, a journal-length treatise on nationalities that became a classic of Communist literature. Troyanovsky's hospitality would one day lead the USSR's dictator to forgive his former benefactor's Jewish ethnicity.

Troyanovsky was posted as ambassador to Tokyo while Romm was on home leave. One of the envoy's duties was to direct the spies who used various official positions as cover. He was especially intrigued by the *Tass* correspondent. Their initial conversation took place a few days after Romm's return. Troyanovsky found him intelligent, articulate and, best of all, a practical man rather than one of those wearying ideologues whom the Party seemed determined to foist on the foreign service. Despite his breeding Romm didn't affect an air of superiority, nor did he needlessly humble himself. Best of all, not once did he try to disguise ignorance with dogma or doubletalk, the irritating qualities that made so many officials useless, even dangerous when there were crucial decisions to be made. The USSR needed people with brains, verve and, most importantly, a realistic sense of their limits, and this comrade seemed more than qualified on each count.

There was one problem. The embassy's chief security officer reported that Romm spent most weekends nesting with a young Japanese lady. Although this shacking up seemed no more objectionable than the security man's own deplorable habit of getting blindingly drunk in licensed whorehouses (that information came from the other member of the security team), not reporting his relationship with a Japanese citizen was a serious breach of regulations. Troyanovsky could have sent him back to Moscow in an instant, yet he hesitated. In only a short time he had grown fond of Romm, an affinity that he was certain came from much more than their shared heritage.

A purge was on, and Moscow's determination to strip the Party of all but its most ideologically committed acolytes was causing a lot of grief. Only an hour earlier the chairman of the committee overseeing the process dropped Vladimir's personnel folder into Troyanovsky's in-basket. A brief note was clipped to the folder. He was reading it when Romm walked in.

"Sit down."

Vladimir normally briefed the ambassador each morning. But this time his superior's welcome seemed unusually terse.

"Comrade Ambassador, if there's a better time…"

Troyanovsky put Romm's file away. "No, stay. Tell me, how's your Japanese comrade's wife doing?"

"Much better. Our money paid for a doctor and medicine. But I'm afraid there's nothing that can save the Japanese Communist Party. My agent's been all over Tokyo trying to organize the few comrades who haven't been arrested. Those he found are too busy watching their backs to be of any use."

Troyanovsky grimaced. So much for the Comintern's grandiose plans! "So what's this you said about your driver? Isn't he just another of the Tokkō's men?"

"Of course. But he's been making some helpful noises."

Troyanovsky was intrigued. Developing a source inside Japan's supposedly impregnable security police would be a major coup. "Are you sure they're not just trying to plant a double?"

"I'm certain they are. But doubling is a tricky business; you never know how it might turn out. Ichiro's curious and very bright. His father lost his seat in the Diet years ago for arguing that Japan's caste system was leading the Empire to promote fools and yes-men."

"He got kicked out? It's verified?"

"Pardon me for saying so, Comrade Ambassador, but I wouldn't have otherwise mentioned it."

Some might have bristled. Not the ambassador. Bone-tired of the yes-men who infested the Communist ranks, he recognized in this officer the spirit that propelled the Revolution. Shortly after their marriage, Troyanovsky's young wife took part in helping the Tiflis robbers get away. She was arrested by the Czar's secret police and but for a stroke of luck would have been imprisoned or hanged. Well, those times were long gone. Nowadays no one made a move without signed approvals in quadruplicate.

Troyanovsky cleared his throat. "Go ahead, but be careful. By the way, when did you last have contact with Karl Radek?"

Vladimir was astonished. Where did this come from? "It's been years. He wrote once from exile. I never answered."

Troyanovsky gave Romm the note from his in-basket. "What am I to make of this?"

Alexander Antonovich!

I am forwarding the file for Romm, Vladimir Georgievich, *Tass* correspondent to Tokyo. Our committee has decided to recommend that he be denied re-enrollment in the Party for the reason of his anti-Communist activities, specifically, his association with Karl Radek, and his signature on the Trotskyite "Declaration of the Eighty-Three."

Your comments and recommendations are solicited and will be attached to our report to the Central Control Commission in Moscow. Please inform Romm of this communication. Please also advise him that he has two weeks to file a written reply and to petition for a personal appearance to plead his case, should he so desire.

With Communist regards,

Orlov, Chairperson

Vladimir paled. "Comrade Ambassador, signing the declaration was perfectly legal! My name was one of thousands!"

Troyanovsky was dismayed. For all his excellent qualities, Romm could be strangely clueless. "Comrade, this isn't about what's legal – it's about loyalty! If the Party decides that only comrades with horns sticking from their heads can be members, so be it!"

"Are you suggesting, Comrade Ambassador, that I grow a horn?"

Troyanovsky sighed. "No, Volya, I couldn't expect you to do that. Maybe pretending to have one will be good enough."

Vladimir and Fumiko had an awkward reunion. Before leaving he made the mistake of sharing something of his feelings. She pretended to take it as flattery, but on his return made certain to mention an imaginary boyfriend, a small untruth that would hopefully bring Vladimir-san to his senses. She had heard of other girls being beaten, even killed by jealous lovers and was relieved when he took the news calmly. In any event, their time together was now limited. Fumiko was no longer a novice. "Auntie" had placed her in the service of a wealthy Japanese industrialist, and she was available only when he was out of town.

He hadn't seen Fumiko for nearly a month when word came that she would be free that weekend. Vladimir found her busily writing in her Russian workbook. Her progress was remarkable: only weeks into study the bright college student was dispatching intricate conjugations with startling efficiency.

"This verb ending should be feminine." It was Fumiko's singular error in an otherwise perfect essay. Years of experience with Japanese characters lent Fumiko a wonderful dexterity of hand, and she was already writing Cyrillic in the cursive, her finely sculpted handiwork proving more than a match to what a Russian might produce.

"Thank you, Vladimir-san." She quickly made the correction. "I'm embarrassed to be so careless!"

Vladimir took out a newspaper clipping. "Your work is wonderful. And here's your reward!"

Mary Pickford and Douglas Fairbanks, Fumiko's favorite Hollywood couple, were on a worldwide tour. They were scheduled to appear at a screening in Asakusa that very evening. Vladimir obtained two tickets for the event from the embassy's cultural affairs attaché, who was happy to accept an expensive flask of sake in return. Why someone might care that much about bourgeois American film stars was none of his concern.

Fumiko screeched and ran off to get ready. The prepositional case would wait.

Caught in another gridlock, the embassy car inched along the Ginza. Vladimir watched as fashionably-dressed pedestrians promenaded by. Most men were attired in suits, but nearly every woman wore clogs and a kimono.

"Why do the genders dress so differently, Ichiro?"

"Don't let our modern skyline fool you, Vladimir-san. Japanese culture hasn't been as affected by outsiders as some think. The other day I saw a teenage girl in pants. Everyone was pointing and laughing. It was horrible! Anyway, kimonos are much more comfortable. I always throw one on when I get home."

Vladimir's thoughts drifted to the previous evening. He smiled at the thought of Fumiko's reaction to "The Gaucho." Not only had Douglas Fairbanks played a decidedly un-heroic role, but Mary Pickford, his real-life wife, had only a bit part. Fumiko took the snub as an ill omen of the stars' reputedly stormy relationship, even if they did seem lovey-dovey together.

Ichiro braked sharply as a pedicab darted from the curb. At this pace it would take an hour to get to Asakusa. Vladimir settled back to think. His life was so weighed down with obligations and cluttered with misunderstandings that finding his way through the maze seemed hopeless. His infatuation with Fumiko had taken on a disturbing quality. Whenever he was in her presence he felt frighteningly vulnerable, like a lovesick boy. Until this moment, in the cacophony of a Tokyo afternoon, he had never understood why a man would take a mistress. Perhaps he still didn't.

And if that wasn't headache enough, there was his not-so-little disagreement with the Party.

The plainclothesman set down his newspaper. Romm was coming his way. Ignoring basic tradecraft, his quarry didn't scan the sidewalk but looked straight ahead, and when he reached the subway entrance rushed straight down, just like an ordinary commuter, his mind apparently on other things.

Excellent!

A few hours later the officer was back at headquarters.

"I wasn't sure they were together until I spotted them sitting side by side in the subway car."

The inspector nodded. "Romm's companion was carrying something?"

"He had a large envelope when they boarded at Asakusa. But his arms were free when we exited at Tawaramachi."

"So Romm must have taken it!"

"It would seem so, Inspector-san. The car was crowded and I didn't want to accidentally lock eyes, so I can't be positive."

"He didn't exit?"

"No. As far as I could tell Romm remained aboard. Only his contact got out. I followed him to the junkyard. He let himself in with a key. I lost sight as he neared a shack."

"Well, that's good enough for me." The inspector's bulky frame jiggled as he approached the map. "Show me where this junkyard is."

Vladimir entered the embassy conference room. He was dreading the encounter. Within a few days the three officials politely shaking his hand would be sending on a recommendation that could end his career.

"Let's begin." Comrade Orlov, the chairperson, was a feared ideologue, an ambitious *apparatchik* who got ahead by finding fault in others. "This, Comrade Romm, is your opportunity to make a case for remaining in the Party. We're aware of your technical work, which I think everyone agrees is satisfactory, so there's no need to get into that. What we'd like to hear are your views about communism. If you'd like to throw in a candid self-assessment, we're all ears."

"Thank you," Vladimir replied. He made eye contact with each member of the panel. While Orlov was by the most influential, decisions were by majority rule.

"For the last two years I've been *Tass* correspondent to Tokyo. I've also been working with Alexander Antonovich on a certain matter of the highest secrecy. What I've learned makes me more certain than ever that it's vital for the government and the Party to speak with a single voice. Anything that threatens unity only arms our enemies. I may not have always seemed committed to this principle, but I assure you that's a lesson that's sunk in."

A committeeman interrupted. "Do you include our hosts among these 'enemies', comrade?"

"The Empire's cruel suppression of Japanese communists speaks for itself. My dispatches for *Tass* document a disturbing tendency towards ultra-nationalism, not much different from what I observed in Germany. Unless Japan curbs these impulses they will come into conflict with many nations, not only ours. So we must be prepared. Unity is essential."

Orlov had little use for Romm, whom he considered a pretentious upstart. But he didn't expect that the man would embrace the same principles that were being advanced to discredit him. "No one can disagree with unity, comrade. But weren't you encouraging factionalism by signing that despicable document?"

"Yes, although not purposefully. I thought that bringing in other voices would strengthen the USSR. Now that I know better I intend to do everything in my power to support a unified approach."

"That all sounds well and good, comrade, but there is no longer any such thing as a "loyal" opposition. What if you don't agree with a particular course of action?"

"As far as I'm concerned, once a decision is made its merits have been settled, so there can be no disagreement. You mentioned self-assessment. Well, here's mine. My vanity led me astray. It's an error that I'm determined not to repeat."

Orlov glanced at his committeemen. They seemed ready to decorate the fool. He rose, signaling that the hearing was done.

"Thank you, Comrade Romm. You've certainly given us a lot to think about."

Other than for Orlov, who probably smelled a rat, Vladimir thought that it went well. His insipid, fawning comments noticeably softened the other committeemen. There was no greater fear in the Party than disunity and factionalism, and no better way to reassure apprehensive comrades than by artfully applying a healthy dose of self-criticism.

His assessment was confirmed several days later when Troyanovsky called him in. The ambassador was in an expansive mood. He poured vodka for both and raised his glass.

"*Za vashe zdorov'ye!*"

Surprisingly, the vote was 3-0 in Vladimir's favor. Troyanovsky, who secretly lobbied for Romm with a committeeman he knew, learned that Orlov went along to avoid an embarrassing split. Still, there was a quota to fulfill, so in the end the committee proved its mettle by voting to purge a different comrade. Unanimously, of course.

Troyanovsky then turned to a matter of real importance.

"This, my friend, is either the best piece of intelligence that I've seen for years, or the biggest pile of crap." He held up a special report that Vladimir had just completed. "Let me get it straight. Two years ago, give or take, Baron Tanaka, the Japanese Prime Minister, wrote a memorandum to the Emperor. This document was supposedly so explosive that its contents were to remain strictly between them. Somehow a copy landed in the lap of the Chinese secret service. It then made its way, again no one knows how, to the intelligence chief of the Japanese Communist Party, who buried it – and here we're speaking literally – in his mother-in-law's yard, under her prized cherry tree. He gets snatched by the Tokkō during the roundup, but not before telling the story to his wife. She then unearths the memo and gives it to your agent, the one who lives in the junkyard. Have I got it right?"

"Yes, Comrade Ambassador. As you know, this document sets out Japan's long-range strategy for conquering, well, the world. I'm quite certain that Chinese intelligence passed it on to the Japanese Communist Party hoping that they would reveal its contents and make the Empire look bad."

Troyanovsky was perplexed. "But didn't you say that the document is probably a forgery?"

"That doesn't make it valueless. Whether or not Tanaka wrote it, it's stuffed full of salacious insider detail, things that only a few highly-placed Japanese know. Our analysts are convinced that regardless of its authenticity it accurately reflects the Prime Minister's imperialistic views."

Troyanovsky skimmed the report. "Conquer Manchuria...then China...then the USSR...then America. Of course they hate us – the War of 1905 was no picnic. Of course they covet our mineral deposits and fisheries. But their anger at the U.S. is mind-boggling!"

"America's stiff import tariffs have affected everyone, Comrade Ambassador. Japan depends on exports for survival. And now that the U.S. is throwing around its weight in the South Pacific..."

"You know, that came up last week. When I told the American consul that Japan didn't appreciate having frigates flying the Stars-and-Stripes cruising in its backyard, you know what he said? 'Who cares what they think? We'd swat them like a fly'!"

"Well, if all we had on our borders were Canada and Mexico, we'd probably feel equally confident..."

An ear-splitting whirring sound interrupted the conversation. The intercom buzzed.

"Comrade Ambassador, it's the flying ship!"

Everyone went outside to watch a fly-over by Germany's monumental Graf Zeppelin, a hydrogen-filled cylinder more than two-hundred meters in length.

Troyanovsky squinted. "I heard that they were coming for a visit. That's *another* country we ought to be taking seriously! Well, comrade, we've done enough for a day. Let's eat!"

Vladimir 's personal life felt hopelessly muddled, but now that his party card was secure his career prospects once again seemed promising. Over dinner the ambassador reemphasized his support and asked whether Romm and his family would be interested in accompanying him to Washington once diplomatic relations were established. Vladimir was flattered. It was an open secret that Troyanovsky was one of the General Secretary's favorites. One could do far worse than ride his coattails.

Too wound up to go to sleep, Vladimir hailed a cab and asked the driver to take him to the movie district in Asakusa. On the way his thoughts turned to Fumiko. Feeling reckless, he had the taxi swing by to see if she was home. As they pulled up he noticed that her apartment was full of college-aged Japanese, probably classmates, talking and listening to music. Fumiko was obviously throwing a party for her friends. He was only a client. Vladimir felt as humiliated as if he had already been sent away.

Fumiko watched the cab drive away. There was no question as to who was in the back seat. Why did he leave? She would have been delighted to introduce her Russian tutor. Men were so delicate!

Vladimir was at the movies when he realized that he hadn't heard from Katsuo for several days. To be sure, other issues had distracted him, but there was no excuse for abandoning his most important asset. There might be ways of smuggling the man and his wife to Vladivostok. He made a mental note and turned back to the film.

His concern was well-placed, if far too late. As Vladimir escaped into an American western, his star informer was in an interrogation room buried deep within Tokkō headquarters.

"Please tell me again," a police inspector asked, "how you received these injuries."

Katsuo's face was puffed out to twice its size. Two front teeth were missing, a cheekbone was crushed and his right eye was swollen shut.

"In...police car...coming from junkyard..."

The inspector glared at a plainclothesman. "Is that correct?"

"No, inspector. I mean, he resisted..."

"In the car?"

"No, during the arrest."

"Really. Must have been quite a fight." The inspector turned to Katsuo. "Why would an accountant and his wife abandon a nice apartment in Kodenmacho to live in a hovel?"

"Ah..."

"Please tell me, Katsuo-san, exactly what you were doing in Asakusa."

"I went to buy medicine for my woman..."

"Why didn't you use a pharmacy in your prefect? Aren't there drug stores in Tawaramachi?"

"Ah...medicine very expensive there..."

"What was in the envelope? Where did it go?"

"No envelope..."

"You're lying!" the plainclothesman screeched. "We watched you..."

"If you please." The inspector's stern tone froze the officer in his tracks. "We're done. Get a guard."

Katsuo was led away. The plainclothesman bowed. "I apologize for interfering with your examination, Inspector-san. It was just that..."

A fist flew, sending the man crashing to the floor. The inspector rubbed his knuckles. "As you can see, a strike from a right-handed man lands on the left. But the prisoner's most serious injuries were on the right. You're the only left-handed man in the squad, if I'm not mistaken."

The officer got on his knees. "I deeply apologize, Inspector-san. I didn't think..."

"No, I guess you didn't. We could have turned him into a double agent, maybe roped in that Soviet clown, but after what you and your boys did he's worthless. So tell me how you propose to make up for your stupidity."

"I will do anything you ask of me, Inspector-san. Anything."

"Fine. Go finish what you started. Then report back. We're not done with this Romm guy yet."

Ichiro broke the news the next day. He and Vladimir were in the embassy car, headed for an interview with a local official.

"Katsuo-san will turn up dead in some alley, the victim of 'hoodlums.' I don't understand, Vladimir-san. You had to know that the communists were finished. How could you place him in such danger?"

How, indeed. Vladimir felt ill. The man trusted him, and would now pay the price.

"What about his wife?"

"They left her in the junkyard. I have a friend who works in a hospital. They sent an ambulance."

"And you, Ichiro-san? Are you in trouble?"

"No, at least not yet. But you are in great danger. You must leave immediately."

"I can't turn tail and run," Vladimir protested. "It would be like admitting guilt!"

Ichiro maneuvered into a parking space and shut the engine. He turned to face the foreigner whom he had grown to consider a friend. He would extend himself one more time.

"Beg your pardon, Vladimir-san, but as far as the authorities are concerned, you *are* guilty. And for the Inspector this is personal. His father was killed in the 1905 war with Russia, and his anger at your country knows no bounds. He's already made plans to avenge Japan's honor. It would happen, just as surely as the sun rises. You wouldn't be the first *Gaijin* to turn up dead in a whorehouse."

Lubyanka prison, 16 January 1937

Leonid returned from his session with Radek. He looked ashen. For hours he lay on his bunk, staring at the ceiling. He hardly touched his dinner and even ignored our pet. He finally told me what happened.

Tamm's troubles began much like Stein's. In 1933 the second Five-Year plan set wildly unrealistic targets for mineral extraction. Managers were dismayed. Those foolish enough to warn that cranking things up that high would cause havoc were told to keep their mouths shut. The ones who persisted were fired or arrested as "wreckers."

Leonid's most recent job was as technical director at a Ukrainian chemical plant. Production quotas were absurdly high. Safety precautions were expensive and slowed things down, so they were ignored. Accidents were commonplace. Twice there were fatal gas explosions, both caused by broken exhaust fans. Everyone was aware of the risk of not venting fumes, but even if there had been money to buy replacement parts (there wasn't) interrupting production was unthinkable. The Plan abides no delay!

Tamm's superior was Ordzhonikidze, the same man to whom Stein reported. Thanks to his boss, Leonid managed to ride out the first catastrophe. He was even awarded a nice car – a Packard – for helping to contain the damage. But then there was a second accident. This time the authorities insisted it was sabotage. Relations with the Reich had turned sour, so despite the fact that Leonid was born in Russia, his German ancestry made him a natural target. His role is to point the finger at the man who purportedly recruited him to blow up the plant, a defendant named Pushin.

Leonid is scared witless. After finishing his story he lapsed into such deep sobs that jailers came to see what was wrong. These are not all bad fellows, and they escorted him to their bathhouse to tidy up. I later told Leonid that if he felt so poorly about testifying he could always refuse and take his chances. He shook his head sadly. Like the rest of us, Tamm fears for his family. He also feels hopelessly boxed in. Pushin, the man he is to falsely accuse, will be taking the stand to confess, and in so doing will denounce Leonid. That's exactly the embrace that I'm locked in with Radek.

Everyone, witness and accused alike, is in the same predicament. It's a masterful trap.

Berck-Plage (1930-31)

Otto's thoughts drifted to the joys of that morning's third croissant. The doctor had warned him about slathering butter on a delicacy that was already mostly that, but eating it dry – *mon oeil!* As for that other bit of unsolicited advice, to lose forty kilos...

"Inspector!" A tidy, impeccably groomed man wound his way through the lobby. He grabbed the rotund policeman in a friendly hug. "It's been a while! How's the *Sûreté* treating you?"

Otto tried to be heard above the din of foreign tongues. "Flying a desk is easy, Jean-Philippe. And you?"

"Ah, in this business nothing ever changes. Our borders are a sieve. They pour in, we send as many back as we can. Come." The French immigration chief led his visitor to a spacious office.

Otto settled into an ostentatious, excruciatingly uncomfortable period chair. "Louis Fifteenth?"

"Fourteenth, I believe. There are warehouses full of the stuff. We could furnish Versailles a hundred times over." He removed a folder from an intricately carved secretary and handed Otto a cable. "I suppose this is what you're after. It's from our office in Japan."

LE MINISTRE DES AFFAIRES ÉTRANGÈRES...Tokyo, 4 Novembre 1930...The Japanese Foreign Ministry advises that V. G. Romm, correspondent of the *Tass* news agency, hereinafter referred to as VGR, was well regarded and would be welcomed back...They extend their best wishes to him, his family and to the family member whose illness required VGR's sudden departure...But a trusted source in the Japanese government paints a wholly different picture...VGR was allegedly engaged in a disinformation campaign against the Empire...By day he posted acerbic comments about Japan while by night he worked with local communists to destabilize the

257

labor sector and impede the economy...He tried to recruit Japanese nationals including an officer of the foreign ministry as agents and succeeded in at least one instance...That agent's capture led VGR to fear he might be arrested so he fled the country under pretext...Considering the above it is urged that VGR be denied entry...M. Dupont

Otto brightened. "Well, I guess that's that." He rose to leave.

The immigration man didn't budge. His tone was grave. "Sit down, my friend."

"*Mon dieu*, Jean-Philippe, please don't tell me that..."

"We advise, the Minister decides. His point is that if we deny this Romm fellow a visa the Soviets will retaliate by denying entry to one of ours. Then we'll even the score, and so on and so forth. And after all's been said and done and we've kissed and made up, whomever they send will still be a spy. For now I'm afraid that we're stuck with him."

Otto hadn't heard about Romm for years when the request came in to investigate his application for a diplomatic visa. Such matters were usually assigned to junior detectives, but he did this one himself. His report, including a detailed account of the episode in Essen, ran a full ten pages. It was more than enough, he thought, to permanently bar the Bolshevik spy from contaminating the sacred soil of France. Alas, the inexplicable ways of diplomacy dictated otherwise.

He reluctantly conceded defeat. "When's our Bolshie set to arrive?"

"In spring. Actually, there is some good news. Romm's accredited to the disarmament talks in Geneva, so the conditions of his visa only permit him to be in France during breaks. He is cleared for Paris and Berck-Plage." The officer produced a medical form. "It's been verified by our Moscow office. Romm's boy suffers from tuberculosis of the bone. He'll be taking a cure at a children's sanatorium in Berck-Plage. His mother and grandmother will be in residence nearby."

Otto returned to his office. Persistence was the hallmark of a real detective. If he couldn't keep Romm out, he could at least try to make his life miserable. With fresh determination he inserted a fresh sheet of letterhead into the typewriter.

RÉPUBLIQUE FRANÇAISE

DIRECTION DE LA *SÛRETÉ* GÉNÉRALE

à Monsieur le Procureur Général de *la Confédération Helvétique*

10 Novembre 1930

I am pleased to furnish to our law enforcement colleagues in Switzerland the enclosed dossier on Vladimir Georgievich Romm, a Soviet journalist accredited to the League of Nations who we have learned will be attending the preparatory meetings for the forthcoming world disarmament conference in Geneva. In fact, Romm, a former revolutionary and political officer in the Soviet military, is a highly-regarded member of the Guépéou, the Soviet secret police. His disruptive activities in the Ruhr, which I personally investigated, and in Japan, where he pretended to be a *Tass* correspondent while running secret agents and promoting the Communist line, resulted in major diplomatic incidents.

It goes without saying that it would be highly useful for the security services of France and Switzerland to monitor Romm and share information about his activities and those of his fellow provocateurs. Naturally, the best solution would be to exclude him from Switzerland altogether. However, if that proves impossible, it is my opinion that Romm is worthy of very close observation.

We would be most grateful if you could apprise us of your decision in this case, and we pledge to keep you informed of any developments.

/s/ Giroux

Bouville was one of a string of sanatoria set along the French North Atlantic coast. Located on a steep rise not far from the water's edge, the immense architectural fantasy of red brick, stone columns and decorative balustrades housed three-hundred victims of the malady that was wreaking havoc on the children of Europe. Even in winter, when bitterly cold Channel winds engulfed the Pais de Calais, the porch was filled with young patients taking in the air whose professed curative powers held out what little hope there was in overcoming the dreaded disease.

Vladimir, Galina and Georgie strolled along the beach. In front lay an expanse of sand several kilometers in length. Every so often they passed by groups of youngsters playing in pools of water that collected on shore. Watched over by white-gowned attendants, the children seemed unusually frail, as though they could be knocked over by a good breeze. Riding atop his father's shoulders, Georgie felt an odd affinity. No one had explicitly said so, but he sensed that he would soon be among them.

Geneva was preparing to host the World Disarmament Conference, sponsored by the fledgling League of Nations. Vladimir was part of the Soviet delegation, purportedly a correspondent for *Tass*. He intended to accompany Galina, Ludvika and Georgie to the sanatorium at Berck-Plage before pushing on to Switzerland.

For reasons that he could well guess at France dithered issuing the necessary visas, stranding the family in Germany. In March 1931, when they had just about given up, approval finally came through and the Romms hurriedly resumed their voyage to the French coast.

Georgie was asleep on the veranda when the taxi pulled up. Ludvika watched her prickly daughter kiss Vladimir good-bye. France was a wonderful change from grim Moscow. Passing one's years in a tiny flat occasionally going to funerals was a dreary thought, and she was happy to have come along. Galina and Ludvika would stay in a local *pension* while Georgie received his treatments. Hopefully the boy's health would be sufficiently improved by summer so that the family could reunite in Paris when the conferees took their break.

An ear-piercing squeal of metal on metal signaled the train's arrival. Vladimir looked up from his English workbook. He was trying to reacquaint himself with the language, which he had studied at the university. A young man sitting across from Vladimir stirred awake. His eyes fell on Romm.

"Let me guess. Journalist?"

Vladimir extended a handshake. "Vladimir Romm. Correspondent for *Tass*, the Soviet telegraph agency. Sorry, my English is poor."

"I assure you it's better than my French." They shook hands. "John Whitaker, *New York Herald-Tribune*. I assume we're here for the same reason."

For someone so young the American seemed unusually self-assured. "Are you with the U.S. legation?"

"I'm just tagging along. The political climate in the U.S. isn't favorable to internationalists, and they're terrified of what I might write. I'm mostly treated like a mushroom."

It took Vladimir a moment to get it. "I think many in our profession feel the same."

"I'm happy to see that the Soviet Union is here. Have you been invited to join the League?"

"Not yet. We're observers, like the U.S. Unlike the U.S., it's not by choice."

"We've suffered from a bad case of isolationism since the Great War. So what do you think: will the talks bear fruit?"

Vladimir knew that his words could appear in the morning paper. He framed his response carefully. "The USSR is committed to peace, so we have hope. Of course, verification may be an obstacle. Is everyone willing to grant full access to their most secret military facilities? And how can we be sure that's all they have?"

"*Passeports, s'il vous plaît.....Reisepass, bitte.*" Nattily dressed Swiss border guards worked their way through the aisle. When one saw Vladimir's credentials his manner instantly stiffened. "*Citoyen Soviétique!*" he called out, alerting his superior and everyone else in the car.

Vladimir wasn't surprised. In the West, his passport always produced the same response: a flash of dread followed by a look of distaste, as though its bearer harbored a communicable disease. One glance at the seal with the star on top was enough to transform the most lackadaisical immigration inspector into a fierce warrior ready to protect his homeland from the claws of the bear.

A senior officer approached. His lips curled. "*Venez avec moi!*"

Vladimir was ushered inside the terminal through a side door. He wound up in a tiny room, its purpose made obvious by the small, bare table and two chairs.

"*Asseyez-vous!*"

Within minutes an enormously tall, perfectly bald official with a pencil-thin mustache entered the room. He carried a thick file. Vladimir noticed that as with other large men his hands were huge, the knuckles large as walnuts.

"My name is Bächtold," he announced. "Your visa, Herr Romm, was issued with the understanding that you are a bonafide correspondent for the *Tass* telegraphic agency."

"I am a correspondent."

The man held up a finger. "If you interrupt me again you will be placed in a cell. Do you understand?"

Vladimir nodded. "Excuse me. I only wish to clear up any confusion."

The man opened the folder. "Before the Revolution you were a Socialist Revolutionary. You switched to the Bolsheviks, for whom you campaigned in Vilna. You served in a Revolutionary Tribunal, and then performed special assignments for Soviet military intelligence and the GPU in Germany, France and, most recently, Tokyo, where you posed as a *Tass* correspondent. You left under highly questionable circumstances. Have I left anything out?"

Vladimir struggled to keep calm. It was as though the Swiss had his personnel file! "Like I said, Herr Bächtold, I'm a correspondent accredited to the League of Nations."

"No! You, Herr Romm, are a Soviet..."

A border guard cracked open the door and handed the official a note. He grimaced and rushed out. Soon there were sounds of a heated conversation, then the slamming of a door. Moments later the guard reappeared. He returned Romm's passport and ushered him to the street.

Whitaker was waiting in a taxi. "Jump in!" he yelled. As soon as Vladimir sat down the brash American leaned towards the driver. "*Schnell!*"

The cab sped off. Whitaker nervously peered through the rear glass. He kept quiet until they were well clear of the police station.

"Your luggage is in the trunk."

"Thank you." Vladimir wondered whether he was better off. Rescued by an American! How would that play in Moscow?

"My pleasure, comrade. Look, I behaved in a way that my paper wouldn't understand. So I won't mention it if you don't."

"That is very gracious."

"They can't touch us once we're in Geneva proper. If you didn't notice, they really, really don't like you, Mr. Romm."

"Please, call me 'Volya'."

"Great! You can call me 'Jack'."

"I thought your name was 'John'."

"It is. 'Jack' is like 'Volya'."

Vladimir smiled at his new friend. "Yes, I'm beginning to think so."

Lubyanka prison,
17 January 1937

Earlier today a guard took me to an office where Radek was awaiting with a heavily marked-up version of my testimony. Putting our past unpleasantness behind, we worked for hours, excising here, simplifying there, doing what we could to avoid the pitfall of contradiction, which is an easy trap to fall into when making up things on such a grand scale.

We ate lunch. It was the same meal as the guards, thick slices of bread and a bowl of *real* stew, with large chunks of meat and potatoes, the broth so much richer than prisoner gruel that I drank it like a beverage. Finally, a good belch!

Radek let on that Molchanov and Vyshinsky are seriously frustrated with my roommate. Ironically, they were counting on Leonid's evident political disinterest – he's never been a party member – to enhance his credibility when he testifies. He was assigned a vital role in the script, as an intermediary who passed on orders from the Reich Chancellery to the workers who sabotaged the mines. But Tamm chokes at the prospect of pointing the finger at others. That makes him worse than useless, for if he clams up on the stand or, even worse, backpedals, it could unravel the entire case. Radek pleaded for my help. "Leonid Evgenevich trusts you," he begged. "Please tell him to do the right thing."

Well, self-loathing is a condition to which I've become accustomed, but a man can only sink so far, and the thought of encouraging that gentle soul to join me in Hell was utterly disgusting. Radek noticed my reaction and, perhaps with a certain memory in mind, stopped pushing.

Sad to say, that wasn't the end of it. When I returned to my cell Leonid was pacing back and forth, ill with worry. He had detected dissatisfaction and feared that the bus might be leaving without him. "Please, I can't think straight," he pleaded. "Tell me what to do!"

His plaintive tone broke my heart. This terribly ethical man was entitled to an honest assessment. "This isn't just about a trial," I said. "Your wavering threatens a system that relies on falsehoods. Lies are no longer just the means: they're the ends, too."

Tamm went perfectly still. One could sense the wheels turning.

"Are you saying that communism is a lie, Volya? Is that what you mean?"

It was an odd moment to become politically enlightened. But there were more practical issues at hand. "Look, all I'm certain of is that if we don't cooperate, we're finished, and our families will have a very rough go of it."

"And if we go through with it? What then?"

My first instinct was to lie to my cellmate just like I've been lying to myself. For some reason, I couldn't. "Dmitry's right. We're probably done either way. It's never been about us."

Leonid sat down. His beaten-down look gave way. Now that he understood exactly where we stood, he could choose. In the end he decided to cooperate. If one can't stop the train, standing on the tracks is not an option.

Of course, by expressing myself honestly I accomplished exactly what the villains hoped for. May God help us.

Geneva (1931)

Switzerland's reputation for non-alignment made it a perfect home for the League of Nations. And Geneva was the natural host city. A prosperous, tolerant place, the pre-eminent principality of *la Confédération Helvétique* reflected the aspirations of a world still reeling from the bitter consequences of the Great War.

Lofty intentions, though, aren't enough. After more than a decade of high-minded oratory world peace and security seemed no closer at hand. Determined not to yield a smidgen of their precious sovereignty, the League's member states squabbled endlessly over the least consequential matters, leaving little hope for resolving the festering disputes that threatened to ignite another ruinous war. Economic issues proved especially contentious. When the worldwide depression took hold the industrialized powers responded with tariffs and trade barriers, wreaking havoc on smaller economies and fueling the rise of reactionary movements in the future Axis states of Italy, Germany and Japan. As a resurgent Germany worked feverishly to reconstruct its industrial base and military might, a fearful France demanded that the League commit to defend its members from aggression, by force of arms if necessary, a move that the geographically less vulnerable British vehemently opposed.

Forty-two nations formed the League in 1920. Germany was admitted six years later. America would never join, while the Soviet Union's entry was delayed until 1934, one year after Germany and Japan withdrew. Every nation of significance, including America and the USSR, was represented at the 1932 disarmament conference. It was active until 1934, when bitter quarreling effectively rendered it moot.

Romm and Whitaker kept climbing. They lost count, and most of their wind, somewhere around the one-hundredth step. Their reward finally came into view: Geneva, as it could only be seen from the North Tower of the Cathédrale St-Pierre, the church where Calvin announced his reformist agenda more than three and one-half centuries earlier. From their vantage point atop the Old City the man from *Tass* and his counterpart from the *Herald-Tribune* followed the progress of two of Europe's great rivers; the mighty Rhône, spanned at Lake Geneva by the majestic Point du Mont Blanc, and a few kilometers upstream the meandering Arve, its playful curlicues resembling something out of a Picasso sketchbook.

Vladimir caught his breath. "If you don't mind my asking, what did you tell the border guards to get them off my back?"

"I told them the truth: that every correspondent is a spy in one form or another, but that in Geneva we're only interested in stealing from each other, not from our hosts."

"That did the trick?"

"Well, I did threaten to make your detention front-page news. Switzerland's pretense of neutrality is an economic bonanza. Have you noticed the size of their banks? They're certainly not anxious to look like they're playing favorites. Their attitude about you, though, did seem a bit extreme. Did you upset an important Swiss, perhaps in a prior life?"

"Impossible," Vladimir quipped. "In the USSR we only go around once. But since you apparently believe otherwise let me take you somewhere truly extraordinary."

A few minutes later they were in the magnificent *Auditoire*, the historic lecture hall where Calvin held his gatherings. "His powerful sermons got city leaders so worried about losing control that they banned him from the municipality."

"I'm surprised you're interested," Whitaker said. "I didn't think religion played much of a role in the USSR."

"It's not nearly as influential as it was under the Czar. Oh, you still have *babushkas* huddling in monasteries, lighting candles and murmuring their prayers. In the USSR citizens are guaranteed the free exercise of religion. But its importance as a political force is gone, hopefully for good. Separation between Church and State is essential. That's in your own Constitution, isn't it?"

Vladimir was actually playing hooky. Days earlier, when he first paid his respects at the Soviet legation, Litvinov's secretary loaded him up with an armful of briefing materials. She refused to let Romm in to see his superior until he knew everything about the pending talks: their historical context, the positions of each major player, and, most importantly, why the concept of disarmament was such a tricky business. Vladimir holed himself up in his room, and other than for daily trips to the League library and his jaunt with Whitaker he stayed close to the Soviet compound. It took him a week before he felt prepared.

"Back so soon?" the secretary smirked.

"I'm ready to see the Comrade Commissar."

The secretary wasn't impressed. "I hope so. Just remember that you've been warned."

Vladimir had a card up his sleeve. Like Troyanovsky, Maxim Maximovich Litvinov was a Jew. It wouldn't make up for everything, but in the ideological minefield that was Stalin's Russia, where the most subtle shifts in dogma could endanger one's health, all bonds were welcome, and that of ethnicity most of all.

Litvinov welcomed Vladimir warmly. Clean shaven and impeccably attired, his round spectacles, formal manner of speech and habit of furrowing his brows at the slightest excuse lent the portly Commissar of Foreign Affairs a distinctly professorial air. He was anxious to judge for himself whether this comrade twenty years his junior was everything that Troyanovsky claimed. His initial impression was favorable. Vladimir carried himself well. He was respectful without being obsequious, and his face radiated intellectual vigor, an increasingly rare characteristic in the engorged bureaucracy. A top-down mentality had produced a generation of toadies, "yes" men whose capacity for innovation and independent thought had been bred out like horns from cattle. Hopefully this one would be different.

Litvinov folded his arms across his ample midsection. "Comrade Romm, you've been in Geneva for a week. What do you think?"

"The Old City is marvelous, Comrade Commissar. That's all I've had a chance to see. I've spent most of my time in my quarters, and in the library."

Litvinov smiled. "I meant, other than as a tourist. I trust that my secretary loaded you up with homework. In one sentence, tell me what you learned."

"I learned that the League doesn't seem eager to take up the Commissar on his daring proposal."

Litvinov's eyes twinkled. "Good. Tell me more."

"You suggested that everyone get together, gather up their guns and dump them in the ocean. Plop, finis!"

The Commissar smiled playfully. "So I did! Is that so complicated?"

"Perhaps not. But disarmament is an inexact concept. It can mean different things to different people. There's also a concern that relying on the good faith of others makes honest participants vulnerable. Did they really bring all their guns? Are they concealing something?"

Litvinov innocently wiped his spectacles. "I admit these can be problems. But isn't it why we have verification?"

"In theory, yes." Vladimir sensed that he was being tested by a very cagey man. "But rascals will always find ways to hide things."

"Of course they will! So if disarmament is, as you imply, fundamentally impossible in a society where 'rascals' exist, then why are we here?"

Vladimir hesitated. Any reasonably smart person who was willing to do the research would have gotten this far. But Litvinov could not possibly want a parrot. It was time to articulate his own vision.

"As I see it, Comrade Commissar, communism frightens the capitalists. Fearful adversaries are unpredictable and dangerous. If we get to know each other better it reduces the chances of a lethal misunderstanding. One can never know too much about one's friends. Or enemies."

Litvinov beamed. Troyanovsky was right. Soon would come the hard part: to place principles into practice. He peered out the window.

"Do you think it's a beautiful city? Certainly the architecture is impressive. But where's the esthetic appeal? All the buildings look like vaults."

"An American I met thinks it's that way on purpose, to convince the rich that everything they leave behind will be waiting when they return."

Litvinov broke into a wide grin. He returned to his desk. "Comrade Troyanovsky told me of your concerns about Germany and Japan."

"Both are on the same path. Germany's fallen under the spell of the Nazis; Japan, of its military. Meanwhile the Communist International is trying to stir their workers. These efforts would be laughable if they weren't so counterproductive."

Litvinov enthusiastically slapped his desktop. "That's exactly what I told the General Secretary! All that those infants have accomplished is to raise nationalistic fervor to a fever pitch. Their blunders – what happened in Germany is a perfect example – have made France, Great Britain and America reluctant to deal with us. Can you blame them? Our failure to compensate them for the Empire's debts hasn't helped, either. But that's what happens when you become a captive to your own ideology."

Vladimir was transfixed. Had he uttered such sentiments to the Party committee he wouldn't have simply been expelled – he would have been arrested!

Litvinov took a chair next to Romm. "Speaking my mind hasn't made me many friends, comrade, but no one will ever accuse me of having a hidden agenda. You'll report directly to me. Write a couple routine dispatches for *Tass* each week to keep up appearances. As for this American, stay on him! What has he heard? What does he know? Get to know all the Americans. It's vital that we break them of their bizarre, self-defeating isolationism before it's too late."

"What about the Brits?"

The Commissar sneered. "During my years in London I learned that the only thing those weak-kneed pansies are interested in is their afternoon tea. They won't even promise to help their neighbors, the French, who are sweating buckets over Germany's intentions. When war breaks out – that's right, *when* – how long do you think it'll be before Nazis are belting out *Deutschland über alles* on the *Champs?* Incidentally, how's your English?"

"Needs improvement. I often switch to French."

"Well, keep working on it. You'll find that Americans have little ear for other tongues."

Vladimir grew fond of visiting the fine shops along the *Rue de Rhone*. He was enchanted by Swiss craftsmanship, from the exquisitely detailed furniture to the intricate clocks and timepieces, their endless ticking heralding the rhythms of an industrious culture. By day the Swiss were all about business. Evenings, though, brought on a remarkable transformation. It was as though he was back in Berlin. Prostitution was technically illegal, yet as long as decorum was maintained the police hardly bothered, the bawdiness giving the normally buttoned-down citizens of Geneva and their foreign guests a chance to loosen their cravats and blow off a little steam.

Swiss were also crazy about the movies. Whitaker was a big fan, and on weekends he and Vladimir frequented the opulent palaces showcasing the latest French releases. They were occasionally accompanied by Dr. Max Baer. A former university professor, he had left his native Germany to pursue diplomacy, but his dream stalled in the obscure backwaters of the League's Secretariat. On this occasion Max had convinced his colleagues to forego the silver screen in favor of Wagner's "Die Walküre," which was being performed at Victoria Hall. Vladimir, who had little stomach for droll German opera, went along to visit the world-renowned venue. Built in 1891 by the British to honor their queen, the ornate, neo-baroque house boasted a massive organ, two balconies and enough gilded ornamentation and sculptural details to make a palace proud.

At intermission the friends gathered at the bar. Max quickly drained his mug and tapped the counter for a refill. "Isn't this a wonderful change from the cinema? And it's a real German company, too!"

Vladimir winked at Whitaker. "Max, why didn't you warn us about Germany's horrifying new weapon?"

"What weapon?"

Whitaker cut in. "Our Bolshevik friend is referring to your obvious tolerance for pain, Herr Doctor. Imagine massive speakers pouring out Wagner on the battlefield. What enemy would fail to surrender?"

"Ach, you two are nothing but savages!" The lights flickered, signaling that the performance was about to resume.

"Well, at least we're halfway," Vladimir groaned.

Baer wiped the foam from his lips. "What do you mean, 'half'? Didn't you read the program? There are *two* intermissions!"

Summer was on its way. Galina packed for the voyage to Paris. Georgie's treatments had gone well. Diet, exercise and the brisk climate imbued the youngster with color and a new vigor. Doctors said that his ankle would require permanent support, but they seemed confident that with regular therapy and a good diet the child's prognosis was good.

Berck-Plage had also done wonders for Ludvika. She had been spending her free hours with a retired French military man, one of the many pensioners who had given up Paris for the quiet pleasures of the southern Pas de Calais. One day he loaded up his old Citroën and drove Ludvika and Galina to Flanders, where many of his comrades had come to rest. They spread their lunch on the grass. Galina gazed at a nearby field. Headstones covered the ground, extending as far as the eye could see. "Now that there's a League of Nations, nothing like this need happen again."

"One prays," the veteran said. He pulled a fat mushroom from the rich soil. "Nature doesn't care whose remains fertilize the earth. French, German, Flemish – they're all equal. Too bad people aren't like that. Everyone's convinced they're special. If it's not nationality it's religion, and if not that it's some 'ism', capitalism, socialism, communism..."

"That's not so," Galina objected. "People *are* different. But that doesn't mean they have to quarrel! In my country nationalities are given homelands where they can follow their own traditions and live at peace with their neighbors."

The veteran snickered. "Those trials of saboteurs that we hear about, that doesn't seem so harmonious."

Ludvika took her male friend's hand. "Henri, don't be so gloomy! After that horrible war everyone is certain to find common ground. I mean, how dumb can people be?"

For a moment the only sound was the humming of a bee. Finally the veteran spoke. "A few months ago an old military buddy came here on vacation. He's now a big-shot scientist. His conscience must have been bothering him, and one night he couldn't stop talking. You know what he said? They're developing bombs that are dropped from airplanes and can set fire to entire cities! A whole city – imagine that! How can anyone justify that? No, the next war will make the last look like a warm-up."

On a sultry day in late August Vladimir, Galina and Georgie strolled in the *Jardin des Tuileries*, Paris' majestic central park. Vladimir studied a visitor brochure.

"Queen Catherine's palace would have been about here. Can you imagine what it would be like to have gardens like these as your front yard?"

"Why aren't they still here, Daddy?" As usual, Georgie was riding on his father's shoulders.

"Oh, some people burned it down."

"Were they bad people?"

His son's question begged for a simple answer, but Vladimir wasn't sure how to respond. Had the leftists of the Paris Commune done good or evil? Or a bit of both?

A squirrel scampered by, saving the day. "Put me down!" Georgie said. Brace or not, he was about to give the creature a run for his money.

While the League was on summer hiatus the family sublet an apartment in Paris. Vladimir went into the *Tass* offices each day to check for messages but otherwise had little to do. Ludvika remained behind in Berck-Plage on vacation. Age was certainly no bar to romance!

Vladimir, Galina and Georgie had dinner at a restaurant on the *Rue de Rivoli*. They were joined by Alexander Romm, who was in Paris researching his first book, a biography of the artist Matisse.

Alexander kissed Galina's cheeks. "Your wife is a miracle worker, Volya. She got me an expedited visa. I'll be interviewing Matisse. Shchukin, too!"

Galina bristled. "Do you mean the rich guy who fled Russia during the Revolution? The one who left behind housefuls of paintings?"

"One and the same. Shchukin was collecting Picasso, Cezanne and Matisse before they became popular. The Trubetskoy Palace, where he and his family lived, is stuffed full of their works. My two favorites are 'La Danse' and 'La Musque,' which Matisse painted especially for him."

"You sound like a fan," Galina reproached.

"Me? Never! I've got plenty of questions to ask the scoundrel..."

A matronly diner at an adjoining table cut in. "Excuse me for interrupting, but I know the Shchukins. They're wonderful people, support many charities, are very generous to the *Assistance Publique*. Mr. Shchukin told me that his family was heartbroken to leave Russia but feared for their lives. Is it true that he was never compensated for his home or paintings?"

Alexander cleared his throat. "Well, Madame, it's not like he paid for the palace. His father gave it to him as a wedding present! Whether we – I mean, the Government – reimbursed him for the artwork I can't say, but rest assured that everything he left behind is being cared for on behalf of their real owners, the citizens of the USSR."

The woman was visibly miffed. "Is that what you plan on telling him when you meet?"

"Perhaps a trifle more sympathetically. You can't blame a man for being born into money, only for how he spends it."

Vladimir glared at his brother. "I'm relieved to hear you say that, Sasha. Thinking back, I don't remember us running around in rags."

Georgie was quietly taking it all in. "Are you arguing?"

Vladimir put the child on his lap. "Of course not! We're just discussing things!"

"It sounds like arguing."

Vladimir, Galina and Georgie walked to their apartment.

"I envy Alexander for his belief system," Vladimir said. "It's much less complicated than mine. Maybe we should trade jobs!"

"What do you know about art?"

Vladimir bought his wife in close. "I know it when I see it."

Galina laughed. "Flatterer!"

A black Citroën was idling in front of their building. A balding, heavyset Frenchman peered out from the passenger side.

"*Bonsoir, monsieur.*"

"It's the police," Vladimir whispered. "Wait here." He approached the car. "Hello, Otto. Fancy meeting you here."

The man from the *Sûreté* grinned wickedly. "Greetings, comrade. I trust that you and your family are having a pleasant stay in France. By that I include your brother Alexander Georgievich, of course."

"Of course. I take it that you've passed on your concerns about my welfare to the Swiss?"

"*Mais, oui!* Can you believe it? They're equally as anxious to assure your safety!"

"I appreciate that. Is there something I can do for you this lovely evening?"

Otto gestured to the back seat. "Get in and we'll talk."

Vladimir stayed put. "The weather's better here, Inspector."

"Look, Bolshie, if we wanted, you'd disappear. But we don't want. Come take a ride to my office. There's something you ought to hear. I promise to behave."

Vladimir pecked his wife's cheek. "I'll be at the *Sûreté*. Take his tag number. If I'm not back by morning call the embassy."

They arrived at a large, nondescript building bristling with antennas. Otto led Vladimir to a room in the basement. A huge, glowing shortwave console gave off enough heat to warm the entire building.

Otto whispered to a sweaty radio operator. He delicately nudged a dial. Vladimir donned a pair of headphones.

"...This is the BBC world service...The Japanese army has invaded China and captured Mukden... Japan claims it was protecting its citizens living in Manchuria from brutal treatment by the authorities...Governor of Manchuria Chang Hsueh-liang ordered his troops to stop resisting...China claims that Japan had been planning the move for months...The League of Nations called an emergency meeting to review the situation..."

Otto poured coffee for Vladimir in his office. "You heard what the whole world will know in the morning. What do you think?"

"Isn't there anyone from your delegation you could ask?"

Otto solicitously patted Vladimir's knee. "You know why I'm so good at my job? Because I don't sit in echo chambers! Japan invaded China. How do you interpret the move?"

Vladimir sipped the strong, bitter brew. Why the mighty USSR couldn't produce decent coffee was a mystery that not even the GPU had solved. "I know the Japanese. They're in China to stay. Once the League condemns their aggression, as it eventually must, they'll quit the League. Their new German buddies won't be far behind."

"So, we agree on something! Japan's occupation of Manchuria puts your country in a very difficult position. With fascist Germany on one flank and the Empire breathing down on the other the Soviet Union is caught in a dangerous pinch."

"Sure. But consider *all* the geography. Your country and the krauts share a border. Germany won't dare take us on as long as there's an independent and potentially hostile France."

"Well said! Since our futures are intertwined, we must actively cooperate at all levels. Including ours, *n'est ce-pas?*"

Vladimir got up. "Otto, you're dreaming. Our revolutions came to precisely opposite conclusions. How I wish that they hadn't, but they did."

On the return trip Vladimir rode in front. They pulled to the curb. Otto gently placed a hand on his adversary's shoulder.

"Look, Romm, it's none of my business, but I really hope your kid gets better. Any time you want to get to Berck-Plage we'll expedite. Maybe our little ones will make less of a mess at it, eh?"

Galina was in bed reading. "It's late, Galya. You should be asleep."

"Easy for you to say. How did it go?"

"Very well, actually. The *Sûreté* has offered to protect me from untoward advances while I'm in Paris."

His wife flipped off the light. "I hope you told them to start tomorrow!"

Lubyanka prison,
18 January 1937

This morning they took the five of us to the guards' bathhouse to wash and change clothes. We were then brought before Molchanov, who spoke about the trial. He started by emphasizing the importance of our roles, as "the eyes of the world will be on the USSR." Early each morning they will take us to the Trade Union Building. We will wait in a room near the Hall of Columns, the cavernous assembly room where the Socialist Revolutionaries were tried fifteen years ago. One of us will testify on each of five days: Dmitry first, then me, Loginov, Stein and Tamm. Our testimonies will be interwoven with appearances by the defendants. We're subject to recall, so all of us must be present the entire time. We will be brought back to our cells each evening.

Molchanov was very specific about what to expect in court. "Two bailiffs will escort you to the podium: one will lead, the other trail. Don't look at the judges or the crowd, not even for an instant. Keep your eyes on the officer to your front, and while you testify, on Comrade Vyshinsky. Return your attention to the bailiff when you leave."

Radek and Piatakov came in late. Their guard mumbled an apology; it seems that Piatakov has been throwing up.

"Are you ill, comrade?" Molchanov asked. His faux-solicitous tone dripped with sarcasm.

The once-great leader of Soviet industry was pale as a ghost. He shook his head. "Only nervous," he mumbled.

Molchanov handed out the scripts. They were neatly bound, making them convenient to carry. Naturally, the thickest by far went to the trial's principal defendants, Radek and Piatakov. But Loginov's was also quite substantial.

"These are the final versions. Study them carefully and bring them with you each day."

My cellmate stared at his script. "Comrade Molchanov," he asked, "there are only two days left. How can we memorize...?"

"No!" Molchanov barked. "Remember what I've said all along: no memorizing! You are not to seem rehearsed! Say these things but use the words that come to you. Do you understand?"

"But these *are* our words," Leonid objected, "they're just not our *thoughts*."

Leonid didn't mean to be funny, but we barely avoided laughing. The living dead have a peculiar sense of humor! Naturally, Molchanov puffed up like one of those fish. One dreads to think what might have happened weeks earlier. But with the trial only days off it was far too late to be replacing witnesses.

"Comrade Tamm, we ask only that you do your best. Is that fair?"

Leonid nodded. He seemed in shock.

Molchanov left and returned with Vyshinsky. The Procurator-General was beaming, as though he couldn't be happier to be with us.

"Good morning. I trust that Comrade Molchanov has enlightened you." He looked around the room. "Any questions?"

Dmitry spoke up. "Comrade Prosecutor, I was arrested and accused of participating in a plot of which I am absolutely innocent. They refused to give me any details because everything supposedly remains 'under investigation.' I understand the importance of being a witness, but when will my own case be resolved?"

Vyshinsky sighed. He knew that every witness had that question in mind. "Comrade Bukhartsev, the period of investigation set by law is still running, so I'm prohibited from discussing the case. Once it ends, everything will be explained to your satisfaction." Before anyone else could speak up, the Procurator-General of the Soviet Union homed in on me.

"I'd like to ask Comrade Romm, who's had personal experience with the Germans and Japanese, to give us his honest evaluation of their intentions. Are the fascists getting ready to attack the USSR, or not?"

I was stunned. To be placed in this spot was the last thing I expected. Somehow I managed to utter a few inanities. Boiled down they amounted to this: war is inevitable.

"Thank you." Vyshinsky scanned the room, making eye contact with each of us. "That's why we're here. Conflict can erupt at any moment, yet England and America are still wallowing in their isolationist fantasies. They're really convinced that when hostilities break out they'll somehow avoid getting caught up in it. That's why your testimonies are crucial. They will alert the peace-loving countries of the world to the threats posed by fascism. I'm confident that each of you will do your part to help."

And that was it. When Leon and I returned to the cell our little friend was on my cot, and when I brushed him off he took to a corner and stared. I felt poorly and rounded up a snack, and he hopped right back up. I suppose we're still friends.

Leonid's slip of the tongue sticks in my mind. Hasn't the gap between our thoughts and deeds been the problem from the start? By meekly parroting the "correct" line year after year – decade after decade – we've so deadened our senses that doing what any decent person would find unthinkable becomes second nature.

No, not second – first!

Dreams of Peace (1932-34)

Anna's brother told the GPU the truth. When weeks passed without word from her husband she left Dnepropetrovsk and took the twins to a friend's apartment in Moscow. Her friend's husband, a Soviet Army colonel, agreed to take in the children but insisted that Anna leave. If a fugitive was found in his home the repercussions would be extreme. In the end she had little choice. Anna held the boys close and promised to return. Jarek and Mikolaj eagerly went back to playing with toy soldiers collected by their "uncle," a fascinating man with tall boots and a chest full of medals.

Anna looked at the return address on Galina's letter. Vladimir was a journalist, a person of influence: certainly he could fix things! She picked up her bag. It was a long walk and by the time she got to the apartment it was well past midnight.

Walter Duranty of the *New York Times* was in Kazakhstan enjoying a junket arranged by the Soviet government to trumpet its progress on the Five-Year plan. As his convoy turned a corner it happened on a company of soldiers. They were guarding a passenger railcar sitting on a spur. Through its dirty windows he saw that it was packed with shabbily-dressed men and women. When its occupants spotted the visitors they started frantically gesturing at their mouths and bellies, the unmistakable, universal plea for food.

Duranty considered the Russian peasantry hopelessly backward. He also thought of himself as a compassionate man and was troubled by the depth of the human misery that was playing out in front of his eyes. Still, as his good friend the General Secretary frequently pointed out, in this impossibly underdeveloped land everyone had to contribute to the maximum of their abilities. There was little choice but to relocate *kulaks*, malcontents and counterrevolutionaries to places where they could grow food, extract minerals, lay railroad track, and in other tangible ways help advance the great Soviet state.

Anna watched as the vehicles carrying the journalists receded in the distance.

After turning herself in she had become just another drop in the waves of human flotsam washing over Russia's Far East. When the locomotive's couplers slammed into the car, signaling the resumption of her journey, she scrambled to regain a bit of floor space. Had she known that a famous American journalist would later describe her and her companions as "more like caged animals than human beings, not wild beasts but dumb cattle, patient with suffering eyes," she would have readily agreed.

As Duranty scratched out his observations Vladimir and his colleagues were having drinks at the Place du Molard, a picturesque square in Geneva's Old Town. It was April 1932. After many months of preparation and interminable delays the disarmament conference was finally underway. It proved a rocky start. Although Germany was technically still bound to the Versailles accords that ended the Great War, it loudly threatened to rebuild its military unless all nations disarmed to its level. Meanwhile the Japanese were busily cementing their conquest of Manchuria, flooding the area with troops and installing a puppet regime led by China's deposed former emperor.

Whitaker sipped his favorite beverage, a steaming mug of chocolate topped with a shot of vodka. "Vladimir, you know the Japs. Do you think they'll be satisfied with Manchuria? Or are they intending to take a bigger bite?"

Vladimir was enjoying his vodka straight. "The Empire's appetite knows no bounds, Jack. There's a reason why the USSR is rushing troops to Siberia. Now that Japan's getting ready to make common cause with Germany, we'll be vulnerable from the East *and* West."

Baer slammed his stein on the table. As a "real" German he refused to drink anything that wasn't brewed. "That business about us and Japan is ridiculous. We have nothing in common with them. Germany isn't trying to make trouble. All it wants is to be left in peace."

Whitaker groaned. "Peace? Hitler and his Nazis are screaming to rearm. That doesn't seem so peaceful. What if your boy wins the presidency? What if he's appointed Chancellor?"

"So what if he is? All Hitler wants is for the fatherland to be able to defend itself. What's wrong with that? Once Germany feels secure, it will be an even better international partner. You'll see."

Vladimir shook his head. "Max, you've been away too long. Do you have any idea what the Nazis are like?"

"Please don't fill my head with your Communist prattle, Vladimir Georgievich.

Germans are a cultured people, not like your flaming Bolsheviks. I've kept in touch with the National Socialists. Incidentally," he added, "they've tentatively selected me to become the Minister of Propaganda."

Vladimir and Whitaker were stunned into silence. Whitaker finally spoke up. "For Heaven's sake, Max, you're Jewish!"

Max impassively drained his stein. "So?"

Although it would never join the League, America recognized the importance of the disarmament talks and sent a team of observers led by Secretary of State Henry Stimson. Allen Dulles came as chief legal counsel. Not yet forty, the slender, patrician lawyer was on his second visit to Geneva, where he had once participated in an arms trafficking conference. Grandson of one Secretary of State and nephew of another, Dulles eagerly took leave from his older brother John Foster's law firm to partake in the excitement of diplomacy. It wasn't as though he was given a lot of discretion. To satisfy a prickly Congress that was determined to keep America from being drawn into another war, his marching orders were explicit: do not agree to anything that could possibly entangle the world's beacon of democracy in a "foreign" dispute.

Stimson reached for a humidor. Its lid was engraved with crossed field guns, the insignia of his branch of service, the American artillery. That and a bad case of tinnitus were the Secretary's only keepsakes from the War to End All Wars.

"Have a seat, Allen. Care for a smoke?"

"If you don't mind I'll just suck on my pipe, Mister Secretary."

"Please, my boy, you're going to wear out my title. Then I'd have nothing left!" Stimson was of course joking. As members of the upper crust there was little chance that either he or Dulles would ever stand in a soup line.

Stimson displayed a surveillance photo. "Courtesy the Swiss."

Dulles looked hard at the snapshot. "It's that Bolshie correspondent."

"Vladimir Romm." Stimson retrieved a thin file. "A Jew, but of rather distinguished lineage. Spent a few years in Germany and France for Soviet military intelligence, then two in Japan for the GPU."

"He's still with them?"

Stimson visibly stiffened. "Once GPU, always GPU." He slid over a thick report. "It's our most recent assessment of the Soviets. We're seriously thinking about exchanging diplomats but their behavior has the President worried. You know, those improbable trials of 'saboteurs,' their on-again, off-again chumminess with the krauts, etcetera. Either something's getting lost in translation or they're the most self-defeating people on Earth. This Romm fellow has been pressing to interview me for *Tass*. Why don't you sit in? You could take it from there."

America had been out of the spy business for years. Ironically, it was due in large part to Stimson, who was so antagonistic to intelligence gathering that he once quashed an American code-breaking effort because "gentlemen don't read each other's mail." Dulles, on the other hand, was raring to run a full-fledged intelligence shop. This could be an opening. He examined the photo.

"The man's a spy, Henry. He'll know what's up."

"Great! Then you won't waste a lot of time circling each other. You know how I feel about the cloak-and-dagger, Allen, but Hoover wants to know what's on their minds."

Vladimir thought that the interview went as well as could be expected. He asked his questions and Stimson responded as vaguely as he could. A hunch that his audience was granted for more than one reason was confirmed when Dulles took him aside and suggested that they meet later.

Litvinov was intrigued. "What do you think they want?"

"I'm not sure. Their Congress is badly divided over the issue of recognition. Hoover's going to be standing for reelection. Maybe our bride's getting nervous. Maybe she needs more reassurance before committing."

"I agree. After all the stunts the Politburo's pulled over the years I'd have problems with recognizing us too. Go on your date, Volya. Reassure Dulles of our intentions. Even if nothing comes of it he might prove useful later."

Vladimir found his counterpart amiable but in some ways naïve. An old-money blueblood with the easy, disarming manner of his class, Dulles displayed a nearly childish enthusiasm for the cloak-and-dagger.

"Have you heard of the 'Ivies'?" Dulles asked.

"Ivy? That's a plant, right?"

"It's how we describe our best private schools: Princeton, Harvard, Yale. Their walls are covered with ivy."

"And yours was...?"

"Princeton. Do you realize what a terrific intelligence corps our graduates would make?"

And so it went for another ten minutes. Vladimir tried a different tack. "Allen, Americans have a wonderful expression. It's called 'beating about the bush.' So let's stop. Our countries were set to exchange ambassadors. Then the U.S. began stalling. What will it take to close the deal? What does your Secretary want to know? Your President?"

Dulles nearly choked on his drink. Trying to keep up with a Russian was perhaps not such a great idea. "O.K., Vladimir, I'll take you up on that. Mind you, this is only a guess, but your friendship with the Germans raises a red flag. We understand that your general staffs are on a first-name basis."

"Absolutely, over the years officers on both sides have become friends. That's a good thing: it makes dangerous miscalculations far less likely. Keep in mind that in the USSR, like in America, the military keep completely clear of politics. Of course, now that the Nazis have gained a majority in the *Reichstag* and tilted Germany to the extreme right, we must reassess the alliance. But you can't expect the USSR to go it alone. Really, we're puzzled by America's posture. Rejecting the League of Nations is bad enough, but staying neutral in the face of what the Japanese have done to China..."

"You're changing the subject," Dulles complained. "In my country there's no equivalent to your General Secretary. One man doesn't call all the shots. Our citizens are dead set against getting mixed up in any more foreign squabbles, and they've made that clear to their representatives. As for recognizing the USSR, why should we play nice with an ideology whose endgame is the fall of capitalism?"

"Comrade Stalin has repeatedly emphasized that our intentions stop at our borders. I can't make it any clearer than that."

"No offense intended, Vladimir, but his word doesn't carry a lot of weight in Congress, which must approve all treaties. We've got plenty of Senators and Representatives who'd like nothing better than to sit back and watch the Germans and Japs tear the Soviet Union to pieces."

Vladimir grimaced. Words had consequences; if these were passed on to his superiors they could set back the relationship between America and the USSR to the dark days of Archangel. Still, he knew that he'd want to stick close to Dulles. Their brief conversation had furnished invaluable insights into what made America tick. It boasted of being an egalitarian society where anyone could succeed through hard work, but was in fact burdened with a class system that, while lacking in titles, was as rigid as anything the Czars could have dreamed up. That's what let a man like Dulles, who had trouble passing the bar exam, advance so quickly.

"Well, Allen, I hope you don't mind if I keep some of this to myself." Vladimir glanced at his watch. "Some of us are going to the cinema to see 'Dr. Jekyll and Mr. Hyde.' Why don't you come along?"

In July the conference went on hiatus. Vladimir joined his wife in Paris while Ludvika and Georgie remained at Berck-Plage so the child could continue receiving special treatments.

Vladimir and Galina passed the time enjoying the beautiful city. At midday they often picnicked on the vast lawns of the *Invalides*, watching curly-haired young men in jerseys and knee socks entertain their sweethearts with vigorous games of football. In the evenings they frequented the cafés lining the *Champs*.

They were sipping drinks, admiring the splendid *Arc de Triomphe* when Galina noticed someone staring at them from another table.

"It's Walter Duranty!" Vladimir said. "I'll go get him."

Vladimir returned with the famous *New York Times* correspondent. Galina was delighted. "We're honored, Mr. Duranty."

Duranty turned on the charm. "Please, call me Walter."

Galina blushed.

Only a few months had passed since the newsman's receipt of the Pulitzer Prize for a series of reports on the Soviet Union under Stalin. His work was cited for a "profound and intimate comprehension of conditions in Russia and of the causes of those conditions. They are marked by scholarship, profundity, impartiality, sound judgment and exceptional clarity, and are excellent examples of the best type of foreign correspondence." In his acceptance speech Duranty said that his experiences in the USSR cured him of "viciously anti-Bolshevik" sentiments. Stalin, he was convinced, was "a really great statesman."

"I read your interview with the General Secretary," Galina said. "It was fascinating!"

"Thank you! You know, he's a very deceiving fellow. Plain-spoken, to be sure, but with an intellect that's sharp as a knife. No matter where one stands on things it's impossible to listen to Stalin without gaining a new appreciation for the USSR's policies. Really, there's only one figure who comes close in influence. That's Kirov, the Party chief in Leningrad. I just got back from interviewing him. A fascinating man! Young, for such a lofty position. Wildly popular, too, maybe more than some might prefer."

Vladimir was fascinated. If only Soviet reporters were free to probe with such abandon! "Do you see him as a possible competitor?"

"To Stalin? Absolutely. Kirov's rugged and brainy. Once he becomes better known he'll give the General Secretary a run for his money."

Vladimir imagined a bull's eye hovering over Kirov's chest. Or more likely, his back. Galina interrupted before he could pry further. "Are you working on something special, Walter?"

"Actually, yes. It's a long piece based on my recent trip to Siberia. It was fascinating! We went to mines, factories, collectives. What's being accomplished is nothing short of miraculous. It should make an excellent counterpoint to those ridiculous articles by the British agronomists."

Galina was ecstatic. "You don't know how pleased that makes me! It's incredibly frustrating to hear about all that anti-Soviet propaganda."

Duranty nodded sagely. "Britain hates the USSR, so you've got to take what those pudding-eaters say with a grain of salt. Seriously, the notion that millions in a region as bountiful as Ukraine could perish from food shortages is so far-fetched as to defy the imagination. What would it accomplish for the authorities to plunder farms and confiscate grain? Of course, if you're stupid enough to believe *Deutsche Welle* and the B.B.C...."

A stunning brunette walked up to Duranty. She pecked him on the cheek.

The newsman got up. "Sorry, folks, but I've got an engagement at the theatre. Toodle-oo!"

Galina watched Duranty leave. Vladimir detected a hint of jealousy.

"All that chatter about starving peasants," Galina said. "You have no idea how often I've been asked if it's true. Really, how could anyone believe that Comrade Stalin would ignore a famine?"

Vladimir's return to Geneva coincided with *La Fête de l'Escalade*, an annual celebration commemorating the defeat of the House of Savoy in 1602. At a picnic hosted by the League he watched costumed Swiss soldiers stage mock battles near the Arve, the river that the invaders used to sneak into the city. Vladimir passed the time chatting with Rose, the secretary to the American delegation. Handsome and full-figured, with hazel eyes and champagne hair, the recent divorcée had a pair of the most exquisitely formed ears he had ever seen. That she was a few years his senior only added to her appeal. When the fireworks show got underway they drifted together, and as the dazzling display lit the sky their fingertips touched.

When conferees reassembled in February 1933 things had changed, and not necessarily for the better. Two notable coronations had taken place: of Franklin Roosevelt, who trounced the clueless Hoover in American presidential elections, and of Chancellor Adolf Hitler, the beneficiary of a power-sharing arrangement that marked the beginning of the end for the Weimar Republic. And that wasn't all. Miffed by a report that concluded their conquest of Manchuria was illegal, Japan quit the League. Germany would follow shortly.

Vladimir was propped up on a pillow studying a Soviet legal document.

XVII. Thornton, Leslie Charles, born in 1887 in Leningrad to a privileged family, married, a British subject, is charged as follows: That during the years 1928-33, while working in the USSR as chief installation engineer of the British firm Metro-Vickers, he took the following steps as a member of a counterrevolutionary group:

1) He collected secret, technical information of State and military importance from Russian engineers and technicians;

2) Both personally and through subordinates, including the British engineers MacDonald and Cushny, he induced Soviet engineers and technicians to carry out wrecking activities and acts of diversion with the object of damaging equipment and causing breakdowns in electric power stations in the USSR..."

Trade disputes and a host of mutual slights had driven relations between Great Britain and the USSR to a new low. Moscow demonstrated its displeasure in the usual way, by arresting eleven Russian workers and six British engineers and charging them with sabotage. As expected, the Soviet citizens promptly confessed. But the stubborn British were not so easily bullied: four steadfastly protested their innocence while two, Thornton and MacDonald, made partial confessions then quickly recanted.

Rose rolled away from the light. "Volya, darling, it's late!"

Vladimir patted Rose's pleasing behind. She insisted on sticking to her diet even during their stolen weekend at a mountain resort. He would never understand why Western women were so determined to shrink body parts that were best left alone.

"I'm almost done."

Rose scowled. "I didn't know you liked fiction. You know, they're laughing about it at the legation."

"Is that what your side thinks? That it's funny?"

"Come on, sweetheart, everyone knows that..." Rose stopped herself. Her most important ground rule was – no politics!

Vladimir was himself skeptical of the trials. And why did the Lubyanka feel compelled to stage them right in the middle of delicate negotiations with America? Stalin must surely be at the controls. What could he possibly be thinking? Western correspondents besieged him with questions. Were the accusations payback? A sly way to excuse shortfalls in productivity? Had Soviet workers been pressured to confess? And what about the foreigners – what would happen to them?

"Whatever the merits – and I can't imagine we made it all up – it's put us in a tough spot, Rose. It could easily poison relations between our countries."

Rose delighted in Vladimir's worldliness and good humor, and seeing him in a funk made her want to help. Surely a bit of reassurance couldn't hurt. "You're too gloomy. As far as I know the Secretary still favors recognition. But don't be surprised if our side insists that Americans get special legal standing, meaning no midnight visits from the Guépéou." She stroked Vladimir's stubble. "Unless on special request, of course. *Now* can we go to sleep?"

Vladimir turned out the light. He didn't notice that Rose was wide awake.

A few days later Vladimir was in Litvinov's office. His superior decoded a cable. "The sentences came in...Thornton got three years, MacDonald, two, and the other Brits were deported."

"I don't get it. All our heavy machinery is foreign. If we start sending guest workers to prison who'll be left to do the repairs? We might as well seal the mines."

"Exactly. That's why in the end they'll simply kick them out, and then hire twice as many at higher salaries. With a depression on the West has to send its surplus workers somewhere. You know anyone else who's hiring?" Litvinov kept decoding. "Here are our citizens' sentences...Three got ten years...three others eight. Ah, that reminds me of something!" Litvinov pulled an old issue of *Pravda*. "Guess who said this at the end of the trial: 'The crimes committed by Gussev, Oleinik and Sokolov are immeasurably grave. They came here to answer for these crimes. And Oleinik found the proper words with which to describe his own conduct, and that of his friends: nothing can be more vile'."

"Their lawyer?"

"Correct! Defense counsel Kaznacheyev, to be exact. With advocates like these, who needs prosecutors? Think of the gains in efficiency!" Litvinov tossed the message into the burn basket. "Let's move on. What did you find out about the Americans?"

"They think our treatment of the British is humorous. Expect them to ask for guarantees that will protect their employees from arrest."

"Good! You know, Volya, if there's one thing I've learned it's that nations are incredibly selfish. America might feel compelled to raise a fuss, but as long as it doesn't threaten their interests they couldn't care less what we do to the English, or anyone else." The Commissar tossed Romm an envelope.

Vladimir opened it. He had been assigned to take an advanced English course at Moscow State University. Litvinov slapped him on the back. "If all goes well, this time next year you'll be in Washington."

Just then an aide hurried in with a radiogram. Litvinov frowned before passing it along. "I'm very sorry, Volya. I lost my mother-in-law not long ago."

Lubyanka prison,
19 January 1937

This morning a guard dropped off my brother Alexander's book on Matisse. It's simply entitled, "Henri Matisse." He signed the title page. Every other bears a censor's initials, confirming, I suppose, that the contents are ideologically inoffensive and don't include instructions for a jailbreak.

As I read the work (the text runs only seventy pages) its message is obvious. Socialist realism lives, although not in the works of Henri Matisse. Hardly a page goes by without at least a passing reference to the detrimental effect of the artist's bourgeois roots – Matisse came from a family of merchants, and then studied law – on his artistic accomplishments. Here's one of the least strident passages. It comes early, on page nine:

> The observer must merely contemplate – he must think of nothing, remember nothing, he must be wafted into an abstraction world of color and form, extinguishing all senses but the visual. This principle is, in essence, an escape from reality. This is the tranquility that Matisse gives in his art. In his fantastic decorative world he calms the soul of the bourgeois, gives him forgetfulness of the social dangers of modern life, whispers to him of eternal well-being.

Alexander's objections to Matisse's infatuation with the decorative, "art for art's sake" aspects of the painterly craft aren't just a paean to the Party. He genuinely believes that all citizens, including artists, are duty-bound to advance the proletarian ideal. Evsey argued with him endlessly, but Alexander stubbornly refused to concede that any realm transcends the material, and the sooner we get used to it the better. Perhaps a night in the Lubyanka would help him realize that even the staunchest Communist might occasionally need to escape, figuratively speaking of course.

Leonid said he is a great fan of Matisse and asked to see the book. He adored the illustrations but was equally put off by Alexander's analysis, which he found profoundly disturbing. Leonid then asked me a question that had nothing to do with the book but everything with why I'm here.

"Volya, you don't seem to be an ideologue at heart. If you don't mind my asking, why did you join the communists?"

"Like I told you, the Socialist Revolutionaries lost influence. I suppose that with world revolution just around the corner I didn't want to be left out."

"But the cruelty, the ruthlessness..."

"I don't mean this as an excuse, Leonid Evgenevich, but those were difficult times. We were under the thumbs of miserable tyrants, and they weren't about to go quietly. To prevail one had to be...I don't know...single-minded, even vicious. Many of us had suffered personally or had family members that were repressed, and in the heat of things our anger and resentment made it easy to justify the most brutal acts."

So far my explanation seemed logical – I had used it on many occasions when dealing with the Western press, and mostly believed it myself. But dear, non-political Leonid quickly detected a fundamental flaw.

"Volya, it's not that I don't follow your reasoning, but it still doesn't help me understand why I'm here."

How to explain why communists turned on each other? Why the life of the revolution was sucked from within? Why we're staging these ridiculous theatrical events, except that their cast members really die?

"No, it doesn't," I conceded. "If there is a reason why we're here, it probably has more to do with man than with ideology. Movements draw in a lot of questionable characters. Even the best-intentioned can be carried away by the seductions of power. We all want to be the last dog to pee on the tree. That sort of thing."

"Volya, you're describing human nature! Are you saying that my being here – *our* being here – was inevitable?"

I had to think about that. "If not us, there would have probably been others. But there's hope. Look how long it's taken for the French to recover from their upheavals. One day there will be a new Russia. They'll look back on this and wince."

Leonid thought about it for a moment.

"Then they'll probably do it all over again."

"Yes. Probably."

America (1934)

When the worker picked up the cutting torch he could not have imagined that his ordinary act would soon become key evidence at a major show trial. Not that it would matter to him personally, because the tool's first spark marked his last living moment and those of the two comrades working alongside him.

Leonid Tamm was in his office at the fertilizer works when the ground shook so violently that it toppled his bookshelf. Gorlovka's chief engineer bolted out the door. As he arrived at the scene of the latest mishap his worst fears were confirmed. Three charred forms lay on the ground. He recognized one. It was Leonid Feodorovich Kurkin, only twenty years old but already a Stakhanovite, a prize-winning "shock worker." Tamm remembered the ceremony when Ordzhonikidze, the Commissar of Heavy Industry pinned the medal for productivity on the young man's neatly pressed shirt. That keepsake and a photograph are all that would be displayed at the funeral, as his body was far too disfigured to place on view.

Workers covered in soot streamed from the plant. "Don't go in, Comrade Engineer! The fire is spreading to other chambers. Everything will blow up!" Tamm knew that was precisely why he had to shut off the gas, and quickly. He placed a wet cloth to his face and plunged in. Stumbling through the smoke-filled interior, the plucky engineer located the valves that the workers had failed to close in their haste to flee.

Gorlovka was saved for another day.

Vladimir heard of the explosion before leaving for America. He feared that it would lead to another sordid tale of spies and wreckers, and perhaps give the USSR's antagonists another reason for delaying recognition. This time, though, the circumstances were ruled accidental and the event quickly faded from notice. His going-away luncheon took place right on schedule.

"My colleagues have already informed you, Mister Romm, of the infinitely greater privileges you will enjoy in Washington than what us poor Western wretches endure here in Moscow, so I won't bore you by repeating them."

After a heavy meal and endless toasts it was time for the obligatory roasts, and the American correspondent's light-hearted reproach drew laughter. It even got a smile from the event's host, the normally humorless Constantine Oumansky, chief of the foreign office press section. The tipsy newsman raised his glass in Oumansky's direction. "Perhaps," he continued, "when Vladimir Georgievich informs you how well the United States treats its guests, the Soviet Union will find it in its heart to reciprocate!"

"But we've already reciprocated," Oumansky insisted. "We've let you live!"

The guests roared.

It was Vladimir's turn. Nikolai Bukharin, chief at *Izvestia*, tapped his elbow. "Keep it brief," he whispered. "And for goodness sake, don't give Karl Berngardovich an opening. He'd have us here for hours!"

Radek was at another table, chatting with Duranty. Four years after his return from exile the voluble Communist journalist was back in the swing of things, writing trenchant pieces for party journals and working at the newspaper *Izvestia*, Vladimir's new employer of record. Romm was dismayed when he found out that the character who caused him so much grief would be his editor. He hoped that his stay in America wouldn't require too much journalism.

Before the ink had dried on the recognition protocols, the Soviet Union flooded America with spies. Most were so-called "legals," with official titles and embassy cover. One was Vladimir Romm, the USSR's inaugural correspondent to Washington. His mission was to gain entrée to policy makers and convince them of the urgent need to support the USSR as it tackled the threats to world peace posed by Germany and Japan.

Vladimir wasn't sanguine about his prospects. His selection was a great honor, but it carried a tremendous responsibility. He knew that softening amateurs in a neutral zone like Geneva was far different from doing it in the eagle's lair, where the drumbeat of isolationism was deafening. Fortunately he was already friendly with Allen Dulles, who was back in private practice after his frustrating sojourn in Geneva, and hoped that he would introduce him to other persons of influence, both inside and outside government.

Vladimir badly missed Rose. Raised on a farm in a fertile region that Americans called the "Midwest," a land not so different from Ukraine in its better days, the warm and gracious woman reminded him of Anna and the peasants that he once championed. On parting he gave her an extravagant, hopelessly delicate Swiss watch, a gift she instantly recognized as a guilty man's peace offering.

"Oh, Vladimir, it's so beautiful," she said, holding it to her wrist. She placed it in his hands. "The thought is lovely but please give it to your wife. She's the one who's earned it."

Thanks to his studies Vladimir's English had greatly improved. Galina, though, found the language a great challenge.

"Wed-nes-day. What's wrong with that?"

Vladimir pointed to a pronunciation guide. "The first 'd' and the 'e' are silent."

Galina was dumbfounded. "But it's not always so. How can you know?"

"It must be memorized. We have similar things in Russian. You know, as in sounding out the letter 'o'."

Galina sneered. "At least that has a rule. This 'd' and 'e' business is just like the West. Complete chaos!"

Vladimir, Galina and Georgie boarded the British-flagged passenger liner R.M.S. Majestic at Cherbourg on June 13, 1934. At nine-hundred eighteen feet and fifty-six thousand tons the magnificent three-stack vessel was the largest steamship in the world, ferrying one-thousand crew members and as many as twenty-six hundred passengers across the Atlantic. Litvinov's wife badgered her husband to authorize first-class travel "so that dear Georgie would be comfortable," and for the next six days the family enjoyed a beautifully appointed cabin and service so efficient that Vladimir found it bothersome. He noticed that it didn't take long for his wife to get used to the pampering.

"Soviet workers paid for it," she said, making her second call for cabin service that day, "so we might as well use it!"

Calm seas and fine weather made for a pleasant journey. Midway through the trip Vladimir was lounging on the deck, practicing his English reading the *New York Times* while Galina and Georgie played miniature golf, an odd pastime that involved striking a hard little ball with a lethal stick known as a putter. Dulles told him that Americans played the adult version of the sport at country clubs, their vast manicured grounds proving an ideal venue for striking important business and government deals. Perhaps it was something he would take up.

Vladimir flipped the page. His eyes were drawn to a headline. "Galya, come look at this!"

SOVIETS TO SEND FIRST PERMANENT REPORTER; AMERICANS TELL HIM THERE IS FREEDOM HERE

One of the most significant visitors from the Soviet Union to the United States since the Bolshevist revolution will depart for Washington next Thursday. He is Vladimir Romm of the newspaper *Izvestia*, who will be the first permanent correspondent of the Soviet press in the United States. Both American and Soviet newspaper men hailed him at a luncheon given in his honor by the board of editors of the *Izvestia*, headed by the famous Nicolai Bukharin...Another correspondent, who also has had Washington experience, was called on and assured Mr. Romm that "you will also have the advantage of writing with no censorship..."

"Hah," Galina huffed. "And they accuse *us* of being propagandists!"

On the voyage's final morning an announcement over the loudspeakers brought everyone on deck. The first thing that came into view was the torch, looming high over the harbor, and when the rest of the Lady broke through the fog thunderous applause greeted the icon that welcomed the oppressed from all corners of the Earth.

Georgie was enthralled. "What's that, father?"

"It's the Statute of Liberty. It was a gift to America from the people of France."

"Why is everyone cheering but us?"

Vladimir slapped his forehead. "We forgot!" he exclaimed. He and Georgie clapped vigorously, Galina a bit less so.

They were met at the customs area by the driver for the Soviet legation. A bulky, friendly fellow decked out in a smart chauffeur's uniform, he like most embassy employees was a Soviet citizen, a fact that was broadcast by the Lenin pin on his lapel. They were soon in the ambassador's resplendent black Cadillac limousine, a vehicle twice the length of anything on the streets of Moscow.

Georgie pointed outside. "Papa, don't people get dizzy in those?"

"Let's ask!" Vladimir slid open the partition that separated the driver's compartment. "Comrade, have you been to the top?"

"You mean the skyscrapers? Of course! It's like being a bird in a nest. When the wind kicks up you feel a slight swaying. There is an observation platform on the

tallest, the Empire State Building. Perhaps you can take your boy there one day."
Georgie clapped excitedly. "Papa, can we go?"

"Now we're headed to Washington. But when we come back to visit, it will be our first stop."

Galina couldn't take her eyes off the skyline. Neither movies nor photographs could do justice to the profusion of indescribably tall buildings, the countless roadways and bridges bristling with cars, trucks and buses, their movement miraculously choreographed by a dizzying array of signals and traffic control devices. It was a performance worthy of the Bolshoi. She had seen some of this in France, but here the level of development was nothing short of amazing. Hours of study in party libraries educated her about America's exploitation of its workers and the shocking gap between rich and poor, but as one motorcar after another sped by she realized that not every occupant could be a rich industrialist. Even in the middle of a ruinous depression the awesome, wealth-producing power of free enterprise was overwhelming. Comrade Stalin's admonition to concentrate on building socialism within the USSR made sense. Toppling capitalism would be a tall order indeed.

It was dark when the limousine turned into a tree-lined street. They parked in front of a fashionable building faced in limestone. In the distance the dome of the Capitol cast a brilliant glow.

A uniformed attendant came running from the canopied entrance. He exchanged a few words with the driver. "Welcome home," the chauffeur announced. "Your apartment's on the second floor."

"Are Ambassador Troyanovsky and Madame still in temporary quarters?" Vladimir asked.

"They finally moved into the embassy. It hasn't been used since the Provisional Government, so it took time to get ready. The furniture only just arrived. It's mostly leftovers from the time of Nicholas II. But I'm sure the Czar of All Russias wouldn't mind."

Early the next morning Vladimir awoke in a room whose dimensions equaled the size of their Moscow apartment. Georgie had crawled in bed with them and he and his mother were still asleep.

Vladimir slipped out of bed. Making a mental note to thank Elena, Troyanovsky's wife for her thoughtfulness, he grabbed a cold glass of milk from the well-stocked refrigerator and checked out the apartment. When he and Galina first laid eyes on the place they were certain it had been assigned in error. "There must be a mistake," his wife insisted as she came across a third bedroom. "It's just us and Georgie!"

The chauffeur shook his head. "One bedroom is for you. Another is for the boy. The third – they call it a 'den' – is to use as you wish. It could make a nice sewing room or study."

Vladimir was checking out a plush leather couch in the living room when someone knocked on the door. It was Troyanovsky's driver, nattily decked out in a white jacket. He rolled in a serving cart brimming with pastries and beverages.

"Welcome to America, Comrade Romm!"

That evening the ambassador and his wife hosted a welcoming reception for the Romms at the newly refurbished Soviet Embassy, situated not far from the White House. Idled for more than a decade, the massive structure had been transformed into a showcase of Imperial excess, replete with crystal chandeliers, intricately carved French furnishings and acres of tapestries. Oleg, the hosts' well-mannered teenage son hustled Georgie off to the game room while Elena led Galina to the parlor, where ladies sipped tea to the sounds of soulful peasant tunes crooned by the chauffeur, now plucking a balalaika.

Galina was bemused. "My, the comrade certainly wears many hats!"

"Around here everyone does, Galya. My husband is very security conscious; the fewer outsiders we take in, the better."

Troyanovsky herded the guests into his study. A large, lightly decorated room, it once housed the massive sword collection of the representative of the Provisional Government.

Drinks poured and cigars lit, the ambassador proposed a toast. "To Comrade Stalin, who sent us here to deliver the Soviet Union's message of friendship and secure America's cooperation in achieving peace and prosperity for the workers of the world!"

Everyone raised their glasses. "To Comrade Stalin!"

"Thank you for helping me welcome the newest member of our staff. I promise not to spoil the evening with business, but our gathering presents a splendid opportunity to reflect on our goals. One must concede that at this precise moment we probably need America more than she needs us. We need her credit, her armaments, her raw materials, and, yes, her technical expertise. More than one thousand of her engineers work in our mines and plants, and we could use thousands more. Regrettably, powerful forces have conspired to sabotage this blossoming friendship. I'm referring, of course, to Germany and Japan. And who's been working tirelessly on their behalf? Trotsky! His supporters have infiltrated Socialist movements, spread scurrilous rumors, called our beloved General Secretary a dictator and accused us of unimaginable repressions. So my challenge to you is simple. Be vigilant! Let no false or disparaging remark go unchallenged. We are all ambassadors charged with disseminating the truth about the USSR. Discredit the fascists and their handmaiden Trotsky however, wherever, and whenever you can!"

Troyanovsky held his glass high. "To Vladimir Georgievich!"

"To Vladimir Georgievich!"

That night Georgie didn't complain about sleeping in his own room, which was stuffed full of presents brought by the guests. His favorite was tucked in next to him, a fluffy brown bear that the ambassador christened with his own diminutive, "Sasha." Georgie was old enough to realize that adults were being especially kind because of his infirmity, and he was smart enough to appreciate it. He had never felt so happy.

Romm wasn't so intoxicated as to ignore the exquisite, sheer nightgown that his wife wore to bed. His reaction drew soft laughter, the likes of which he hadn't heard for some time.

"So you like it, right?"

"Where did you get it?"

Galina affected surprise. "Me? When did you know me to buy something so extravagant? It's a present from Elena. It came from a shop on Fifth Avenue, a fancy street in New York. She promised to take me there one day."

The next afternoon Vladimir was in Troyanovsky's office. Instead of vodka the ambassador poured coffee, a custom that he was encouraging the staff to emulate during working hours.

"I understand that your wife will be teaching dance and putting on shows for our families."

"Yes, you were very kind to arrange it."

"You can thank Elena for that. She's in charge of our cultural program. And how is Georgie?"

"Wonderful. He slept with your bear."

Troyanovsky was an experienced diplomat, exquisitely attuned to nuance. "Tell me, Volya," he asked, switching to the familiar, "I detect a bit of an undercurrent. Is it about your presentation to the journalists?"

As a new member of the capital's corps of foreign correspondents, Vladimir was expected to deliver an address to his counterparts about the Soviet press. Anxious to make a good first impression, he worked many hours preparing a draft. So when he checked his embassy mailbox he was disturbed to find an envelope containing the speech, in its full form. As he read it he was dismayed to recognize Radek's unmistakable diction.

"I found my talk in the mail, Comrade Ambassador."

"Karl Berngardovich worked hard on it. Is there a problem?"

"It's stiff and laden with exaggeration. Far too dogmatic, I think, for its intended audience."

"No problem, give it back, I'll have the translator polish it."

"Actually, I worked up a speech on my own. I'd be happy to bring it in."

Troyanovsky frowned. "I'm sorry, there's not enough time. They intend to publish this lecture in an academic journal. What you say carries the weight of official policy, so the full text must be approved by the Central Committee. Is there anything else?"

"I've been fielding calls about Ukraine. What is our position about reports of mass starvation?"

"Our position is the truth!" Troyanovsky gestured to a stack of newspaper clippings piled high on a table. "They're reprints of Duranty's articles from the *Times*. He calls the famine for what it is: a shameless lie propagated by the Soviet Union's enemies. Why don't you take a few?"

Troyanovsky watched his subordinate leave. He sank deep into thought. Litvinov had praised Romm's performance in Geneva to the skies. True enough, the comrade was skilled and intelligent, if perhaps sometimes overeager, but his politics had hardly progressed since his rescue from the jaws of those party hacks in Tokyo. That ego! It really was a shame.

Vladimir delivered the address a few days later. "...Our press is not simply a means of distribution and circulation of news or of ideas; it is a powerful factor of organization and education of large masses of people for new forms of work, and for a new collective consciousness...Common crimes, accidents, gossip and so on have no place in the Soviet press except, perhaps, in the judicial chronicle. But some occurrence showing inefficiency or loss because of bad management, or reflecting remnants of racial or national prejudice, would be given prominent space...Journalists mostly get regular salaries plus special payments for various articles; some are guaranteed a stable monthly minimum amount a month for a certain number of articles...They, as well as the members of their families, enjoy full social insurance, paid by the paper or review. In short they have every right possessed by other working persons in our country."

A moment passed before the audience realized that he was done. They reacted with tepid applause. He wasn't surprised. Troyanovsky had relented and asked to review his version of the talk, but when it was returned several paragraphs were missing from the end, thus the abrupt conclusion. He was reluctant to irritate the ambassador any further, so he read the speech as is.

It was time for questions. Vladimir recognized the man from the *Washington Post*.

"Mister Romm, you didn't mention censorship, an irritating fact that our correspondents in your country deal with on a daily if not hourly basis. Would you comment on that?"

Vladimir glanced at Troyanovsky and his top two assistants, Counselor Boris Skvirsky and First Secretary Alexis Neymann. From their expressions it seemed as though they smelled a burning fuse.

"I'd be happy to," Vladimir replied. "Our newspapers are run by official organizations. *Pravda* is the organ of the Communist Party. My paper, *Izvestia*, is published by the Central Executive Committee, which oversees the bureaucracy and sets government policy between Congresses. There are also papers put out by the trade union council, the Communist Youth League, and so forth. Just like publishers in the U.S., each decides what gets printed, the difference being that in America the decisions represent corporate interests, while in the Soviet Union they represent the people's interests."

Troyanovsky beamed. He poked at his companions, who smiled broadly.

"Are you saying, Mister Romm," the reporter persisted, "that there's no difference between the function of an editorial board, which sets a paper's tone and direction, and your government censors, who rule over content?"

"Setting a newspaper's 'tone and direction' limits content in a far broader and more encompassing sense than anything our censors do, sir, which is to vet accuracy and safeguard secrets."

Romm joined Troyanovsky for dessert. "Great job, Volya!" the ambassador exclaimed, patting his apparently reformed protégé on the back. He gestured toward the reporter from the *Post*. "I think that idiot's still picking up his teeth."

Troyanovsky's toadies chuckled as if on cue.

Vladimir dug into his apple pie and ice cream. Regrettably, it was sometimes necessary to speak from the head instead of the heart. Matching wits with a hostile reporter was amusing, but only a fool would think that Soviet journalists were free to write or say what they wished. Press freedoms disappeared under Stalin, whose demands for conformity made prevarication the norm, and not only when dealing with outsiders. Fostering illusions was distasteful enough; to pretend that they were real...

Someone gently tapped his shoulders.

"Mister Romm? I'm Paul Ward, from *The Nation*."

Lubyanka prison,
20 January 1937

Leonid and I have been passing the time exchanging anecdotes. Here's one that was making the rounds when I served as a lay member of a revolutionary tribunal:

"A judge finds a colleague laughing his head off. "What is it?" he asks. "I just heard a hilarious anecdote," the friend replies. "Tell me!" the judge begs. His friend sadly shakes his head. "I can't. I just gave someone five years for it!"

Poking fun at the absurdities of Soviet life is a popular way to let off steam. So popular, in fact, that at one point the Central Committee banned deprecating humor as counterrevolutionary. Naturally, the edict spawned a host of new quips. Standing in line day after day for life's necessities can make anyone miserable, so if poking fun at the inanities of socialism helps keep us sane, where's the harm? Here's a brief personal favorite:

"How do we know that Adam and Eve were Russian? Homeless, naked and with only one apple between them, they thought they were in Paradise!"

My cellmate's never been outside the USSR, so he's shown a lot of interest in my travels. Today he asked about the Japanese. If they're as artsy and refined as everyone says, how could they have treated the Chinese so savagely?

It's an excellent question. I'll never forget that first occasion, not long after my arrival, when I came across a clearly well-to-do Japanese woman in one of Tokyo's exclusive department stores. Carefully made-up and attired in a splendid kimono, she was carrying a little tyke dressed in an elaborate military costume. My driver Ichiro shrugged it off as nothing special. (He was probably afraid to say anything lest the event find its way into another hit-piece.) Ichiro would probably disagree, but I came to regard the proud, upper-caste mothers and their uniformed babes as a reflection of the regrettable extent to which Samurai values pervade Japanese life.

What makes this preoccupation with the martial so odd is that it coexists with an esthetic sensibility that is second to none. Everyone knows about the Japanese infatuation with flower arrangement and with origami, a technique for folding paper squares into imaginative shapes. I came to appreciate their understated, elegant homes and offices, which foreigners brought up on clutter and mindless ornamentation might at first think sparse, and the ubiquitous, lovingly tended gardens, many unavoidably tiny due to the crowding, but no less striking for their size. In spring there was an explosion of cherry blossoms, while in the fall everyone rushed to the country to experience the symphony of maple leaves turning their impossible shades.

How to reconcile all this with the Empire's ruthless militarism? That was Leonid's question, and in the end I was stumped. Japanese are as much an enigma as the industrious Germans, who brought us both Beethoven and Hitler. Now that they've joined causes (let's not forget Italy and that bizarre Benito character as well) their intentions seem frighteningly clear.

Is it true, as Vyshinsky insists, that the trials are being staged to wake the world to the threat of fascism? Perhaps America and the Brits really have swallowed the Nazi lie that Germany simply intends to regain its ancestral lands. What seems far-fetched is that these absurd court proceedings will help bring around the American Congress, which punctiliously turns over every rock to assure that no foreign obligation lurks underneath. In fact, their obviously fabricated nature could easily have the opposite effect.

Leonid and I may not be the most impartial observers, but we've come to the conclusion that what really lurks behind the trials is a certain comrade's ambitions. Who were the principal accused last August? Kamenev and Zinoviev, may they rest in peace. Who are they this time? Piatakov and Radek. Who's at home waiting for the other shoe to drop? *Izvestia* editor-in-chief Nikolai Bukharin. All are one-time top Bolsheviks, and each had opposed Stalin's agenda before his coronation, when the Soviet Union was ruled by a triumvirate. He dispatched its two other members at the 1936 trial, and now he's gunning for the rest.

There's an explanation for this show, and it's got nothing to do with spies and wreckers. It's a liquidation. It's about who's left standing.

Chicago, Cleveland (1934-35)

"Kirov's been killed!"

Lev looked up from his desk. "What's that you say?"

"Kirov!" the agitated militiaman repeated. "Leningrad Party Chief! Murdered!"

Lev's desk was stacked with reports of that week's mayhem, mostly brawls that occasionally ended with a drunkard's brains staining the sidewalk. Now that pistols were commonplace many robberies were also ending badly. But the killing of a top official was unprecedented.

A plainclothesman came in. "It's pretty straightforward, boss. It happened just outside his office. Witnesses say they weren't arguing. The guy walked up to Kirov, drew a pistol and shot him twice point-blank. He then dropped the gun, collapsed over the body and started bawling like a baby. That's how the militiamen found him."

"So it wasn't a robbery?"

"Doesn't look that way." The officer flipped through his notebook. "Nikolayev, Leonid Vasilyevich. Thirty years old, ordinary worker. Clean record."

"So why did he do it?"

"Wouldn't say. You want to talk to him?"

Lev was flabbergasted. "He's *here*? Kirov was a party bigwig! They're the NKVD's responsibility!" That year the GPU was supplanted by a new internal security apparatus. What hadn't changed were the bullies.

"We had to get him out of there, chief. A drunken mob was forming. They would have killed him."

Lev followed his officers to the interview room. Two uniformed officers watched over a bony young man with dirty black hair. He was slumped in a chair.

"I'm Lev Alexandrovich, chief of..."

"Who cares?" the suspect snarled. "Just shoot me and be done with it."

"Everybody out!" Lev ordered, shutting the door. He pulled up a chair so close that his and the killer's knees touched. No man could ignore that. Nikolayev's eyes blinked rapidly.

Lev spoke softly. "Oh, you'll be shot all right, comrade, but not by me. Those kinds of things are done by specialists. While we wait for them to arrive, why don't you tell me why you did it?"

The killer wetted his lips. He hadn't expected that his future would be laid out with such certainty. A note of hesitation crept into his voice. "Why should I?"

"To satisfy my curiosity. How about it?"

Tears ran down the man's face. "My girlfriend. Ah, she's so beautiful..."

"What, you killed her too?"

"No! Not that I didn't want to, the bitch!"

Lev heard footsteps. There was no time left. "What? What are you saying?"

"He was screwing her! That big, important comrade could have anyone! Why did he pick on..."

The door swung open. Medved, the secret police chief, barged in. He was trailed by three malevolent-looking men in black coats.

Medved was outraged. "What the hell are you doing, Lev Alexandrovich?"

"I'm interviewing the prisoner. It's what detectives do."

Medved smirked. "Go back to your drunks, mister policeman. We'll take it from here."

Lev watched them drag off the youth. His assistant approached. "Did he say anything, chief?"

"No. Not a thing."

Early the next morning a special train bearing a phalanx of top officials pulled in to Leningrad. Medved was there to greet them. Stalin walked up. He slapped the secret policeman hard in the face.

It was December 31, 1934. The Romms and Troyanovskys were on vacation in New York City. While the wives window-shopped on Fifth Avenue, the ambassador, Vladimir and Georgie headed for the Empire State Building.

They were on the observation deck, huddling against the cold East River wind.

"We're higher than the birds!" Georgie exclaimed.

"That's because we're on top of the tallest building in the world," Vladimir said. "And do you see that bridge in the distance? It's the George Washington, the longest in the world. What do you think of that?"

Georgie laughed. "Papa! Why are you fibbing? Everyone knows that the best and biggest of everything are in the Soviet Union!"

Troyanovsky smiled. "He's got you there, Volya."

Georgie's attention was drawn to a pair of gulls circling lazily over the Hudson. "They're not beating their wings. How can they stay up?"

"They're floating on air, Georgie. It's like when Mama takes you swimming, except then it's the water that holds you up."

Georgie looked to "uncle" for confirmation. Troyanovsky nodded his assent. "Listen to your father, Georgie. He's often right."

That evening the families joined the thousands who packed Times Square to watch the descent of a brilliantly-lit iron ball.

The ambassador pulled out his pocket watch. "Georgie, what time is it back home?"

The boy's brow wrinkled. He carefully studied the timepiece. "If you mean Moscow, uncle, it's tomorrow...seven-thirty in the morning. In Vladivostok it would be much later, of course...ah, two-thirty in the afternoon."

Troyanovsky was delighted. "Excellent!"

Thanks to the ambassador's influence, a new tuberculosis sanatorium in rural Maryland offered to treat Georgie for a nominal fee. A spread-out affair with an open design, it had a special wing for children, and discreetly hidden from view, its own mortuary. Vladimir and Galina were hopeful, but in the end its therapies turned out to be essentially the same as at Berck-Plage: rest, nutrition and fresh air. Doctors were always hinting at promising new approaches but no real answer seemed close at hand.

After the show ended Vladimir and his superior detoured to a tavern for a chat. Events in the Soviet Union had taken a frightening turn. Kirov's killing was framed as an assassination, the slap in the face a rebuke for failing to prevent it. Leningrad's secret police chief and his underlings wound up in Siberia for dereliction of duty. Dozens of low-level functionaries were accused of anti-party activity and shot. Nikolayev also got a bullet. Before his execution he gave the regime a going-away present, testifying in open court that the murder marked the initial phase of a campaign orchestrated by the country's enemies and directed by Trotsky to topple Stalin. Widely reported in the newspapers, the killer's words shocked the nation. It was the first time that Trotsky, a controversial but for many heroic figure had been maligned this way.

It wouldn't be the last.

Troyanovsky ordered a round of drinks. "Georgie seems to be well informed, politically speaking."

"His mother drags him to a lot of Party meetings."

"You know, women have always been our staunchest revolutionaries. They were tossing bombs while we were children. Elena and I were hardly married when the *Okhrana* arrested her over that business in Tiflis. What a mess! I didn't know it, but she had been running messages for the bandits."

Vladimir raised his glass. "To a heroine of the Soviet State!"

Troyanovsky was deep in thought. His subordinate's quip about party meetings made the ambassador wonder. Was the man always so careless? In the current climate every utterance was subject to being parsed for its ideological implications.

"I'm not sure how to say this, Volya. You know I hold you in the highest regard. Your heart's in the right place, but you must learn how to paddle in unison with others, in directions you might not prefer. It wouldn't hurt to watch how you express yourself, either. Moscow is just getting warmed up."

Vladimir remained in New York City for a few days to cover the North American automobile show. Set in a cavernous military armory, the wildly popular exhibition featured twenty-five American makes, including for the first time both Ford and Chevrolet. Gazing at the lustrously polished fenders of a twelve-cylinder Packard cabriolet, he wondered at the resiliency of a system that could produce such miracles, let alone in the middle of a depression. America had to come to the Soviet side. It simply had to.

William Bullitt was determined otherwise. Ebullient and optimistic when he first arrived in Moscow, the purges, arrests and trials soon convinced America's first Ambassador to the USSR that Stalin was madman. In a move that he considered a serious breach of protocol, the Communist International – pretending, as usual, that it was not an instrument of the USSR – invited American communists to participate in the Comintern's summer 1935 World Congress in Moscow. Coincidentally, the University of Chicago planned a conference on the USSR about the same time, and as a special draw invited Karl Radek to be the keynote speaker. To retaliate, Bullitt at first refused to grant Radek a visa. When he finally relented, reportedly under pressure from Roosevelt, who had turned a deaf ear to his envoy's misgivings, Stalin decided that it was more important for the fiery Bolshevik to stay home to work on the USSR's new constitution. Radek's talk would have to be given by someone already in the country.

That someone turned out to be Vladimir Romm.

In June 1935 the Romms and Troyanovskys journeyed by rail to Chicago. As the train approached Harpers Ferry Vladimir referred to a guidebook. "We're coming to the town where more than ten-thousand Union soldiers surrendered to the great Confederate General, Stonewall Jackson..."

"Why was he so 'great'?" Galina asked. "Wasn't the South fighting to keep Negroes in chains?"

Troyanovsky laughed. "Looks like you get it from all sides, Volya."

"Galya's right. It still makes me uneasy to get on a bus and watch them stare from the back."

"It's all quite odd," Elena offered. "Negroes have their own neighborhoods, their own schools, their own hospitals, even their own university. Oh, the politicians claim that everything is equal but that's nonsense. I mean, all you have to do is go to these places and have a look. What's amazing is that the colored don't revolt. They act as though they prefer to be separated. I asked one of the cleaning ladies about that. You know what she told me? 'No offense, missus, but the less I have to do with white folks the better'."

"Paul Ward took me to the courthouse the other day," Vladimir said. "We sat all morning watching them bring in prisoners to be read their charges. Most were poor Negroes. On our way out we passed by a statute of a woman holding a scale. I asked Paul why she was blindfolded. He said it was supposedly to guarantee that people would be treated equally, but that it was really from embarrassment."

Romm and Troyanovsky were in the observation car as the train neared Cleveland. It was a sobering sight. They rolled past one idled plant after another, their decaying state laying bare the impact of the economic malaise on the great industrial belt of the Northeast. Vast lots where prosperous members of the working class once parked their automobiles were overgrown with weeds, the only signs of life being the few guards who lazed about, trying to keep looters from stripping the buildings and carting away what little remained.

"The depression's handiwork," Troyanovsky muttered. "One can only imagine what's befallen the workers."

A neatly-dressed man in his early thirties made his way from another row. He offered the men a calling card.

"I'm Jim Thornton from the *Cleveland Plain-Dealer*." He turned to Troyanovsky. "Please forgive me, but I'm certain that I've seen your picture..."

"Ambassador Alexander Antonovich Troyanovsky of the USSR, at your service. Please meet my colleague Vladimir Romm, correspondent from *Izvestia*."

The men shook hands. "You gentlemen headed West?"

"We have a meeting in Chicago," Troyanovsky explained. "Please, join us."

Thornton sat down. They chugged past another dormant factory. "I couldn't help notice your reactions. Believe me, as someone who lives here it's very close to my heart. More than a third of Ohio's workers are unemployed. Imagine – a third! City men are hounding farmers for work! Our unemployed have no benefits, so families are losing their homes and going hungry. In America!"

"Are you on your way back from Washington?" Vladimir asked.

"Yes. I was covering the social security hearings. It doesn't look good. That heartless bastard Hoover got kicked out, but the fat cats are still in the driver's seat. Whenever Roosevelt tries to do something for ordinary people they scream 'socialism' – no offense intended, gentlemen – and throw another bundle of cash at their congressman."

Whistles signaled the train's arrival. The reporter scribbled a note. "It's my home address and phone number," he told Vladimir. "Give me a call when you come back through. I've got friends who'd love to meet you. If nothing else, we could both get a good story out of it."

The honored visitors were quartered on campus. Vladimir and Galina woke early to take a stroll. They stepped into a fantasy of medieval spires, towers and fierce gargoyles that stretched as far as the eye could see.

Galina gazed at the extraordinary sight. "It's as though we've gone back in time!"

"Rockefeller said that it was the best eighty million he ever spent."

"Rockefeller? What do you know about him?"

"Capitalism is catching, Galya. Did I tell you about the car show?"

Galina pecked her husband's cheek. "Yes, Volya. Many times."

That afternoon Vladimir and the wives sat in the front row of a lavishly appointed auditorium as Troyanovsky delivered the opening address.

"...but this policy of friendship and peaceful collaboration is so vital an ingredient of our theory and practice that it is impossible for us to renounce it in favor of the doctrines of hostility, nationalism and domination. Such ideas can have no part in our foreign policy..."

He went on this way for about ten minutes. Reassured by the intelligent, well-spoken diplomat that peace and reasonableness were the Soviet norm, a pleasing lull settled over the several hundred students and academics patiently waiting for the speech to run its course.

"...I believe I may say that in the USSR we have no racial prejudices..."

Audience members sat up. Things were finally getting interesting.

"...In my country Slavs, Mongols, Jews, Caucasians, Chinese, northern nationalities, and others – over one hundred and eighty national stocks in all – live on friendly and peaceful terms. The presumption of superiority of one race over another is absent from the minds of our population. In some countries racial hatred may be regarded as a virtue; I am glad to say that in the Soviet Union it evokes general contempt and indignation, and its active manifestations are held to be criminal acts and regarded as such by the people. Anti-Semitism, for instance, is looked upon as a barbarity incompatible with a civilized society – something left behind in the dark period of Russian history."

The audience erupted in applause. Vladimir, Galina and Elena glowed with pride. Even if the rosy picture that Troyanovsky painted was a slight exaggeration – after all, the lands reserved for ethnic groups were mostly in the East and shockingly poor – the USSR was indisputably ahead in the one area that America, which boasted about liberty and freedom, chose to ignore.

Vladimir was next. His speech, prepared by Radek under the watchful eye of party hacks in Moscow, was an elaborate puff piece that bragged about the Soviet Union's heroic economic advances during the five-year plans. As a non-economist he was apprehensive about presenting figures that, if experience proved correct, were wildly inflated at a university renowned for its economics faculty, of whom many would assumedly be in the audience. But Troyanovsky was right when he said not to worry, as unlike some of their government counterparts, many American scholars were partial to socialism. Scheduled just before a lavish reception, Vladimir's talk didn't draw a single challenge.

"We read that you were at Smolny when Lenin spoke."

Vladimir smiled at an attractive, auburn-haired professor demurely snacking on toast and caviar. "Yes, I was. Actually, we were in different parties. He was a Bolshevik, while I was a Socialist Revolutionary..."

"*Revolutionary?* Oh, my word!" The woman looked as though she might faint.

Troyanovsky watched faculty members gather around his star correspondent. Socialism had taken hold of the American *intelligentsia* to a far greater degree than Moscow thought possible. Many Americans felt battered by capitalism; desperate for a Utopia, they saw in the promises of communism a perfect fit. And it wasn't all about the economy: his remarks about bigotry, which Moscow had thought chancy, drew a wonderful response. None of it should have been a surprise. Intourist, really an arm of the secret police, busily hosted American writers and educators on "fact-finding" tours of Soviet factories, collectives and historical sites. These carefully orchestrated events didn't disappoint, generating a rash of books and journal articles that gushed about social and economic advances under Stalin. Meanwhile the U.S. badly lagged in counterintelligence capability, making the pickings ridiculously easy.

The Ambassador of the Soviet Union kissed his wife's glowing cheek. The exercise was a success! Alexander Antonovich Troyanovsky and his sidekick Vladimir Georgievich Romm, preachers of the new world order, found their choir in America's heartland.

Who would have thought?

Jim met Vladimir at the Cleveland train station two days later.

"We're thrilled that you decided to visit."

"Ambassador Troyanovsky said it would be a great opportunity to mingle with working Americans. I'd be crazy to miss it."

Jim placed Vladimir's bags in the trunk of a newer Ford coupe.

"Is this the eight?" Vladimir asked.

"Nah, it's the four. A lot easier on the pocketbook. What do *you* drive?"

Vladimir stared at his host. He didn't know whether to laugh or cry.

They drove into the suburbs where large, new housing tracts were rapidly displacing farmland. Before coming to the U.S. Vladimir assumed that Hollywood movies exaggerated the living standards of ordinary workers. He had since visited the homes of some of his Washington colleagues. Nearly all were larger and better appointed than Alexander and Elena's apartment, which was considered luxurious by Soviet standards. But what he saw here was startling. Row after row of new single-family homes, most with flower beds, lush lawns, white picket fences and a car in the driveway. Despite the harsh economic times, many Americans were apparently living quite well. It seemed almost an affront.

They drove by one of the larger homes. A beautiful new Auburn was parked in front.

"That's where my in-laws live. He's a retired editor."

Vladimir stared at the sleek automobile. "He worked in a *newspaper?*"

"He was my boss. I met my wife Sally at one of his parties."

They parked in the driveway of a tidy beige bungalow with clapboard siding. A panting mass of golden fur bolted out.

"Jim, bad boy!" A slender young woman with black hair walked up, laughing.

"Volya, meet my wife Sally." Jim vigorously rubbed the retriever's head. "Sally raised him from a pup. He was 'Jim' before we got together."

"Doesn't it cause confusion?"

"Not really. When my wife calls we both come."

They were relaxing after dinner. Vladimir learned that Jim was a third-generation American of English ancestry. Sally, a schoolteacher, was also native born. Her grandparents emigrated from Italy as teens.

"Some Americans are frightened of the Soviets, but not us," Jim explained. "Prick any American, chances are that out will flow European blood."

"Not your Negroes, though."

"No, not them."

Flames licked from the fireplace. A creased and faded photograph of a young soldier wearing an old-fashioned uniform was on the mantle.

"Who is the military man?" Vladimir asked.

"My grandfather," Jim said. "He was with the Eight Ohio Infantry. They fought Pickett at Gettysburg. It's a famous battle from our Civil War."

"He was a Union soldier?"

"Yes. Ohio went with the North."

"So your state was against slavery?"

Jim turned to his wife. "You're the teacher, sweetheart."

"It's complicated," Sally explained. "Not all Ohioans favored abolishing slavery, but most feared seceding from the Union even more. It hadn't been that long since the Revolution and people yearned for stability."

"It's like that with us, too," Vladimir agreed. "Fears of breaking apart can be very strong." His eyes fell on a photograph of a pale child with red hair and freckles. "And that beautiful young lady? Who is she?"

Sally took Jim's hand. "That's Jim's sister, Christy. She died from T.B."

Vladimir paled. "It happened long ago. We wouldn't display the picture if we didn't want guests to ask."

"Thank you, I understand." Vladimir struggled to find the right words. "You see, we have something special in common."

Jim and Sally took Vladimir to the local shopping district, a block-long strip sporting a grocery, hardware, drug store and cinema. They sat at a chrome and steel soda fountain where Vladimir enjoyed his first-ever root beer float.

"How did you like it?" Jim asked as they returned to the car.

"Very tasty. But I noticed a child having one. I didn't know that alcoholic beverages could be served to persons so young."

Sally broke up. "Volya, 'root beer' is a soft drink. There's no alcohol."

Vladimir feigned disappointment. "None? It would have made such a great story!"

Jim smiled at his spouse. "*Now* do you believe he's a reporter?"

On the last day of his visit Vladimir accompanied his hosts to a barbeque at the home of Sally's parents. When they arrived a dozen guests were chatting and munching on snacks. They looked at Vladimir curiously. Jim lent him some casual clothes, but a Bolshevik in sandals and walking shorts was still a Bolshevik.

Vladimir was peppered with questions. Mindful of Troyanovsky's friendly reminder, "whatever happens, don't land on page one!" he tried to steer the conversations clear of politics. Vladimir worked his audience with a well-practiced charm, delighting them with such tidbits as the Russians' taste for American cars and cinema, and his own love of gangster films.

Sally's father had some bad news. "Under the new movie code, in the end bad guys always have to lose. Your hero Cagney may have to start playing more heroic roles."

"Movie code? What's that?"

"An agreement to tone down content. There were complaints that the cinema was getting too risqué, threatening public morals."

Vladimir thought about it for a moment. "Who's that detective with the beautiful rich wife and the small, annoying dog?"

A guest answered. "You're thinking of the 'The Thin Man,' Mister Romm. Nick Charles, his wife Nora and her dog Asta."

"Yes, they made a wonderful movie. It's the first one that my wife and I saw after arriving. Well, Nick likes to drink. Is that also against the rules?"

"Oh, I think that's still OK. But sex, bad language and the wrong guy winning are out."

"I understand. Two of those I agree with."

Everyone roared. Vladimir thought he had them in the palm of his hands when a tipsy middle-aged man intervened.

"You know, comrade, they've been throwing you softballs. So far no one's asked you anything of importance."

The guests quieted. A woman tugged on the man's sleeve. "C'mon, Harry, let's take you home."

He shrugged her off. "Pay no attention to my spouse. Like that detective character, I'm at my best when I've had a few."

Vladimir tried to tone things down. "Do you work at the paper?"

Harry grinned, displaying a missing tooth. "Nah, I'm just a working stiff who lives next door. One of those prole-somethings you commies carry on about."

"That's proletarians," his wife corrected. "And Mister Romm is not a 'commie,' he's a Communist, dear."

"Whatever." Harry drew closer. "Do you know what an electrician is, chum?"

Vladimir warily sipped his drink. Going to blows with an American was not part of his assignment. "Of course. It's a wonderful trade. Many fine American electrical engineers work in our mines."

The drunk bored in. "They're not Americans – they're traitors, every last one of them! I'm a *real* American worker. And I can prove it." He pointed to a small, deep wound in his forearm, then to a matching lesion on the other side. "Guess how it happened!"

"You were shot?" The guests tittered. Even Harry grinned.

"Some idiot didn't cut the power. Zap! High voltage A.C., burned all the way through. I suppose it's not something that commie intellectuals have to worry about."

Vladimir stepped back. He lifted his shirt to reveal an ugly, ragged scar running across his back.

There was a collective gasp. Even Harry was shocked. "How the hell...?"

"Red Army bayonet. You see, I wasn't always an 'intellectual'."

Dmitry Bukhartsev, *Izvestia's* correspondent-spy in Berlin, was in his second year of writing poisonous articles about the Nazis. As a Jew and a Soviet his access to

German citizens was severely limited. He was also increasingly beset by plainclothes security agents who were eager to find a good reason to expel the pesky Soviet from the Reich. With only so many ways of describing food shortages and goose-stepping soldiers Dmitry was running out of ways to annoy his hosts.

Then the most fascinating assignment of his career landed in his lap.

"My father despises Hitler but there's little he can do. Americans are so caught up with themselves that they don't recognize the Nazis for what they really are. It's up to Socialists to lead the way."

As the earnest and attractive young woman rambled on, Dmitry understood why Boris was smitten. While many bored, over-privileged Westerners dabbled in communism to assuage their class guilt, few embraced the ideology as wholeheartedly as the daughter of the American Ambassador to Germany. A woman of hearty appetites, Martha Dodd's plunge into socialism would not have been complete without sharing her favors with at least one attractive representative of that great proletarian movement. After auditioning a few she settled on Boris Vinogradov, the charming, good-looking press officer at the Soviet Embassy.

Then the unexpected happened: Boris asked his superiors for permission to marry. Having dodged repeated entreaties by the NKVD to turn his girlfriend into an agent, the love-struck official was eager to sweep her off to Moscow to wash his underwear. The thought of throwing away such a potentially valuable source drove the secret police crazy. Enough was enough, and when Boris brushed aside their umpteenth request they did what comes natural. Boris was recalled to Moscow, secretly arrested and thrown into the Lubyanka. Bukhartsev was quickly impressed to salvage the contact.

Martha immediately took to Dmitry; as far as is known, not in an intimate way. Their initial meeting was arranged under pretext of conveying a message from Vinogradov. In fact, Boris did write a letter. Dictated by his jailers, it said that he was called away on urgent business and would return as soon as he could. Whether Martha was disappointed is hard to say. What's known is that she quickly began giving Dmitry correspondence and secret materials from her father's office. She also reported on her other boyfriends, including a high-ranking S.S. man. Thanks to Bukhartsev this thoroughly modern girl was well on her way to becoming one of the Soviet Union's top intelligence assets.

Boris would have to be kept alive a little while longer.

Lubyanka prison,
22 January 1937

Only one day to go until trial! Have I mentioned that they've been fattening us up with extra rations? This morning there were also new fashions to go along with our new bellies. After a big breakfast they herded us into a supply room, where we rummaged through piles of clothing, selecting shirts, pants and jackets that prisoner tailors altered right on the spot. We also got shoes, stockings and underwear, all previously worn but in excellent shape. One hates to think about the prior owners. Molchanov referred to the garments as 'donations'. Then pity the poor donors.

We were also fitted with belts and ties. I've grown so accustomed to draw strings that fastening my pants in the proper way felt like an impossible luxury. For reasons that one can guess at these items won't be distributed until we're in the assembly room, then collected afterwards. In the meantime we stumbled around holding up our trousers.

Once everything was laundered and pressed it was time for a bath. We even enjoyed the luxury of a small dollop of shampoo, a rare enough commodity on the outside. Barbers – again, each a prisoner – trimmed our hair and clipped our nails, scissors and such being normally forbidden lest prisoners use them in a socially unapproved way.

It's amazing how quickly good food, hygiene and decent apparel can transform a passel of filthy characters into something approaching swans! I mean this not only in terms of appearance but for its effect on our morale. As much as one resents being exploited, it's hard not to feel more hopeful about things after a bath and shave.

What more could Vyshinsky hope for than five reasonably content liars?

Liquidation (1935-36)

"Volya, darling!" A rustle of silk, that unforgettable scent and all-too-familiar hug. Rose! What was she doing here?

"You seem shocked," Rose smiled. "Am I unwelcome at Embassy receptions?"

"Of course not. I'm just a little surprised," Vladimir conceded. "Are you here with Allen?"

Rose laughed heartily. "Goodness, how desperate do you think I am?" She pointed to a stocky, bearded man getting drinks at the bar. "My fiancée. Unless you have a better idea," she teased.

Galina watched curiously from a distance. She was chatting with Troyanovsky's wife and the *Times'* Walter Duranty when she heard a woman call out her husband's pet name.

"Who is that?"

"I'm not sure," Elena said. "Do you know her, Walter?"

"She worked for Dulles, I think. Maybe you ought to go check her out, Galya," he winked.

Rose greeted Galina with a friendly handshake. "I'm so happy to meet you. I was a secretary for the American legation in Geneva. Your husband and my boss were pals."

"Still are!" Dulles stepped in. He knew that Rose and Vladimir had enjoyed more than a simple friendship, but why let that spoil things? The famous lawyer deftly plucked a fat mushroom off a passing waiter's tray. "Delicious! You know, Volya, I told Rose that you could help her and Rolf get to Saint Petersburg for their honeymoon. Did I over-promise?"

"Not at all." Vladimir scribbled a note on the back of a calling card and handed it to Rose. "Take this and your passports to the Intourist office. It should see the both of you through all the 'Red tape'."

Dulles addressed Galina. "Mrs. Romm, would you mind if I borrowed your husband?"

Vladimir led his friend to a private office next to the Embassy library. He fetched a bottle of vodka from the liquor cabinet and poured drinks.

"Thanks for the save, Allen."

"You're welcome. Actually, there's something I've wanted to discuss. How long has the ambassador been gone?"

"Four months." Vladimir had been asked more than once. Troyanovsky's prolonged sojourn in Moscow – he left for "consultations" in October 1935 – had tongues wagging. His absence spoke poorly of the prospects for the new alliance, to say nothing of the possibility that, as some speculated, it might have been a pretext for Troyanovsky's arrest.

Dulles refilled their tumblers. "Look, this is very unofficial, but I've been asked to do some fact-finding."

"Well, Allen, if you're looking for unofficial, I couldn't think of a better person to ask."

"Terrific! Here's the gist of it." Dulles counted out with his fingers. "One, the Communist International. Two, the USSR's debts."

Vladimir tensed. "I'm listening."

"First, as to the Comintern. You will never, not in a million years convince the West that the International is anything but a Party organ. Its reckless promotion of communism outside the USSR is very irritating and goes completely against the spirit of recognition."

Vladimir laughed bitterly. "There are plenty in the Party who would agree with the 'reckless' part. But communism is inherently international. Anyone who thinks that it's possible to convince us otherwise is dreaming. What's number two?"

"America wants its money back. Ninety million bucks isn't chicken feed."

"Allen, I'm a correspondent, not a diplomat, so I can't speak for my government. But as far as the Soviet people are concerned, the debt run up by the Czars is not the Soviet Union's, and any moral obligation we might have had to make it good was cancelled when your troops landed at Archangel."

Dulles was taken aback. "That was before your Revolution, Volya."

"That's not so long ago. America's a youngster. Our history began in the days of Muscovy. And how can the U.S. claim to be our friend when it enacts laws like the Neutrality Act? When your President constantly reassures Congress that America will not, under any circumstances, get involved in what he called 'other people's wars'?"

"You know darned well that I have no quarrel with you there."

"That's not what you said in your book."

"Hamilton and I couldn't get the publisher to let us criticize isolationism. All we could write – and it took a fight to get it in – is some circumlocutory nonsense, that America mustn't rule out its options by declaring it would never intervene. You almost need a law degree to understand that!"

"Well, when your President sends as his first ambassador someone as openly hostile as Bullitt..."

Dulles was perplexed. He was a lawyer. How did he wind up on the defensive? Was Romm that good? Or was there more to diplomacy than met the eye?

"Bullitt and his backwards-thinking crowd are part of the old guard. Roosevelt wants a more progressive approach, and if he's reelected I'll be helping recruit people for the State Department who recognize that. Our President very much wants to support the USSR, and France, and Ethiopia, and everyone else who's threatened by fascism. In this political climate, though, he can't be rattling sabers. Heck, there are plenty in Congress who would impeach him tomorrow over the New Deal. Once he gets a second term you'll start seeing some real progress. But Congress needs some flowers and candy. And most importantly: no bad surprises. It's hard to argue for partnering with a country that's holding purge trials. If Troyanovsky has disappeared into the dungeons, your mission here is effectively done."

Vladimir and Galina found Georgie and his babysitter fast asleep. The couple let them be and went to bed.

Galina slipped into a nightgown. "Where did you and Dulles wander off to? Walter was hovering around me like a bee."

"Perhaps if you dressed more modestly," Vladimir teased. His wife's beaded, daringly low-cut gown was crafted by Elena's favorite couturier.

"Don't change the subject. You didn't exactly push that woman away."

"In this world you can't get too many hugs, Galya. Anyway, to change the subject, did Walter share anything interesting?"

"Actually, there *was* something. Did you hear that Lev Alexandrovich is in the Lubyanka?"

"Lev's locked up?"

"No, not that way! He was let go from his detective's job. They sent him to Moscow as a prison guard. Walter said that considering the Kirov mess, Lev got off easy. It's all very strange, don't you think?"

Vladimir was disgusted. "Strange" and "commonplace" were increasingly interchangeable. "You know, I never thanked you for interceding with him. If you hadn't, he might be guarding me."

Galina softened. "I didn't think you knew. But you're welcome."

Troyanovsky had come back from Moscow and things seemed back to normal. Vladimir couldn't feel more guilty over the favor that he was about to ask.

They were in the ambassador's study. Elena was hosting a party to celebrate Georgie's birthday, and sounds drifted in of children at play.

"Volya, I completely understand. Overseas assignments can place a terrible strain on a family. Just hear me out, and if your mind's still made up we'll bring in a replacement right away. Now, what I'm about to say you must not share, not even with your wife."

"You have my word, Comrade Ambassador."

Troyanovsky lowered his voice. "While I was in Moscow the secret police arrested a gaggle of young communists for conspiring to assassinate the General Secretary. Believe me, the kids were serious enough, although whether they could have actually carried it through is uncertain."

"Did they get all of them?"

"Oh, sure, the cell had been thoroughly penetrated. There's never a shortage of informers. According to my source – this, Volya, is in the strictest confidence – there is compelling evidence that Trotsky was behind the plot."

Vladimir was floored. "Trotsky inciting a pack of Russian youngsters to murder Stalin? How could it be possible? The lunatic's been running around Europe for years with our dogs on his tail!"

"Look, I've not tried to make sense of it. All I know is that something big is brewing. This isn't a good time to be close at hand. Understand?"

So that was it, Vladimir thought. To rekindle counterrevolutionary hysteria the secret police got an agent-provocateur to fire up a bunch of hapless teens. Pinning the blame on Trotsky was bad news for all who had ever been in any way connected with the radical, a group that comprised half the employees at *Izvestia*, from Bukharin down to, regrettably, himself.

Strangely, Radek, the man once thought closest to the renegade, was just promoted to head the group drafting the USSR's new charter. Go figure!

Troyanovsky gave Vladimir four theater tickets. "They're from our cultural attaché. Elena reminded me that Jascha Heifetz is a Vilna boy. Take some friends, have a good time."

Vladimir, Galina and *The Nation's* Paul Ward and his wife Dorothy approached the grandly colonnaded entrance of Constitution Hall, the magnificent new home of the National Symphony.

Galina was ecstatic. "Oh, my word! It's just like Smolny, where Comrade Lenin made his speech!"

"My wife's homesick," Vladimir said. "Everything looks like Moscow."

During intermission an usher handed Vladimir the musician's calling card. A note on the back invited the couples backstage after the concert.

Vladimir explained. "Our families were casually acquainted through events at the publishing house. He's five years younger so we never spent time together. I didn't know about his accomplishments for many years, when I read that 'Vilna's boy wonder' was performing at Carnegie Hall. He was still in his teens!"

When the concert was done the couples were escorted to the musician's dressing room. Vladimir recognized the famous performer from publicity photos. Far from handsome, with brooding eyes, a high forehead and a toothy smile, Heifetz had a presence that Americans called "star quality." Being filthy rich didn't hurt, either.

They exchanged pleasantries. "Your ambassador sent a note. It mentions that you're related to the film director Mikhail Romm."

"He's a distant cousin, a generation younger," Vladimir said.

"Really! You know, I saw his 'Rushka' in Saint Petersburg during my '34 tour. It was a masterpiece!"

"Do you miss your homeland?" Galina asked.

"Not really. I was only a boy when we left. That one time I went back it was cold and gloomy. We were greeted by dour-faced officials who acted as though I should have been grateful to be let in. I cheered the Statute of Liberty just like an immigrant when we got home."

They ended the evening at the Romm's apartment. Vladimir paid the babysitter while Galina readied coffee and pastries.

"Was he what you expected?" Paul asked.

Vladimir thought about it. "There's a big difference between being 'from' Vilna and 'of' Vilna. But what I'd give to have a smidgen of his talent!"

Galina grimaced. "I didn't find him all that admirable. He seemed to think very little of Russia, where he learned to play the violin. It's well known that he lives extravagantly."

Vladimir bit into a strudel. "He's left the old country behind, Galya. Nicholas was still in power when an American impresario heard the boy play and brought him and his family to the U.S. Heifetz thinks of himself as an American. All he wants is a bigger house and a fancier car."

Dorothy took offense. "That's a pretty broad brush, Volya. Do we really seem that obsessed with material things?"

"Excuse me, it's probably jealousy talking. We certainly don't live like this in Moscow. Other than for you and Paul we've made few American friends. To tell the truth, I often feel as though we landed on the moon."

Georgie had let himself out of bed. He was in his pajamas, staring at the sweets.

"Hello, Georgie, I'm Paul. Do you remember me?"

"No. Are you an ambassador like Uncle Alexander Antonovich?"

"No, Georgie, I'm a journalist like your father."

"Oh. May I have a strudel?"

Galina gave him a taste of hers and took him back to bed. Paul laughed. "Volya, do you remember when you were that direct?"

"Sure. I always said what was on my mind before I got married."

Galina took her time settling the boy in. She had never adjusted to the American way of things and badly missed Moscow. Vladimir had also seemed eager to go back, but their plans were on hold. Something happened at his talk with Troyanovsky, for he returned with plans for a working vacation at a national park in far-off California. It was clearly a consolation prize.

In August 1936 delegates from France, Great Britain, the U.S., Japan, China and the USSR met at Yosemite to discuss the explosive situation in the Far East. Anticipating that its takeover of Manchuria would be the main topic, Japan dispatched a large contingent that included ranking members of its foreign office. Litvinov, who doubted that the talks could accomplish anything, sent two representatives: Vladimir and a "geographer" from Moscow.

Their trip was uneventful, their arrival a bit less so. They had barely settled into their cabin when a *New York Times* stringer appeared at the door. He was there to get a comment on a news bulletin from the previous day. Vladimir had heard nothing of the matter until that moment.

Troyanovsky was at his desk in the embassy when the call came through. He instantly guessed its purpose.

"Hello, Volya. How was your trip?"

"Fine, Comrade Ambassador. And the lodgings are fine, too. But that's not why I'm calling..." Troyanovsky heard a newspaper rustling. *"New York Times,* dateline Moscow, fourteen August. "Soviet indicts sixteen as a terror band guided by Trotsky... Zinoviev, Kamenev and four others already in prison are among the accused...plot on Red chiefs seen...Moscow government charges exiled revolutionary sent five agents into Russia."I was just ambushed about it by a reporter. Did we know it was coming?"

Troyanovsky took a deep breath. "You were already on your way when we got the message."

"But Comrade Ambassador! Heroes of the Revolution consorting with Trotsky? It's madness! Zinoviev and Kamenev were Stalin's colleagues on the *troika* while Comrade Lenin was incapacitated!"

"Volya, I'm not a policeman. Obviously there must be something to it. Look, leave these things to others. You're an observer at an important conference. You have more than enough on your plate."

Troyanovsky regretted ending the call so abruptly. But there was no purpose agonizing about things that one couldn't control. He went back to the personnel evaluation he was working on:

> Comrade Romm is a well-qualified officer, fluent in English, German and French. During his time in the U.S. he has made good contacts in journalistic and intellectual circles. He has been a firm supporter of the Embassy line and takes every opportunity to speak out against the counterrevolutionary Trotsky-Zinoviev factions. He is disciplined and politically well prepared. Romm has studied the U.S. and achieved significant results. His relationship with comrades is good.

Vladimir had performed well in Chicago and his attempt to win over Dulles was promising. Yet his voicing skepticism so openly and over an unsecured channel was disturbing. Admonishing him to be careful had little effect. Troyanovsky knew that this document was as much a reflection on him as his subordinate. It would be one of the first things that Moscow would look at if Romm ever got into trouble. Troyanovsky reluctantly appended a paragraph.

It should be noted that during 1925-28 Romm belonged to the Trotsky opposition and signed the Platform of the Eighty-three. In 1928, while *Tass* correspondent to Tokyo, he renounced Trotskyism verbally and in writing and submitted the appropriate application for reenrollment to the Party Control Commission. He was retained on the rolls. Since then Romm has behaved appropriately and with careful monitoring should continue to be a valuable member of the Party.

The USSR's pair of envoys observed meetings, occasionally asked questions, and otherwise mostly wondered why they were there. Japan deflected all questions about the Empire's territorial ambitions. Its delegates refused to discuss Manchuria or the rumored alliance with Germany, dismissed without further comment Soviet worries about getting boxed in, and insisted that Japan's expanding navy and air force were only meant to deter imperialist aggression, like the kind that America, France and Great Britain once practiced against the fledgling Soviet state.

At the close of another day's futile efforts Vladimir headed to the cabin. As soon as he walked in a young man wearing a Japanese military uniform jumped off the couch.

"Vladimir-san!"

Ichiro enthusiastically hugged his favorite *Gaijin*. "Your lovely wife was kind enough to let me wait. She is very trusting!"

Galina laughed. "My husband told me plenty about you, Ichiro-san. Anyway, I've always had a soft spot for men in uniform."

Vladimir recognized a familiar insignia on his friend's jacket. "Flight wings?"

"Soon after you left I lost my job and enlisted in the Imperial Navy. They needed fly-boys, and I did so well in training that they kept me on as an instructor and test pilot. I'm here because of my language skills. By the way, thank you for not recognizing me at the meetings."

"I thought it best to be discreet."

Galina knew that the men wanted to talk privately. She took Georgie for a walk.

"You have a lovely family," Ichiro said.

"Thanks. And you?"

"It's not possible, at least not yet. I'm only a Lieutenant junior grade, and what little I make goes to my mother. Perhaps once I'm promoted."

Vladimir toasted. "To the next Admiral of the Fleet!"

"That won't be me, Vladimir-san. I've found my niche, and as long as I can play with my toys I'm happy. I could probably be shot for telling you this, but I've been testing a new carrier-based plane. If its fuselage holds up, we'll rule the skies!"

Vladimir was alarmed. "Is Japan preparing for war?"

Ichiro downed his drink. "For now it's a trade war. In the end the consequences for the loser are the same. What the Treaty of Versailles did to Germany, tariffs are doing to Japan. It's unrealistic to expect our military to sit back while the Empire is strangled."

Galina and Georgie passed the days pleasantly, enjoying hearty breakfasts in the lodge, and then strolling to a nearby waterfall to read and relax. They spent afternoons traversing the valley on tour buses and horse-drawn carts, marveling at the crisp, free-flowing streams, half-mile tall granite walls and towering trees thousands of years old. At dusk someone would usually spot a bear, an event that never failed to please Georgie, who like all Russian children was enthralled with the powerful creatures.

During their first weekend the family took a rafting trip down the Merced. Georgie stuck his hand in the water.

"It's freezing!"

An elderly woman turned to face him. "It starts as snow high in the mountains," she explained in perfect Russian. Her arm swept across the landscape. "Do you know what made this beautiful valley, sweetheart?"

"Some people say it was God," Georgie replied, "but our family isn't superstitious."

The stranger's eyes twinkled. "Well, then, if you're a scientist you must know all about glaciers."

"What's a glacier?"

"A great big chunk of ice. We're in the trench that a glacier dug as it scoured the ground."

Georgie stared transfixed at the river. The woman introduced herself. "I'm Ludmila Ivanovna. Please forgive me; it's hard to stop being a teacher."

"Do you live in California?" Vladimir asked.

"Los Angeles. My husband and I – Lord have mercy on his soul – emigrated from Kiev in eighty-two." She pointed out two ladies sitting in front. "My daughters. And you?"

"I'm Washington correspondent for *Izvestia*, my wife teaches at the embassy."

"How interesting! Are you enjoying yourselves?"

"Very much," Galina said. "People have been very kind."

"Yes," the old woman agreed. "When Pasha and I immigrated everyone helped us get settled. Then as we got on our feet they tried to make sure that we became *real* Americans. You know, the pancakes for breakfast kind."

Galina was charmed. "Did you?"

"Maybe a little. But I also had influence! Before long our American friends were coming by to ask, "Ludmila, when are you making more *blini*? More *pelmeni*?""

"Do you ever think about going back?"

The woman gently patted Galina's hand. In her wrinkled smile one could see the lush, endless landscapes of Ukraine. "Oh, sure. Who wouldn't? But there doesn't seem to be much room left for God-fearing people. No, I think I'll just hold on to the memories."

Georgie was getting bored with adult company, so one day Galina dropped him off at a day camp to play with other children. With a few hours on her hands she went to the lodge and sat down to coffee. The only thing to read was a *New York Times*.

Galina gasped. A large photograph depicted Kamenev and Zinoviev casually strolling with Stalin. She immediately recognized the picture as one taken a decade earlier, when the three were still partners. A frightening headline was set immediately below the picture.

RUSSIANS DEFEND EXECUTIONS

But the Mystery That Hung Over the Trials is not Dispelled for Foreign Observers

Moscow, Aug. 28. – The execution of Gregory Zinoviev, Leon Kamenev and fourteen of their fellow-accused at the conclusion of the Soviets' greatest and most sensational trial undoubtedly meets the approval of a majority of citizens, at least in Moscow. Conversations with individuals indicate a general feeling that justice has been done. It has been a shocking thing, of course – the condemnation and shooting of "Old Revolutionaries," including men who had once occupied posts of highest honor. But no one knew better than Zinoviev and Kamenev the only possible penalty for even plotting the downfall of the present regime, not to speak of planning the assassination of Stalin and actually carrying out that of Kirov...Knowing the Russian talent for stage management and acting, some wonder whether some of the testimony was not framed in some way. Such observers have evolved several interesting theories, among them that several [accused] were agents provocateurs acting a part and that they will be secretly released after their execution is announced. But if that is the case foreign diplomats, correspondents and ordinary spectators never would have been admitted to the trial. There is too much danger that we would have encountered one or more of them sometime afterward and guessed the trick...

Not wanting to spoil the family's time in Yosemite, Vladimir had kept news of the trial to himself. The article didn't tell the whole story. Authorities had also struck on another front, placing a handful of old Bolsheviks under investigation for conspiring with Trotsky and the usual "foreign elements" to commit the usual crimes: "wrecking" and sabotage. One of their targets was a man only a step removed from Romm. His name was Karl Radek.

Lev's decision to keep quiet undoubtedly saved his life. Nikolayev's explanation of why he shot Kirov, which he conveyed during their brief tête-à-tête, was irreconcilable with the wildly improbable Trotskyite arias he later sang in court. Perhaps neither version was true. There were even hushed suggestions that Stalin was behind the killing. One day, when truth returned to fashion, Lev could go back to being a detective. For now being a prison guard would do.

If only his duties weren't so excruciatingly dull! Nearly all the "counterrevolutionaries" were intelligent men, nonviolent and pathetically eager to return to the Party's good graces. Their desire to please didn't mean that they lacked courage. Lev arrived just as a team of brutes led by Molchanov was unsuccessfully trying to persuade Kamenev and Zinoviev to take on starring roles at a trial. Teams of interrogators mercilessly browbeat the poor souls around the clock, keeping them awake for days with no success. Molchanov finally ordered the plumber to turn up the heat in their cells. *Way* up. A couple days later Vyshinsky was walking around wearing a cat's grin. Fearful of being cooked alive, Stalin's one-time ruling partners had thrown in the towel.

Their trial took place in August 1936. Lev was kept busy running prisoners to and from court. Then came that morning, one day after the circus was done, when he showed up for work and learned that the last-minute reprieves that everyone assumed would come in, didn't. In the middle of the night, guards on extra pay marched Kamenev, Zinoviev and fourteen others down remote corridors, shot each one once in the back of the head, then left the bodies so their fluids would empty down floor drains. In a single nauseating evening executing top Party leaders became no longer unthinkable. What's more, their cells were already being occupied. Each day Black Marias brought in a fresh batch of poor wretches and the same ugly business of extracting confessions began anew. Radek surprised everyone. He held out for a week, then two. Guards wagered about how long he'd last. Then one day the General Secretary stopped by. Soon the once-celebrated Communist journalist, although still a prisoner, was running all over the place getting others to confess. Then the great Piatakov folded.

Another trial was brewing. It was crazy! From Shakhty, where ordinary engineers were recast as "wreckers", to the Lubyanka, where once-celebrated Bolsheviks were treated like rabid dogs, the madness had enmeshed Lev and his colleagues in events that were beyond comprehension.

Weeks passed. One day secret police brought in one of Ordzhonikidze's deputies, a frightened engineer whose brother was a scientific big-shot. He was quickly followed by a German fellow, also an engineer, then by an obscure bureaucrat who kept yelling about his Order of Lenin. Their files were stamped "witness," a meaningless distinction that the guards thought hilarious. Only that morning someone mentioned there were two more, both foreign correspondents. Lev glanced at their names.

His heart froze.

Lubyanka prison,
25 January 1937

The full weight of this mess has finally sunk in. I suspected that something bad was brewing soon after the 1936 trial when authorities announced that Radek and Bukharin were under investigation. Even after they grabbed Radek and Piatakov I still wouldn't listen – not to myself, nor to my friend Paul Ward, nor at the last moment to Galina, who next to Alexander has been the family's most enthusiastic Socialist. Even Troyanovsky, who must have been under strict orders to keep quiet, had thrown a few hints.

Every Moscow resident has seen black prisoner wagons speeding through the streets. Two days ago I got the thrill of riding in one to the House of Trade Unions, where the trial is being held. When we arrived they locked us in a large, windowless room and told us to study our scripts. After dinner – they're running two sessions, the first at eleven, the second at six – they called Dmitry to the stand. He returned about an hour later, not looking so well. He didn't talk about what happened and we haven't asked.

Yesterday we brought books from the prison library to help pass the time. We found out that the trial is taking place in the Hall of Columns. That's where Lenin's new regime once tried the leaders of my old party, the Socialist Revolutionaries. Vyshinsky's forerunner Krylenko, a man with whom I had a bad run-in, was the prosecutor. Piatakov, now a defendant, was the chief judge. Imagine how he must feel!

My turn came last night. Molchanov turned me over to a squad of uniformed militiamen who marched me off as though I was a member of the French nobility on his way to the guillotine. When we reached the hall I was handed off to a set of bailiffs who took me the rest of the way. As I entered the immense, brightly-lit ballroom my heart beat furiously. There was a sea of spectators, at least several hundred. It occurred to me that Walter Duranty, the *New York Times* man, was probably among them. If so, he must realize that he's watching a farce. Of course, after getting a Pulitzer for glorifying the General Secretary's handiwork, he's unlikely to say so.

On my way to the lectern I passed next to the prisoners, two rows of cadavers in ill-fitting suits. Yuri Piatakov, leader of industry, once a judge in this very chamber. He seemed so thoroughly beaten-down that one had to look twice to be sure that his chair was occupied. Grigori Sokolnikov, founding member of the Soviet Union, a military leader, lawyer, economist and top diplomat, most recently the number two man in light industry. Nikolai Muralov, a Bolshevik from the start, a fierce fighter, top agronomist and educator. Leonid Serebryakov, not well educated but an enthusiastic revolutionary, later a key transport official. Like some of the others his career was repeatedly stalled and reborn because of his support for Trotsky. Before they transformed the General Secretary into a Czar it was perfectly acceptable to align with whomever one chose. Amazing how such things can be retrospectively counterrevolutionary!

Then of course there was Radek, sitting with the accused but in reality worlds apart. He tipped his head and grinned insouciantly as I walked by, as though he had fixed things. Perhaps he did – for himself.

I got a passing glance at the judges, who were sitting behind a high bench. The chief judge is a military man named Ulrich, who had also presided over the 1936 trial. Maybe one day he can be as well-rounded as Piatakov, who's been accorded the privilege of experiencing both sides of the process.

There's little to say about my testimony other than it went as expected. It was my first time being questioned by Vyshinsky, but after a moment's hesitation I lapsed into a kind of trance, mechanically mouthing the well-practiced responses – trying not to sound rehearsed, of course. I'm embarrassed to say that the lies frothed from my lips quite easily. It proved remarkably easy to recite nonsense, the truth being buried under so many layers of deceit that it hardly registered. Was I tempted to recant? Not really. Who would believe a lone holdout? If there's any consolation it's that I'm not the only Bolshevik who capped off his career as a ventriloquist's dummy.

One thing stands out in my mind. Before Vyshinsky excused me he asked the three defense lawyers if they had any questions (most of the accused were "voluntarily" going without counsel, but I suppose that not having any at all might seem too provocative). Although the outcome was predetermined, I still feared that I would fold like a pretzel under the slightest challenge. Naturally, not one of these worthless attorneys had anything to ask, and after a moment's hesitation – was it really over? – I meekly stumbled off after the bailiff.

This morning it was Loginov's turn. He was gone for a long time, and when he returned the defrocked *apparatchik* looked strangely invigorated. Bukhartsev put down his book. The look in his eyes made me apprehensive.

"You seem mighty pleased with yourself, Comrade Loginov. Did they promise you another bauble to keep your Order of Lenin company? A Hero of the Soviet Union, perhaps?"

Loginov pretended to be absorbed in a novel. "Doing one's socialist duty is reward enough."

"Oh, that. Please forgive me; I must have missed the directive that authorizes comrades to falsely accuse each other of capital crimes." He turned to the rest of us. "Anyone remember it?"

I stepped in. "Please, Dmitry, this isn't the place. Settle it later." As usual our guard was in the hall, chatting with colleagues. It was pleasant not to be constantly monitored, and my friend was set to spoil it.

"My quarrel isn't with you, Vladimir Georgievich. It's with this turd whose insufferable company I've been blessed with."

Leonid put his hands to his ears. "Stop it! What difference does it make who's accusing whom? We've *all* sold out!"

Bukhartsev sidled up to Loginov. "Yes, but with far less pleasure! And there's something else. This comrade has volunteered for another trial!"

"They're going to make us do it *twice*?" Leonid squealed.

"No, my friend, only *him*! Vladimir Feodorovich thinks it might prolong his worthless life to condemn another group of unfortunates." Dmitry slapped Loginov's skull. "Isn't that so, *comrade*?"

Loginov cowered. "I told them we'd do it together! I was only trying to help you!"

Bukhartsev became enraged. "Help *me*?"

The guard burst in. "What's going on?"

Loginov bolted for a corner. "Nothing," Dmitry said. "There was a rat, but it's run off."

The guard looked around. "At it already?" he smirked. "And I thought that traitors stuck together." He fastened his eyes on Bukhartsev. "Don't make me come back."

The guard left. Dmitry slumped in his chair. "Ah, Leonid Evgenevich is right," he sighed. "We bargained with the Devil; we deserve what's coming."

Leonid walked over. "It will be all right," he soothed. "You'll soon be with your family."

Dmitry's eyes glistened. His voice quavered. "You really think so?"

I had always thought of Leonid as a timid sort, but his expression was...I don't know, *serene*. Then I remembered that he wasn't a Party member. He couldn't be – the man was devoutly Orthodox.

Leonid gently placed his hand on Bukhartsev's shoulder. "Believe it, Dmitry Pavlovich. Believe it."

Show Trial (1937)

Dorothy suspected something was terribly wrong when the first thing Paul did when he walked through the door was to hand her the newspaper:

PLOT WITH REICH AND JAPAN CONFESSED
AT SOVIET TRIAL

Trotsky Planned to Provoke War and Upset the Regime, Accused Say –
All 17 Admit Full Guilt

By Walter Duranty, Moscow, Jan. 23. – In a clear, colorless voice, as precise and unemotional as that of a professor addressing his class, Gregory Piatakov, former Assistant Commissar for Heavy Industry, today threw away his life and the lives of his sixteen fellow-accused as their trial as conspirators against the Soviet regime began...Finally there will be witnesses – not many and not wholly independent – like Bukhartsev and Vladimir Romm, *Izvestia's* American correspondent, who Radek said carried the first letters from him to Trotsky and back again. They are both under arrest, or anyway "held as material witnesses." But they are evidence, nevertheless, in addition to the confessions.

Dorothy couldn't put down the article. Tears streamed down her face as she read it again and again.

"My God, Paul! Vladimir, a traitor? It's crazy!"

"Crazy or not, I tried to warn him when they visited. Maybe if I had been more forceful..."

"The poor man! His family! Maybe we can send them money to hire a good lawyer."

Paul stroked his wife's hand. "I'm not sure that would help. Their system's really different, hon. They've scheduled a special meeting about the trial at *The Nation*. I'll volunteer to write a piece about Vladimir."

William Bullitt was no longer Ambassador to the Soviet Union. Irritated by the respected diplomat's poor opinion of Stalin, Roosevelt replaced him with Joseph Davies, a wealthy corporate lawyer whose most obvious qualification was that his wife Marjorie, a General Foods heiress, had contributed generously to the President's reelection campaign. Appalled that someone with no diplomatic background would be given such a key post, State Department officials nonetheless did their best to brief Davies about Stalin and his henchmen. They could have saved themselves the trouble. Roosevelt and his aides had already convinced their new envoy that the retrograde, disparaging views of the USSR held by the gloom-and-doom boys at Foggy Bottom were plain old bunk. To assure that there would be no one left to poison Davies' mind, by the time that the Troyanovskys saw the amateur diplomat and his socialite spouse off at New York harbor an American-style cleansing of the State Department's Soviet desk was well underway.

Joseph and Marjorie Davies arrived in Moscow in January 1937, only days before the trial began. They took up residence at Spaso House, the mansion in central Moscow that served as the U.S. Ambassador's official residence. Eager to make his picky mate's stay in the unglamorous city more tolerable, Davies spent copiously from family funds to redecorate the residence. After all, it would be months before their family yacht would arrive in Leningrad.

Davies sat transfixed through the week-long proceedings. On January 24, at the end of the second day of testimony, he invited the American correspondents to dine with him at Spaso House. Thanks to the enormous supply of provisions that the couple hauled from the U.S., they would dine on fried chicken and mashed potatoes, to be prepared by their appalled Russian chef.

After the meal Davies and the newsmen repaired to the smoking room for brandy and cigars. First among equals was Walter Duranty, with whom the rookie ambassador had become exceptionally close. The correspondents listened as he read a cable:

> All members of the Washington newspaper corps have read with anxiety of the arrest of our colleague, Vladimir Romm of *Izvestia*. In our dealings with Romm we found him a true friend and advocate of the USSR. Never once did he even faintly indicate lack of sympathy for or disloyalty toward the existing government. He did more than any other Soviet envoy to popularize Stalin's regime in this country. We hope this estimate can be

strongly certified to his judges and that you will ask Ambassador Davies also to transmit these representations.

All eyes fell on Davies. The ambassador-naïf cleared his throat.

"Gentlemen, only yesterday, before Romm's testimony, my opinion might – and I emphasize, *might* – have been different. As I wrote to Roosevelt, the trial clearly illustrates the superiority of our way of doing things. But this afternoon you heard the man confess. I'm sure that we all agree that his detailed, compelling and damning admissions make it impossible for the United States Government to step forward on his behalf. Really, it's out of the question. Look, I'm no great fan of this Trotskyite wreckers stuff, but Romm was calm, articulate and seemed awfully well-fed, and unless he's the best gal-darned pretender in the universe he was sure persuasive."

Duranty jumped in. "Romm's testimony dovetailed perfectly with Radek and Piatakov's. They were convincing, to a degree that you simply couldn't make up. Considering what happened to the accused last summer, confessing might seem strange to the folks back home, but this is a very peculiar culture. Just look at their literature, say, Dostoevsky. Sinning and repenting are the staff of Russian life."

Davies smiled broadly. "Hear, hear! That's precisely my view. But let's open it for discussion. Anyone else?"

His guests stirred uncomfortably. Word was out that America's envoy was a hopeless lightweight who had already managed to dispirit his own staff. His embrace of the famine-denying, Stalin-loving Duranty made him an object of ridicule. But few newsmen were willing to go toe-to-toe with Davies. In the hostile environment of the Soviet Union every American depended on the ambassador's goodwill.

A reporter finally spoke up. "With all due respect, Ambassador Davies, I dealt with Romm in Washington. He seemed like a regular guy, pleasant and helpful. I must say that when it came to the Soviet Union he was an unswerving patriot. Whenever someone criticized Stalin or the USSR he always jumped to their defense. To think that he was a 'counterrevolutionary' defies common sense."

An older newsman agreed. "Absolutely correct. I once asked Romm if he thought that the 1936 trial was staged. He nearly bit my head off."

Davies smiled pleasantly. "Fellows, I don't pretend to be a journalist, but everyone knows that traitors keep their real thoughts to themselves. In any event, this trial is an internal Soviet matter. If you really think they rigged it, well, you're entitled to your opinion, but unless there's hard proof of the man's innocence – and I think that's highly improbable – we'd only be making fools of ourselves to object. It's Diplomacy 101: don't start a fight you're sure to lose. Anyway, best I can tell he's only a 'witness'; I'm sure that when the trial's over they'll let him go."

Duranty excused himself to go file his report. It was published the next day:

It is a sad and dreadful thing to see your friends on trial for their lives. And it is sadder and more dreadful to hear them hang themselves with their own words...Today Mr. Romm came into court as a witness, but he was between two guards because he had been arrested and had confessed that he was a member of the Trotskyist conspiracy. He told how he had conveyed letters hidden in books and in other ways from Radek to Leon Trotsky and back again...He spoke with the same charm and courage that made him popular among Washington newspapermen – one of the most exclusive and intelligent groups in the world and one that would never tolerate anyone shoddy or second rate. Mr. Romm is not on trial – not yet, at least. But he is not a good risk for life insurance...

Dulles dropped a twenty-five cent piece in the newsboy's hands.

"Hey!" the vendor yelled. "Your change!"

"Keep it!" Dulles hurried into the lobby of a luxurious office building. He returned the guard's salute and boarded an elevator that would take him to the penthouse. Until war came and he could get to do some real intelligence work practicing law would have to do.

His morning *café au lait* waited on the sideboard. Dulles blew off the foam and settled at his desk. There it was, on page three. "Life insurance," indeed. How could they honor the stooge with a Pulitzer? He unlocked a drawer and took out an envelope. Inside was a single sheet of *Queen Mary* stationery:

November 5, 1936.

Dear Mr. Dulles, I feel very sorry to have missed before I left. I am going now to Moscow to talk things over as my paper wants me to go to London. I hope I will have the pleasure of meeting you again somewhere. Meanwhile, I wish to thank you for the kindness shown to me in Geneva and in the USA. I will always remember with pleasure our talks. With best wishes and regards,

Very sincerely yours, V. Romm.

P.S. Have you read John Whitaker's book? I found it very amusing. I see that he has spared you, at least!

In fact, Dulles *had* read the book. Whitaker's tart comment about "too many rich idlers" clogging America's diplomatic pores stung, but it was a perfect fit for that fool Davies. Dulles and Vladimir lost touch not long after the party in the Soviet embassy. Romm's letter, apparently written on his way home, arrived a couple weeks after Dulles learned of his arrest. He wished there was something he could do. Vladimir was great fun and quite the raconteur, but it would take more than a way with words to get out of this jam.

The Soviet Embassy was besieged with letters from government officials, journalists and ordinary citizens whose lives had been touched by the popular Soviet correspondent. Most, like the newspapermen in Cleveland, received a polite, noncommittal response. Dulles' note led to a call from Troyanovsky, who promised to convey the lawyer's views to Moscow. But when a courier dropped off a petition signed by editors of every major daily on the East coast the ambassador thought it best to arrange a personal meeting. American newsmen were unpredictable, and he was anxious to ward off any negative press.

Troyanovsky knew how to flatter self-important men. So when the delegation arrived he personally led them to a sitting room. A valet rolled in a self-service coffee cart. Troyanovsky took a seat among his guests. He would pretend to be just another ordinary man doing an ordinary job.

Felix Morley, the Pulitzer-prize winning editor of the *Washington Post* led the group. "Our purpose, Mister Ambassador, isn't to meddle in Soviet affairs. All we wish to do is correct any mistaken assessments that might have been made about Mister Romm. To say that we were dismayed by his arrest is an understatement. In all our dealings he vigorously defended the policies of the Soviet government. He seemed in every respect an absolutely loyal servant of the USSR."

Troyanovsky went around the room topping off his guests' cups. "Let me start by saying that I welcome your concerns and take them very seriously. I too have the greatest respect for Comrade Romm. You know, he wasn't originally a Bolshevik. He began with the Socialist Revolutionaries, a group with whom we, meaning the Bolsheviks, often quarreled. Perhaps I shouldn't mention it," he continued, "but I once interceded to save Comrade Romm's career. In the late 20's he signed a document supporting Trotsky's platform. I found out about it later, when I was Ambassador to Japan and he was in Tokyo as correspondent for our news agency *Tass*. By then of course, Trotsky was in exile; you probably remember that the madman wanted to take over the world..."

"Excuse me, Mister Ambassador," an editor said, "but wasn't supporting Trotsky once perfectly legal?"

"That's something we'd need a lawyer to decide," Troyanovsky quipped. "In any event, considering what we've learned since, Comrade Romm's conduct was a serious lapse in judgment. With my encouragement he renounced the traitor, and after his heartfelt plea to a local committee – and my personal recommendation – the Party agreed to keep him on the rolls. I stuck my neck out for the man and for the longest time was certain that his infatuation with counterrevolutionaries was history. Then, in open court, he admits running messages and performing other evil deeds for Trotsky's infernal syndicate!" The ambassador shook his head. "What's that expression? 'You could have bowled me over with a feather'."

Pleased that the meeting went smoothly, Troyanovsky went to the embassy kitchen for a midday snack. He ran into his teenage son. "Mom's come down with a migraine. I think that Romm business hit her hard."

Troyanovsky hurried to their bedroom. Elena's eyes were swollen from crying. "Galina and I made all those plans to get together in London..."

"It's not your fault, sweetheart," he cooed. "How could anyone know what that swine was up to? Just be thankful he wasn't doing it while working for me!"

Elena blew her nose. "What he said in court made me ill."

"That wasn't half of it. Did you read Radek's testimony? Now *there's* some treachery!" Troyanovsky solicitously propped up his wife's pillow. "I'll have the cook make you something light. How do scrambled eggs sound?"

Radek was undeniably the star witness. His testimony had been meticulously prepared, yet on his very first day on the stand he seemed to veer wildly off course. Radek surprised the courtroom – and supposedly, Vyshinsky – by insisting that he had broken with Trotsky and was about to bring in his helpmates and cooperate, but that the indignities of the arrest changed his mind.

Vyshinsky went on the attack. "For how many months did you deny everything?"

"About three months."

"The fact remains that you, who were supposedly itching to come clean and surrender your people to justice, didn't, and when you yourself fell into the hands of justice you categorically denied everything. Is that a fact?"

"Yes."

"Does that not cast doubt on what you said about your vacillations and misgivings?"

"Yes, if you ignore the fact that you learned about the terrorist program and about Trotsky's instructions only from me, of course, it does cast doubt about what I said."

Radek's assertion that he alone provided the underpinning for the case electrified the hall. Yet Vyshinsky didn't skip a beat. "The important thing to establish," he fired back, "is that your initial denials were a lie. Has that fact been established?"

Radek paused. The tension was electrifying. Would he step back from the brink?

"It has," he conceded.

Observers made much of the exchange. Was the duel a genuine battle between two prideful men? Or was it a scripted attempt to convince the gallery that there really was no script, and that Radek's ultimate comeuppance reflected the truth? When he was first named as a suspect Radek bitterly denied involvement. Now here he was, supposedly at the plot's center. Beyond witnesses, Vyshinsky needed a compelling performance from his star defendant. However that came to be, whether accidentally or on purpose, he got it.

It was January 27, 1937, the fifth day of trial and the last in which testimony was scheduled to be heard. Vyshinsky was examining one of the lesser defendants, a railroad official named Knyazev. With four more accused plus Tamm still to take the stand, the Procurator-General of the USSR was in a hurry.

"Accused Knyazev, did you in 1934 join the Trotskyite underground organization?"

"Permit me first to tell something about internal activities the Trotskyite organization was connected with..."

"Just tell me what you did as a member."

"I will deal with this in detail."

"Did you take part in diversionary and wrecking activities on the railways?"

"I did."

"What *kind* of wrecking activities?"

"Organizing train derailments, damaging the tracks and locomotives..."

By the time that Vyshinsky got bored and cut him off, the petty bureaucrat had single-handedly drawn in more than two dozen innocents into the pretend conspiracy.

"...Levin, assistant manager of the traffic department, Dolmatov, manager of the maintenance department, Bochkarev, my inspector, and engineer Shcherbakov... At my instructions these persons formed a terrorist organization...In the traction department the following were involved in Trotskyite counterrevolutionary work: on the Kurgan section – Nikolayev, chief of the depot, his assistant Andreyev, engineer Starostin, and Mogilny, a foreman in the department of locomotive service. On the Zlatoust section there was..."

All told a splendid performance. Unfortunately, not everyone was as voluble as Knyazev.

"Tell me, please, how old are you?"

"Thirty-five, I will be thirty-six."

"If you are thirty-five, then of course you will be thirty-six."

"I mean that I will be thirty-six within a few days."

Vyshinsky gritted his teeth. They should have dropped Tamm long ago. Unfortunately, Radek had placed the frightened engineer smack in the middle of things. Now it was up to the timid soul to corroborate the confession of defendant Pushin, whose testimony had already implicated both men in the conspiracy.

"How did you learn of Pushin's criminal activities?"

"I worked with him from the autumn of 1932 until his departure from Gorlovka in the middle of 1933."

Vyshinsky sighed. "I am asking you, where did you learn about Pushin's criminal activities, and what do you know about them?"

Tamm glanced around the magnificent hall. Designed as a ballroom for the nobility, its imposing Corinthian columns infused the proceedings with a disconcerting flair. He peeked at Pushin, looking for a sign – any sign – of the doomed man's approval.

Pushin blinked.

Tamm sighed. "He himself told me."

"In what context?"

"Pushin and I had a number of anti-Soviet talks."

"How did you come to have these talks?"

"I knew that his sentiments were anti-Soviet."

"How did you know?"

"It was evident from all his conversations, from the remarks he dropped."

"Was he a member of the Party?"

"Yes."

"And were you?"

"I was non-Party."

Three technical experts followed Tamm to the stand. None were under arrest. Their accounts were nearly identical:

"Was the explosion due to accident or to malicious intent?"

"In view of the existence of strictly prohibitive instructions and special permission to perform such work from the technical director or the superintendent of the department – the fact that these instructions were ignored cannot be regarded as accidental, but must be regarded as due to malicious intent."

In Stalin's Russia, workers didn't have "accidents".

Vyshinsky delivered his closing argument on the sixth evening. His speech, which ran fifty-four closely-spaced pages, ridiculed and profaned the accused in the style that had become de rigueur for political trials:

> This trial has revealed and proved the stupid obstinacy, the reptile cold-bloodedness, the cool calculation of professional criminals. As they waged their struggle against the USSR these bandits stopped at nothing – neither wrecking, nor diversions, nor espionage, nor terrorism, nor treason to their country...This trial revealed the underground criminal activities of the Trotskyites, the entire mechanism of their bloody, treacherous tactics. It revealed the face of real, genuine Trotskyism – this old enemy of the workers and peasants, this old enemy of socialism, this loyal servant of capitalism.

As might be expected, Vyshinsky reserved special scorn for Radek. His merciless articles demanding that the accused in the first trial be "crushed" lent his current circumstances a certain irony:

> What did Radek write at the time of the trial of Zinoviev, Kamenev and the others, of the trial of the traitors who had been exposed in their anti-Soviet criminal struggle? Of the "Trotskyite-Zinovievite fascist gang and its hit man – Trotsky" (these were his own words) he wrote that "the stench of corpses" pervaded the courtroom in which the case was tried, and he exclaimed with passion: "Crush the vipers! It is not a matter of exterminating ambitious men who have gone to the length of committing a great crime, it is a matter of exterminating the agents of fascism who were prepared to assist in igniting the conflagration of war, to facilitate the

victory of fascism in order to receive from its hands at least the shadow of power." This is what Radek wrote. Radek thought he was writing about Kamenev and Zinoviev. A slight error! This trial will rectify Radek's error. He was writing about himself!

Vyshinsky had one final issue to address. At the first trial there was a murdered politician to point to, the beloved Leningrad Party leader Kirov. Not this time. But who needs one dead man when there were all those killed and crippled by the brutal five-year plans? Transformed into victims of "wrecking" and sabotage, they got to serve the state once more:

> I am not the only accuser! Comrade Judges, I feel that by my side here stand the victims of the crimes and of these criminals: on crutches, maimed, half alive, and perhaps legless, like Comrade Nagovitsina, the switch-girl at Chusovskaya Station, who appealed to me, through *Pravda*, today, and who, at 20 years of age, lost both her legs in averting a train disaster organized by these people! I do not stand here alone! I feel that by my side here stand the murdered and maimed victims of these frightful crimes, demanding of me, as the State Prosecutor, that I press the charge on all points! I do not stand here alone! The victims may be in their graves, but I feel that they are standing here beside me, pointing at the dock, at you, accused, with their mutilated arms, which have moldered in the graves to which you have sent them! I am not the only accuser! I am joined in my accusation by the whole of our people! I accuse these heinous criminals who deserve only one punishment – death by shooting!

And that was that. Vyshinsky actually toned it down from the 1936 trial, when his unforgettable closing words, "I demand that dogs gone mad should be shot – every one of them!" shocked the fragile sensibilities of the Western press.

It was time for the defense lawyers to speak. Had one not known otherwise, they could have easily been mistaken for assistant prosecutors. Here is what Knyazev's attorney had to say:

> First of all, Comrade Judges, the Counsel for Defense is a son of his country. He, too, is a citizen of the great Soviet Union, and the great indignation, anger and horror which is now felt by the whole population of

342

our country, old and young, the feeling which the Procurator so strikingly expressed in his speech, cannot but be shared by Counsel...In this case, Comrade Judges, there is no dispute about the facts...I am defending Knyazev, chief of a railway, who, on behalf of the Japanese secret service, derailed trains carrying workers and Red Army men. I will not conceal from you that when I read the material in the case, when I perused the documents, when I heard Knyazev's evidence I thought I could hear the crash of the wrecked cars and the groans of the dying and injured Red Army men...The gravity of Knyazev's position is made still more grave by the fact that he is a person who is almost physically, directly guilty of these wholesale, sanguinary murders...

Then came the defendants. Piatakov, the most senior Party member on trial, went first. A practiced Communist, he had self-criticism down to a tee:

I am too keenly conscious of my crime, and I do not venture to ask you for clemency. I will not even make bold to ask for mercy. In a few hours you will pass your sentence. And here I stand before you in filth, crushed by my own crimes, bereft of everything through my own fault, a man who has lost his party, who has no friends, who has lost his family, who has lost his very self. Do not deprive me of one thing, Citizen Judges. Do not deprive me of the right to feel that in your eyes, too, I have found strength in myself, albeit too late, to break with my criminal past.

There were sixteen more. Each impaled himself in a similar fashion. The three judges – due to the nature of the charges all were military men – retired to deliberate at seven in the evening. Sentences were announced six hours later. Thirteen, from the mighty Piatakov to the lowly Knyazev, were to be shot. Radek and two others got ten years; a lesser figure, eight. Stalin had long foreclosed the right to appeal in such cases, so every execution was carried out within a few hours.

During the preceding weeks a relentless propaganda stream convinced ordinary Muscovites of the rightness of the verdicts, and jubilant crowds gathered at loudspeakers set up on Red Square to hear the sentences pronounced. Rallies and celebrations followed. Newspapers were already running articles about another show trial. To take place in 1938, it would be the third and final of the set.

It wasn't just Moscow. Soviet Russia was awash in counterrevolutionary plots and conspiracies. Kirov's murder had set off a frenzy of activity in the countryside, with NKVD agents competing to unmask terrorist cells and arrest "saboteurs." Worried about backlash from families and the loss of skilled workers, Stalin finally put the brakes on the frenzy in 1938. By then hundreds of thousands of innocent citizens had been shot or dispatched to join the "*kulaks*" and other socially undesirable elements slogging away at labor camps in the East.

Reaction was mixed. Stalin's boosters celebrated the trial, while Trotsky and his supporters criticized it as a charade. In the U.S. the socialist Pioneer Publishers issued a pamphlet condemning the proceedings; an ideological rival, the Communist Workers Library, distributed a monograph extolling its virtues.

In all, thanks in part to the testimony of Romm and the other "witnesses," the 1937 trial did have a "markedly better press" than the first. In an unsigned editorial, "Behind the Soviet Trials," *The Nation* explained why:

> One reason is that the incredulity has decreased before the relentless piling up of the testimony. Another reason is that the defendants in the second trial – especially Radek, Piatakov and Serebryakov – were men of more stubborn strength and greater integrity than those of the first trial, and their confessions were therefore more impressive. Finally, the suspicion that the confessions might in the first trial have been extorted by a promise of freedom was weakened when the executions were carried out and when it became clear that the defendants in the second trial made their confessions while facing what they believed to be certain death. It would have been possible for Radek to say a few words of repudiation in open court in the presence of foreign correspondents and the diplomatic corps, and with those words to electrify the whole world. That he did not do so carries considerable conviction.

Duranty's spin on things was predictable. Anxious to preserve what was left of his reputation, his last dispatch from the Hall of Columns tried to project an image of dispassion and balance. Still, while he bemoaned the trial's opaqueness, there was little question where his sympathies lay:

> None of the accused beat his breast in self-condemnation or indulged

in the fulsome praise of Joseph Stalin that disgusted observers at the previous trial. All spoke with dignity, restraint and courage and gave a genuine impression of telling the truth. Nevertheless, it is a pity from the Soviet viewpoint that no documentary evidence was produced in open court, as a letter and a Photostat copy of a letter from a Japanese envoy and, it is said, other important material held back for the secret session last Wednesday night. Moreover, Mr. Vyshinsky in his speech Thursday made too many references to the secret session that had no convincing effect. Taken all in all, however, the trial did "stand up" and should go far to justify Sokolnikov's statement that Mr. Trotsky is now revealed before the workers of the Union of Soviet Socialist Republics and the rest of the world as an ally of fascism and a preparer of war and, therefore, definitely finished as a force of international importance.

Duranty's Pulitzer wasn't a grant of immunity. Immediately below his piece an editor inserted, without further comment, a message to Soviet prosecutors from a Socialist member of the Norwegian Parliament. It essentially called the account of Piatakov's visit to Trotsky a work of fiction:

> This is to inform you that it has been confirmed officially that no private or foreign plane landed in Oslo in December 1935. I confirm in my capacity as Trotsky's host that there was no meeting in Norway during December, 1935, between Trotsky and Piatakov.

Ambassador Davies was perplexed by the irregularity of the proceedings and the oddly ritualistic capitulation of the accused. Even so, he was convinced that the defendants were indeed guilty:

> Assuming, however, that basically human nature is much the same everywhere, I am still impressed with the many indications of credibility which obtained in the course of the testimony. To have assumed that this proceeding was invented and staged as a project of dramatic political fiction would be to presuppose the creative genius of a Shakespeare and the genius of a Belasco in stage production...

Davies would later write in his memoirs of a certain man who "...gives the impression of a strong mind which is composed and wise. His brown eye is exceedingly kind and gentle. A child would like to sit in his lap and a dog would sidle up to him."

He was referring, of course, to Stalin.

Dorothy was furious. She wasn't surprised about *The Nation's* editorial, which was consistent with the left-leaning weekly's steadfast support for Stalin. But she could not fathom her husband's long piece in the same issue. It was entitled, simply, "Vladimir Romm."

"How on Earth could you write such drivel, Paul? "I can contribute little bearing upon his innocence or guilt." He and his lovely family were our guests! Did you forget the beautiful note he sent us from the ship?"

"Look, honey..."

"First you tell the whole world that Galina was 'a stauncher revolutionist than her husband,' then you accuse the American newsmen who met with Troyanovsky of being naïve for suggesting that her husband 'could not have been a conspirator because he never let any of his friends here in on any of the alleged plotting.' Do you have any idea how that could be used? Just whose side are you on?"

"You're taking it out of context! Maybe my remarks were a bit caustic, but I also wrote that Vladimir never said or did anything even remotely disloyal. Quote: 'his intellect was such that it is as hard to associate him with the fantastic plot Vyshinsky laid bare as it is to associate Radek with it'."

Dorothy stared at her husband. "For God's sakes, Paul, did you just hear yourself? Your beautifully crafted sentence equates our dear friend with a lunatic! Do you really feel that Vladimir and Radek came from the same mold?"

Paul sat down. In an ideal world one's writings would not be taken so literally, but that's not how ordinary people read, never mind those in a position to decide Vladimir's future. Dorothy's objections were leading him to wonder. Had *The Nation* turned a blind eye to Soviet excesses? Had he been censoring himself, shifting his tone to please his bosses? Was his fondness for communism affecting his objectivity? He mused about the trial. Could something that elaborate be nothing more than a cruel hoax? If so, it would bring into question the very essence of that great experiment, one that promised to forever strip those disgusting notions of "haves" and "have-nots" from the human lexicon.

"Line up, comrades, line up!" It was pitch-dark as guards herded the sleepy-eyed prisoners into the hall. Through the magic of radio, even those slogging on the banks of the Amur River, a remote region a stone's throw from China, could be kept apprised of the trial's progress. Now that the verdicts were in and the sentences had been carried out it was time for them, too, to celebrate.

"Great news!" the political officer announced. She was standing on a stool, addressing prisoners whose ideological rehabilitation was her responsibility. Not that there was any great urgency to the task, as the Five-Year Plans depended on a ready supply of slaves, and sentences were for all purposes forever.

"The trial is done! All are guilty!" She donned her glasses and read from a list. "Piatakov, Yuri Leonidovich. To be shot! Serebryakov, Leonid Petrovich. To be shot! Muralov, Nikolai Ivanovich. To be shot! Drobnis, Yakov Naumovich. To be shot...!"

Silence gripped the hall. A few workers crossed themselves. For an instant the commissar faltered. What was the point of trying to enlighten these imbeciles? Let them rot!

"To commemorate this milestone in the struggle against fascism we will take a day off to reflect and receive Communist instruction. Assemble in two hours. Dismissed!"

A woman lingered behind. She approached the officer.

"Comrade Commissar, did you find out what happened to the witness Romm?"

The prisoner's plaintive expression took hold of something in the official's heart. In a sense they were both captives, and they were both women. "No, Anna Mikhailovna, you've asked before and nothing has changed. If I hear something I will tell you, all right?"

"You don't think they will shoot him?"

"Don't be ridiculous! Like you said, he was only a witness!"

Lubyanka prison,
10 February 1937

My lawyer Comrade Kutuzov came to see me after I testified. I've finally calmed down enough to write about it. I quickly realized something was wrong. It wasn't his physical appearance, which is unexceptional. He's chubby, has a receding hairline, a goatee and wears glasses; think a stocky Lenin and you'd be close. What struck me as odd was his attitude, which seemed far more impersonal than what one would expect from an ally. I'm afraid that as far as Soviet justice goes, the notion of "defense" has lost all meaning.

We met in an interrogation room. Kutuzov offered a limp handshake then quickly reached into his briefcase for a *Pravda*. He pointed to an article about the trial. "Was this your testimony?"

I winced. Oh, my words were reported accurately enough, but reading them wasn't exactly pleasant. "Yes. So?"

Kutuzov looked at me strangely. "So? Your brothers assured me that you were innocent. So did your wife."

"But I *am* innocent. There was no conspiracy! It was all political theater. *Bad* political theater. Wasn't it obvious?"

I have a pretty good idea of what play-acting looks like. Comrade Kutuzov's reaction was depressingly genuine.

"You lied?"

"Please, Comrade Kutuzov. How could anyone believe such a strange tale? Trotsky, a handmaiden of Germany and Japan, secretly meeting with top Bolsheviks while in European exile?"

My "lawyer" took a deep breath. The veins in his neck seemed like they were about to pop. "You're saying that the Procurator-General of the USSR staged a daydream? That thirteen accused were shot for *nothing*?"

The next thing I remember I was in a corner, retching. We have been confined to our cells since the last day of testimony and had no word of the outcome. I assumed, of course, that everyone would be found guilty. But it was the first I'd heard of any executions.

"Radek is dead?"

Kutuzov snickered. "Relax. Your buddy only got ten years."

My nerves slowly steadied. At least Radek's blood wasn't on my hands. Then a terrible thought came to mind. "What about Pushin?"

"Pushin? Why do you care?"

"My cellmate, Leonid Tamm, testified against him."

Kutuzov sighed. He glanced at his notes. "Pushin was shot," he sneered. "Look, I'm a lawyer, but a patriot first. I sat through the trial, heard the evidence. Everyone confessed. You and the others corroborated their testimony, and at great length, I might add. Now you're saying it was all made up?" He got right in my face. "What kind of an idiot do you take me for?"

Indeed, how many kinds are there in the USSR? Before I could begin counting Comrade Kutuzov snapped his briefcase shut and got up. He was leaving! Under the circumstances the threat of losing my only tangible contact with the outside world felt like a mortal blow.

"Please! You asked my family to make sure that I cooperated, and I did!"

"I'll be back when you're ready to tell the truth. Until then there's nothing I or anyone else can do."

I had to think fast. "Will you help me if I don't recant?"

Kutuzov paused. "No more crazy talk?"

I shook my head. What could I do but give in? "No more denying. I confess to everything!"

My words frothed with cynicism, but Kutuzov didn't seem to care. Whether in court or in a cell, in the Soviet Union it's what one *says* happened that's important.

He sat back down and pulled out a sloppily typed document. "It's the petition I prepared before trial."

I skimmed through it. It was based on my Party file and on interviews with Galina, my father and brothers. "What about Ambassador Troyanovsky? Comrade Litvinov? Unshlikht? Berzin?"

Kutuzov's eyes narrowed. "Your friend Troyanovsky's last evaluation is already in the file. To be candid, I'm not sure it's of any help. I've already asked him and the others to furnish letters of support. But don't expect too much. I'm sure they wish you the best, but after what you said in court you really can't expect high officials to be bailing you out."

He handed me paper and a pen. "Go back to your cell. Write down your side of it. Explain why you became a traitor and beg for forgiveness." He gathered his things. "I'll start preparing for trial."

I felt dizzy. "A trial? Radek said we'd be let go!"

"Let go?" Kutuzov got up to leave. "Well, who knows, Karl Berngardovich might be right. After all, he only got a tenner!"

"Wait!" I implored. "Aren't we going to...I don't know...go over the evidence?"

Kutuzov paused at the door. He grinned malevolently. "Really, comrade, can't you remember your own testimony?"

Leonid besieged me with questions. I tried to avoid mentioning Pushin. Having one's assigned defendant shot is an ominous sign. My cellmate is no dummy, though, and he guessed that I was holding back.

"Please, Vladimir Georgievich, tell me the truth. Was Pushin shot?"

I stared into the man's sad eyes. All I could do was nod. I'm such a coward!

Leonid shrugged, as though it was exactly what he expected. Maybe there's an advantage to working things out with a higher power.

He lay on his bunk. "I figured that Radek would dodge the bullet. His kind usually does."

I was overcome with guilt. After all, I was the "political" one, not Tamm! "How can our lawyers buy such drivel?"

"Volya, what do you expect? They're all loyal Party men. They don't worry about 'facts'; they just do what they're told. Anyway, there have been other trials. You were in a position to know. What did *you* think?"

"I suppose I chose not to."

The Trial of Vladimir Romm

"Accused Romm, were you given a copy of the Indictment?"

"Yes."

"Have you read it?"

"Yes."

"How do you plead to the charges?"

Vladimir knew the question was coming, but it rattled him nonetheless. He glanced at his lawyer. Kutuzov's scowl conveyed the expected reply.

"Guilty. But I wish to explain..."

"There will be time for that later." The tribunal's president turned to the secretary. "Let the record reflect that Vladimir Georgievich Romm, born 1896 in Vilna, charged with treason, espionage, preparation of terrorist acts, and membership in a counterrevolutionary terrorist organization, has entered a plea of guilty. *To everything.*"

Vladimir struggled to stay calm, but his shirt was already soaked with perspiration. By happenstance the rude "trial" was being held in the same room where policemen and prisoners once colluded to persuade the whole world that the USSR was under siege, from enemies without and within. But this was no rehearsal; infinitely worse, the three stern-faced men sitting on the improvised podium, each wearing the uniform of a military jurist, were there to judge *him*.

Lev was also present. He stood quietly in the back, watching over guards whose bored looks and slouched postures conveyed the perfunctory nature of the proceedings. Here in the bowels of the Lubyanka there was no need to convince foreigners of anything. Each day hordes of prisoners charged with treason were herded in and, within minutes, swiftly ushered out. Careers in the security services were being built on the backs of unfortunates whose petty misconduct was being elevated to capital crimes. Given the incessant demands of the Five-Year Plans, those not shot became a cheap source of labor. In time the toll on specialists would become a drag on productivity and lead Stalin to order a reassessment. But that day was still well in the future.

The president addressed Vladimir's lawyer.

"Comrade Kutuzov, as the Procurator-General is preoccupied elsewhere, he submitted his proof in the form of testimony given by your client, two months ago, in the case of the anti-Soviet terrorist centre, where he appeared as a witness. Do you have the transcript?"

Kutuzov rose. "I do."

"Does the defense concede that the accused's own words prove each charge in the present indictment to the extent required by law?"

"They do."

The president leaned back. Not that he had expected a different response, but it was nice to have things run this smoothly. He'd have to put in a good word for this comrade.

"Fine. So let's move on to the final plea. Accused Romm?"

Vladimir had steeled himself for the indignities of a trial, but the unseemly haste caught him by surprise. "Um, yes?"

"Do you have anything to add to the written submissions furnished by your lawyer?"

Romm was aghast. Was he really *that* disposable? He struggled to answer.

"I commanded Red Guards in Vilna. Our efforts were instrumental in the Red Army's..."

"We have your Party file," the president interrupted. "We're well aware of your background. It includes, if I'm not mistaken, a side trip to Archangel, where you worked against the revolution."

"That was before I began my career as a Communist," Vladimir pointed out. "My file contains many commendations. Colonel Unshlikht..."

"You mean Iosif Unshlikht, the former chief of military intelligence?"

"Yes. He and I worked together in Germany..."

Vladimir paused. The judges seemed amused. Even the guards were smiling.

"Your one-time superior, prisoner Romm, is hardly a good character reference, inasmuch as he's now cooling his heels pending trial for counterrevolutionary activity."

Vladimir fought against panic. "Well...there are others. Comrade Troyanovsky..."

The president's patience was wearing thin. "Vladimir Georgievich, even your biggest booster had his concerns. Alexander Antonovich now considers his intercession in Tokyo, which saved your Party card, a serious error. Even back then, his evaluation of your performance criticized your failure to live up to Party standards. He called it 'Bohemianism', but I think we can now safely call it by its real name, 'Trotskyism'."

Comrade Kutuzov rose. "Citizen judges, as you well know everything relevant in this case has been submitted in writing. However, Galina Romm is present should you wish to question her about her statement."

Vladimir was startled. Kutuzov had said nothing about calling his wife.

The judges conferred briefly. The president tucked all the documents back into a file. "That will not be necessary. The Court will adjourn for deliberation."

The judges left. Kutuzov approached Vladimir. "Look, I cut you off for a reason. There's nothing to be gained by irritating the judges."

"When will they announce the sentence?"

"Whenever they choose. It could be a few hours, it could be tomorrow. I'll personally deliver their judgment. It will be my final service." Kutuzov walked off.

The next thing Vladimir knew, he was facing Galina.

"We'll be outside," Lev said, taking the guards with him. "You have five minutes."

Husband and wife stared at one another. A moment passed, then another.

Galina placed her hand on Vladimir's face. She gently stroked his beard. "Remember when you sang me that ballad? You know, from *Stenka Razin*? Do you have another?"

Vladimir collapsed in her arms, not like a man reclaiming his wife, but as a frightened child. He sobbed deeply.

Galina finally pulled away. "Volya, there is little time."

Romm slumped in a chair. He struggled to form a coherent thought. "Georgie...?"

"He's fine. We're still at Evsey's. They send their best."

"Forgive me. I'm just so...surprised. And grateful."

"Thank your lawyer. You know, he's taking quite a risk..."

"Kutuzov?"

"He's been wonderful! He has kept us informed at every step. Your brothers and I had copies of your testimony long before it appeared in *Pravda*."

Vladimir was appalled. He stared at his wife. "My...*testimony*? Galya, does everyone really think I'm guilty?"

Galina had feared it would come up. She had always been a loyal Communist.

Was he asking her to choose?

"Why is it necessary to speak of this now?"

"Because it is! What could be more important?"

Galina willed herself to calm down. "Are you saying that none of it happened? That you didn't..."

"I was never a traitor. *Never.*"

"But you confessed! Not only you: Radek, Piatakov – everyone! It was so convincing! Kutuzov brought us articles by Walter Duranty, Paul Ward...they believed it, too. And now you say it wasn't true?"

"It wasn't! Not a word! They made it all up!"

"But...the Party's been so good to us! We've lived such wonderful lives! We've been to France, to America. And now you say that..."

"Yes. That's exactly what I'm saying."

"But, *why?*"

"You'd have to ask them. Please, Galya, you must believe that I did it for us. For Georgie, for you."

"For *me?* Volya, do you have any idea what it's like to be the spouse of an 'enemy of the people'? My career is ruined. Everyone whispers! I can't leave the apartment without getting dirty looks. I've been told that after you're sentenced I'll be exiled to a camp in the east!"

Vladimir looked stricken. "I'm so sorry. I really had no choice."

"No *choice?* Did someone put a gun to your head?"

Vladimir sighed. "It wasn't like that."

"So why, Volya? Why would you lie?"

Lubyanka prison,
7 March 1937

Leonid was tried a few days ago. He never came back. Guards later came by to clear out his things. They told me that once prisoners are sentenced they're moved elsewhere, and I hope that wherever he wound up he's all right. I worry, as the poor wretch he testified against was shot. My former cellmate is a fine, sweet man, and I hope that his sentence will be brief.

As for me, hours have passed and I've yet to learn of my sentence. I'm very nervous. Just before trial Comrade Kutuzov said it would probably fall somewhere short of Radek's "tenner." Somewhere short? Radek boasted that he was Trotsky's right-hand man and a key driving force behind the plot, while my script – which he wrote – made me out to be nothing more than a "facilitator" (Kutuzov's word, not mine). But the chief judge's hostility fills me with dread. Who could have guessed that they would strike down a brave Communist warrior like Unshlikht? My lawyer reassured me that both Litvinov and Troyanovsky, who remain very much in favor, also filed written statements on my behalf, and while I've not been allowed to read them I fervently hope that they will encourage the court to be lenient.

Galina's presence came as a shock. Had I known she would come I would have behaved much better. Thanks to me, her circumstances, and those of my son, are quite rotten. But I was so preoccupied with myself and with what others think of me that I asked little about her. Before I knew it our time was up, and things ended awkwardly. I fervently hope to make up for it one day. Yes, dear wife, I'll sing you a song. I'll compose it myself!

Yet I can't shake her parting question. Why would I lie? One can't count the number of times that Radek and Molchanov assured us that we were being... patriots! In effect, that the execution of innocents would bring us glory! Sure, it now seems outlandish, but we were desperate. Dangling such an enticing rationalization was an ingenious move. Despicable, but ingenious.

Patriotism isn't a new excuse for loathsome behavior. My mind still burns with the images of those goose-stepping Storm Troopers marching past the restaurant in Berlin. *They* were patriots!

So what about *me*? Why did I lie? Was it a misplaced love of country? Fear of what might happen to my loved ones if I didn't cooperate? Or was I so anxious to resume my illustrious "career" that I was willing to do anything to be given a second chance?

May my father and Hillel the Elder forgive me, but what was hateful to me, I *did* do onto others. If this happens to be my last writing, it will at least be the truth.

The Next Morning

Lev's wife stayed up all night to make sure her spouse didn't try to telephone the Lubyanka. Neither did she let him go to work unusually early.

"Don't make a scene. It's not only you who would suffer."

She was of course correct. At times like these doing anything out of the ordinary was summoning trouble. No one was immune from the vicissitudes of the Great Terror. And the moment he arrived to take over his shift, Lev knew that it had claimed a very special victim.

"I'm terribly sorry, Lev Alexandrovich."

Instead of his normal early-morning condition – drunk and asleep – Boris was sitting at the desk, wide awake. The plump, good-natured night-shift supervisor knew that Lev and the prisoner Romm had been acquainted. His colleague had obviously thought well of the man, and that was good enough for him.

Lev sat heavily on the couch. He couldn't stop the tears from flowing.

Boris draped a beefy arm around the grieving man. "The bastards took him about midnight. May they choke on their extra rations!" He offered a handkerchief and helped Lev to the desk. "Best tidy up before someone comes. There's something for you in the drawer."

Lev removed a crumpled sheet of paper bearing the handwriting he knew so well. "I cleaned out his cell myself," Boris explained. "It's not on the inventory."

"Thank you."

"Ah, forget it. *Please!*" Boris poured two shots of cheap vodka. He raised his tumbler. "To Vladimir Georgievich!"

"To Vladimir Georgievich!"

Just then two beefy secret police goons barged in. They had a manacled, terrified man in tow. He was still in the fine silk pajamas that he had been wearing when they dragged him from his soft bed.

An agent handed Lev the man's identity card. But there was really no need. The new lodger in the political isolation section of the Lubyanka prison was George Molchanov.

Moscow (2002)

The old man brought a tray of snacks, then settled into an easy chair. A schnauzer promptly jumped on his lap. "I'm astonished that anyone still cares. We used to complain about having socialism stuffed down our throats. Since that drunkard Yeltsin it's been all about money. Be careful what you wish for, I say!"

Oleg and Larisa helped themselves to tea and cakes. Oleg, a senior professor at Moscow State University, did pretty much as he pleased. And what pleased him most was to immerse himself in the dark recesses of Stalin's Great Terror. His youngish, politically attuned dean couldn't fathom why someone would spend their entire career delving into such a gloomy topic, to say nothing of dragging along a gang of graduate students on the dismal journey. Several, including an opinionated young woman, were now busily seeking answers to all manner of embarrassing questions, playing right into the hands of unpatriotic, Western-leaning groups that stubbornly refused to let bygones be bygones. Really, if dredging up past injustices was all that important, President Putin would let them know. He was an expert at such things.

"Mother's been gone ten years, and for the last two she never left the apartment." The old man's voice was hushed so as not to wake the dog, who was farting in its sleep. "You say that you found her name in a ledger?"

Larisa showed him a photocopy of a page dated 12 September 1980. "Is this her signature?"

Oleg glanced at his star pupil. They met three years earlier when she appeared without appointment at his office. He would have shooed her away but for the yellowed, badly creased sheet of notepaper, protected in cellophane, that she brought for him to examine. He would later chuckle at the memory of the telephone call. Larisa had changed her course of study from economics to history. How, her father demanded to know, could someone make a living doing that?

Larisa persevered. After earning baccalaureate and master's degrees in record time – with the highest honors, no less – she enrolled in the doctoral program, then wrote a prospectus so compelling that the dean, who looked on the Soviet era more as a communicable disease than a legitimate object of study, had no choice but to admit her to candidacy. And here they were.

The old man shook his head in amazement. "That's my mother's writing, all right. You say it's from the cemetery at the Donskoi?"

"From the visitor's register. Anna Mikhailovna went to Tomb One several times a month, even in winter. She was the only one dedicating prayers in his memory."

"It kind of makes sense," the old man admitted. "Every so often mother would be gone all day to visit a 'friend.' She never volunteered who it was, and I sensed it was best not to pry; I mean, even old people are entitled their privacy. Say, could this have something to do with the camps?"

Larisa was startled. "The camps?"

"It's not the kind of thing one likes to talk about. I guess I'm old enough not to worry what people think. It was about 'twenty-eight, when they started collectivization. My father shot a couple Bolshevik thugs who came to take the farm. Mother grabbed me and my brother – his name was Mikolaj, may he rest in peace – and ran away. She dropped us off at a friend's house and turned herself in. They exiled her to a labor colony, where she spent the war."

"And your father?"

The dog stirred. The old man gently stroked it back to sleep. "He was shot, of course."

Larisa blanched. "Oh, I'm so sorry."

"Thank you. You know, there were countless victims. But I guess the most powerful number is still one." His eyes returned to the document. "I've been racking my brain since you called. That name still doesn't ring a bell. Vladimir Georgievich Romm. Why would she honor *him*?"

Oleg threaded his decrepit Lada through the busy streets. Once empty except for buses, trolley cars and the occasional Zil limousine, Moscow's roadways were now thick with Mercedes and BMWs, the trophies of an oil-rich economy run amok. But take one step outside the city and it was as if time had stood still, the roads crumbling, the peasants still riding in carts pulled by donkeys. Some said that capitalism was a poor match for the Russian soul. Oleg thought it more likely that the well-connected had again snatched the loaf, leaving ordinary people the crumbs.

He turned to Larisa. "Did you get what you needed?"

She wrinkled her nose at the cigarette smoke. If they could only get their mentor to quit poisoning himself! "There must have been a relationship, don't you think? Maybe if..."

Oleg laughed. "You've got a dissertation to finish, Lara. Focus!"

"Oh, I will. I was just hoping that I could make it more, you know, *personal*."

"When your work comes out every historian in the motherland will be jealous. How many had a grandfather who smuggled a prisoner's diary from the Lubyanka?"

"Finding it was sheer luck. I was looking through his things, and there it was."

Fashionably dressed teens darted across the road, forcing the professor to brake. "You're too modest. If it wasn't for your curiosity and persistence the man's words would have ended up in the trash!"

He parked at the high-rise where his pupil and her schoolmates shared a tiny flat. Larisa stepped out. Her smile couldn't hide her disappointment.

Oleg caved, like she knew he would. "Old-timers like Jarek and me use the personals to find lost connections," he said. "Maybe someone will know how his mother and your Romm guy were connected. Or know someone who knows. Come Monday we'll place ads in the Moscow and Saint Petersburg papers. If that doesn't work I'll get a reporter to run a story. All right?"

Larisa's face lit up. "Thank you!"

It was midnight. Oleg couldn't sleep. Easing from bed so as not to wake his wife, he went to the study and settled in his favorite armchair. He flipped on the lamp, opened a folder and began to read. "Lubyanka prison, 27 November 1936. My cell is a narrow, rectangular affair, three meters wide by four meters in length..."

A Little Bit of History

This section offers a factual account of the events following the 1937 trial, including the outcomes for the witnesses and the accused and for the prosecutors, secret police agents, *apparatchiks* and other Party stalwarts who implemented and, at least for a time, benefitted from the terror.

All seventeen defendants of the 1937 trial were convicted on their pleas of guilty. Thirteen were promptly shot. Four – Karl Radek, Gregory Sokolnikov, Valentin Arnold and Mikhail Stroilov – received prison sentences ranging from eight to ten years. But none survived to tell their stories. Radek died in prison in 1939. As the man who "knew too much," the precise circumstances of his demise remain a matter of suspicion. Accounts have him fatally injured in a fall or beaten to death by other inmates, some say on instruction of the authorities. Sokolnikov also died or was murdered in prison in 1939. Arnold and Stroilov were executed in 1941.

Vladimir Romm was tried in a closed military tribunal on March 7, 1937 and sentenced to death. He was shot the following day. It is unknown if he was represented by a lawyer. Witnesses Dmitry Bukhartsev and Leonid Tamm were also promptly tried and shot. The bodies of Romm, Bukhartsev and Tamm were taken to the Donskoi monastery on the outskirts of Moscow where the government had built a cremation facility to dispose of the remains of the repressed. Their ashes were interred in a common grave, known as Tomb Number One.

In accordance with Soviet law, Vladimir's wife Galina Romm, Dmitry's wife Raisa Gerchikova and Leonid's wife Nina Bunkova were arrested and exiled to

Siberia. Evsey Romm was reportedly arrested in 1937 and released the following year. Alexander Romm and his wife, both well-known Moscow art critics, went apparently unmolested. Alexander continued to write and publish books about famous artists. He died in 1952.

Witness Vladimir Loginov was not shot immediately after the trial. Instead, he was impressed to testify at the trial of a fictitious Ukrainian terrorist center. Loginov did his duty and was shot on October 11, 1938.

Alex Stein was the only of the five witnesses who was not shot, at least not by the Soviets. In January 1940, after serving three years of a 25-year term, the German guest worker was expelled to his homeland. Several coworkers whom Stein had falsely accused of spying and wrecking were also liberated, and when they arrived in Berlin they complained to the Gestapo. Stein was promptly arrested. He had no choice but to confess all over again:

> When I consider that I bragged about my Communist orientation for nothing but personal advantages, by denigrating the Führer, by the painting, the Soviet star and by falsely accusing German engineers of wrecking activities I have to call myself a scoundrel...I see now that I deserve severe punishment. However, I believe that my long imprisonment in the Soviet Union and my psychological suffering is punishment enough. I desire to go back to work as soon as possible. In view of my age I beg for your mercy...

Stein disappeared into Germany's internal security apparatus. His fate is unknown.

Try as he might, Commissar of Heavy Industry Sergio Ordzhonikidze couldn't get Stalin and the Politburo to put a halt to the "spy" and "wrecker" madness that was consuming the USSR and stripping it of many of its best and brightest citizens. Convinced that his own arrest was imminent, Leonid Tamm's boss committed suicide on February 18, 1937. He had already delivered a farewell address. In a bitter speech to subordinates two weeks earlier he mocked the evidence being used to justify the repressions:

> On the 20th of this month, the Plenum of the CC of our party will hold its session. The agenda will include the results and the lessons of this filthy business [the wrecking]...Have you given me evidence showing how you are trying to put an end to the sabotage, what sort of measures you are undertaking? No, you aren't doing a damned thing...No, comrades, you must dig deep, surely there must be big or small cells everywhere in our organization which have committed filthy deeds. Look at Barinov [he was present]. Several of his derricks collapsed. It could have happened that a scoundrel overturned several derricks by himself and said that they were overthrown by the snowstorm. A most interesting question keeps nagging at me: How could this have happened? You and I have been working together for so many years...So how could it have happened that Piatakov was on our staff and yet no one, by God, saw through him?...Could it really be that this happened because we had become so blind?

Soon after the 1937 trial, American supporters of Trotsky's competing brand of Communism, the "Fourth International," formed a committee to examine the evidence presented during the 1936 and 1937 Moscow show trials. It was chaired by the renowned educator and philosopher John Dewey. Known as the "Commission of Inquiry into the Charges Made against Leon Trotsky in the Moscow Trials," or the "Dewey Commission" for short, it publicly deposed Leon Trotsky, who was then living in Mexico, and sent investigators to gather documents and interview witnesses throughout Europe. In 1938 the committee published a thick volume concluding that the trials had been completely falsified. Based on affidavits, ticket purchases, ship records, rental receipts and news accounts of Trotsky's movements in Europe, commissioners concluded that neither Trotsky nor his son could have met Romm, as they were never in the same place at the same time, and that Piatakov could not have flown in to meet Trotsky as no aircraft landed in Oslo during the month in question. Former inmates of the Soviet gulag furnished detailed accounts of abuse and torture. Foreigners who had worked in the Soviet mines spoke at length about poor safety conditions and the unrelenting pressure to increase output:

There were continuous minor breakdowns, mostly at the beginning, and due to poor material and workmanship, and later on, due to the habit of which they have of forcing production too fast, inexperienced men, machinery that has not been properly tuned up to put it rapidly into operation. And even after they get started, after the machinery is tuned up, by over-loading...It is characteristic of all their industry to force everything too fast, speed it up too much, and that caused many breakdowns.

Committee staff deposed the mother of defendant Valentin Arnold. She spoke of a woman her son mentioned in his confession:

She was an old woman who never left Riga, and had nothing whatever to do with politics. I often sent Valentine to her to collect money. For this reason I think that he mentioned the first name that came into his head, happening to recall the old lady.

Stalin's purges didn't end with the Party. Fearful that military men who once supported Trotsky might stage a coup, Stalin ordered that Marshal Mikhail Tukhachevsky, Deputy Commissar of Defense and seven top subordinates be tried for spying for Germany. They were shot on June 12, 1937. Had the top ranks of the Soviet General Staff really turned into Nazi collaborators? That's what Stalin's admirer, American Ambassador Joseph Davies apparently thought:

In view of the character of the accused, their long terms of service, their recognized distinction in their profession, their long-continued loyalty to the Communist cause, it is scarcely credible that their brother officers... should have acquiesced in their execution, unless they were convinced that these men had been guilty of some offense. It is generally accepted by members of the Diplomatic Corps that the accused must have been guilty of an offense which in the Soviet Union would merit the death penalty.

The madness didn't stop there. Dozens more Soviet officers were soon arrested and shot. Among them was hero of the Revolution General Vladimir Antonov-Ovseenko. He had just been appointed Commissar of Justice.

Another sordid tale of spying and sabotage opened in Moscow on March 2, 1938. In the third and final show trial, twenty-one officials were charged with participating in a Trotskyite plot to overthrow the USSR on behalf of Germany, Poland and Japan. Among them were *Izvestia* chief editor Nikolai Bukharin and Genrikh Yagoda, the secret police chief who helped stage the first trial. To give Vyshinsky victims for his closing arguments several physicians were included as defendants. They were accused of purposefully providing incorrect treatments and of poisoning top Party officials, thus introducing the fascinating new concept of medical wrecking.

Naturally, everyone confessed. Eighteen were shot, including Bukharin and Yagoda. Three were imprisoned; they were shot three years later.

Other clean-up work in 1938 included the executions of Boris Vinogradov, the Soviet official who had wanted to marry Martha Dodd, and Nikolai Krylenko, the prosecutor at the 1922 trial of the Socialist Revolutionaries. Semenov, the secret policeman who was the main witness in that case, was also arrested. He was used in other cases and died in prison.

Propelled by the example of the Moscow trials, spy and wrecker hysteria swept through the USSR. Citizens and bureaucrats denounced one another with wild abandon. Security officials competed to make the most arrests, turning the countryside into a killing field and the Soviet Union into a land that was said to be resting on graves. According to an authoritative account authorities arrested 1,575,259 persons during 1937-38, including 1,372,832 for counterrevolutionary crimes. A staggering 681,692 were shot.

Thousands of secret policemen got a taste of their own medicine, thus assuring their perpetual silence. One of those executed was George Aleksandrovich Molchanov, the principal interrogator at the 1936 and 1937 trials. Arrested in 1937, he was denounced as a "rightist conspirator" by his former boss Genrikh Yagoda at the 1938 trial. Romm's former superiors, General Yan Karlovich Berzin, Colonel Iosif Stanislavovich Unshlikht and secret police official Vladimir Andreevich Styrne were arrested as spies and traitors in 1937. Styrne was promptly shot; the others didn't meet their Maker until 1938.

As the killing machine ground on the slaughter of the educated class was imperiling the USSR's development. In the waning months of 1938 Stalin went to the spigot, issuing decrees that prohibited mass arrests and ordered improvements in the "quality" of investigations. But as this memorandum from the Supreme Court to the General Secretary attests, the time-tested techniques of Soviet "justice" were not being abandoned:

> During the past several months a great number of cases concerning members of rightist-Troskyist, bourgeois-nationalist, and espionage organizations have been received for judicial review...Taking into consideration the fact that... the majority of the defendants, citing the harsh conditions under which the investigations were carried out, have recanted their testimony at the judicial hearings and...attorneys for the defense, a significant number of whom have yet to be politically evaluated [may discover] the methods employed in [our] preliminary investigations...I consider it advisable, as a rule, not to allow attorneys for the defense access in [such cases].

By 1939 the "Great Terror" was over. No, the Gulag didn't close; scores of citizens continued to be arrested for political offenses and sent to camps to provide cheap labor for the Soviet industrial machine. But the murderous struggle within the Party was done. Its legacy seems remarkable. A majority of the nearly two-thousand delegates to the 1934 Party Congress were arrested as counter-revolutionaries. Ninety-eight of 139 members of the 1935 Central Committee, the second-highest stratum of the party, were shot.

Stalin was at the helm of a new Party, a new internal security apparatus and a new military leadership. He continued as undisputed ruler until his death from natural causes on March 5, 1953.

On August 20, 1940 a Soviet secret police agent wielding an ice pick murdered Trotsky at his villa near Mexico City.

In 1941 Joseph E. Davies published "Mission to Moscow," a memoir of his service as American Ambassador to the USSR between November 1936 and June 1938. His fawning account justified everything from the show trials to the executions of the General Staff. President Roosevelt was delighted with the book and pulled strings to have it made into a major motion picture. Released in 1943, "Mission to Moscow" featured an all-star cast, with Walter Huston in the lead role as Davies and Anne Harding playing his wife. Howard Koch wrote the script. Years later, when the Cold War broke out, Koch's work on the film got him blacklisted as a Communist stoolie and forced him to relocate to Great Britain. Koch later shared an Academy Award for writing "Casablanca," now honored as the pre-eminent screenplay of American cinematic history.

Former prosecutor Andrei Vyshinsky died from natural causes in November 1954. His death occurred at a luxurious apartment on New York City's Park Avenue where he lived while serving as Soviet ambassador to the United Nations.

In 1953 the USSR's new leader, Nikita Khrushchev orchestrated the arrest and execution of Stalin's last secret police chief, Lavrenti Beria. Three years later, in February 1956, he went after the rest of the old guard. In a major address to Party officials known as the "secret speech" he condemned Stalin's cult of personality and the injustices that took place under his regime:

> Many thousands of honest and innocent communists have died as a result of this monstrous falsification of such "cases," as a result of the fact that all kinds of slanderous "confessions" were accepted, and as a result of the practice of forcing accusations against oneself and others…When the wave of mass arrests began to recede in 1939, and the leaders of territorial party organizations began to accuse the NKVD workers of using methods of physical pressure on the arrested, Stalin dispatched a coded telegram [stating], "The Central Committee…explains that the application of methods of physical pressure in NKVD practice is permissible from 1937 on…It is known that all bourgeois intelligence services use methods of physical influence against [our representatives] and that they use them in

their most scandalous forms. The question arises as to why the Socialist intelligence service should be more humanitarian against the mad agents of the bourgeoisie, against the deadly enemies of the working class...

Khrushchev began his career in 1931 as a staunch Stalinist. He became Moscow Party secretary in 1935 and by 1938 was helping carry out purges in Ukraine. During the war he served as a political commissar. Khrushchev was elected Party First Secretary in 1953 and Premier five years later. Policy disputes, including concerns about his handling of the 1962 Cuban missile crisis, and worries about his mental condition led to his ouster in 1964. Unlike other losers in Soviet turf battles, Khrushchev was granted a pension. He succumbed to a heart attack seven years later.

After her flings in Berlin Martha Dodd returned to the U.S. and married Wall Street tycoon Alfred Stern. She promptly converted him to the Soviet cause. In 1957 American authorities charged both with espionage. Tipped off that something was brewing, the couple had already slipped away to Mexico. To avoid extradition they fled to Czechoslovakia and spent the remaining decades of their lives in the Soviet orbit, mostly in Prague, with detours to Cuba and the USSR. Alfred Stern died in Prague in 1986; Martha passed away in the Czech capital four years later. A prolific essayist, she authored "Through Embassy Eyes," a 1939 non-fiction account of her years in Berlin, and, in 1945, "Sowing the Wind," an anti-fascist novel.

On February 22, 1958 the Military Board of the Supreme Court of the USSR posthumously rehabilitated Vladimir Romm and set aside his conviction. In a letter to the party Galina Romm asked that it reinstate her husband so that she would become eligible for his pension:

To the Party Central Control Commission
From Romm, Galina
City Minusinsk, Krasnoyarsk Region
Oktyabrsaya Street, Building 58
9 October 1958

My husband Romm, Vladimir was in the Party since 1918. From 1922 until November 1936 he worked abroad — Germany, France, Japan and USA fulfilling special orders and also as a correspondent for *Tass* and *Izvestia* (break from 1925-1927 when he worked in the newspaper *Trud*.) In November 1936 we came back to Moscow from the U.S. and after three days my husband was arrested and disappeared. Until March 1958 I knew nothing about him. In March 1958 I got the letter from the Military Board of the Supreme Court of the USSR from which I saw that he was sentenced in 1937, not being guilty, and in February 1958 he was rehabilitated. I am asking you to make him a member of the Party again – of the Party he served honestly all his life. I also ask you to send me the extracts from the personnel file of my husband about his length of service because I need this to ask for his pension.

Galina Romm's request was apparently granted. Soviet police files indicate that she had no surviving relatives and moved in with friends in Moscow. Galina later told a Gulag memoirist that she met with her husband once while he was in prison. Georgie apparently lived with Alexander and Elena while she was in exile. He reportedly died from an unspecified disease after graduating from college. Galina died in a Moscow hospital in August 1983.

In December 1958 Igor Tamm, brother of witness Leonid Tamm, was co-recipient of the Nobel Prize in physics. Hero of Socialist Labor, three-time winner of the Stalin prize, leader of the team that developed the Soviet hydrogen bomb and mentor to Andrei Sakharov, the renowned theoretician was honored for explaining "Cherenkov" radiation, produced by the travel of objects at speeds faster than light. According to descendants, secret police chief Beria told Igor Tamm that Leonid died in prison while serving a ten-year term. Igor Tamm didn't learn the truth – that his brother was shot soon after the trial – until after Beria's execution.

On September 27, 1960 the Military Board of the Supreme Court of the USSR posthumously set aside Bukhartsev's conviction. Two years later his wife requested that he be readmitted to the Party, most likely to qualify for his pension. Minutes

kept by the Party Control Commission convey a sobering account of her travails
with the pitiless system:

> Moscow, 9 August 1962
>
> The wife of Bukhartsev – Gerchikova, R. M. – was arrested by the NKVD
> in 1937 and sentenced as a family member of those sentenced for political
> crimes to eight years in a labor camp. She was released in 1947. In 1950
> she was re-arrested and exiled to Siberia. In 1957 she was rehabilitated. At
> the present she doesn't work and receives a pension as an ordinary citizen.
>
> Decided: To posthumously rehabilitate B.D.P. [Bukhartsev, Dmitry
> Pavlovich]

Gerchikova's dead husband was once again a good Communist.

In 1990 the *Solovetskii*, a large stone taken from a Soviet labor camp was installed
across from the Lubyanka to serve as a memorial to the victims of the repressions.
Dzerzhinsky's statute was removed from its honored spot in front of the secret
police headquarters less than a year later. On October 18, 1991, shortly before its
dissolution, the USSR passed a law providing for the restoration of civil rights
and financial compensation to the victims of the Soviet terror. A similar law was
later enacted in Ukraine. Since then several hundred thousand persons have been
officially rehabilitated.

On October 30, 2007 Vladimir Putin, President of the Russian Federation,
attended a memorial ceremony at a former secret police shooting range near
Moscow where more than twenty-thousand of the victims of the Great Terror
are buried.

Author's Notes

Some years ago, while reading accounts of the Great Moscow Show Trials of 1936-38, I came across an interesting aspect of the second trial, which took place in January 1937. In addition to the customary string of confessions by penitent defendants, the prosecution put on five "witnesses," one for each day of testimony. Since each was under arrest and freely admitted participating in the plot, to bring them in as purportedly impartial observers seemed odd. But Procurator-General of the USSR Andrei Vyshinsky was caught in a dilemma. Many Westerners had reacted skeptically to the earlier trial, in August 1936, because it relied nearly exclusively on confessions. Determined to prop up his next house of straw, Vyshinsky decided to corroborate the accused using the only means available. It was a criminally brilliant move. As Soviet law allowed no privilege against self-incrimination, the witnesses inevitably created abundant legal justification for their own liquidation, thus assuring their perpetual silence. It was a "win-win" all around.

The two most prominent witnesses were Vladimir Romm and Dmitry Bukhartsev. Both were secret policemen who had been posted as foreign correspondents, Romm in Washington and Bukhartsev in Berlin. They were tasked with corroborating the confessions of the two principal accused, Karl Radek and Yuri Piatakov. (Indeed, the trial, which had seventeen defendants, is known as the Radek-Piatakov trial.) American Ambassador to the Soviet Union Joseph E. Davies and the *New York Times"* Walter Duranty, both unabashed Stalin fans, were present throughout the proceedings. They bought the tales hook, line and sinker. Indeed, Davies went so far as to participate in "Mission to Moscow," a major motion picture, released in 1943, that glorified Stalin's brutal regime and endorsed the trials. Until Soviet Premier Nikita Khrushchev blew the whistle on the travesty two decades later, many in the West continued to believe that the improbable accounts of "wrecking" and sabotage were true.

Little has been written about the witnesses. I sought to learn more. Who were they? What were their social, cultural and political backgrounds? And most importantly, how did their lives come to intersect in a Moscow courtroom three-quarters of a century ago?

A colleague's visit to the Russian Archives of Socio-Political History in Moscow yielded detailed biographical and service-related information for the three who were card-carrying communists: Romm, Bukhartsev and Party *apparatchik* Vladimir Loginov. Since Romm and Bukhartsev served in Europe, and Romm in America, there was considerable mention of them in the immigration and internal security archives of France, Switzerland, Germany and the U.S. Two descendants of the large and notable Romm family were also located and interviewed in Russia.

A fourth witness, Leonid Tamm, wasn't a Party member. His brother Igor, though, was a Soviet physicist and Nobel Prize winner. An article commemorating the anniversary of his death led to an interview with descendants, including one who met Leonid when she was a child.

The fifth witness, Alex Stein, was a German national. He was also the only one to be released after the trial (regrettably, into the arms of the Gestapo). A German archivist uncovered an internal security file that included an account of Stein's interrogation when he was repatriated.

Historical fiction is occasionally criticized for placing truth on the back-burner for the sake of a good read. As this is the first known attempt to document the lives of the five witnesses, and one of only a handful that examines the show trials in depth, I resolved to describe historical events accurately, inventing dialogue and using other tools of fiction to bridge the many gaps in the record and assemble an appealing and enlightening narrative.

Romm is the main protagonist. Thanks to the archives it was possible to follow him through his postings in the Soviet Union, Japan, Europe and, finally, the U.S. At each step he was inserted into actual events, in effect yielding a guided tour of the interwar period from the perspective of a loyal servant of the Soviet state.

When real persons are portrayed – and in this account only a handful of characters are fictional – there is concern that lives are being distorted for the sake of a good story. One workaround would be simply to give everyone a fictional identity. Here that would have been an awkward solution, as this work incorporates a large body of fact. Trusting that readers will remember that this is a novel and that there was no intent to harm anyone's reputation, real names were used. Those who wish to better disentangle truth from fiction and learn more about the era should refer to the following paragraphs, which provide sources for further reading and identify passages where the narrative departs substantially from fact.

Documentary Evidence

Vladimir Romm's French visa application, September 1930.
National Archives of France. Reproduced with permission.

Galina Romm's French visa application, May 1934.
National Archives of France. Reproduced with permission.

11/5/36

Foreign Dept.
Izvestia,
Moscow
Cunard White Star
R·M·S·"Queen Mary"

Dear Mr. Dulles,

I feel very sorry to have missed before y° left. I am going now to Moscow to talk things over as my paper wants me to go to London.

I hope I will have the pleasure of meeting you again somewhere. Meanwhile, I wish to thank you for the kindness shown to me

in Geneva and in the USA.
I will always remember
with pleasure our talks.
    With best wishes and
regards
        Very sincerely yours
        V. Romm

P.S. Have you read John
Whitaker's book? I found
it very amusing. I see that
he has spared you, at
least!

Vladimir Romm's letter to Allen Dulles, written on the RMS *Queen Mary* on November 5, 1936

Allen Dulles Papers. Mudd Manuscript Library. Department of Rare Books and Special Collections. Princeton University Library

Lubyanka prison, 27 November 1936

Vladimir Romm, Alexander Troyanovsky, Karl Radek, Leon Trotsky, Paul Ward, and Allen Dulles are historical figures.

Testimony from the 1936 and 1937 trials is based on *The Case of the Trotskyite-Zinovievite Terrorist Centre* (People's Commissariat of Justice, 1936), a narrative with testimonial excerpts, and *The Case of the Anti-Soviet Trotskyite Centre* (People's Commissariat, 1937), a verbatim transcript. Both were translated into English and published by the Soviet government. While they are believed to mostly accurately represent what was said in court, it has been said that some of the reported testimony may have been "sanitized" and inserted after the fact.

Information about the trials is from Robert Conquest, *The Great Terror: a Reassessment* (Oxford University Press, 1990), and Roy Medvedev, *Let History Judge* (Columbia University Press, 1989).

Vladimir Romm's family members are as described. His wife Galina's portrayal was inspired by Paul Ward's article, "Vladimir Romm," published in *The Nation* on February 6, 1937. The depiction of his brother Alexander draws from Alexander's book, *Henri-Matisse* (Isogiz, Moscow 1937). His brother Evsey's portrayal was influenced by an interview with a descendant. His son Georgie Romm's tuberculosis of the ankle was noted in French and American immigration records.

Vladimir Romm wrote about his return to the USSR in a letter to Dulles dated November 5, 1936. It is on *Queen Mary* stationery, suggesting it was written during the voyage. The letter is in the Allen Dulles collection at Princeton University.

Witnesses Dmitry Bukhartsev, Leonid Tamm, Vladimir Loginov and Alex Stein are historical figures. Soviet archives indicate that Stein was arrested on November 4, 1936, Tamm on November 6, and Romm and Bukhartsev on November 25. Loginov was also arrested during this period; the exact date is unknown.

Vilna (1905)

Vladimir Romm's arrest as a young boy is fictional. It was inspired by his claim in a Party biography that he helped his brothers carry out duties for a Socialist Revolutionary cell in Vilna. Vladimir also asserted that his father George Romm was a member of the Bund, a party of Marxists, and that his uncle Il'ya was a member of the outlawed but officially tolerated Constitutional-Democrat Party, commonly known as Cadets. In 1906, following a year of unrest, Russia formed its first parliament, the Duma, a consultative legislature subordinate to the Czar. Cadets won nearly a third of its seats.

Grand Duke Sergei's murder by Ivan Kaliayev is described in John C. Perry and Constantine Pleshakov, *The Flight of the Romanovs* (Basic Books, 1999).

Yevstolia Ragozinikova reportedly shot and killed a prison warden named Maximovsky, then unsuccessfully tried to set off a bomb hidden under her clothing. See Isaac Steinberg, *In the Workshop of the Revolution* (Rinehart & Co., 1953).

The Combat Brigade, a secretive terrorist cell led by Boris Savinkov and under the nominal control of the Party of Socialist Revolutionaries, orchestrated many assassinations of Czarist officials. It has been said that some of its members were mentally troubled youths. See Anna Geifman, *Revolutionary Terrorism in Russia, 1894-1917* (Princeton, 1993).

Lubyanka prison, 6 December 1936

Witnesses summoned to testify at the invented conspiracy that formed the basis for the 1937 show trial were arrested on related charges, but their cases were kept separate. They were jailed under provisions that allowed pre-trial investigations to run for many months, with no access to a lawyer. Once their services were no longer required the witnesses received summary trials in closed proceedings. Since there was no privilege against self-incrimination their testimony during the 1937 show trial was used against them. For more about Soviet criminal law and procedure of the era see Judah Zelitch, *Soviet Administration of Criminal Law* (University of Pennsylvania Press, 1931.)

The Romms (1906-07)

The scene at Sofia Romm's residence in Saint Petersburg is fictional.

Information about George Romm's medical career and his official postings are from Imperial records. According to a distant relative, he and his wife wound up living separate lives, with George Romm in Vilna and Sofia and their three sons in Saint Petersburg, where she participated in the art scene and studied piano. Vladimir Romm reported in his party autobiography that he was born in Vilna and lived in that city with his brothers, suggesting that his mother may have relocated, at least for a time. It has also been suggested that Vladimir was actually born in St. Petersburg but that his birth was recorded in Vilna because of edicts that restricted where Jews could live.

Vilna Governor-General Victor Von Wahl is a historical figure. Imperial records revealed that he wrote a letter dated December 12, 1897 to a member of the nobility conveying his decision not to appoint George Romm as head physician of the Vilna Jewish Hospital because of his ethnicity, and selected a Catholic doctor instead.

Vladimir Romm's party files indicate that his father served a term of imprisonment, presumably in connection with his membership in the Bund.

George Romm's prison encounter with Stalin and Vyshinsky is fictional. Stalin's prison stretches at Bailov and at Batumi, where he was locked up with Vyshinsky, have been widely reported. See Dmitri Volkogonov, *Stalin: Triumph and Tragedy* (Forum, 1991), and Arkady Vaksberg, *Stalin's Prosecutor: The Life of Andrei Vyshinsky* (Grove Weidenfeld, 1991).

There are conflicting accounts about Stalin's involvement in the Tiflis robbery. Some claim that he was a double-agent, simultaneously working for both the Bolsheviks and the *Okhrana*, the Czar's secret police. It has also been said that he personally supervised the robbery. For more about the robbery and socialist politics see Robert C. Williams, *The Other Bolsheviks: Lenin and his Critics* (Indiana University Press, 1986), and Robert C. Tucker, *Stalin as Revolutionary, 1879-1929* (Norton, 1973).

According to a descendant, George Romm and his first wife Sofia divorced after his release from prison. He then married a nurse and they emigrated to Switzerland. George Romm's second wife later died and he resettled in France. In 1926 he reportedly returned to the Soviet Union and moved in with Evsey and Esfir in Leningrad. A genealogical account indicates that he passed away in 1929.

Lubyanka prison, 9 December 1936

George Molchanov, Vyshinsky's principal interrogator for the 1936 and 1937 show trials, and his superior, Nikolai Yezhov, are historical figures.

Vladimir Romm's confession is based on the 1937 trial transcript.

Journeys (1915)

Vladimir Romm's position at the *zemstvo* in Minsk and his induction into the military are mentioned in his party file. Anna and her family are fictional characters.

Lubyanka prison, 12 December 1936

Stalin's visit to Radek and the latter's active role in preparing the 1937 trial have been reported by several authors, including Conquest. Their common source was

Alexander Orlov, a Soviet intelligence agent who defected in 1938. His account, *The Secret History of Stalin's Crimes* (Jarrolds, 1954), is largely hearsay but believed accurate.

The Commissar (1917)

The era of the Russian Revolution can be traced to 1905, when food shortages and widespread anger over the disastrous war with Japan led to strikes and demonstrations. Lenin seized on the discontent and tried to mount a *putsch*, which failed due to poor preparation and lack of public support. The second and third stages of the revolution took place in February 1917, when the Czar capitulated and was replaced by a liberal Provisional Government, and that October, when the Bolsheviks (later known as Communists) overthrew the Provisional Government. For comprehensive accounts of these events see Richard Pipes, *The Russian Revolution* (Vintage Books, 1991), and Perry and Pleshakov.

"Order No. 1" is an edited version of the actual document. See John R. Boyd (trans.), "The Origins of Order No. I," *Soviet Studies* (Vol. 19, No. 3, January 1968).

Vladimir Romm's service as a Socialist Revolutionary Commissar in the 177th Infantry Reserve Regiment is mentioned in his party files. Maxim Feodorovich is a fictional character.

Lubyanka prison, 13 December 1936

Yezhov's written order to Romm is fictional. It was inspired by accounts of members of the secret police who were arrested, planted at trials and ordered to provide false testimony.

A New Order (1917)

Events of the October Revolution are based on Pipes, and on Perry and Pleshakov.

Vladimir Romm mentioned in his party file that he was a delegate to the Second All-Russia Congress of Soviets. He also wrote, possibly self-servingly, that he often favored the Bolshevik line and quarreled with his Socialist Revolutionary comrades over dogma.

Isaac Steinberg, a historical figure, is one of the few Socialist Revolutionary leaders who survived the Soviet period. His views are from his autobiography, *In the Workshop of the Revolution*.

Lenin's decree of 28 November 1917 is a historical document. Its depiction is based on Nicolas Werth's translation in Courtois et al., *The Black Book of Communism* (Harvard University Press, 1999).

The account of how Vladimir Romm met his future wife Galina is fictional. His party file contains a disparaging assessment by Ukrainian communists, who described him as a spoiled elite and his wife as a "ballerina." It is unknown if she was a dancer. There are indications that she was employed as a schoolteacher.

Vladimir Romm's party autobiography notes that he briefly served on a revolutionary tribunal. Their workings are discussed by Pipes, by Peter H. Juviler, *Revolutionary Law and Order* (Free Press, 1976), and by Christy Jean Story, "In a Court of Law: The Revolutionary Tribunals in the Russian Civil War, 1917-1921" (Ph.D. dissertation, UC Santa Cruz, June 1998). Her descriptions of real trials inspired the account of the fictional trial observed by Vladimir Romm.

Socialist Reality (1918)

In 1918 the Bolsheviks were renamed the "Russian Communist Party of Bolsheviks," or communists for short.

Vladimir Romm was a member of the Party of Socialist Revolutionaries and remained with its Left faction after the split. His autobiographical and, likely, self-serving comments in Communist Party files indicate that he left the Socialist Revolutionaries because he disagreed with their principles and methods.

Kaplan's attempt on Lenin's life is a historical fact. Its account is based on various sources, including Pipes and David Shub's *Lenin* (Pelican Books, 1966). Conspiracy theories about the crime abound; some even deny that Kaplan was the killer. For example, see Semion Lyandres, "The 1918 Attempt on the Life of Lenin: A New Look at the Evidence," *Slavic Review* (Vol. 48, No. 3, Autumn 1989).

Stenka Razin is one of the first post-revolutionary ballets. Its significance in the transition of the Soviet ballet to a socially-conscious art form is discussed in James Von Geldern, *Bolshevik Festivals, 1917-1920* (University of California Press, 1993), available full-text at http://ark.cdlib.org/ark:/13030/ft467nb2w4/.

Lubyanka prison, 17 December 1936

Like other purported correspondence between Vladimir Romm and his family members, Alexander's letter is fictional.

In 1937 Alexander Romm published *Henri-Matisse* (Isogiz, 1937). This biography reviewed the artist's work from the perspective of socialist reality and criticized his supposed preoccupation with the bourgeois, decorative aspects of the craft.

Return to Vilna (1918)

Vladimir Romm's party resume indicates that he spent time in occupied Archangel. British, American and French military contingents took control of the city during the Russian Civil War and assisted Socialist Revolutionaries and the White armies in efforts to oust Communists and topple Lenin's regime. Romm's resume indicates that he then switched sides. He traveled to Vilna, joined the Lithuanian Communist Party and led a Red Guard detachment.

The account of the Polish-Lithuanian-Russian struggle is based on Norman Davis, *White Eagle, Red Star* (St. Martin's Press, 1972). Vilna's social and economic situation is based on Israel Cohen, *Vilna* (The Jewish Publication Society, 1943).

Lev Alexandrovich is a fictional character.

Communists (1918-1919)

The Soviet Union's 1919 capture of Vilna and its retaking by the Poles several months later are historical events. The city's political situation and its residents' views of the occupation and the occupiers are based on Davis and on Cohen. According to party records, Romm led a military revolutionary committee after the city fell to the Red Army. His actual activities are unknown.

Empress Petrovna's views are from Zvi Gitelman, *A Century of Ambivalence: The Jews of Russia and the Soviet Union, 1881 to the Present* (Indiana University Press, 2001).

Tambov (1920)

Vladimir Romm's assignment to Tambov as a military intelligence officer is mentioned in party records. His actual activities are unknown.

The situation in Tambov and General Antonov-Ovseenko's controversial role are based on Seth Singleton's "The Tambov Revolt (1920-1921)', *Slavic Review*, Vol. 25, No. 3 (September 1966). The General's subsequent service as a prosecutor and his own trial and execution are mentioned by Medvedev.

Lubyanka prison, 21 December 1936

Solzhenitsyn also borrowed books from the Lubyanka's library. See D. M. Thomas, *Alexander Solzhenitsyn: A Century in his Life* (St. Martin's Press, 1998).

The Comrade (1921)

Accounts of the Red excesses during the Russian Civil War are from Pipes, Story, and two articles by Nicholas Werth, "The Dirty War" and "From Tambov to the Great Famine," both in *The Black Book of Communism*.

Severny's encounter with Princess Olga Paley is based on her book, *Memories of Russia, 1916-1919* (reprinted by Royalty Digest, 1996, available full-text at www. alexanderpalace.org/memoriesrussia/chapter_XXXIV.html). Vladimir Romm's mission to reform Severny's unit, his encounter with the woman lodger and the Ukrainian Communist Party's hostile reaction to his activities are based on detailed accounts in party files.

Lubyanka prison, 23 December 1936

Testimonies of Piatakov and Radek are adapted from the 1937 trial transcript.

A Struggle Within (1922)

For an authoritative account of the 1922 trial of the Socialist Revolutionaries see Marc Jansen, *A Show Trial Under Lenin* (Martinus Nijhoff, 1982).

Semenov's life as a revolutionary and a spy is discussed in Sergei Zhuralev, "Little People and Big History: Foreigners at the Moscow Electric Factory and Soviet Society, 1920s–1930s," *Russian Studies in History* (vol. 48, no. 3, Summer 2005). Conspiracy theories about the attempt on Lenin's life and Semenov's alleged role are discussed by Iurii Fel'shtinskii in "The Mystery of Lenin's Death," *Russian Social Science Review*, (vol. 45, no. 3, 2004).

Nikolai Krylenko is a historical figure. According to party files, Vladimir Romm was an intelligence section chief in Moscow between January and August 1922. His involvement in the Trial of the Socialist Revolutionaries and his meeting with Krylenko are fictional.

Nastasia Feodorova is a fictional character.

Moscow Center (1922)

Relations between Germany and the Soviet Union are discussed in Jon Jacobson, *When the Soviet Union Entered World Politics* (University of California Press, 1994), and in Conan Fischer, *The German Communists and the Rise of Nazism* (St. Martin's Press, 1991). Soviet military assessments and Berzin's views draw from Raymond Leonard, *Secret Soldiers of the Revolution: Soviet Military Intelligence 1918-1933* (Greenwood Press, 1999).

Radek's role in the failed *putsch* is well known. For a detailed account see Warren Lerner, *Karl Radek: The Last Internationalist* (Stanford University Press, 1970).

Lubyanka prison, 27 December 1936

Biographical information about Bukhartsev and his parents are from party files.

Berlin (1922-23)

This section was inspired by Vladimir Romm's party files, which indicate that he performed "illegal work" (meaning not under embassy or official cover) for military intelligence in Berlin and Paris during 1922-24. His actual duties are unknown.

Depictions of Berlin's cultural life and of its Russian émigrés are based on Otto Friedrich's account of Berlin in the 1920's, *Before the Deluge* (Harper and Row, 1972). Accounts of the hyperinflation of 1921-23 are from Friedrich and from Fischer. Information about German militias, the *Freikorps* and the rise of Nazism is from Fischer.

Radek's views on German communists, his ideological meanderings and the thrust of his infamous "Schlageter" speech – that communists and Germany's "nationalist masses" shared a common cause – are mentioned by Lerner, by Jacobson, and by Fischer.

The USSR's large scale spying efforts in the Reich are discussed by Jacobson and by Leonard.

Lubyanka prison, 28 December 1936

Accounts of Bukhartsev's postings are based on information in party files. Bukhartsev authored at least two books and several monographs, all seemingly supportive of the lines taken by Stalin. One book criticized the Dawes Plan, while another took on the economist Nikolai Bukharin, an acolyte of Lenin and one of the principal defendants in the 1938 trial. Complaints by the Nazi propaganda ministry about Bukhartsev's acerbic reporting were found in the German Federal archives.

Essen (1923)

France's invasion of the Ruhr, its relations with Germany, the circumstances in Essen and the killing of the strikers are based on Conan Fischer, *The Ruhr Crisis, 1923-1924* (Oxford University Press, 2003).

According to party files, Vladimir Romm was in Germany during this period working undercover for Soviet military intelligence. His actual duties are unknown.

Radek's complex (some might say, wildly inconsistent) views about the German situation are discussed by Lerner.

Lubyanka prison, 30 December 1936

Like most everything about the 1937 trial, Piatakov's alleged meeting with Trotsky was a fabrication. For a detailed analysis of the authenticity of the evidence from the perspective of Trotsky's supporters see *Not Guilty: Report of the Commission of Inquiry into the Charges Made Against Leon Trotsky in the Moscow Show Trials* (Harper & Brothers, 1938).

The Colonel (1923)

Otto is a fictional character.

Unshlikht is a historical figure. His service in the secret police and military intelligence, dealings with Stalin and Dzerzhinsky and role in the German uprising are discussed in Leonard and in Viktor Suvorov's *Spetsnaz: the Story Behind the Soviet SAS* (Hamish Hamilton, 1987), full-text at http://militera.lib.ru/research/suvorov6/index.html.

Vladimir Romm's duties in Germany are unknown. He listed Unshlikht as a reference in his party files.

Lubyanka prison, 1 January 1937

Details about the alleged role of the mysterious, and as it turns out, fictitious journalist "Stirner" are from the 1937 trial transcript.

Hamburg (1923)

Moishe Stern (aka Emil Kleber) is a historical figure. His fascinating career in the Soviet military is set out in Walter Krivitsky, *In Stalin's Secret Service* (Enigma Books, 2000). Stern's role in the abortive revolution, the failure to adequately prepare the Proletarian Hundreds and the foul up that led the Hamburg cell to revolt all by itself, with disastrous consequences, are based on Leonard, on Fisher, and on Chris Harman's *The Lost Revolution: Germany 1918 to 1923* (Bookmarks/ Socialist Workers Party, 1982).

Vladimir Romm was posted in Germany during this period. It is unknown whether he participated in the revolt.

City of Light (1924)

Party files indicate that Vladimir Romm performed intelligence work in Berlin and Paris during 1922-24. His actual duties are unknown.

Soviet secret police surveillance of exiled royals, monarchists and Whites in Europe is discussed in Dziak, in Leonard, and in Christopher Andrew and Vasili Mitrokhin, *The Sword and the Shield* (Basic Books, 1999).

Accounts of the activities of exiled Grand Dukes Kyril and Nikolasha are based on Perry and Pleshakov. Depictions of Paris in the 1920s and of its community of Russian expatriates are based on Elliot Paul, *The Last Time I Saw Paris* (Random House, 1942), and on William Wiser, *The Crazy Years: Paris in the Twenties* (Atheneum, 1983).

Lubyanka prison, 6 January 1937

Vladimir Romm's rehearsal testimony is based on the 1937 trial transcript.

Savinkov (1924)

Savinkov fell prey to the GPU largely as described, although not, as far as is known, with Vladimir Romm's help. Accounts of his capture can be found in many sources, including Dziak and Andrew. His cooperation with authorities and final plea are based on Walter Duranty's first-person account, *The Curious Lottery* (Coward McCann, 1929). For an authoritative biography of Duranty see S. J. Taylor, *Stalin's Apologist* (Oxford, 1990).

Vladimir Romm's party records reflect that he left military intelligence and joined the GPU Foreign Department in late 1924, with no reason given. His dissatisfaction with military intelligence and clash with Berzin are fictional elements.

Le Train Bleu, Ballets Russes and the company's place in dance history are explored in Lynn Garafola, *Diaghilev's Ballets Russes* (Oxford University Press, 1989).

Trud (1924-25)

Vladimir Styrne is a historical figure. For an account of his activities see Christopher Andrew and Oleg Gordievsky, *KGB: The Inside Story* (Harper Collins, 1990).

Vladimir Romm's brief stint at GPU headquarters, immediately followed by his assignment to *Trud,* are mentioned in his party autobiography. He was likely planted at the paper's foreign desk to monitor things, a common practice.

Aspects of trade union development and government policy during the time of the New Economic Policy (NEP) are from Jay Sorenson, *The Life and Death of Soviet Trade Unionism 1917-1928* (Atherton, 1969). The role of the Soviet press during this period is discussed by Matthew Lenoe in *Closer to the Masses: Stalinist Culture, Social Revolution and Soviet Newspapers* (Harvard, 2004), and by Jeffrey Brooks, *Thank You, Comrade Stalin! Soviet Public Culture From Revolution to Cold War* (Princeton, 2000).

The anecdote is paraphrased from William H. Chamberlin, "The Anecdote: Unrationed Soviet Humor," *Russian Review* (Vol. 16, no. 3, July 1957).

Party files indicate that Bukhartsev wrote for a workers' newspaper. The article attributed to him is fictional.

The described trial is fictional. It was inspired by Lenoe's accounts of similar proceedings. Many such trials took place during the NEP's later stages. Punishments were usually mild.

The Manifesto (1926-27)

Vladimir Romm's meeting with Bukhartsev is fictional. It is unknown if they were acquainted before the 1937 show trial.

Bukhartsev's party records mention his posting at *Komsomolskaya Pravda.* Other comments in the file suggest that he had been working as an intelligence agent for some time. Bukhartsev is mentioned in A. Kolpakidi and D. Prohorov, *Vneshnya razvedka Rossii (Russian Foreign Intelligence),* a Russian-language encyclopedia of Soviet-era intelligence officers published in Moscow in 2001.

For a succinct account of the struggles between Stalin and Trotsky see Michael Kort, *The Soviet Colossus: History and Aftermath* (M.E. Sharpe, 2006).

Vladimir Romm's sympathies with the Trotsky opposition and his troubles at *Trud* are mentioned in party files. Pressures on the Soviet press to conform to Stalinist doctrine are discussed by Lenoe and by Brooks.

Radek's meeting with Romm is fictional. Radek's extensive participation in the Trotsky opposition is discussed in Lerner. The Declaration of the Eighty-Three (also known as the Platform of the Eighty-Three) is a historical document that was widely circulated among Trotsky's supporters and was ultimately endorsed by thousands, including Vladimir Romm.

Lubyanka prison, 11 January 1937

Information about Loginov was drawn from party files. Loginov's persona was inspired by his extensive role in the trial, as evident in the transcript, and by his appearance as a defendant/witness in a subsequent terrorist trial in Ukraine, mentioned by Conquest. His interactions with Romm and Bukhartsev are fictional.

Lev (1928)

Depictions of the Shakhty trial draw from Medvedev, from Duranty's *The Curious Lottery*, and from Duranty's running account of the proceedings as published in the *New York Times* in June and July 1928.

Romm's firing from *Trud* for "not being completely devoted to the line of the Central Committee" and his reassignment as *Tass* correspondent to Tokyo are mentioned in his party files. They contain no further explanation.

Lubyanka prison, 12 January 1937

According to the transcript of the 1937 trial, all those mentioned testified essentially as stated. "Mr. L" is Yakov Abramovich Livshitz; "Mr. R" is Stanislav Antonovich Rataichak.

Siberia, Ukraine, Tokyo (1928)

Loginov's exile and the circumstances of his reinstatement are based on a detailed account in party files. His letter to the party, his activities while in exile and the incident in his youth involving his brother are fictional.

Anna, Idzi and the farm encounter are fictional.

Party files give no explanation for Romm's posting to Japan as *Tass* correspondent only a few months after his departure from *Trud*. Correspondence in the files of the French Ministry of the Interior conveys the belief that Romm was sent to Japan as a spy.

Ichiro is a fictional character.

Political, economic and social circumstances of interwar Japan are based on Edward Sidensticker, *Tokyo Rising* (Knopf, 1990); George A. Lensen, *Japanese Recognition of the USSR* (Sophia University, 1970); Katharine Sansom, *Living in Tokyo* (Harcourt Brace, 1937); and Keiko Packard, *Old Tokyo* (Oxford, 2002).

In a volume of recollections from Gulag survivors, Galina Romm suggests she accompanied her husband to Tokyo. See See Milutin, T.P., *People of My Life*, online at http://www.sakharov-center.ru/asfcd/auth/?t=page&num=1318.

Lubyanka prison, 13 January 1937

Leonid Tamm was not a party member. Most of what is related, including the encounter between Tamm's father and the Red Army, was mentioned by Igor Tamm's descendants during an interview.

Minutes of the Political Bureau contain few details of the case against Leonid Tamm other than the date of his arrest, November 6, 1936. According to Conquest, Radek and Piatakov had been taken into custody in September 1936, a full two months earlier. It is believed that Piatakov encouraged others to testify. His interaction with Tamm is fictional.

Fumiko (1928)

Depictions of social and economic conditions in Tokyo during the early Shōwa period are drawn from Sidensticker; Sansom; Packard; Koji Taira, "Urban Poverty, Ragpickers, and the "Ants' Villa" in Tokyo", *Economic Development and Cultural Change* (17:2, January 1969); and T. Hasegawa, "The Population of Greater Tokyo," *Review of the International Statistical Institute* (1:2, July 1933).

Fumiko is a fictional character. Troyanovsky's evaluations criticized Romm for "Bohemian" tendencies. There is nothing to suggest that he had an affair while in Japan.

Accounts of the liquidation of the Japanese Communist Party and the waves of arrests in 1928 are based on Lensen and on Elise K. Tipton, *The Japanese Police State: The Tokkō in Interwar Japan* (University of Hawaii Press, 1990).

Lubyanka prison, 14 January 1937

Comrade Kutuzov is a fictional character.

Georgie (1928-29)

French immigration records mention Georgie Romm's tuberculosis and his visits, accompanied by his mother and grandmother, to a sanatorium in Berck-Plage. Georgie's condition was also noted in the ship's manifest documenting the family's arrival in the U.S.

Diagnostic and treatment protocols of the period are based on H. Herzog, "History of Tuberculosis," *Respiration* (65, 1998) and on William Campbell and Le Grand Kerr, *The Surgical Diseases of Children* (Appleton and Co., 1912).

Romm's period of leave is fictional. According to party files he was in Tokyo for three years, from mid-1927 to May 1930. A recently discovered account suggests that he was accompanied by his family.

Events at the farm are fictional. They were inspired by historical accounts of the dispossession and exile of *"kulaks"* ("rich" peasants) during Stalin's collectivization campaign. For examples see Werth's "From Tambov to the Great Famine," and Kort.

Lubyanka prison, 15 January 1937

Accounts of Stein's treatment by Soviet authorities are based on records in German Federal archives of his interrogation by the Gestapo. His testimony is based on the 1937 trial transcript.

Stein's interactions with Romm and Bukhartsev are fictional.

The Tokkō (1929-30)

Troyanovsky's service in Japan is mentioned by Lensen and by Jacob Kovalio, "Japan's Perception of Stalinist Foreign Policy in the early 1930s," *Journal of Contemporary History* (19, 1984). His interactions with the young Stalin are based on Roman Brackman, *The Secret File of Joseph Stalin* (Routledge, 2000) and Arkady Vaksberg, *Stalin Against the Jews* (Knopf, 1994).

Troyanovsky's assessment of Romm was inspired by the ambassador's written evaluations in party files.

Party files reveal that Vladimir Romm was severely reprimanded for signing the Declaration of the Eighty-Three. The note to Troyanovsky from the party committee investigating Romm is fictional. Romm's letter to the Party was inspired by the explanation and apology he wrote while in Japan.

According to party files Vladimir Romm gathered valuable intelligence about China while posted in Japan, but the nature of his activities is unknown. His intelligence exploits and the Tokkō's response are fictional. During this period Romm represented the USSR at an international conference in Kyoto. Historians report that this is where China first intended to publicize the "Tanaka Memorial," a prophetic, by most accounts forged document that set out Japan's ambitions to seize Manchuria, control Siberia and hobble America and the West. For details see John J. Stephan, "The Tanaka Memorial (1927): Authentic or Spurious?" *Modern Asia Studies* (7:4, 1973). Events leading to Japan's invasion of Manchuria are discussed in C. Walter Young, "Sino-Japanese Interests and Issues in Manchuria," *Pacific Affairs* (1:7, December 1928).

The depiction of Romm's sudden departure from Japan is fictional. It was inspired by a report in French intelligence files that Romm was forced to flee Japan when authorities discovered that he was doing more spying than journalism.

Lubyanka prison, 16 January 1937

Detailed accounts of the mine explosions are in the 1937 trial transcript.

Ordzhonikidze's intervention on Leonid Tamm's behalf and the gift of a Packard automobile were mentioned by Igor Tamm's descendants.

Berck-Plage (1930-31)

French police alerted their Swiss counterparts in writing of Vladimir Romm's activities in Tokyo and reputation as a spy. The memo from the French attaché in Tokyo and the letter from the French to the Swiss are fictional; they were inspired by correspondence in the French archives.

Vladimir Romm's postings to Paris and Geneva are reflected in Soviet archives.

The circumstances of Romm's arrival in Geneva, including his "rescue" by John Whitaker, a historical figure, are fictional. However, Romm and Whitaker did meet in Geneva. In his book, *And Fear Came* (McMillan Company, 1936), Whitaker describes his conversations with Romm while both served as foreign correspondents at the disarmament conference.

Lubyanka prison, 17 January 1937

According to the 1937 trial transcript Leonid Tamm was by far the most resistant of the witnesses, causing Vyshinsky to lead him through his courtroom testimony. Tamm wound up implicating himself and others, but only vaguely.

Geneva (1931)

Discussion of the League of Nations and Disarmament Conference draws from *A Brief History of the League of Nations* (League of Nations Association, December 1934); F. P. Walters, *A History of the League of Nations* (Oxford University Press, 1952, 1960 and 1965); and F. S. Northedge, *The League of Nations* (Leicester University Press, 1986). Period depictions of Geneva are based on Paul Chapponière, *Geneva* (B. Arthaud, 1931), and Marcel Rosset, *Rambling in Geneva* (Éditions du Griffon, 1952).

Max Baer is a historical figure. Interactions between Whitaker, Romm, Baer and Duranty were inspired by passages in Whitaker.

Litvinov is a historical figure. His fictional discussion with Vladimir Romm reflects well-known views held by Litvinov, Troyanovsky and other Soviet officials about the threats posed by Germany.

The retired French soldier Henri is a fictional character.

French archives contain mention of several trips by Galina, Georgie and Ludvika to Paris and Berck-Plage. While in the capital they lived on the Rue de Vaugirard near a city children's hospital where Georgie may have been a patient.

Sergey Shchukin is a historical figure. His activities as a collector of French paintings are mentioned in Beverly Kean, *All the Empty Palaces* (Universe Books, 1983).

Japan's invasion of Manchuria is a historical fact.

Illusions of Peace (1932-34)

Duranty's account of a train car in Siberia packed with persons being transported to labor camps is based on his memoir, *I Write as I Please* (Simon and Schuster, 1935).

Japan's invasion of Manchuria and its effect on Soviet-Japanese relations are based on Kovalio. Soviet-British relations are discussed in Keith Nielson, *Britain, Soviet Russia and the Collapse of the Versailles Order, 1919-1939* (Cambridge University Press, 2006), and in Michael Carley, "Down a Blind Alley: Anglo-Franco-Soviet

Relations, 1920-39," *Canadian Journal of History* (Vol. 29, April 1994).

Baer's surprising quest to be Hitler's propaganda minister (a position later filled by Goebbels) was mentioned in Whitaker.

Allen Dulles and Henry Stimson are well-known historical figures.

Vladimir Romm's party file and French immigration records indicate that he split his time between Paris and Geneva.

Information about the Metro-Vickers case is from Gordon W. Morrell, *Britain Confronts the Stalin Revolution: Anglo-Soviet Relations and the Metro-Vickers Crisis* (Wilfred Laurier University Press, 1995). The paragraph from the indictment and the quotation from the defense lawyer paraphrase the official transcript, *Wrecking Activities at Power Stations in the Soviet Union* (Modern Books and State Law Publishing House, 1933). Thornton and MacDonald spent three months in custody after their verdicts before their sentences were commuted to expulsion.

Vladimir's affair with Rose, a fictional character, was inspired by an entry in a Swiss Federal police file suggesting that he was involved with a female secretary to the American legation.

Lubyanka prison, 19 January 1937

Alexander Romm's *Henri-Matisse* was first published in 1937. A 1947 edition by Lear, New York, is subtitled "A Social Critique." Three letters from Matisse to Alexander Romm are mentioned in Jack D. Flam, *Matisse on Art* (E.P. Dutton, 1978).

America (1934)

The accident at Gorlovka is a fictionalized version of the actual incident as described in the 1937 trial transcript. Leonid Kurkin was one of the named victims.

Constantine Oumansky is a historical character. The going-away luncheon for Romm is based on the actual event as reported in the *New York Times* (June 2, 1934, p. 19).

For a discussion of the mid-1930's Soviet initiative to infiltrate spies into the U.S. see Weinstein and Vassiliev.

It is unknown why Ludvika Ossipovna, Vladimir Romm's mother-in-law, didn't accompany the family to the U.S. Her passing is fictionalized.

Dates of the Romm family's embarkation and arrival on the Majestic are from the ship's manifest. They identify the travelers as Vladimir, Galina and Georgie and list their nearest relative as Alexander Romm in Moscow.

The *New York Times* headline and excerpt are verbatim quotes from an article published on June 2, 1934.

Depictions of the Soviet Embassy and accounts of its officials are based on a series of articles in the *New York Times* between July 16, 1933 and November 29, 1934.

Oleg Troyanovsky, son of Ambassador Troyanovsky, is a historical figure. He was an alumnus of the Sidwell Academy, a prominent Quaker (Friends) school in Washington, D.C.

Vladimir Romm's welcoming reception is fictional. It was inspired by his bylined article, "The Press in the USSR," *Journalism Quarterly* (XII:1, March 1935), which includes the quoted excerpts. Written in the first person, it was probably first delivered as a speech.

Chicago, Cleveland (1934-35)

Sergey Kirov is a historical figure. While few deny that Nikolayev was the killer, many scholars, including Conquest and Medvedev, suggest the murder was a plot hatched by Stalin. For a book-length argument to that effect see Amy Knight, *Who Killed Kirov?* (Hill and Wang, 1999). For opposing views see Matt Lenoe, "Who Killed Kirov and Does it Matter?" in *The Journal of Modern History* (74:2, June, 2002), and Alla Kirilina, *L'assassinat de Kirov: Destin d'un stalinien, 1888-1934* (Seuil, 1995).

Bukhartsev's party files briefly mention that he "converted" the daughter of the American Ambassador to Berlin. His recruitment of Martha Dodd is mentioned by several sources. This account is based on Allen Weinstein and Alexander Vassiliev, *The Haunted Wood* (Modern Library, 2000). They also discuss Martha Dodd's later activities as a Soviet agent.

Ambassador William Bullitt's voyage from hopefulness to despair about Stalin is described in Dennis J. Dunn, *Caught Between Roosevelt and Stalin: America's Ambassadors to Moscow* (University Press of Kentucky, 1998).

Romm wrote a long piece about the New York car show for *Izvestia*; the account here is fictionalized.

In June 1935 the Harris Foundation sponsored a lecture series on the USSR that was hosted by the University of Chicago. Addresses given by Troyanovsky, Vladimir Romm and others were published in Samuel N. Harper, Ed., *The Soviet Union and World Problems* (University of Chicago Press, 1935). In a monograph entitled "Reinventing Government: Fast Bullets and Culture Changes" (full-text at www.sovereignty.net/p/gov/Hillmann-book2.html) Robert P. Hillmann reports that Radek was originally scheduled to attend.

Newsman Jim Thornton is fictional, as is Vladimir Romm's stopover in Cleveland.

Liquidation (1935-36)

The embassy episode and Georgie's birthday party are fictional.

Bullitt's view of Stalin and his disagreement with Roosevelt's policy of appeasing the Soviet leader are from Dunn.

Information about the Komsomol young Communist plot and events preceding the 1936 trial are from Conquest and Medvedev.

Heifetz's debut performance at Constitution Hall took place in 1936. His meeting with Vladimir Romm is fictional. The musician's life and work are described in Artur Weschler-Vered, *Jascha Heifetz* (Schirmer Books, 1986).

The August 1936 Yosemite Conference of the Institute of Pacific Relations is a historical gathering. Its proceedings are in W. L. Holland and Kate Mitchell, eds., *Problems of the Pacific, 1936* (University of Chicago Press, 1936). For a concise account see Quincy Wright, "Yosemite Conference of the Institute of Pacific Relations," *American Journal of International Law* (30:4, October 1936). Vladimir Romm and D. E. Motylev of the Soviet Academy of Sciences were the USSR's sole representatives.

Ludmila Ivanovna is a fictional character.

Troyanovsky's evaluation of Vladimir Romm paraphrases the ambassador's actual remarks as preserved in party files.

Accounts of the 1936 trial were published in the *New York Times*, August 15-20, 1936. The excerpt about the executions is a condensed version of correspondent Harold Denny's dispatch, published August 30, 1936, page E-5.

Lubyanka prison, 25 January 1937

All trial information is from the transcript. Loginov's participation in another trial is mentioned in Conquest.

The interaction among the witnesses is fictional.

Show Trial (1937)

The interaction between the Wards is fictional.

News clips are from the *New York Times*.

Bullitt's travails with Roosevelt, his replacement by Davies, the latter's views and his conflicts with knowledgeable Russia hands are based on Dunn and on Davies' memoir, *Mission to Moscow* (Simon and Schuster, 1941). Davies' meeting with Duranty and the other newsmen, his reaction to Vladimir Romm's testimony and the correspondents' appeal on Romm's behalf are based on *Mission to Moscow*.

The cable that Duranty purportedly read out loud was published in the *New York Times*, January 23, 1937, p. 28.

Duranty's "It is a sad and dreadful" story was published in the *New York Times* on January 25, 1937, page 3.

Romm's letter to Dulles, quoted verbatim, is from the Allen Dulles archives at Princeton University. Whitaker's "rich idlers" comment is from *And Fear Came*, p. 111.

Troyanovsky's meeting with the correspondents was an actual event. Its depiction was inspired by an article in the *New York Times*, January 27, 1937, p. 10.

All trial testimony, including Vyshinsky's clashes with Radek, the statement by Knyazev's lawyer and Piatakov's plea are verbatim or lightly edited excerpts from the official transcript. Radek's explosive comment and Vyshinsky's reply are from pg. 135.

For a detailed account of the self-criticism rituals that pervaded Party life see J. Arch Getty, "Samokritika Rituals in the Stalinist Central Committee, 1933-38," *The Russian Review* (Vol. 58, January 1999).

Public celebrations at trial's end were widely reported by Soviet newspapers and in dispatches by Western correspondents. (One account, written by Duranty, was published in the *New York Times* on February 6, 1937, p. 67.) Equal scenes of madness took hold in the countryside. See Sheila Fitzpatrick, "How the Mice Buried the Cat: Scenes from the Great Purges of 1937 in the Russian Provinces," *The Russian Review* (Vol. 52, July 1993).

The episode with Anna is fictional. Depictions of labor camp life and the inmate-built rail line are based on "The Empire of the Camps" in Courtois et al.

For a pro-Stalin assessment of the trial see William Z. Foster, *Questions & Answers on the Piatakov-Radek Trial* (Workers Library, 1937). For a pro-Trotsky view see *Why Did They Confess* (Pioneer Publishers, 1937).

Excerpts from *The Nation* are from its February 6, 1937 issue.

Duranty's last courtroom dispatch and the accompanying wire story were published in the *New York Times* on January 30, 1937, p.1.

Davies' quotes are from his memoir; "human nature" is on page 43; "kind and gentle" is on pages 356-357.

Lubyanka prison, 10 February 1937

Romm's former superiors General Yan Karlovich Berzin and Colonel Iosif Stanislavovich Unshlikht were arrested in 1937 and shot in 1938. See Heinrich E. Schultz, Paul Urban and Andrew Lebed, *Who Was Who in the USSR* (The Scarecrow Press, 1972).

Trial of Vladimir Romm

According to Gulag memoirist T.P. Milutin, Galina Romm said that she visited her husband in prison shortly before his execution.

7 March 1937

Romm was reportedly tried on March 7 and executed on March 8. There is no indication that any Soviet official interceded on his behalf. Litvinov and Troyanovsky served out their diplomatic careers and died of natural causes. Troyanovsky's son, Oleg, also served as a Soviet diplomat, ultimately as ambassador to China.

The Next Morning

This episode is wholly fictional.

Moscow (2002)

The characters referred to in this section are fictional, as is the diary. Tomb Number One at the Donskoi Monastery, which reportedly holds the ashes of Romm, Bukhartsev, Tamm and countless other victims of the Soviet terror, is regrettably not.

A Little Bit of History

Biographical information about officials who were victims of the Terror was compiled from Conquest; from Medvedev; from J. Arch Getty and Oleg V. Naumov, *The Road to Terror* (Yale University Press, 1999); and from Schultz, Urban and Lebed.

Ordzhonikidze's suicide was widely reported. His speech is an extract from Document 90 in Getty and Naumov.

Fates of Romm, Bukhartsev and their wives are from party files and information compiled by *Memorial*, a celebrated Russian human-rights organization that was formed to document and investigate Stalin's abuses (http://www.memo.ru/eng/index.htm). Information about Evsey and Alexander Romm and Leonid and Igor Tamm are from interviews with descendants. Supplemental information about Galina Romm and Georgie are from correspondence with Galina's daughter from a second marriage and from Galina's conversation with the Gulag memoirist.

The Dewey Commission issued two volumes: *The Case of Leon Trotsky* (Harper & Brothers, 1937), essentially a transcript of Trotsky's deposition, and *Not Guilty* (Harper & Brothers, 1937), a detailed exposition and analysis of the evidence presented during the 1936 and 1937 trials. Extracts are from *Not Guilty*.

Ambassador Davies' quotes about the trial and the execution of the Generals are from *Mission to Moscow*, pg. 201.

Information about the 1938 trial is from Conquest and the official transcript, *Report of Court Proceedings in the Case of the Anti-Soviet Block of Rights and Trotskyites* (People's Commissariat of Justice, 1938).

Loginov's role in the trial of the Ukrainian terrorist center and the fact of his execution are from Conquest.

Statistics on arrests and executions and information about the memorandum to Stalin are from Getty and Naumov (see Document 195).

Circumstances of the deaths of Trotsky, Radek, Stalin, Beria and Vyshinsky have been widely reported.

A copy of Stein's statement to the Gestapo was supplied by the Federal German Archives.

"Secret speech" extract is from its translation in Khrushchev, Nikita, *The Anatomy of Terror: Khrushchev's Revelations About Stalin's Regime* (Public Affairs Press, 1956). For an online version see http://www.fordham.edu/halsall/mod/1956khrushchev-secret1.html.

Boris Vinogradov's fate is mentioned by Weinstein and Vassiliev and, in more detail, by Shareen Blair Brysac in *Resisting Hitler: Mildred Harnack and the Red Orchestra* (Oxford University Press, 2000).

Igor Tamm's Nobel citation is a matter of record.

Letters from Galina Romm and Raisa Gerchikova and the decisions taken by the Party are from Russian archives.

Praise for Lenin's Harem

Born to an aristocratic life of wealth and privilege, but driven from the family home by resentful Latvian peasants, a young German struggles to survive and protect his love from the brutalities of a domineering brother, class struggle, war, and communist rule. The attention to historical detail and depth of introspection are worthy of Pasternak or Solzhenitsyn. Enthralling, reads as true as my grandfather's letters.

Daniel Wagner, former Dean of the CIA's Sherman Kent School for Intelligence Analysis

William Burton McCormick vividly depicts the tragedies of the 20th century through eyes of a single Latvian Rifleman. With Wiktor Rooks, we witness the destruction of traditional society and its seemingly conservative values, to be replaced with new social, political and national ideas, innovations all ultimately perverted to hell by their adherents. The novel considers the eternal problems of humanity as cast through the dark prism of actual historical events.

Professor Kaspars Klavins, Riga Technical University and Fellow, Royal Society of Arts (UK)

William Burton McCormick takes us right inside lives that would otherwise be not simply invisible to us but unimaginable.

Suzannah Dunn, author of *The Confession of Katherine Howard*

An engrossing and well managed piece of writing, chronicling a fascinating and turbulent period of Russian and Latvian history while never once losing sight of the need to drive the narrative through the personal tale of its hero, Wiktor Rooks.

Martyn Bedford, Costa shortlisted author of *Flip*

LENIN'S
HAREM

A NOVEL

WILLIAM BURTON McCORMICK

Chapter One

My brother always said they were watching us. From the fields, or the forest, or roadside, wherever they did their chores. I never gave it much thought. He was the heir and they were his concern. I, heir to nothing, could pardon watchfulness.

What happened afterwards, though, even Jesus would not forgive.

While our parents entertained the guests at the two-day Christmas ball inside, I sat on the manor's steps that evening distributing glasses of champagne to late arrivals, well-wishers and friends who'd enjoyed a walk in the crisp winter air of the Courland countryside. Unchaperoned for most the night, I'd frankly had more than a few glasses myself, too much for an eleven-year old boy.

It was in those later hours that I caught the voices on the wind. Far down the road, in the hollow, I could hear the singing of the working folk, those Latvians who spent their days farming the land for our family and the other Baltic Barons. Their Christmas songs drifting between frost-covered fir trees, harmonies moving slowly along as unseen carolers passed through the night. Voices, it seemed, from another world, one that touched ours daily but remained forever closed. How I wished to understand those Lettish songs.

With little to entertain me at the party, I got off the steps and found the old highway leading toward the peasant farms. Sipping champagne, by the time I reached the little thatch and log farmstead at which the carolers gathered, I was slightly cold, reasonably drunk, and completely surprised at the spectacle before me.

These Christmastime revelers were out in costume, Courland's native people *mumming* through the winter night. Letts of all ages wore animal masks, most in elaborate home-made disguises. Hairy stitched bears pranced on chains held by the mythic hero, helmeted Lāčplēsis. Ceramic goat horns rested on the heads of adolescent girls who danced with fake Jews in black hats and painted-on beards. I spied tiny old men whose trailing cotton beards sprang from their baby faces when they stepped upon them, while women dressed as spirits spun about me, the green stripes of their festive dresses showing beneath ghostly white sheets. All-in-all, a grand procession of adults and children, some dressed for the holiday season, others wrapped in their workers' clothes, marching together from the snow-covered fields toward the Latvian villages. All singing hymns of Christmas, a joyous chorus reverberating throughout the winter countryside.

My young eyes widened in wonder. Though I could not understand a word, these Lettish harmonies elated my spirit, brought me closer to the season than my family's stuffy, aristocratic ball ever had.

Why had my parents forbidden me to come here?

Fascinated, I could not resist following this procession as the mummers wound their way along the moonlit path. A Yule log dragged behind, they stopped at every home in forest or field, families dressed in red and green casting a year's worth of problems onto the timber as it passed.

For hours, through a string of villages, I trailed this parade. Fantastic figures and singing families joining at every stop until the alleys of the last town were swollen with costumed bodies. Funnelled into a narrow street, the crowd pressed so close my cap was jarred from my head, the champagne glass knocked to the muddy stones by a trio of deliriously dancing ghosts. With no pause to retrieve them, the tide swept me forward, breaking through on the far side of town where the land at last reopened into my father's fields. They came to rest in the yard of a most ancient farmhouse: stocky square timbers, a four-sided thatched roof and double smoking chimneys at the crown. A faded coat of arms hung from a wooden pole, reminding all that Letts were freemen, serfs no longer.

The march over, the singers gathered around the sacrificial Yule log, preparing for the celebratory burning. As the leaders toiled to light the icy log, the crowd at last seemed to consider my presence, masks turning my way, eyes lingering a bit too long. I suddenly felt outlandish in my fine jacket and shoes, far more foolish than the most absurd of these mummers. How I wished I were dressed as them, devoid of identity, free to mix undetected. How many recognized me as Rudolf Rooks's son, youngest child of the family that kept them for generations? So many faces, surely, would be familiar without their masks: Father's stablemen, farmworkers, woodcutters, perhaps even an elevated house servant down for the celebration. They all must be here. Yet there were no greetings, no holiday salutations, not even in the common Russian language. Their Lettish words buzzed mysteriously by my ears, the people passing close, but not once calling my name.

There was, however, an uncomfortable air of recognition in one silent watcher. Intense eyes beneath a swine mask, he clutched a drunken woman to his chest, her own camouflage slipping low, revealing her reddened face. I saw only a glimpse – Mrs. Bata, the wife of my father's foreman – then the Yule log caught fire and an eclipsing blaze rose up between us.

While last year's troubles burned into memory and the dancing mummers cast bizarre shadows over the snow, I tried to peer through the flames. There stood Mrs. Bata, now alone, her feline mask righted, but her man was gone. For a moment.

"Why are you here?" he shouted, appearing from the crowd, grabbing my shoulder and shaking me harshly. The voice was surprisingly familiar, the language not unknowable Lettish or even Russian but German, my native tongue!

This mummer squatted on his haunches, lowering down to my height. He shoved up his mask revealing the frowning face of my older brother.

"Otomars," I gasped.

"Wiktor, what are you doing here? At this hour?"

What was *he* doing here? Among the peasants. "I…I heard the songs."

He pulled me close, cold nose against my cheek, sniffing my breath. "You're drunk."

So was he, so what? "Mother let me have some champagne at the Christmas ball. Why are you dressed as a pig?"

Conscious that all the Letts were staring, Otomars lowered his voice, changed the tongue from German to a less conspicuous Russian; the adjustment difficult for my tipsy mind, I was not the language master he was.

"Wiktor, pay attention to me." He snapped his fingers in my face. "Does Father know you're down here?"

"No."

"Well, I'm taking you back."

So stern for a man in a pig mask. "Why?"

He didn't answer, simply dragging me from the crowd. He eighteen, I eleven, it was no contest. His face now visible, the Letts gave him a wary distance. Mummers silently watching as he stole me away into the night. Cowed and kidnapped by the first-born son.

"Why Otomars? Why can't I stay?"

We were a half kilometer from the village when my brother finally relented. The Latvians long out of sight, their beautiful songs only a memory, I didn't understand why we had to leave. "I want to hear them sing."

"Wiktor, listen to me," he said, voice firm as Father's. "There've been incidents all over Courland. In Livland too. I need you inside."

Incidents? What incidents? "I was only in the village, I go every day."

"Not alone, not past midnight, not when they've been drinking," with his free hand he cuffed my neck, "or you have."

"It wasn't much," I tugged at his grip. "You've had more than me."

He dragged me on. My resistance fading, we fell into silence, listening to the rhythmic crunching of our shoes in the snow. We were close to home now, the high windows of the manor house peeking over the bare trees.

I played my last card. "Then I'll just have to tell Father about Mrs. Bata and the housekeeper..."

He smiled, as if I weren't even in the game. "Do that and I'll mention where I found you tonight. Passed out drunk."

"I wasn't."

He shrugged. "Who's to say?" His grin had triumph. As always.

I was trying to conjure a worthy retort, some offsetting counterattack, as we arrived at home. Pale yellow and brown by day, the manor house was painted in midnight hues of silver and white, tree-limb shadows clawing across the front. The ground-floor windows darkened, the fires dead in the yard cauldrons, there were still a few trailing voices inside, the tinkling of piano keys from the parlor. Anne, at least, was still up.

In the worn slush before the steps, a crushed bouquet of roses. Flattened petals trampled under a man's boot print, an arc of purple and red leaves throughout the yard. Down the path toward the stables lay a dozen naked stems, most of them broken. Erich Kaltenbach had been here. Anne had rejected him again.

"Will he ever stop?" I said.

"Our sister's captured his heart, Wiktor," said Otomars, pulling a petal from the slush. "That's not an easy thing to forgo."

Yes, especially for a spoiled baron's son used to getting his way. "Maybe, Father should speak with Erich?"

"No, I will. Tomorrow." Otomars let out a sigh, warm breath rising in the winter air. "Let's get you inside."

I climbed the steps alone. "Aren't you coming?"

He remained at the bottom, brushing snow over the roses with the side of his boot. "No."

"Why can you stay out, but I have to turn in?"

He stretched out his hands. "Because I'm a man and you're still a boy."

"If you're a man, why are you dressed as a pig?"

He laughed, something in him warming at my remark. Otomars came up a few steps, pulled the mask from his head, slipped it gently over my face.

"I'll tell you what: Go inside, stay inside, and tomorrow night – after our parents are asleep – we'll trek down to the village together. Agreed?"

I couldn't see in this thing. "I…"

"One 'oink' for 'no.' Two for 'yes'."

"Oink, oink."

"Good piggy."

He tapped my nose through the mask, playfully mussed my hair, all with a charm that made it almost alright, as only he could. "And nothing more about Mrs. Bata."

By the time I got the eye holes righted, he was gone, far down the path under the cover of trees. I was alone.

I considered going back, breaking my word, and following Otomars down to the Latvian villages again to make a point. But I was cold, a bit sleepy. Enough adventure for the night, tomorrow there'd be another volley.

With voices in the parlor, I could not risk detection. Probing questions at this hour, in this state, would be most unpleasant, especially from my parents. So, I went around the side of the house to rap on Erene's window and ask the faithful housemaid to let me inside in confidence.

As I passed round the corner, I gazed over the expansive lawn, divot-ed snow stretching down to grey stables. Still a few sleighs and carriages parked in the shadows, some guests yet to leave, or perhaps, staying the second night.

Beyond lay the little path that led to the main road to Mitau, a screen of fir trees running along one side. A man hanging by the neck from a branch.

I recoiled in horror, surprise, one thought in my mind: Erich.

The roses, the rejection…

I sprang from the porch, my mind not on the dead man, but on my sister. The guilt she'd feel.

But as I ran through the snow, I cast off the blinding mask, the corpse became clearer, a focusing silhouette against the moon behind. It wasn't Erich or even a man...

It was a burlap sack, stuffed and tied in the shape of a man. Dressed in an old coat, the collar buttoned to the chin, a painted waistcoat and knee-high boots to finish the illusion. The hallmark clothes of a Baltic-German gentleman, it could have been my father, or Erich, or Otomars; any of the landowners who ruled Courland.

I felt the deathly chill of the hour, took a few tentative steps forward, stood beneath the dangling thing, hoarse breath and drumming heartbeat the only sounds.

Rail spikes pierced the effigy at the head and chest, painted blood snaking down its icy form. And at the center, three words. Running from breast to belly:

Free

Latvia

Now!